CRY WOLF

Also by Ian Stuart Black

In the wake of a stranger (Dakers, 1953)
The passionate city (Heinemann, 1958)
The yellow flag (Hutchinson, 1959)
Love in four countries (Hutchinson, 1961)
The high bright sun (Hutchinson, 1962)
The man on the bridge (Constable, 1975)
Caribbean strip (Constable, 1978)
Journey to a safe place (Constable, 1979)
Creatures in a dream (Constable, 1985)

We must kill Toni: a comedy in three acts
(Evans Plays, Acting Edition, 1953)

CRY WOLF

Ian Stuart Black

Constable · London

First published in Great Britain 1990
by Constable and Company Limited
10 Orange Street London WC2H 7EG
Copyright © 1990 Ian Stuart Black
Set in Linotron Palatino by
CentraCet, Cambridge
Printed in Great Britain by
St Edmundsbury Press Ltd
Bury St Edmunds, Suffolk

British Library CIP data
Black, Ian Stuart
Cry wolf
I. Title
823'.914 [F]

ISBN 0 09 469460 3

Dedicated to Wrightington (NHS)
West Lancashire
in admiration.

And for J.G., T.B., and R.B.

Part 1

'I know a trick you can't do,' said Henry. He pointed a finger challengingly at his uncle.

'Now watch this penny,' replied Edward. 'I can take it in one hand and with a twist of the wrist . . .'

'That's stupid,' said Henry. 'Anybody can do that.'

'I know how you do it,' scoffed Caroline.

Edward feigned surprise. 'You know how this magic works?'

Henry dismissed him. 'This trick is really good. I saw a man turn himself into a wolf!'

'That's easy!' declared Edward.

Henry challenged him – all four feet of him, and all eight years.

'All right, you do it. Do it now.'

'Yes,' echoed his sister. 'You do it! Do it now.'

Their mother could hear them across the lawn. 'Don't speak to your uncle like that.'

They were too involved to notice her. Edward absorbed them: he was a citizen of their world. The same values held good for him, the same logic.

'Have you ever seen a man turn a horse into a field?' asked Edward.

'That's stupid,' Henry repeated.

'Henry!' called his mother reprovingly.

The boy kept his large serious eyes on his uncle. 'I'm telling you about a real trick. I saw it happen.'

'I saw it happen, too,' said Caroline.

'Where?' asked Edward. He was lying in a hammock in the sunshine, his eyes closed. If it hadn't been for his nephew and niece he would have been asleep.

'From the tree-house,' said Henry triumphantly.

'You've been told to be careful in the tree-house,' called his

9

mother, weeding one of the flower-beds some distance away. She had good hearing where her children were concerned.

'It's all right, Mother,' Henry called back. 'It's perfectly safe.'

'It doesn't shake a bit,' called Caroline.

'Your father says it needs some repair,' their mother replied. But they sensed that the warning was mere ritual.

'Very well,' said Edward. 'Where was this wolf?'

'He was a man,' said Henry. 'At least he was a man at first.'

'All men are wolves,' said Edward sleepily. 'You'll find that out later. Or rather, you will, Carrie.'

'Do you mind, Eddie! She's only six,' called his sister.

'I'll soon be seven,' Caroline corrected her.

'Okay,' said her uncle. 'Where was he?'

'Well,' Henry marshalled his argument, 'we were up in the tree-house. It hangs over the river . . .'

'I know where it is,' his uncle told him. 'I helped to build it when I was here two years ago.'

'Well,' said Henry – he drew a deep breath – 'we were there. I was reading. Carrie was doing something . . .'

'I was reading, too.'

'Get on with it,' said Edward.

'You know you can see across the river.'

'I know.'

'You can see through the trees to the big wall.'

'Even in summer?'

'What d'you mean?'

'Can you see with all the leaves?'

'Well, just. Anyhow,' said Henry – he was a dogged reporter, hanging on to the thread of his story, sensing his uncle's mockery even in somnolence – 'I heard this noise.'

'I heard it, too,' said Caroline.

'Near the wall.'

'The wall round Sir Whatnot's estate?'

'He's been dead for years,' his sister called.

'Who lives there now?' asked Edward.

'It's been empty for eighteen months. There used to be a school there, but that folded.'

'So there's no one there now,' Eddie prompted his nephew.

'There is. I could hear someone moving through the bushes. Then we saw him,' said Henry.

'The man or the wolf?' asked Edward. He wasn't sure he was

going to last till the end of the story. His eyes were heavy with afternoon sleep, product of seven years in siesta countries.

'A man,' said Henry. 'Just mooching about, not doing anything much. I think he was just taking a look at the place. I don't think he'd been there before.'

'Maybe he's going to buy it?' suggested Edward.

'Anyhow,' said Henry, 'he just looked around, you know – over his shoulder – in case someone was following. Then he saw no one was there, so he turned himself into a wolf.'

'Just like that?'

'Yes.'

'Before your very eyes?'

'Well, he did move a bit behind the branches.'

'Out of sight?'

'Not really. Not completely. Except, of course, there was the wall.'

'It's a very high wall,' said Edward sleepily.

'Anyhow, you have to admit, it was a good trick,' said Henry.

His uncle nodded. 'Very good. Especially as he didn't have an audience.'

'He did have an audience,' Caroline pointed out. 'He had us.'

'I was forgetting,' murmured Edward.

'Wake up, Uncle Eddie,' coaxed Henry. 'What d'you think about that?'

'Leave your uncle alone,' called his mother softly. 'He's very tired.'

'Why is he?'

'He hasn't recovered from his travelling.'

The children looked resentfully at the sleeping man. They would dearly have loved to shake him, for he had brought excitement into the long days of their holiday. But with their mother so close, they restrained themselves, and went off, a little sullenly. 'He just makes jokes,' muttered Caroline. 'He doesn't believe anything we tell him.'

They glared towards the hammock. Edward could just be seen, his dark hair falling over closed eyes, sun-tanned, round-faced, of medium height and build; wiry, powerful across the shoulders, and toughened by days of labour, working, as he liked to do, with the men of many races whom he employed. He appeared young for his twenty-seven years, and anyone who looked as fit and strong as Uncle Eddie, they thought, shouldn't need a daytime sleep. It was just one of his little schemes!

'We'll show him,' said Henry. 'He thinks he's clever, Eddie does, but I bet he can't do *that* trick.'

As John Warwick pulled up outside the house, he could hear the children playing. They were having an argument about something, but that was par for the course. He liked the holidays, when he was able to see something of them before they were chased off to bed.

He was tired after the journey from town and the drive from the station. The hot weather and the crowded train would stay with him, he guessed, until that first quick drink. Besides, he'd had only sandwiches and coffee all day at an office conference that had lasted for ever.

He felt a sharp pang of irritation as he left the car. Further along the drive he could see the Porsche his brother-in-law drove parked in the shade of the tall aspens. He had already commented to Edward: 'That's a bit extravagant, isn't it?'

'I'm just hiring it,' Edward had told him.

'Still a bit over the top, don't you think?'

'Well, I'm used to them,' Edward had excused himself.

'Used to them?'

'I've been driving one out in the Gulf. They aren't all that expensive in some parts of the world.' They had left it at that.

'Daddy! Daddy!' the children shouted as they heard him come into the house. They raced down the stairs.

'Hello, kids! How's it all going?'

As Caroline launched into a series of complaints about one of her friends, John left them. 'I must have a shower,' he told them, over his shoulder.

'There *is* something,' said Henry.

'Later!' their father called back.

'Later' was considerably later, after John, Margaret and Edward had settled in the little porch which caught the still-warm rays of the slanting sun. Both Henry and Caroline had had their supper, but they were allowed a token fruit drink because their uncle was there.

'Eddie says there's nobody living in Park House,' Henry informed his father.

'It was your mother who said that,' Edward protested.

'Well, there isn't,' said Margaret, who had the ability to conduct a conversation without giving it too much attention.

'Eddie says there's been no one there for eighteen months,' persisted Henry.

'What a shocking fib!' said Edward. 'I never said that.'

'There *is* no one there,' said Margaret, as she poured drinks.

'Well, he's wrong, we know he is. Because we've seen someone there.'

'Time to go to bed, my loves,' said their mother.

'I've seen someone, too,' Caroline said loyally.

'What do you mean? Down at Park House?'

The children were pleased to have caught their father's interest. 'Yes. Over the wall . . . in the trees. There was a man there.'

'We saw a man there. Walking.'

'I'm not surprised,' said John. 'Some people took the Park a week ago.'

'You didn't tell me,' said his wife.

'I forgot. Someone told me in the village. Foreigners or something, coming from abroad. I didn't know they were there yet.'

'You see!' said Henry in triumph, pointing at Edward. 'I told you so.'

'You told me one or two things,' said Edward drily.

'And they're all true,' claimed Henry.

'That's enough. Time for bed,' said his mother.

As they left they called: 'Will you come and say good-night to us, Daddy?'

'Of course.'

John sat on the bed and viewed his son. Henry often surprised him, his serious little face earnest, eyes concerned, sometimes talking like an adult, pressing some point with his own special logic. A childish logic, but nonetheless persuasive.

'The trouble with Eddie . . .'

'Uncle Eddie,' suggested his father.

'Uncle Eddie, is that he thinks he's always right.'

'It's a common failing,' agreed his father.

'You tell him something, and he just makes fun.'

'Uncle Eddie teases,' said his father.

'Mother said there was nobody in the old house, and Eddie just took her word for it.'

'My fault.' John ruffled his son's dark hair. 'I should have passed on the information.'

'So he was wrong about the man, and he was wrong about the wolf.'

'What wolf?'

'The wolf over the wall. The wolf in the Park House garden.'

John grinned at him. 'There was a wolf in the garden?'

'Carrie saw it too,' said Henry.

'I saw it, too,' Caroline called from the bedroom across the landing.

'I don't suppose there'd be a wolf there,' said John. 'Not a real wolf. Not walking about in a garden.'

'I didn't see it walk,' admitted Henry. 'It was just there for a moment.'

'How do you know it was a wolf?'

'I saw a wolf at the zoo. You took us.'

'Oh yes. I'd forgotten.'

'Well, this wolf . . .'

'Was it with the man you saw?'

'Sort of. Well, he was there, then . . .'

'It would be a dog,' said his father with a smile.

'It was too big for a dog.'

'A guard dog. A German Shepherd dog. An Alsatian.'

Henry shook his head. 'It wasn't like *any* dog.'

'Alsatians are very like wolves. Some people say they are just one generation away from wolves. If it was walking round the Park House gardens it must have been a guard dog.'

'Why would they have a guard dog?'

'If they come from abroad, and don't know how peaceful and law-abiding we are in Sussex, these new people – foreigners, you know – might think it necessary to have a big dog. This chap you saw was probably showing the dog the area he had to look after. Dogs have a strong instinct to mark out a territory; then that's theirs and they protect it. A lot of animals and birds do that . . . people do it, in a way, as well,' he added thoughtfully.

Henry had an important point to make. 'But this man and this dog weren't together. Not actually *together*. He was there one minute – one second really – and then this wolf, this dog, was there. Suddenly! In exactly the same place.'

14

They could hear someone coming up the stairs.

'Good-night, old fellow.' John gave the boy a kiss.

Edward appeared at the door. 'I've come to say good-night too.' He was holding something behind his back.

'Don't get them excited,' said John, 'or they'll never go to sleep.' He left Edward standing at the foot of the bed, and Henry watching his uncle suspiciously.

'I was thinking about what you told me,' said Edward. 'About the man doing that trick. So I thought I'd better show you I'm just as clever as he is!' He spun round with a fanfare: 'Ta-ra! Man into wolf! I told you I could do it!'

'Let me see! Let me see!' Caroline called from her room. She appeared in the doorway and gazed at her uncle with contempt. 'That's just Mummy's old fur.'

'It isn't even a wolf-fur,' said Henry coldly. 'It's a fox-fur . . . and it doesn't cover your face.'

'I can see you easily,' said Caroline. 'No one would think you were a wolf.'

Her mother called from downstairs: 'Are you out of your bed, Caroline?'

'Just going!' She raced back to her room.

Edward put his head round her door. 'Sweet dreams,' he called.

She turned away. 'That was just stupid,' she pronounced. They heard him chuckle as he went down the stairs.

Henry called softly to her: 'I know what I'm going to do.'

'What?' Caroline was totally convinced of her brother's infallibility.

'I'm going to show him the man doing it.'

'How?'

'I'll take him there.'

'Up into the tree-house?'

'Yes. We'll hide. We'll stay and wait. If the man lives there he'll have to come back. Like last time, he won't see anyone – so he'll do the trick again. He'll turn himself into a wolf.'

A few seconds later they were both asleep.

Henry had much of his father's approach to a problem. At worst it could be a plodding resolution, but at best he showed signs beyond his years of an ability to plan.

He hurried through his breakfast without comment.

'Are you all right, Henry?' asked his mother.

'Of course. I just don't want any more.' He slipped out into the garden.

But Caroline was aware of everything her brother contemplated – not in detail, but in embryo. It was as though she were switched to the same wavelength, but slightly out of tune. She was after him in a flash.

'Where are you going, Henry?'

'I told you. I'm going to show Eddie I was right about the man.'

'Where is Uncle Eddie?'

'I haven't told him yet.'

'Why not?'

'I'm going to see if the tree-house is big enough for him. One of the sides is a bit broken. I know what he'll say if there's anything wrong. He'll make an excuse, and go away.'

They hurried past the greenhouses and the old stables which now formed the garage. The garden was shaped like a hatchet: the house was surrounded by a large square lawn with artificial dells and a pond, while a long handle of land ran down through woods and azalea bushes, backed by massively high rhododendrons. A stream ran along by the path, and at the end of the property it flowed into what they called 'the river'. This was really only another stream, but wider and deeper, forming the boundary of the garden, with fields on one side. On the other side, some twenty or thirty yards across the river, high stone walls stood bleak and silent. Beyond the fields in one direction they could see a farmhouse, and in the other, in the distance stood a couple of Victorian houses. They had been John Warwick's nearest neighbours these past eighteen months; indeed, for as long as the estate called Park House had been untenanted.

The children knew their way blindfold through the overgrown tangle of weeds and shrubs. Only the path was ever tended in this part of the garden, but they preferred to use their own 'secret' tracks through the bushes.

The garden ended at a low stone wall, covered by ivy and creepers. Beyond it, the stream ran within a few feet, but this summer had been so dry that there was hardly any flow, and the mud beyond the wall was caked and cracked.

'You could walk on it,' Henry had told his father.

'You'd better not,' he'd been warned.

In the very last tree in the garden, the tree-house had been built. It was about eighteen feet above the ground, in a thick and sprawling yew tree whose branches jutted above the wall. The tree-house was partly concealed by a mass of creepers.

'Eddie said he helped to build it,' said Henry, 'when he was here last.'

'I wish he could stay,' said Caroline thoughtfully.

'He can't,' Henry told her. 'He's got business.'

'Daddy has business, but he stays.'

'Eddie has to go round the world or something . . . Right, I'm going up.'

A series of pegs had been driven into the tree-trunk, making it easy to climb. They both scrambled into the wooden structure and Henry inspected it carefully. It was just as he thought.

'I'm going to get some old sacking.'

'Why?'

'The wall has a crack in it.'

Caroline viewed the tree-house's wooden side. 'It's not a big crack.'

'You know what Eddie is like. He'll say it isn't a proper hiding place, and he won't stay. He'll say he isn't going to wait for the man to turn into a wolf unless he's properly hidden.' He started to climb down the tree. 'I know where to get some old fruit netting.'

He hurried away, wanting everything to be finished before his uncle had a chance to find out what was being prepared for him. When he returned to the tree-house, Caroline wasn't there. That didn't surprise him: she often became bored, and went off to do something else. She probably didn't see the point of this preparation.

Henry hung the netting over the side of the planks which, nailed across two branches, acted as a wall. There was plenty of net left over, so he pulled part of it across the top of the house, covering himself completely. This was the first time there had been a roof on the tree-house and Henry was pleased with his morning's work.

Making his way back through the bushes under the rhodo-dendrons, he was quite shocked to come upon Caroline, huddled on the ground behind a clump of ferns. She heard him coming and turned to stare at him. Her eyes were red. Henry couldn't understand it.

'Have you been crying?'

She shook her head.

17

'Then what's the matter?'

She peered back over his shoulder. He turned sharply, but there was nothing there.

'What is it?'

'I want to go back to the house,' she said.

'Well, come on.'

She scrambled to her feet.

'Why didn't you stay in the tree-house?'

'I didn't want to.'

'Why not?'

'Just didn't.' She could be very stubborn.

'That's not a reason.'

Caroline said no more as they made their way through the wood. Henry returned the rest of the netting to the shed, and put his sister's odd behaviour out of his mind. After all, sometimes there was no accounting for what she did.

As he headed back towards the house she fell into step beside him. She spoke quietly at first, and he wasn't sure he heard correctly.

'I thought the wolf was going to follow me,' she whispered.

'What wolf?'

'In the garden,' she said. 'When you went for the netting . . . it was watching me.'

'The wolf was watching you?' He didn't know whether she was making it up.

'Yes.'

'Animals don't watch people,' he suggested.

'I looked in the other garden, and I didn't see it . . . not at first. It was a bit farther away this time. It put its nose through the bushes . . . then it stopped. I knew it had seen me 'cause it kept its eyes very steady. Yellowy-green eyes . . .'

'Wolves don't have yellow eyes,' protested her brother.

'I thought it was going to eat me.'

'How could it? On the other side of the wall.'

She shivered. 'I thought it was going to find a way.'

'What did it do?'

'When I looked again, it had gone . . . so I ran away.'

'Was the man there?'

'No. Just the wolf.'

They were back at the house. Before they went in she said: 'I'm not going there again.'

Shortly afterwards the Porsche was driven sedately up the

18

drive, and Margaret and Edward carried some packages into
the kitchen.

'Hello, you two! What have you been up to?' Edward's
greeting sounded like a challenge to his nephew.

'Nothing much,' said Henry. He had been a little taken aback
by Carrie's story, but he was determined to go ahead with his
plan.

'You helped build the tree-house, didn't you, Uncle Eddie?
Well, it needs some repairs. I've done a bit, but I think you'd
better check it.'

'Check the tree-house?' Edward looked quizzically at him.
'Tell you what, I'll come down with you and hide in it, and see
if the man comes back and does his famous trick.'

Henry caught his breath. However had his uncle guessed
that was his plan?

They left the house together. 'What about Carrie?' asked
Edward. 'Doesn't she want to see this too?'

'Not really.' Henry tried to play down the idea.

'Why not?'

'Well, she's seen it. Besides, she's not very fond of it.'

'She doesn't like the trick?'

'Not really. She thinks it's a bit scary.'

Edward looked down at the boy trotting by his side. 'What
d'you mean? She seemed pretty relaxed about it yesterday.'

'Well, she was down there this morning . . .'

'Ha! I knew you two were up to something.'

'I was patching up the house, I told you . . .'

'What about Carrie?'

'Well, usually she doesn't mind being by herself. She goes off
and hides . . .'

'Get to the point.'

'She was up in the tree-house while I was getting the
netting . . .'

'The what? Never mind. Press on.'

'When I came back she was hiding in the bushes. She said
she'd seen the wolf. She was pretty quiet, 'cause she was
scared.'

As they were going down the path through the trees, Henry
stopped to point out where he had found his sister.

'What was she doing in there?'

'Hiding.'

'Why?'

'She thought the wolf was going to come after her.'

Edward looked sharply at the boy. 'This isn't some stupid game, is it? I mean, you aren't trying to frighten your sister?'

'Of course not.' Henry was scornful.

Edward hesitated. 'Okay,' he said. 'Come on.'

They went the rest of the way in silence, stopping at the foot of the sprawling yew. Edward looked at it with affection.

'I enjoyed building this. With a little help from your dad. Not an expert with his hands, your dad, but willing . . . Now, let's see. Yes . . . the pegs are still here. That just shows – if you're going to do a job, do it properly.'

He climbed easily and swiftly into the tree, Henry following a little more slowly. On the edge of the tree-house he took a careful look across the wall, over the patch of open field with the dried-up stream, into the thickly wooded grounds beyond the tall walls of Park House estate. As far as he could see it was deserted. He wondered what Carrie could have seen to make her so frightened. Perhaps a funny-shaped tree, or a bush – or something like that? In that shadowy, unkempt and overgrown wilderness you could imagine anything. You could think you saw faces; or a bush, moving in the warm breeze, could be mistaken for some sort of animal. But certainly there was nothing there now.

'My, my,' said Eddie softly. 'Time flies.' He ran his hands over the struts that formed the sides of the house. He recalled putting them together with a much smaller Henry at the foot of the tree, determined to climb up . . . and succeeding.

'I like the netting,' he told Henry. 'Splendid camouflage.' There was room for both of them. 'It's smaller than I thought,' he mused. 'Do you use it much?'

'All the time,' Henry told him.

'What do you do?'

'I read here. And when friends come, we play.'

There were a few bits and pieces to be mended. Edward busied himself with them, and time passed quickly. The sun shone through a break in the trees above them; by mid-day it was hot, and Edward lay on the wooden flooring, basking in the warmth. A breeze stirred the branches around them. It was idyllic, he decided . . . a return to the long summer days of childhood, with a dream-like quality about the time and the place. He wondered to what extent that quality had alarmed his little niece. He sat up, and looked towards the walled gardens of their silent neighbours.

'What did Carrie say? She had seen your wolf?'

'Yes. It was watching her.'

'And where did you see the man?'

'Over there.' Henry pointed to a corner of the wall. From the height of the tree-house they could look at an angle into the garden. A small patch of clearing was lit by sunlight, and swaying branches sent a pattern of shadows backwards and forwards over the ground.

'Your father says there are people there now, so perhaps someone was having a look round with a dog?'

'I don't think it was a dog.'

Edward didn't want to go over that ground again. He lay back in the sun. 'I don't think we're going to witness any magic today,' he said drowsily.

'You sleep a lot,' commented Henry.

'Only in the middle of the day,' said Edward. 'Usually I get up very early – six o'clock, while it's cool – work till mid-day, and nod off till about five. Then back to work, till eight o'clock or later, when it's cool again.'

'That's a funny way of doing things,' said Henry critically.

'It works . . .' Edward could feel the uneven floor under his back. 'Some of these planks are loose,' he said.

In the distance a gong sounded.

'That's Mother.'

'Yes?'

'We've to go to lunch.'

Edward dragged himself back from oblivion. 'Okay.' They climbed down from the tree.

Lunch was a salad, a sandwich, and a glass of beer for Edward.

'I'm sorry for John in London in this weather,' said Margaret. 'He doesn't like the heat.'

'Are you finished?' Henry asked his uncle.

'More or less,' admitted Edward.

'Come on then. We have to fix the floor-planks.'

'Leave your uncle alone,' said Margaret. 'He needs a rest.'

'He's had a rest.'

'Okay,' said Edward. 'On your feet.'

They made their way back to the tree-house, carrying the necessary tools.

'Next time I'm back in England,' said Edward, 'you'll be ten. You'll be able to do running repairs yourself.'

'I'm nearly nine now. I have a birthday this month.'

They soon had the planks firmly nailed into place. 'Sound as a bell,' said Edward. 'That'll last another couple of years.'

'What else can we fix?' asked the boy.

Edward looked around. He wanted something undemanding to occupy Henry, because he himself intended to make further use of the peace and solitude.

'The very thing,' he said. 'Some of this netting is falling to bits. I suggest you use the pieces to mesh it together.'

He showed Henry what he meant, and the problem caught the boy's attention. 'I can do that.' He settled down against the trunk of the tree and began to thread together the loops.

'That should take him hours,' thought Edward. He found his place in the sun again. This time it was only a matter of seconds before he was asleep.

'Uncle Eddie . . . Eddie!' Henry was gently shaking his shoulder.

'What is it? What's the matter?'

The boy seemed to have become caught up in the netting, and at first Edward thought that was the problem.

'There's someone there,' said Henry softly.

'There's what?' He wasn't properly awake.

'There's someone over the wall.'

He roused himself. 'In the garden?'

'Yes.'

'Who is it?'

'I just heard voices.'

Both were motionless, straining their ears to listen.

'Not a thing,' said Edward.

'I heard someone.'

'What doing?'

'Talking . . . laughing.'

Edward sat up. He could hear nothing.

'You can start imagining things if you go on long enough,' he said.

'There were voices . . . ladies' voices.'

'Ladies?' That was more precise. After all, there *would* be people in the next-door garden now the place was inhabited.

And there were bound to be women. There was nothing extraordinary about women strolling round their property . . .

The sound of laughter came clearly on the light summer breeze.

'There you are! I told you!'

A moment later there was another wave of laughter, then the sound of voices. It was impossible to make out what was said, but the lilt of speech, the overall sound, was not at all like English. It was more lyrical, a rising sound which finished like music. And they were young voices, Edward decided. More than two, perhaps three.

'One thing for certain,' he said. 'There's not a man's voice among them. Your friend with the wolf can't be there.'

'He might be,' said Henry. 'Just keeping quiet, not saying anything.'

'True,' Edward nodded.

The laughter had died, but the conversation came and went with the breeze.

'It's not nice to spy on people,' said his uncle. 'Besides, what can you see in that overgrown jungle?'

'You might see if they have a dog.'

'A dog? Oh, I see what you mean.' From where he was sitting Edward could see only the top branches of the trees. 'No. There won't be a dog, or it would bark.'

Conversation drifted across the open patch of field.

'I wish you'd look,' persisted Henry.

'There's no point,' Edward told him. 'They must be sitting near the wall. On the other side. Besides, I've told you, it's rude to peer at people.' They sat in silence for a few minutes. There was something most attractive about those women's voices; they sounded completely at ease, as though they were telling a familiar story, or playing some game.

Edward couldn't quite put his finger on the quality that suggested itself to him. It was something seductive. No . . . that wasn't the exact word. Sensual, possibly? Yes, that was more like it. A sensual enjoyment . . . something very relaxed, physical, shared. He was puzzled that such a picture, such an interpretation, should jump to mind . . . Perhaps he was supplying these qualities himself. His interpretation, and not the actual event, might be what intrigued him. Besides, he admitted to himself that there was something exciting about this eavesdropping. These women must think themselves miles from any other human being, and were letting their hair down, unaware of the presence of a man and a boy.

'We should go back to the house,' said Henry. 'We've been here a long time. Mother will be looking for us.'

'Then we mustn't make a noise,' warned Edward. 'It would be very embarrassing if they realized we were here.'

He rose cautiously to his feet, and Henry was about to follow, when: 'Stay where you are,' whispered Edward sharply.

The boy caught the tone of his voice and sat motionless.

'What is it?'

'There's someone there.'

'Can you see them?'

'I think so. Just a moment . . . I'm not sure . . . some trees . . .' He was saying anything that came to mind, standing motionless, holding the netting above his head, shrouded in the shadow of the tree. For a moment he had been uncertain of the scene, for sunlight and shadow did indeed confuse the picture. And a picture it certainly was.

There were three young women – little more than girls – lying on a patch of ground beneath the trees, partly in the shade, partly in the full glare of the sun. They were relaxing at their ease in the warmth of the afternoon; casual, provocative in their carelessness, with an abandon about their attitudes – immodest in their privacy as they sprawled on the grass. They were dark-haired, their bodies very curved and rounded, surprisingly robust and powerful, yet almost exaggeratedly feminine. And they were totally naked.

'Is the man there?' whispered Henry.

Edward kept his voice down – it sounded a little shaky. 'I don't see him.' He was no stranger to nudity: he had lived with it in parts of the South Seas, appreciating, enjoying it. Perhaps it was the unexpectedness of the scene that took his breath away, the very domesticity: the next-door neighbours! The people over the wall!

The boy was about to speak, but Edward motioned him to keep silent.

They were talking again, laughing. One girl rolled over lazily, firm round breasts dropping out of sight as gently curved buttocks turned into view. He had seen many a more lascivious display that had not moved him as this girl did. One of the others squatted on her heels, picking leaves and pine-cones from her hair . . . She was like a siren – she could have sung any man to his death, Edward thought, as he watched her slow-moving, casual unselfconsciousness.

'What are they doing?'

'Just sitting around.' That was true enough.

'Having tea?' suggested Henry.

'Could be,' said Edward softly.

'Well, if the man isn't there, you won't see his trick.'

'I don't suppose I will,' agreed Edward quietly.

Henry was growing impatient. 'Let's go.'

'We mustn't make a noise,' whispered Edward, helping Henry to his feet.

'Let me have a look,' said the boy. He stood on his tiptoes, stretching.

'You can't,' said Edward.

'You could lift me.'

'Another time,' said Edward. He handed the boy through the open trap in the floor and watched him climb down.

'Aren't you coming?'

'I'm on my way.'

He took a last look through the netting.

The girl had rolled back again and was fanning herself with a handful of ferns. The third girl stood upright, and for a moment he thought he had been seen, since she was pointing towards the tree-house. The others stared in his direction, but then she swept her arm in a circle, clearly telling them something. They looked on, mildly interested. They were like three of the Muses, Edward told himself. Three Muses, but with more interest in life than in art; with bodies inviting all that life had to offer, and with bodies that had all there was in life to give. He drew a deep breath. The world was full of unexpected treasures which no one man could hope to possess.

'Come on, Uncle Eddie!'

He climbed carefully down, and they walked back silently towards the house.

Caroline met them at the door. 'Did you see the wolf?' she asked.

'I couldn't see anything,' Henry complained. 'They were behind the wall.'

'Did you see the wolf?' she asked Edward.

'Not exactly a wolf,' he said.

'The man?'

'Nor him either . . . not properly.'

25

'There were just some ladies,' said Henry.

'You didn't see the trick?'

'Can't say I did . . . but I guess you and Henry are right.'

'What about?'

'About that man. Anything could be happening over that wall.'

'A man could turn himself into a wolf?'

'Certainly.' At that moment Edward could believe almost anything.

There was an air of satisfaction about the two children as they joined their mother. They had won an argument against this attractive and provocative uncle.

Later that evening the adults remained at the dining-table after the evening meal, Edward on one side, John on the other, slowly sipping their way through a good Scotch whisky Edward had brought, while Margaret, flitting to and fro, did a multitude of things in an abstracted fashion, joining in the conversation from time to time, standing it on its head as she occasionally mistook its drift.

Both men had wanted to talk, each with a different subject in mind, and somehow they managed to follow the diverse threads.

'Who are these people in Park House?' asked Edward.

'I really don't know anything about them.'

'Have you met them?'

'No, have you?'

'Henry and I heard voices from over the wall.'

'It's good to see you again, Edward,' John assured him warmly. 'The children like you.'

'Good.'

'And they don't have many relations. When's the next trip home?'

'Oh, another couple of years, I suppose.'

'Can't you get away more often?'

'I *can* get away. I mean, there's no one to stop me.'

'Eddie works for himself, you know,' said Margaret as she walked by.

'It's tying things up,' said Edward vaguely. 'I can't just down tools and nip off as the spirit moves. Once I start a deal . . .'

'That's what concerns me,' frowned John. 'I mean, on your own, like that, couldn't you run out of deals?'

'It's not very likely,' said Edward drily.

Margaret was on her way back to the kitchen. 'Tell John what you told me.'

'What was that?'

'About selling all that stuff to the Arabs.' She had gone.

'What stuff?' John tried not to sound disapproving.

'I think Maggie means the scrap-metal business.'

'You've been selling scrap-metal to the Arabs?'

'I've been selling scrap-metal, and a lot of other things, to several Arab states. And to several other countries, including the Israelis, the South Africans, the Greeks, the Lebanese, some Americans, even the Russians. And, believe it or not, a small consignment to the United Kingdom.'

John pulled a face. 'I can't pretend I approve of all your customers.'

'I don't approve of all my customers myself,' said Edward. 'Just the good payers.'

'H'mm,' said John.

'So you don't even know their name?' asked Edward.

'Whose name?'

'Your new neighbours.'

'Just a moment, I did hear it . . . Sorry. They have foreign accents, but someone says they're really English. Been abroad a long time. Something like that.'

'Don't you think you should make enquiries? After all, they're your near neighbours, smack on your doorstep.'

'It's a damn long way off, that doorstep.' John refilled their glasses. 'Do you realize that if you go by road you have to drive halfway to the village before you turn off down the lane that takes you to the Park House gate? And it's been shut for a couple of years. Big iron gates, twelve foot high, a heavy iron chain, rusted solid I should think. I mean, my near neighbours? The whole of the village, the tennis club, the cricket club, those blasted hunt people – they are all nearer to us than that dump.'

'Have you seen it?'

'When we first came here. The old boy was still there, then. Of course, it was in terrible condition. Probably still is.'

'So you don't know anything about them?'

'Not much. You see, the thing is, Eddie, Margaret and I are concerned about your career.'

'I'm not concerned,' said Margaret as she went past.

'It's all very well doing all right while you're young, but you ought to be building something for the future.'

'I've got a bit salted away,' said Edward with a shrug.

'That's not exactly what I mean.'

'How much *have* you got salted away?' asked his sister as she rejoined them.

'You don't ask that sort of thing, my dear,' said John.

'Darling, he's my little brother! Tell me, Eddie – where's it salted?'

'One or two places.' He grinned at her obvious relish. It was good to know that even these years of marriage to John had not dimmed her amusement.

'Like where? The Channel Islands?'

'Well, that is handy for loose change,' he admitted.

'Where else?'

'The usual. Nothing extreme: Switzerland . . . Cayman Islands . . . some Canadian banks are very accommodating . . .'

'What does it add up to?' she asked.

'I get by,' he grinned.

'Have you got your first million?'

'Who hasn't?' Edward feigned surprise.

'I don't think we have, have we, John?'

'We certainly haven't!' Her husband made it sound like a virtue.

'How about two million?' She might have been bidding at an auction.

'What currency are we talking about?'

'Sterling?'

'H'mm.' Her brother winked, but gave nothing away.

'Dealing in scrap-metal is just another way of describing gun-running, I hear,' said John sharply.

'Not gun-running,' said Edward, pretending to look alarmed. 'That's dangerous. No, you mean "arms-dealing".'

'Not much difference, if you ask me,' said John coldly. He found it hard to accept that his young brother-in-law – and Edward was still only twenty-seven, seven years younger than Margaret who was another seven years younger than John himself – this young man had amassed, in the short space of four or five years, more than he could hope to earn in a lifetime . . . And he himself was doing very well. There was something definitely wrong with society and its values if that could

28

happen. John took a deep breath and sank the rest of the contents of his glass.

'Better, darling?' asked his wife. She leant forward and kissed him. 'After all, you have me, darling. And poor Eddie has nothing but a floating population of glamorous girl-friends.' She turned to her brother. 'By the way, who is it now? Anyone we know?'

'I'm out of luck at present,' said her brother. 'Although I must say I've seen a couple of girls – three, in fact – I wouldn't mind getting to know quite well.'

'Local?'

'I doubt it.'

'Pity. But we'll see what we can do about it,' said his sister. 'John's quite right: it's time you settled down.'

'I'm taking the children to buy shoes,' Margaret told Edward next morning. 'There's a discussion about where we go: Tunbridge Wells, Haywards Heath or Brighton. They have friends in all three, so we'll be away for lunch. Do you want to come, or can you manage on your own?'

'I'll be okay. I'll probably go to the pub for a bite.'

'Splendid. See you later.'

He waited until her car had disappeared down the drive, then he went to the stables and collected his own car.

John had said he had to drive half-way to the village before turning down the lane, but that was an over-statement. The lane joined the village road at a T-junction, where stood a dilapidated signpost still marked 'Station'. There had been no station – in fact, no trains and no railway – for many years, but the post remained.

He drove slowly down the lane, still uncertain why he had come and what he hoped to achieve. He was clearing his mind, he told himself, working on instinct.

Across the fields he caught a glimpse of the Victorian house which had been home to his sister since she and John had married. At times it was hidden behind hedges, then was lost entirely as trees obscured it. A little further on he saw the beginning of the high stone wall that bounded Park House. It was a massive structure, and Edward reckoned it would be a couple of miles in length, as it enclosed the entire property. No one could afford to build such a wall today, he mused, and probably very few people could afford even to keep it in repair.

He saw the entrance ahead, set back from the road as the wall curved to make an elegant semi-circle in the centre of which were two massive iron gates. These were shut, and appeared to be locked too, with a length of chain round the lock. They were topped by two decorative figures, but he was uncertain what they were meant to represent.

It was possible to see through the ironwork, which bore a pattern of leaves, ornamental flowers and seashells, and was painted black but flaking with rust. An avenue of trees stretched away on the other side, disappearing into shadow, while just inside the gate stood a small lodge, silent and empty, with its windows boarded up. What a pity, he thought. The dispersal of wealth had brought casualties as well as benefits.

He continued down the lane, keeping the same steady speed. Had anyone seen him, they would not have guessed his interest.

He reached the old station at the bottom of the lane, and could have turned towards the village but he decided to go back the same way.

A couple of hundred yards from the big gates he drew up, got out and inspected the rear tyres. He could see the lodge, and assured himself that no one was there. Back in the car, he drove on until he was almost level with the gate, then left his seat as if still not satisfied, and took another look at his wheels.

There was no sound from within the grounds, and no movement. The avenue curved through a shrubbery; the house itself was out of sight.

Edward didn't know what he had expected – or hoped – as he returned to the car and drove away. The contrast seemed remarkable to him. Yesterday a sense of life, of youth, vitality and laughter had spilled out from this place, yet this morning it was grey and deserted. One would swear that no one lived behind those walls.

Back at the house, he made himself a cup of coffee and sat down as though to plan a campaign. The truth was that he didn't know exactly what the campaign was to achieve. He remembered that once, as a schoolboy, he had watched a woman undressing at a bedroom window, and he had felt guilty about it. But whatever was his present intention, he felt no vestige of guilt. One could walk through a picture gallery or a museum and see representations of beautiful women, feeling nothing but pleasure, appreciation; an assertion of the joy of life. In a way that was what he felt now. Those women – the trio in the garden – had been an assertion of life's meaning.

In a mirror he caught sight of himself, smiling, as he wondered why he was bothering with this justification. The truth was that he had been caught up in a mystery, and he was eager to investigate it. After all, wasn't he really looking for a man and a wolf?

As he finished his coffee Edward was aware of a certain doubt creeping into his mind. He didn't question what had happened – that was undeniable. But he began to wonder whether it had really been all that significant. Three young women had been sunning themselves in what was to them their garden. They thought they had complete privacy, so no wonder they were so casual and relaxed.

As he strolled through the garden and down the path between tall trees, he wondered whether they were sisters. There had been something similar about them. All three were darker than most Europeans – but the family had lived abroad, John had said. They were certainly not the tall, slim ideal of the fashion models. If anything, they were less than medium height, and had stronger bodies, powerful thighs, broader shoulders. There was nothing of the brittle-boned society beauty about them . . . And yet at the same time they were beautiful. More than beautiful: they were compelling – otherwise, Edward asked himself, why was he still thinking about them? He had only to drive up to London and a most attractive actress, girlfriend of many happy occasions, would have been delighted to welcome him back into her life.

But he was plagued with the spell cast by the picture of three girls in the sunshine. As he stood under the yew tree, with the tree-house over his head and one foot on the low wall that overlooked the fields, he wasn't sure whether he wanted the spell to be broken.

He measured with his eye the distance to the Park House wall. He had thought it to be about fifty yards, but perhaps it was a little more. The wall curved away towards the country road along which he had driven that morning, and also ran in the other direction, directly away from where he stood, backing on to the fields. Because of the angle, it was difficult to see the length of that section of the wall, but something in the shadow caught his eye. It took him a moment or two to realize that the shadow was made by a break in the wall, and something that appeared to have been built on top.

Edward checked the ground in the field before him. The stream was a tiny trickle, and the mud was caked. He climbed down and stepped easily across the water. Insects hummed in the dry grass, and a solitary bird sang in the trees nearby; otherwise, it was dream-like and silent. He walked along by the high wall, taking his time. As he approached the break in the wall he saw that there was a modest portico built into the wall, with two decorative figures on top, and he realized it was a gateway; not large like the main gate, but simple and solid. Of course, these fields behind the walled garden must have belonged to Park House in its heyday. This would be the back entrance, so to speak, which the family would have used when visiting their farmlands to keep an eye on their stock.

The gate was designed, like those at the main entrance, with decorated ironwork and with an old rusty lock. There was no chain around it, and Edward thought when he first tried it that it was going to open: the handle turned, but nothing budged. He tried again, but it was as solid as a rock. He crouched down to examine it. It proved to be a tongue-and-groove lock with a massive lever which looked as though it hadn't been used for years. A sprinkle of rust had come off on his hands.

The two plaster figures on either side of the gate had been attacked by the weather, wind and rain having worn away much of their features. They were like gargoyles and very old – older than the rest of the wall, he considered. On one side an animal was leaping down with wings outstretched, and on the other a similar animal was playing a fiddle. This time it was possible to make out what sort of animal it was. Had it not been for the wings, it could have been a wolf.

He had an odd sensation . . . A wolf? He looked again at the figures. In spite of the crumbled plaster they were undoubtedly wolves. The wings were an artist's addition to make the image more fearsome. But wolves? Was it just a coincidence, or did this have anything to do with the children's story? Had they at any time seen these figures? Were the ones on the main gate wolves as well? It was very likely. So if they had seen the figures, if these had stayed in their minds – perhaps in their subconscious – then they themselves might have created the

32

wolf-image. He was increasingly convinced that this was the origin of . . .

Speculation stopped dead! A most unholy sound stunned him. Edward felt his skin prickle . . . his heart jumped.

He was standing in front of the gate, looking up at the figures. Ahead of him, in the garden itself, he could see no sign of life, nothing but a tangle of shrubs and, beyond, untended trees. He looked up again at the flying wolf. It was a mad fantasy! He pressed his face against the gate and tried to look in, but it was impossible to see to left or right. These gates and this high wall might have been designed not so much to keep people out as to keep people in. He was about to step back when he heard something moving in the bushes.

At first he thought it was a man running, but there was too much movement, too many flying feet. Besides, whatever was approaching was too low to be a man. Something was racing close to the ground. Edward crouched down to peer into the undergrowth.

He had a brief glimpse of an animal's legs going fast over the ground, of leaves sprayed up, bushes brushed aside. He was appalled to see how like the legs were to those of a wolf, with thick hair and black paws. The rest of the animal was out of sight. And the unholy sound which he had heard before was repeated – this time at hand, a few yards away . . .

It was an animal howling – an animal on the hunt, and close to the kill!

Edward was galvanized into action. This mad race through the undergrowth, this howl – both were directed at him! He threw himself back from the gate. He was just in time, for the iron structure shook with the impact as the creature threw itself against the bars. The lock shuddered . . . a trickle of stone dust fell. A moment later it shook again as the animal launched itself against it a second time. Edward prayed that the hinges were solid, as the snarling rose to a crescendo only inches from his ear.

But the gate held, and the animal let out a terrifying howl which left Edward sweating . . . Two great paws rested on the iron bars, head-high. It must have been standing on its hind paws, upright like a man. But bigger than a man: it must be huge! It might think he had gone away – but of course it could smell him. Indeed, Edward could smell the brute himself: an odour of sweat and fur, and another smell – pungent, acrid – which he couldn't place.

Strength oozed back to his limbs, and he began to edge away. But even as he moved a pointed snout thrust between the bars. The mouth was open, revealing two rows of vicious teeth. Saliva flowed from the animal's jaws, the upper lip was pulled back in a snarl. It tried to jerk its head towards him, but the gap between the bars was narrow, without space enough to get the snout any further through. The animal couldn't see the man it smelt, and the frustration seemed to drive it into a frenzy of hysterical yelping. Its excitement was terrifying as Edward backed away along the wall.

For a moment the animal vanished from the gate, then the big paws were back . . . then went again . . . then once more the snout came through, and the beast gave tongue to its defeated fury.

Edward knew he was safe; he could now turn and run.

He heard voices and stopped, appalled. Someone might open that gate!

Two male voices were confusedly shouting in a foreign language. Then a man cried: 'Back! Down . . . good dog! Good dog . . . back.' The animal was still snarling, but the howling stopped.

Edward leaned against the wall. He saw a couple of hands grasp the iron bars, and the gate was shaken . . . Then there was another silence, then the sound of something scraping on metal. Someone was trying to unlock the gate, but it remained closed. Hands appeared on the bars again, and another man asked questions. It was obvious that they could see nothing through the bars of the gate.

'Good dog . . . good dog.' It sounded as though they were moving away. The animal – 'dog' they had called it – apparently moved off with them.

Edward waited until they were out of earshot, then hurried to the relative safety of his sister's garden. He stood in the shadow of the tree-house, looking across to the Park House wall. If the gate had been unlocked and that beast had been let out, he wouldn't have given much for his chances, nor for the chances of anyone – man, woman or child.

* * *

34

Margaret returned with the children after tea.

'Did you go to the pub for lunch?'

'No. I didn't feel like it.'

'Are you all right?'

'Yes, thanks. Fine.'

He wasn't quite sure what to tell her.

'We've got new shoes, Uncle Eddie,' both Henry and Caroline informed him. They put them on and cavorted about.

'Like them?'

'Splendid . . . and all the latest style.'

They were so vulnerable, he felt. Only a high wall and a rusty gate stood between them and that murderous brute. He didn't think he could tell Margaret. It would be better to wait and speak to John.

'So what did you do all day?' they asked him.

His instinct was to tease, to mock; that was what they expected of him.

'I just practised a few tricks.'

'You didn't,' Caroline scolded him. 'You didn't do any tricks.'

'Come on, you two,' called Margaret. 'Early tea and early bed. You've had a long day.'

Edward walked round the house. He had an urge to see that the windows were shut properly, and to try the doors.

'How long have these people been in Park House?' he asked Margaret.

'I don't know. John's not sure.'

If they had been there for more than a week, had that dog been there all the time?

'Do the children play in the wood?'

'Of course,' said Margaret.

'I don't suppose they could hurt themselves down there?'

'Hurt themselves? How?'

'Oh I don't know. Fall out of trees . . . fall over your wall . . . get stuck in the stream.'

'They know not to play near there.'

'Do you ever go near the stream?' Edward asked Henry, later.

'No,' said Henry. 'Well . . . not much.'

'It's safe,' Caroline told him.

'It's not,' Edward said.

'It's tiny! A baby couldn't drown in it.'

'Your mother says you're not to go there.'

35

They looked at him in surprise, for he wasn't normally on the side of law and order.

'Well, we don't go near it,' said Henry firmly. 'Not for a long time.'

'Not for days,' said Caroline.

Edward was strangely glad when they were bathed and in the safety of their beds. But surely it was an illusory sense of safety?

He had to say good-night to them several times.

'I'm not sleepy,' said Henry. Later he called: 'Eddie . . . Uncle Eddie!'

'What is it?'

'Did you go to the tree-house?'

He hesitated. 'Yes.'

'Did you see anyone?'

He hesitated again. 'I think I heard someone.'

'Did you see the wolf?'

'Go to sleep,' he called.

Edward went out and walked round the garden until his brother-in-law came home. John joined him on the lawn, looking pleased with himself.

'You were asking about the people next door, weren't you?'

Edward was taken aback. He had intended to bring up the subject, but hadn't expected John to do so.

'Well, I've got news,' his brother-in-law went on, grinning with pleasure. 'They must be damn nice people. Sensible, anway. They haven't been here much more than a week and they've made two subscriptions in the village – one to the Conservation Society and one to our section of Greenpeace.' These were two activities dear to John's heart. 'And what's more, somebody there, the man of the house, I suppose, has given the local hunt to understand, in no uncertain terms, that he will not tolerate them riding or hunting over his land.'

'Who told you this?'

'Common knowledge. Chaps on the train were talking about it. Seems the occupants did some shopping in the village, and were quite friendly – very civilized, rather distinguished, I hear.'

Edward frowned. None of this tied in with his experience of their neighbours.

'I was going to talk to you about them,' he said. 'They've got

36

a large and very fierce dog that roams around their garden, making the most alarming sounds.'

'Like what?'

'Howling. Barking. Going into a frenzy at the sound of strangers.'

'Well, it would, wouldn't it? If it's a guard dog.'

'I was thinking about your two kids.'

'What about them?'

'Are they safe?'

'They don't go down to Park House.'

'The dog might get out.'

'Good lord, old man, there are all sorts of hazards in the country. The farmer had a bull in that field. Maniacs go shooting at weekends. The bloody hunt went through our garden. Kids learn to look after themselves in these parts.' He didn't appear disturbed.

'It was a damn big dog.'

'It would be,' agreed John. 'My guess is they're a wealthy bunch, and they probably have a thing or two worth pinching. Anyone with their wits about them nowadays is wise to have some sort of protection. Burglar alarm, guard dog, something like that.'

Edward shrugged, aware that he wasn't making any impression. 'You haven't seen this dog, have you?'

'No.'

'Nor heard it?'

'No,' admitted John.

'You might change your mind when you do.'

'Doubt it,' said John. 'As a matter of fact, I've often thought of having a dog myself.'

Edward let it go at that.

Over the evening meal John told his wife the same news about their new neighbours. 'Seems they gave a really large subscription to the Conservation people, who were quite shaken. Sounds like our new neighbours have their hearts in the right place. Old-fashioned values . . . retain the countryside . . . protect threatened species . . . and put that bloody Master of the Hounds – or whatever he calls himself – in his place.'

'That's nice,' said Margaret.

'A chap on the train met some of them in the village. A tall

37

chap, grey-haired, very charming, and a woman who was with him . . .'

'How old?' asked Edward.

'Don't know, same age, I think. My friend guessed she was his wife. There were a couple of girls in tow, apparently. According to the chap on the train they were damn attractive. Dark, quiet, didn't say a word . . . all rather turned-in on themselves. But of course they would be, coming to a new place like this. In these parts, you know, Eddie, it takes years before you're accepted.'

Edward wondered whether they had been two of the three he had watched from the tree-house.

'By the way, Eddie,' said John. 'How long are you here this time?'

'I'm in England for five or six weeks. I was thinking of going up to London for a few days. I've got one or two things to do.'

'Stick around,' said John. 'We don't see much of you nowadays. And the children love having you here.' That was as close as John would ever come to saying how much he liked having his brother-in-law around. He looked on him as a young brother; in fact, he had known him as a schoolboy, before Margaret's parents had died. He was a part of the family, and these last five or six years during which Edward had been gallivanting round the world had left a hole in the little clan.

'A noggin?' asked John. His slang was patently out-of-date, but it suited him.

'I'm going for a little drive around,' Edward informed the world. 'Anyone want to come?'

'I can't,' said Margaret. 'The gardener's here today.'

'Can I come?' called Henry.

'Can I come?' echoed Caroline. They danced round him, clutching his jacket.

'Where would you like to go?' They set off, both children squeezed into the front seat.

'Let's go to the sea,' said Henry.

'Too far,' said his uncle.

'London,' said Caroline.

'Don't be stupid,' said Henry.

'How about going to see the old railway bridge,' said Edward.

'And the station. We could climb up to the track, and see where the steam trains used to go?'

'Yes. Let's go on the track,' they agreed.

He was already heading in that direction, turning down the lane as he had done the day before, driving slowly towards Park House.

'I can see our house from here,' said Henry.

'I can't,' said Caroline. 'Show me . . . show me!'

'Over there, silly.'

They were both peering back as the main gates came into view. A large van, drawn up outside, had pulled into the semi-circular area, but still jutted on to the road. Edward came to a halt. The gates were open, and a couple of workmen in overalls were carrying crates into the lodge.

Edward peered out of the window, as though gauging the width of the road ahead.

'Do you have room?' another man called. 'I can get them to move.'

'I can manage,' Edward called back.

The man watched carefully as the Porsche went slowly past. Once clear Edward waved his thanks, and the man bowed and smiled. There was no doubt who he was. Grey-haired, distinguished, tall, an amused smile. The other thing Edward noticed was how expensively dressed he was. Almost too elegant for the countryside.

He had begun to accelerate before he noticed the dog on a chain by the gate. He caught another glimpse of it in the driving mirror.

'See that dog?'

'Yes,' said Henry.

'What do you think about it? Could people mistake it for a wolf?'

'It is a bit like a wolf,' agreed Caroline.

'That's not the proper wolf,' said Henry firmly. 'That's just a *dog*.'

'A very nasty dog,' said Caroline.

Edward drove on to the deserted station. A little further along the road was the old bridge, now no longer serving any purpose as it carried no traffic. The community was split between those who wanted to remove it and those who were determined to preserve it at all costs.

They climbed the embankment beside it and walked along

the desolate track, which was slowly being taken over by nature. Weeds grew through the pebbles. Everything was wild, deserted, silent. In the distance a fox crossed the track. A large bird circled high above: could it be a hawk?

The children spent some time exploring, and racing up and down the track, until Caroline grew tired.

'Right. Back to the house for ice-cream.'

'Is there any?'

'We'll pick some up in the village.'

He drove equally slowly on the way back. He had hoped the van would still be there so that he would have a reason to slow down, but it had gone. The gates were shut. As he drew level Edward remembered that he wanted to look at the figures above the gate. Were they also effigies of flying wolves?

'Tell me what you think these are,' he said as he braked beside the gates, and pointed at the figures on the pilasters at either side. The children peered up at them.

Both figures were eroded but recognizable. They were indeed wolves with wings; one was doing a dance with its tongue hanging out, and the other had something in its mouth.

'What's it eating?' asked Henry. 'Is it a bird?'

'If wolves could fly,' said Edward, 'birds wouldn't have much of a chance.'

At that moment he was aware he was being watched from the other side of the gate. The grey-haired man was standing outside the lodge. And there was another person directly behind him, whom Edward couldn't see properly.

'Excuse us,' called Edward. 'We were fascinated by your devices.'

At first the man didn't appear to understand, then he looked up. 'Oh yes, the figures. Splendid, aren't they?'

'My nephew and niece wondered what they were.'

'Ah . . . your nephew and niece.'

The man moved forward until he was close to the other side of the gate, and smiled at the children. 'The artist has taken a few liberties,' he said. 'He has given them wings, but in other respects we believe them to be wolves. Perhaps in those days there were still such creatures in these parts to model from. Maybe that is why they are so accurate.'

'Wolves eat you,' Caroline informed him.

'Nonsense,' said the man. The smile broadened. 'They have their own natural food on which they live, like every animal –

like you do yourself. Wolves are really frightened of people. They wouldn't eat a charming little girl.' He turned to look at Edward. 'Yes . . . I thought you were too young to be the father.'

'Their father is your nearest neighbour,' said Edward. 'They live over there.' He indicated with a nod.

'Oh, yes, I know.'

Edward could see the person standing behind: a young woman, dark and motionless, with an oval face, expressionless in repose. Her large eyes were fixed on Edward and moved only as he moved. Then to his surprise he noticed the dog at her feet. That too was watching him and the children, with quiet disinterest.

'I hope you are settling in?' said Edward as he turned to go.

'We are very satisfied,' said the grey-haired man. When they drove off, he waved to the children.

Edward called in at the village shop to collect the promised ice-cream. On the way back Henry said: 'Did you know that lady?'

'What lady?'

'At the gate.'

'No.'

'I think she knew you.'

'Why?'

'She was watching you all the time.'

As they left the car, Caroline, who had been unduly quiet, said thoughtfully, 'That was a nice man.'

They divided the ice-cream in the kitchen.

'We can't eat all this,' said Margaret.

'Yes, we can,' Caroline told her.

'We'll keep some for John,' said Margaret. 'Put it in the freezer.'

She didn't take part in the children's conversation.

'You seem a little *distraite*,' commented Edward.

'I'm worried about Horatio,' she said. Horatio was their cat; large and powerful, with a habit of bringing into the house dead rats, mice, an occasional squirrel, and once a vole.

'What's he brought you now?' asked her brother.

'He's off his food,' said Margaret. 'That's two days in a row he hasn't touched his supper.' The cat came and went as it liked, but Margaret always left a bowl of food and some milk

41

for it in the scullery. There was a flap on the back door for its entrance when the spirit moved it.

'Perhaps it hasn't been home,' suggested Edward. 'Come to think of it, I haven't seen the brute for a couple of days.'

Margaret frowned. 'He always comes back at night. That's what's worried me. The farmer at the back – his son, actually – shoots everything on sight. John has complained about it.'

'Does Horatio go that way?'

'He goes everywhere . . . and the field is a favourite place. I hope he hasn't been caught in a trap.'

'Are there traps?'

'There used to be. They were trying to trap foxes. A cub got caught and made a terrible noise. That was reported, and I think the trap was removed.'

'Where was it?'

'You know the big oak in the middle of the field? With a little dell behind it? It was in the dell.'

'I'll take a look,' said Edward.

'Me, too,' said Henry.

'And me.'

'Not on,' Edward told them.

'Why not?'

'Your father doesn't allow you to go into that field.'

'But . . .'

'You're certainly not going,' said Margaret.

Edward was glad of her support.

'Rotten sport,' the children muttered as they wandered off.

Edward felt very much better this time about going into the field. If he met anyone he could tell them he was looking for the cat. Nevertheless he took one of John's walking-sticks – the most substantial one he could find.

He went briskly down the path to the tree-house, stood on the wall and scanned the field. There wasn't a soul to be seen. The far end of the field was out of sight, dropping down in a gentle slope. It was a big field, with the old oak in the middle and more trees on the far side; an idyllic scene.

Edward gave the walled garden a cautious glance before he set off towards the oak, but all was quiet. As he walked further into the field he could see the gate, closed as before, with no sign of any activity. Curiosity overcame him, and he decided to take a path that would bring him close to it. He had thought of calling out the cat's name, but he was unwilling to break the peace that hung over the place. Even the birds seemed to have stopped singing. It was very hot, the sun almost directly overhead.

His attention kept switching from the oak to the gate, then back to the oak, which was huge and ancient, part of the trunk having been split by the weight of a low branch that now rested on the ground. The spread of the tree was enormous, casting a black shadow. He remembered the little dell as a dry, earthy hollow with an unpleasant smell, an ideal place for a fox's lair.

As he glanced again at the gate, he was startled to see it was no longer an empty frame. Figures, static, silent, were watching as he approached. His first instinct was to turn and head for the oak, but that would have given an odd impression to the people watching – whoever they were. There was no sign of a dog. So he continued in the same direction, and at the same speed, looking around, as though searching for the cat.

As he approached, he could make out three figures, none of whom moved. A girl stood in front, her hands on the bars. She was dressed in a dark skirt and blouse, reminding him of peasants in Southern Europe. Behind her were two men, also in dark clothes: slacks, open shirts and light-weight jackets, with wide-brimmed hats that shaded their faces. There was a marked resemblance between them all.

Edward saluted them as he approached.

'Good day!' He made an effort to appear casual. 'I'm looking for a cat.'

They watched blankly, not moving, viewing him silently.

He stopped by the gate. 'We have lost our cat,' he said. 'He sometimes comes into this field. I don't suppose any of you have seen him?'

It was as though they hadn't understood, then one of the men said, 'A cat?' He sounded incredulous.

'Yes. He hunts here,' Edward added cheerfully.

They didn't take their eyes off him. One man shook his head. 'No cat,' he said.

'I see,' said Edward. 'Thank you very much.'

He took his time, smiling, nodding, with a bow to the girl. Her big dark eyes were fixed on him, her black hair swept back; her skin glistened and her lips were parted, showing white, exquisite teeth.

He waved his stick and headed towards the oak, waiting until he reached it, until he was in its shade, to look back. But there was no one at the gate. Perhaps they had been as surprised, as embarrassed, as he himself had been?

He made a search of the area. The dell was overgrown with brambles, and loose stones rolled under his feet. The smell of rotted food and animal droppings hung heavily in the air. Tufts of hair were tangled in the bushes, but there was no sign of a trap, nor of the cat. A great split in the tree-trunk, where some big bird had made a nest, was now deserted and decaying. Edward was sure that Horatio had not come to a sticky end here.

The gateway was clear of onlookers, so he decided to go back the same way. Where had those three figures popped out from, he wondered. Was there a niche on the other side of the gate, which might explain the sudden appearance of people or dogs?

As he arrived within about twenty yards of the gate, he could see the overgrown bushes beyond it. Then the next second the girl stepped into view, much as she had stood before: hands grasping the bars, her face against them, eyes fixed on him. It was so unexpected that Edward stopped in his tracks. He had been thinking about her, of her blank, oval face, its lack of expression – and then there she was! But this time she was smiling, a clear signal of welcome.

For some reason, he didn't know how to react. He turned as if to head towards the stream, as though moving away from her. She still smiled – a small figure, not saying a word and oddly imprisoned behind the bars, yet seeming absolutely sure of herself. The strangeness of it fascinated Edward.

'Any cat?' she said, amused, almost mocking.

'I beg your pardon?'

Her voice was as soft as a purr. 'Any cat? You find any cat?'

He shook his head, wondering how old she was. About sixteen or seventeen? The shadowy look had vanished from her eyes; they were bright, laughing. There was no doubt what the message was, but perhaps it was merely innocence. He guessed by her accent that she was foreign: perhaps such an expression of invitation meant quite a different thing in her country?

She placed a finger against her chest and said, 'Santana.'

He was puzzled. 'Santana?'

She nodded. 'Santana,' she repeated happily. She pointed her finger at him. 'You?'

He understood. 'Edward,' he said.

She looked at him with pleasure. 'Edward,' she repeated. She pressed her face against the bars.

'No cat?' She was smiling, concluding one conversation, inviting the next. Then she motioned with her hand, beckoning him. 'Come and speak,' she whispered.

The two men might still be somewhere around. They might appear as before. Even more alarming, the dog might come through the bushes.

She must have guessed his thoughts, for she smiled. 'No people,' she said. 'No men. Come and speak . . .'

The smell of her was intoxicating. It wasn't perfume, nor even flowers, just the smell of her . . . She beckoned, crooking her finger and lifting her chin, drawing him towards her. One part of his mind protested: this was folly, the gate was locked, the promises – even if sincere – were futile. The invitation was impossible. But he came within arm's length and her hand reached out, catching at his jacket, drawing him against the bars.

He was astonished by her strength. Her hand went round his neck, a soft hand, gentle, delicate, firm, but the power that held him was totally unexpected. He was so startled that he tried to pull away, but a second later his face was against the bars and she drew his mouth down to hers. Suddenly dizzy, he clung to the gate. He had never before been so possessed. It was as if she were the stronger.

She relaxed her arm around him, drew back her head and smiled.

'Edward,' she said.

There was a faint noise some way off. Edward heard it, and stiffened. He backed away as the girl turned to listen, putting her head on one side, the look in her eyes changing to one that was cold, hard, fierce. He guessed that she could see someone in the garden behind. Her pretty lip curled, almost into a snarl.

There was certainly the sound of a snarl from close by. Someone . . . something . . . bore down on them from the bushes. He would have thrown himself aside as he had done the day before, had not the girl been standing in front. But at the last second she pulled away, and then it was too late for him to move . . . too late to get out of the way.

A lean shape came through the bracken to one side of the gate, the loose jaw open like that of the dancing figure of the wolf above the gate, the thick hair matted, the low, shaggy body running towards him with the stamina of its kind.

God! thought Edward, is that the dog Henry saw? Not a German Shepherd dog, more a real wolf. Gathering itself to leap in full flight!

He was still hanging on to the bars, transfixed, and didn't see where the second animal came from. He didn't even see if it too were a wolf. Or perhaps *this* was the dog he had seen yesterday? But the second wolf – if wolf it was – came from the opposite direction, throwing itself on the first animal, gripping it by the throat, rolling over with it in a struggling heap of snarling bodies. The noise was alarming. Dust rose from the dry earth. Both animals disappeared into the bushes, then rolled out again, snapping and yowling. Blood glistened on matted hair . . . The attacker seemed beaten and the fury of the second animal was terrifying.

Edward stood by the gate, bewildered, still holding the bars, hardly breathing. The whole thing must be a dream – no, a nightmare!

Someone was whistling in the distance . . . A long, piercing whistle, again and again, heard above the noise made by the fighting animals. They dragged themselves apart, still furiously snapping at each other; but the fight to the death was finished. The whistle had a power that overcame their fury. They went scrambling, limping away, through the bushes and out of sight.

Edward stood for a long time at the gate. Only gradually did he recover any sense of reality. Eventually he made his way across the field, and into the garden, wondering what had happened to the girl. He hoped she had escaped safely . . . He guessed she had.

It was impossible to go back and face anyone – even his sister and her children. Edward was too bemused to think clearly. He took his time over climbing into the tree-house, where he sat for a long while, looking through the old netting towards the iron gate.

'Good gracious,' said Margaret. 'I didn't mean you to go to all that trouble.'

'What?'

46

'You've been a long time.'

'Oh. Well, I had a look around . . . you know . . . I didn't notice the time.'

'Any sign of the cat?'

He could hear the girl say, '*Any cat?*'

'Are you all right, Eddie?'

'Yes, of course . . . Sorry, I was thinking. No, sorry. No cat.'

'It's not like Horatio,' said Margaret.

If those wolf-like dogs had caught Horatio he would never come home again!

'What have you done to your face?' asked Margaret.

He was surprised. 'Nothing. Why?'

'You've got a mark on it. Like a bite.' She lifted his chin to the light. 'Yes, a bite, on your lip. Didn't you know?'

'No.'

'With a spot of blood.'

'I must have done it going through brambles. A thorn.'

'It doesn't look like a thorn.'

'I'll wash it.'

He went to his room. The mark on his face was quite clear. The girl had bitten him. He remembered her beautiful teeth. He touched his face tenderly, then bathed it, experiencing a momentary pang as it began to fade.

'What were you doing in the tree-house?' asked Henry.

'When?'

'I saw you up in the tree-house this afternoon. You were there for hours.'

'I saw you too in the tree-house,' accused Caroline.

'I was looking for your cat.'

'In the tree-house?'

'You can see a long way from there. You can see all over the field.'

'Did you see anything?'

'No.'

They looked at him suspiciously.

'You're too big to play in the tree-house,' said Caroline sharply.

Edward generally waited for John to return home before he had his evening drink, but this time he poured himself a large Scotch.

'I'll wait for John,' Margaret told him.

Edward went and sat in the garden, in the alcove where the

47

sun's rays lingered warmly. He had already made up his mind what he was going to do – or rather, what he was *not* going to do. These people were his brother's neighbours, new to the village, new to this country, probably. The girl was hardly out of school. He was not going to get involved in any scandal. John was an excellent fellow, but conventional and conservative, and he, Edward, was here only in passing. No matter that what had happened was memorable – breath-taking – that was where it stopped. What a pity he hadn't met the girl at some other place!

The whole thing, he decided, had become exaggerated; a masculine fantasy. This was the first time he had relaxed for a year, and everything was out of proportion. He had worked it all out by the time John arrived home.

He held his glass aloft. 'Either you're late,' he called, 'or I'm suffering from belated jet-lag. My drinking time is out of sync.'

Later, when Margaret had joined them, John was delighted to give them both his latest news. 'This village is going to the dogs,' he said. 'Losing its character. Bad enough all these commuters buying their way in . . .'

'You're a commuter,' interrupted his wife.

'I've been here ten years,' said John. 'Anyhow, commuters are bad enough, but now we have foreigners.'

'I thought you said the Park House people were English,' said Edward.

'Maybe English in origin, but from somewhere abroad.'

Edward would have liked to pursue the subject, but John ploughed on. 'Now I hear another old country house has been taken over by some European.' It was hard to decide how much John's chauvinism was real and how much a joke.

'What house?' asked Margaret.

'You know the Tudor Cottage?'

'Who's bought that?'

'No one has actually bought it. Rented. Some woman, I understand, from some out-of-the-way place.'

'Like where?'

'I was told . . . H'mm . . . got it! Sardinia.'

'That's not out of the way.'

'It's hardly on the beaten track.'

'So that makes two families scattered over this vast stretch of Sussex,' Edward summed up.

'Actually not two families,' said John. 'I understand this lady

48

is alone. Although, for how long – knowing the easy attitude of relationships that some countries have . . .'

'Oh shut up, John,' Margaret said. 'Anyone would think we hadn't lived together before marriage.'

'Margaret, really!'

'Edward's a big boy now,' Margaret assured him.

'I gather the lady from Sardinia is a widow,' added John.

'Poor thing,' said Margaret. She went on to tell him about the cat.

John wasn't impressed. 'Horatio often goes away.'

'Not for two days. Nearly three.'

'He'll be all right.' John turned to Edward. 'Now, about your friends next door . . .'

'Not my friends,' protested Edward.

'They have a furniture van parked at the station. From overseas.'

'Your mates on the train know everything,' said Edward drily.

'They are just interested in their fellow beings! More drinks, you two?'

Edward had hesitated about telling them what had taken place that afternoon. He certainly wouldn't mention the girl, but he could say he had seen people at the gate. The worry was that they might ask questions which there would be no way of answering. But he had to warn them.

'When I was looking for the cat I saw those dogs again.'

'I thought you said there was only one?'

'I think I saw two. I was some distance off, but you can see through the iron gate in the wall.'

'You can't see much through there,' said John.

'They're huge dogs. No wonder Henry thought it was a wolf.'

'Has Henry seen them?'

'Well, he was talking about a wolf.'

'How could he see anything in that garden?'

'Maybe from his tree-house?'

'I doubt it.'

'Anyhow, they seemed to be fighting – kicking up a hell of a din, snarling like wild animals.'

'You tend to exaggerate, Eddie.'

'I don't like the idea of the kids . . .'

'You don't think a dog could jump that wall, do you?'

'No.'

49

'Well, then . . .'

Edward shrugged. There was little more he felt he could say.

John pulled out his diary. 'You've got this meeting tomorrow,' he said.

'What meeting?' Edward frowned.

'You said you had a meeting in London tomorrow,' said John.

He had forgotten. The events of the last two days had obliterated most things. 'Oh yes. That's scrapped.'

'When did you scrap that?'

'Well, anyhow, I'm not going,' said Edward. It would be hard to drag himself away at this point.

'Tell me when it's on again,' said John, 'and we'll meet in town for lunch.'

Edward nodded. In the distance he heard a long howl; it sounded like several animals. But neither John nor Margaret thought it remarkable.

Edward told himself he was looking for a solution but he wasn't sure what the puzzle was. He might be inventing this mystery, to which the answers were probably simple. The newcomers were entitled to keep dogs, and who could complain if an attractive girl should take a fancy to him? Or perhaps she had kissed him as a joke? Perhaps the other girls had dared her? She probably wasn't much more than a schoolgirl, herself.

He volunteered to go into the village for Margaret after John had left for the morning train, and drove the long way round, turning down by way of the station. He timed it to perfection, for a large van was edging its way into the Park House estate. He didn't recognize the little group clustered round the van, and the grey-haired man was not there. He returned from the village the same way by which time some crates had been unloaded and stacked outside the lodge, but a couple of empty ones lay by the gates. One of them had letters painted on its side. He could make out three words: 'Cagliari, Sardegna – Southampton.'

Sardegna . . . Sardinia? That rang a bell. Hadn't John said that the widow who had taken a cottage in the village came from Sardinia? There had to be a connection.

'Where is this Tudor Cottage?' he asked Margaret, as he handed over the basket of groceries.

It was a couple of miles away on the other side of the village, she told him. 'Why? You're not thinking of renting?'

'It's a thought.'

He took his time, first playing with the children, then making coffee . . . He didn't want to draw attention to his interest. It would probably add up to nothing, but perhaps he could prove a connection. Perhaps the grey-haired man would be there, or the girl?

Later that morning he drove through the village, down the hill through beech woods. It was a pretty part of the country, with woods backing on to fields, and lanes wandering off to unmarked destinations. He passed a collection of old farm buildings, then turned along the edge of a belt of trees. Set back amongst them was a thatched house, too large to be called a cottage, though that was the name on the gate: 'Tudor Cottage'. It had recently been painted and rethatched, and the drive was well-tended. Standing in the driveway was a Mercedes, but there was no sign of anyone there.

A little further along the road Edward pulled up outside a pub, went in, bought himself a drink and came out again to drink it in the sunshine. He kept one eye on the cottage.

About twenty minutes later he heard a car door shut and an engine come to life. He put his drink down and was in his own car in seconds.

The Mercedes was taking its time reversing out of the drive. Edward stopped to let it pass in front. The driver thanked him with a little bow. She was a woman in her twenties, fair-skinned, touched by the sun, dark-haired, with large oval eyes and a sharp, anxious face. She looked vulnerable, he thought, with her quick, nervous movements. He sat in the car, wondering why he was becoming involved.

Driving back past Park House, he saw the van still there, blocking the gateway with its collection of crates. There was no sign of the Mercedes. He wasn't sure why he had expected it to be there too.

'So you're not going up to London?' Margaret viewed her brother thoughtfully.

'Not for the time being.'

'What's happened to that nice girlfriend you had in town?'

'Which one?'

'The actress.'

'She's still there.'

'Still friends?'

'I suppose so. Though if you don't see someone except at two-yearly intervals things are inclined to change.'

'I thought you were going to see her?'

'Later on.'

'Oh?'

'My dear Maggie, don't worry, I'll go and see my actress – and any of my old girl-friends who are still around. But right now I like it here.'

She smiled warmly. 'The children adore you. They talk about you all the time.'

'Where are they?' he asked.

'They did say . . . Let me think. Oh yes, they're looking for the cat. I told them not to be late for supper.'

Edward strolled out to the old stables, where Henry had a den in the tack room. They weren't there. He continued down the rhododendron walk to the tree-house, but there was no sign of them. Horatio was an avid hunter; his patch was wide. If they were looking for him, they could be almost anywhere.

'No sign of the kids,' he told Margaret on his return.

'They'll be back as soon as they get hungry.'

He couldn't rid himself of an uneasy feeling as he walked to the main gate and along the thick banks of shrubs that hedged the property from the road. 'What the hell are you worried about?' he asked himself. But the thought of the big house in the walled grounds not far away preyed on his mind.

When he went back to the house Margaret was in the kitchen preparing supper. 'Did you find them?'

'They don't seem to be around,' he said casually.

She glanced at the wall clock. 'They should be back now.'

There was a Victorian walled garden behind the house, which neither the weekly efforts of a gardener nor the erratic attention given by Margaret and John could keep in order. Edward walked round it, then he checked the greenhouses.

Margaret was standing in the sitting-room by the big windows overlooking the lawns as he returned. 'Henry said something like, "We know where Horatio goes," and I said, "Good. Bring him back. Be careful if he's hurt".' She broke off. 'What is it, Eddie? You seem anxious.'

'It's those damn dogs,' he said.

'You think they might have hurt Horatio?'

'It's getting a bit late,' he answered.

52

As they stood there the children walked out of the shadow of the trees.

'Look! They're carrying something.'

They hurried to the front door and out around the house.

'It's not the cat,' said Edward.

Carrie saw them first and started to run towards them. 'Look, Mummy! Mummy! Look what I've got.' She was holding something above her head.

'What is it?' Margaret wondered aloud.

'Looks like a bundle of rags,' said her brother.

'And look what I've got,' called Henry. They arrived together, racing up excitedly.

'Look, Mummy!' Caroline was flushed with pleasure, and holding a doll. It was beautifully modelled, and wore the most exquisite clothes. A first glance told Edward that it was indeed special, with elaborate stitching on the blouse and skirt, and lovely, fading colours. Clearly the doll was clothed in the traditional costume of some Mediterranean country. It seemed to him more a museum piece than a child's toy.

'Where did you get that?' Margaret looked at the child in wonder.

'The lady gave it to me,' chanted Caroline.

'Look what I've got,' said Henry. He had been holding something behind his back, and now displayed it with a flourish. His mother took it.

'What is it?'

'A recorder! But much better than the ones at school. And you should hear him play.'

'Who?'

'The man. The man who gave it to me . . . the old man who spoke to Uncle Eddie.'

Margaret looked blankly at her son. 'Is it a recorder?' She handed it to her brother. It had seven finger-holes and a thumb-hole, and was fashioned out of wood with ivory moulding. Fine decorations encircled one end, and a thin silver band edged the pipe.

'When did he give it to you?' asked Edward.

'He was at the other gate,' said Henry. 'He was just standing there . . .'

'The gate to the field?'

'Yes.'

'You were in the field?'

53

'We were looking for Horatio. Mum said we were to look for him.'

'I didn't say in the field! You know you are not allowed . . .'

Henry interrupted: 'We saw this thing in the distance when we were on the wall – our wall. There was something lying on the grass.'

'I thought it was Horatio,' said Carrie. 'I thought he was dead. It made me cry.'

'I told her it wasn't a cat. But she thought . . . so I went to show her.'

'What was it?'

'A dead bird . . . maybe Horatio killed it. I showed it to Carrie and she stopped crying.'

'So you were both in the field?'

There was no denying it. 'We didn't mean to go.'

'You've been told by your father . . . I don't know what he will say.'

'But it was all right,' said Henry. 'It's quite safe, you know . . . they aren't allowed to keep the bull in there now. There aren't even cows.'

'Then we saw these nice people,' said Carrie. She clutched her doll passionately.

'This lady and the old man,' said Henry.

'And the other lady. A young one,' added Carrie.

'Yes, the girl,' nodded Henry. 'They were just watching and smiling.'

'They were at the gate when you found the dead bird?' The scene presented itself to Edward as though he himself had been there.

'I got a surprise,' said Carrie.

'So did I,' said Henry. 'So I said, "How do you do" to them. I thought that would be polite.'

'You mean they just happened to be carrying this doll with them?' Edward was incredulous.

'Of course not,' scoffed Henry. 'They didn't know they were going to meet us and have a talk.'

'They sent the other lady away,' said Carrie.

'The young one,' said Henry.

'And when she came back they gave us these things.' Carrie cradled the doll with delight, but Henry frowned. He felt he was on tricky ground; the adults were unexpectedly critical.

'I told them we weren't really allowed in the field,' he explained.

'What did they say?'

'The man said it was very wise of my parents. Not because of cattle or stallions, but there might be strangers around, and nowadays people didn't always behave like they should.'

'I thought he meant robbers,' said Carrie. 'And the man said they had dogs to keep robbers away and Henry asked if they were dangerous and the man said, "Only if bad people got into the grounds."'

'Did they open the gate?' asked Edward.

'Of course not. It's locked. They haven't even got a key.' Carrie was positive.

Margaret took the doll carefully from her daughter. 'What are we going to do about this?' she said. 'I think it's very valuable.'

'I love her . . . She's beautiful.'

'It's not really a child's toy.'

'I'll look after it!'

'I don't know *what* your father will say.'

Margaret headed towards the house, the children following, anxious to explain. 'We had to go in the field. The dead bird might have been Horatio.'

'What else did the people say?' asked Edward.

'Not much. Just how nice it was here. How peaceful . . .'

'How near the gate were you?'

Margaret frowned. 'What do you mean?'

'Were they still near the dead bird, or were they close to the gate?'

'That's a funny question,' said Margaret.

'We were right beside the people,' said Henry.

'Right at the gate,' said Carrie. 'They had to pass our presents through the bars.'

It was a bizarre picture, and didn't fit with Edward's own encounter at that gate. He followed the others into the house.

'What about the second lady, the one they sent to get these things. What was she like?'

'She was just a girl,' said Henry dismissively.

'I'll keep these just now,' said Margaret, and put the doll and recorder in her desk.

'Oh Mummy!'

'Till your father gets back.'

She sent the children off to wash before their meal, and Edward examined the presents.

'They must give them back,' said Margaret. 'It could be embarrassing.'

'Perhaps your neighbours don't know the local ways. I mean, if they have come from abroad . . .'

'But it's ridiculous to give children valuable gifts like these.'

Edward shrugged. 'Some countries lavish presents on children. The Italians . . .'

'It's ridiculous,' Margaret repeated. 'Look at this dress.' She held up the doll. 'Look at the work that's gone into it! It must be a replica of the real thing. Carrie would ruin it.'

'She was being very careful with it.'

'And the recorder must be worth a small fortune!'

'Oh, I don't know . . .'

'It's not for a schoolboy to practise on!' she said firmly.

'Perhaps they've got lots of things like these. If they are wealthy they probably think nothing of giving this sort of thing away. Besides, it might be their way of making friends . . .'

She was not impressed, looking coldly at the two gifts. 'We don't even know these people, Eddie.'

'I know what you mean . . . but there are different customs.'

'I don't know what John will say.' This clearly was the dominant concern in his sister's mind.

She intended to bring the problem up as soon as John reached home, but he was full of his own news as he came into the house.

'You'll never guess the latest piece of gossip from the commuters' club.'

'Darling, just a small matter about the children.'

But John was ploughing on. 'You know the Colemans are giving a drinks party tomorrow?'

'Of course I know. You said you didn't want to go, you said they were boring.'

'I met old Coleman on the train, and he's not as dull as I thought. He particularly wants us to go, and take your young brother. They remember you, Eddie, from the last time you were here. Apparently you were a great hit.'

'I don't remember them,' said Eddie. 'Who are the Colemans?'

'Our local tycoon. Chairman of Coleman Cards – you remember? They make these Christmas cards and things. Mother's

56

Day and all that. The huge house on the other side of the village?'

'All pictures and furniture,' added Margaret. 'Rather a show-off place.'

Eddie nodded. 'I remember. I showed someone an Arabic dance. I think I'd drunk a bit.'

'Well, they want you back. And it's going to be interesting: our near neighbours have been asked as well.'

'The people from Park House?'

'Correct. It's a chance to meet on neutral ground. If they're reasonable, we'll ask them here.'

'Are they all going to the Colemans'?'

'What d'you mean?'

'There seem to be a lot of people in there.'

'I don't know. Old Coleman said the owner and his wife, I think.'

'So are we going?' asked Margaret.

'Why not? Should be fun. Anyhow, I said we'd turn up. It's just a pre-lunch drink or two, nothing formal. Might be a few snacks – but you never know with the Colemans. With all that cash they're notoriously mean.' John was about to go upstairs. 'I'll get changed. Pour the drinks, Eddie; I'll be down in two ticks.' He was generally at his most energetic when he returned home on a Friday. The prospect of a weekend in the country always enthused him.

'Just a moment!' called Margaret.

He turned back at the door, and she showed him the doll and the recorder.

'Henry and Carrie were in the field . . .'

'I thought we told them not to!'

'They were looking for Horatio, and they saw the people next door.'

'The Park House people?'

She nodded. 'Apparently they were at their back gate. They had a chat with the children, and for some reason they gave them these. Carrie had the doll, and Henry the recorder.'

'They look rather special,' said John.

'So we thought,' said Margaret. 'I wondered whether we shouldn't give them back.'

John growned. 'Oh, I don't know. It's a friendly gesture . . . but I know what you mean. A bit ostentatious, isn't it? Over the top. I know, when we meet them tomorrow we'll just bring it up, casually. Say the things might be too good for our kids. Say they aren't old enough to appreciate them. We don't want to create problems – let's play it by ear.' He went off to change.

'You never know with John,' Margaret complained. 'Sometimes he's so old-fashioned, insisting on what he calls "the proper way to do things", and sometimes it's anything goes.'

They were on their third drink before John appeared, now in his 'country' clothes.

'Right,' he grinned at his brother-in-law. 'What sort of an exhibition are you going to make of yourself tomorrow? Coleman and friends are looking forward to it.'

Coleman turned out to be a much better host than John had suggested.

'I'd like you to meet another widely travelled guest,' he said to Edward: 'Dr Paul Shannon.'

The tall, grey-haired man smiled and bowed. 'We have already met, my neighbour and I.'

'Splendid,' said Coleman. 'Then I must introduce you to the rest of the family. Edward is merely an occasional visitor, but Margaret and John Warwick are almost on your doorstep.' He moved away into the crowd.

'How are you settling down?' asked Edward.

'A slow process.' The other man smiled as he gave a shrug. 'We are a large family. The house is very satisfactory.'

'Did Coleman say "Doctor"?'

'Not a medical doctor – although I did study a little medicine when I was younger. The title is academic, given, I suspect, by an impoverished and grateful university.'

Waiters with silver flagons ('That was a bit much,' said Margaret afterwards) passed amongst the guests: 'Fruit cup, sir? Or something stronger?'

'I hear you've just come from abroad,' said Edward.

The Doctor nodded. 'We are a little nomadic in our family. Sardinia was our recent home, but we have been forced to move on several occasions.'

'Forced?'

'You would say "forced". For example, some of us were happy to escape from Russia when the Revolution came. Then there were troubles in Macedonia, Croatia . . . as I am sure you know.'

'A little before your time, Doctor?' suggested Edward.

He nodded. 'Then Fascist Italy was unfriendly – wartime London uncomfortable – Eastern Europe could hardly feed itself, let alone immigrants.'

'You went back to Eastern Europe?' That surprised Edward.

'Many of my cousins hold those countries very dear. They feel at home there. Although they are British, they have roots in such parts of Europe.'

'What took you abroad?'

The Doctor was amused by the question. 'Like you yourself, sir, I imagine, livelihood – survival. One needs must go where fortune beckons, and . . . may I call you Edward?'

'Of course.'

'And at first, I think, we went as mercenary soldiers to several countries, many centuries ago. As you know, Edward, spend a few generations in other lands and one is alien in one's own country. Perhaps that is something you should consider yourself.'

Edward grinned. 'I do. But the risks pay dividends.'

The Doctor agreed. 'Of course. We have been involved in many fields. Banking, finance, in the past – but our family found that artificial.'

Edward nodded. 'Money breeds money, but nothing is made.'

'Exactly. We have been in shipping, fruit growing – dried fruits, you understand – in timber mills, farming.'

'Quite a selection.'

'Have you any dealing in such areas, Edward?'

'Not really. I've been tidying up in parts of the world after local disasters – picking up pieces, buying, selling.'

Edward was intrigued by the conversation. The older man seemed surprisingly ready to paint a picture of himself and his family. Was there a purpose behind this open and friendly attitude? He couldn't think what it might be.

'How long do you stay here?' asked the Doctor.

'A couple of weeks.'

'You must visit us.'

'I would like to,' said Edward. He glanced round the room. 'Are you alone?'

'Some of the others are here.' Edward wondered whether that included any of the neighbours he had seen in the garden – or at their gate, for that matter. 'We have also met Henry and

Caroline,' said the Doctor. 'They told us their names. We were charmed by them. It is a happy moment to find such children, so bright, so intelligent – so in this world. Such splendid little people – strong, healthy.' He shook his head with admiration.

'I saw the presents you gave them,' said Edward.

'Gifts from my cousin,' said the Doctor. 'The Countess is always over-enthusiastic and spontaneous. She found the children delightful, and had to show her pleasure . . . I hope there is no problem.'

'I don't suppose so,' said Edward. It all sounded very reasonable.

'She is here,' said Dr Shannon. 'I would like to introduce you to Countess Clara.'

The woman advancing towards them looked about sixty. Her jet-black hair was piled on the top of her head, making her look tall, and she was elegantly dressed, perhaps more than a pre-lunch drinks party warranted, with a necklace, bangles and earrings. But Edward thought she carried it off rather splendidly.

She gestured, spreading her arms as she saw Edward. 'I know! The uncle!' She smiled broadly, not waiting for an answer. 'Henry spoke well of you. "He jokes and does tricks," he told us. An irresistible combination in a man with good looks and youth.'

'You are in England, my dear,' warned the Doctor, 'so one is not permitted to flirt.'

She pretended to draw Edward aside. 'My cousin is out of touch. He forgets the English also move with the times.' Edward wondered whether their charm was turned on especially for him. 'Invite him to see us,' she told her cousin.

'It is done.' He smiled and bowed. They were like a double act. 'But perhaps a little later, when we have settled in properly?'

'No, no. Now.'

Margaret and John joined them, and they were soon surrounded by what John called the 'commuter society'.

'What pleasant people,' said Margaret later, when the three were on their own again.

'Did you mention the presents to the children?' Edward asked.

'Actually I forgot.'

'I spoke about them. I think we shouldn't make too much of it.'

'I'm sure it's all right,' agreed Margaret.

'I very much doubt that "Countess" title,' said John.

'I think she is charming,' protested his wife.

The Countess saw them as they were about to go, and took Edward by the arm. 'I hear you leave soon . . . but visit first, please. You are not married? I know, I have asked about you. Don't be alarmed – not for myself. But I have most attractive nieces . . . quite a number, ten or twelve at the last count. Some are very beautiful, full of fire and vitality. I am sure there must be one amongst them for such a nice Englishman.'

The Doctor moved in behind. Her. 'My dear, this is not the market-place . . .'

'Poof! What does an old man know? I am only telling the truth about my girls . . . and they are not daughters, only nieces, so I have nothing to gain. Visit, and you shall see. I will send an invitation. Will you accept?' She didn't wait for his answer. 'Do the children swim?' she asked, and then swept away.

Margaret drove home, saying, 'John has drunk too much, and you, Eddie, have had your head turned.'

'She's a very charming lady,' Edward agreed.

'I can't see them blending with the local gentry,' said John.

'She said they don't go out much,' recalled Margaret.

As they drove to the front door, Henry and Carrie came rushing out.

'Mum! Daddy! Horatio's back!'

The cat came stiffly down the steps from the house.

'What's the matter with him?'

'He's been bitten, or something.'

'Or trapped or something.'

'He's covered in blood.'

'Dried blood.'

'We tried to wash it off, but he won't let us.'

The cat had a gash along his back, and a cut over one eye. Fur had been torn along one side.

'Poor Horatio.' Margaret tried to stroke him, but the cat pulled away. They watched him limp into the house.

'He must have put up a damn good fight,' said John.

* * *

A large white envelope was lying in the hall when they came in from playing croquet on the lawn, the children incensed with Edward.

'Eddie didn't win! He cheated! He went round the wrong way!'

'He missed a hoop.'

'You owe me money,' said Edward.

'We didn't bet!'

'Five p. each.'

'Dirty cheat!'

'Henry! Language!' Margaret was busy opening the envelope, which was marked 'Delivered by hand'.

'Oh, how sweet,' she said. Then she read out: 'So pleasant meeting our near neighbours. We understand the children enjoy swimming. No one uses our pool on Sunday mornings. Please make use of it tomorrow. Before noon, if convenient. Trusting we see you then.' It was signed 'Clara Savoia.'

'The Countess,' said John.

'Isn't that nice of them!' said Margaret. 'Would you like that, children? D'you want to go swimming?'

They skipped about delightedly.

As they pulled up outside Park House, a man was already unlocking the big iron gates and pushing them back. He bowed and waved the car through.

'I wanted to show you the figures on the gate,' said Edward. 'We'll have a look when we go.'

The man signalled to them.

'He wants us to drive on.' John called across: 'Do we go up to the house?'

He appeared not to understand, then he smiled and nodded. 'Yes, yes . . . the house.' He pointed to the drive through trees. The house could just be seen.

'Thank you.' John drove on. 'I don't think he speaks any English,' he said.

'Lots of people have foreign servants,' said Margaret. 'We could do with an *au pair* ourselves.'

'Good Lord, we're going to have to live up to the Joneses, are we?' muttered her husband.

A woman came from the house as they drew up at the front door.

'It's all very well organized,' John whispered.

She approached the car. 'The Countess is so glad you are able to be here. She leaves a message: she is sorry to be called away this morning, but if you come with me I will show you the swimming-pool and the rooms to change.' She was brisk and efficient.

'I hope it's not inconvenient?' said Margaret.

'Not at all. It is nice you could come today. Another time the Countess will be here to greet you.'

The pool was built in a large annexe at the back of the house. They passed through a conservatory full of exotic flowers, then along a couple of corridors. Everything had been newly painted and carpeted. There were pictures in the corridors, and windows that looked into another conservatory crowded with pot-plants, palms, fig trees and cacti. A dynamo hummed softly close by.

'This has cost someone a bob or two,' whispered John. There was soft luxury all round them. 'They've been here only a few weeks! How did they do it?'

The pool was enclosed and larger than they had expected; transparent water sparkled in the sunlight that shone from windows in the roof.

'If you prefer it more open . . .' Their hostess pressed a wall button, and part of the roof slid back.

'Enough?' she asked, and the pool was left half-open to the sky.

'Here you will find cabins to change.' They were ranged along one side, elegant, shining white cabins with smoked-glass windows. In each were chairs, towels, perfumes, powders.

'You are not to touch those, Carrie,' ordered her mother.

The woman with them smiled. 'Perhaps a little. To experiment for times to come.' She inclined her head. 'I leave you,' she said. 'If you wish anything, please ring.' She indicated the bells in each cabin. 'I am sorry there is no one here to look after you.'

'This is absolutely perfect,' said John.

She smiled her acknowledgement as she left.

'Did you ever see anything like it?' John looked around in admiration. 'They must be absolutely loaded. Wait till the Colemans see this!'

The children were already changing, and a moment later they were in the water.

'Stay in the shallow end, Carrie,' called her mother.

'I can swim, I can swim!' protested Carrie.

They swam up and down for the sheer pleasure of it. The water possessed an especially soft quality – was that just Edward's imagination, or was there something in the water? All around outside was so silent and empty that they were surprised when two boys came into the annexe. Both were in swimming trunks, and they stopped short, equally surprised to find strangers there.

'Excuse,' said one of them, and they turned to go.

'That's all right,' called John. 'Come in. There's plenty of room. And it *is* your pool.'

The boys stood uncertainly by the door, seeming not to understand. John waved them towards the pool. They smiled and nodded, and a moment later they dived in.

'Shows how fit you can get with a bit of regular exercise,' said John. The two boys were supple and strong. They swam the length of the pool, up and down, with a rhythmic crawl that hardly created a splash. Both were tinged brown by some southern sun. One in particular, with dark, curly hair, olive skin and wide, large eyes, reminded Margaret of old Italian frescoes. He could have been the model for some Cupid or god.

Afterwards the boys tried to understand what Henry said, standing beside him, listening, then slowly asking questions. The next time that Margaret was aware of them, Henry was sitting on the beautiful boy's shoulders – 'Well, he was beautiful. Really beautiful,' she insisted later. 'Very strong to lift Henry and Carrie like that. And none of those bulging, over-developed muscles boys sometimes have at that age.'

Henry called across to Margaret: 'This is Marcel. He's a year older than me.'

'He's what?'

'He's nine . . . nearly ten.'

'That's nonsense,' John said to her. 'Henry's got it wrong.' Marcel was certainly older than ten. The down on his chest was soft but plentiful, and the steady look in his eyes as he took in all about him was not that of a child.

A bell rang faintly in the distance. The two boys heard it and prepared to climb out of the water. They clapped Henry on the back and waved to Carrie. On the side of the pool they both gave short formal bows to the adults. 'With your permission,' they said, and hurried away.

'Why aren't *our* kids as well-mannered nowadays?' complained John.

'I think we should get out,' said Margaret. 'We don't want to outstay our welcome.'

'Out, you two!' called John.

'I brought towels,' said Margaret. 'I think we should use our own.'

By the time they were dressed it was mid-day.

'Come on, gang!' John swept the children before him. 'Time's up!' They were excited, skipping along the corridor as they retraced their steps to the car.

'I wonder if we should say goodbye and thank you to someone?' suggested Margaret.

'Doesn't seem to be anyone around.' John climbed into the car. The others followed. Eddie was about to take his seat when Carrie squealed: 'My costume! It's in the shower.'

'She forgets everything,' scoffed Henry.

'I'll get it.' Edward hurried away. The rooms and corridors were empty and silent, the thick carpets deadening any sound. As he went into the annexe he realized that someone was in the pool, and presumed that one of the boys had returned. But this was an even better swimmer than either boy had been.

The figure went through the water with the ease and style of a seal – head down, hardly turning to breathe, long hair streaming over brown shoulders, the rhythm hypnotic, the almost imperceptible paddle of feet sending the swimmer along at speed.

Edward stood watching in admiration. He was so enchanted that it was a couple of minutes before it dawned on him that the swimmer was female. The gently sloping shoulders and narrow waist gave place to wider hips and full, rounded buttocks. Her thighs and legs, curved, firm and strong, plunged her deep in the water as she turned to start each length. He was mesmerized, not just by the beauty of the figure, but by the grace with which she swam.

He was still motionless in the doorway when the swimmer came to a halt at the far end of the pool and swung herself from the water. A towel lay beside her and as she sat on the edge, her feet still dangling in the water, she began to wrap it about her head. He then realized that, apart from the towel, she was completely naked.

She caught sight of him, and for a moment she stopped

drying her hair, her arms still raised, lifting her breasts, exaggerating the full curves, bringing up her nipples to sharp, delicate points. But she didn't move, or seem in any way disconcerted, merely watching him fixedly, a little puzzled perhaps, as if unsure whether or not she knew this stranger.

He felt his throat had gone dry. 'I'm sorry,' he said. 'I didn't know anyone was here.'

She still watched him, silent, unmoving; then she began to massage her hair softly through the towel. She didn't appear concerned that she was naked, or, indeed, as if she were aware of it.

'We left a costume . . . in the shower,' he explained. 'Excuse me. I'll get it.'

He had a feeling she didn't understand what he said, but she gave a little nod, and he went into the shower. Carrie's costume was on the floor. Out of her sight he drew a deep breath. He had seldom seen a girl as beautiful. Her casual manner bewitched him: there was no modesty, false or otherwise, she was completely sure of herself. Body and person were one. That was the only way he could think of her – as unaware and accepting as – as any animal. He caught sight of himself in the shower mirror; he was shaking his head.

She could have gone while he was in the cubicle, but she hadn't moved when he reappeared. She was still drying her hair as it fell from the towel to her shoulders, jet black on to the golden-brown of her skin. He realized with a start that there was something familiar about her, and he stopped to stare across at her.

She was still looking at him, steadily, with interest, but with no great involvement.

It came to him! She was so like the girl at the gate! The girl who had put her arms through the iron bars and dragged him, a willing victim, against the ironwork, against her own body where that was possible – certainly against her mouth. He remembered the sensation – light-headedly, as though he were drunk.

The name she had told him came back to him, and he said it now, doubtfully: 'Santana?' But even as he said it he knew this was not the girl. She stopped drying her hair and let the towel drape over her shoulders. There came a little flicker of expression – the first – across her face. She gave a slight shrug, a little dismissive, but she said nothing.

Edward hurried away. He almost ran along the corridors. God knows what he thought he might meet . . . He told himself he should have seen this was not the same girl . . . and yet they were so similar in many ways. Both had that long, black hair; both had the same slightly blank oval face; both had the same full sensitive lips. And he guessed they were the same height. Both so sensuously feminine. Could they be sisters . . . cousins? Was it a family resemblance?

'What kept you?' asked John.

'What?' He was bemused.

'You've taken your time.'

'Oh, sorry.'

'Eddie got lost! Uncle Eddie got lost!' mocked Carrie.

'Say "thank you" for your swimming costume,' her mother reminded her.

Edward wasn't sure why he didn't mention the girl, either then or later when the children had gone. He usually passed on any amusing or interesting tit-bits to his sister.

This time he said nothing . . . and that surprised him.

A car was standing outside the house when they reached home, and Henry recognized it.

'That's the police car.'

'It's old Parker,' muttered John. 'What the devil does he want?'

Sergeant Parker lifted himself laboriously from his seat as the other car drew up.

'Sorry to bother you, Mr Warwick, ma'am. It's Mr Edward I wanted to see, if you don't mind.'

'What have you been up to, Eddie?' asked John.

The sergeant gave a wan smile. 'It's a bit of help we want, if Mr Edward can spare the time.'

'What's the problem?' asked Edward.

'As I remember, sir, you've been doing a bit of work in Italy?'

'Some time ago,' admitted Edward.

'So we thought you might still know some of the language.'

'A little . . .'

'Got a difficulty with communications,' went on the sergeant. 'There's this lady in Tudor Cottage, new to the district . . .'

'Something happened to her?' asked Edward sharply.

'Not to her, sir. She's shot her dog.'

Edward drove off in his own car, following the sergeant.

'Don't worry about lunch,' called Margaret. 'It's only salad.'

They parked outside the cottage, and Edward followed the sergeant in. The widow from Sardinia was sitting straight-backed on a chair, pale-faced and motionless, and it was obvious to Edward that she was in a state of shock.

'I don't think she's in any condition to answer questions,' he told the sergeant.

'I just want to know if she has a licence for the gun.'

Edward turned to the girl – she was older than he had supposed, maybe in her late twenties. '*Avete uno permesso per questo fucile?*' he asked.

She understood and nodded. She pointed to a desk, then rose from the chair where she had been sitting with her face hidden in her hands, crossed to the desk, and took out a bundle of papers.

'Somewhere,' she said.

The sergeant glanced through them. 'Thank you, ma'am. All in order,' he said.

'What about the dog?' asked Edward.

'That's not really our problem,' said the sergeant thought-fully. 'It was killed on her own property – Mrs Balelli is the present tenant here. The normal practice would be for her to have it buried. Or the vet in the village could take it away.' He handed the papers back to Edward and put away his notes. 'It's not really a police matter, you understand. Of course we like to be of assistance if need be, but it was an accident, no one else was involved, and no one got hurt.'

He took Edward with him to the door.

'Thanks, Mr Glover,' he said. 'I thought it would be easier for the lady if she had someone who could talk her own language – explain things. She won't hear any more from us, since the firearms licence is in order. Can't think what she wanted such a big dog for, anyhow.'

Edward felt uneasy. His recent memory of dogs disturbed him. 'Was it her dog?' he asked.

'It's got her name on the collar,' said sergeant. 'Perhaps you'll have a word with her, sir? Make sure she's understood? I'll drop by in a couple of days to see if she's all right.' He drove off as Edward went back into the house.

'Is there anything I can do for you?' he asked.

The girl looked up. He had noticed when he first saw her

how nervous she looked. Now the pale, strained face showed her alarm. She began to talk rapidly in Italian.

'I'm sorry,' he said. 'I can't follow.'

She began again, slowly, in English. 'I was going to my car. I had to go out. There was this noise . . . like howling . . .' Her fingers twitched nervously, and every now and again she glanced sideways, as though on guard.

'I had heard this before. By day once . . . but especially at night. I thought it was just to frighten.'

'I'm sorry. I don't quite . . .'

'The dog howling,' she said. 'And at night I watched from the window, up there . . .' She pointed to the cottage staircase. 'My bedroom. The garden is wild behind this house. It goes to trees.'

Edward nodded.

'In my room I was safe. Carefully I locked all doors and windows. I know how these things are. From my window I could see in the moonlight trees, bushes, the fence . . . The dog came over the fence, I think. He jumped.'

'Which dog do you mean?' Edward wasn't sure he understood. 'Your dog?'

She shook her head. 'The big dog. It kept in the shadows and howled. To let me know.'

'What?'

'That it was there.'

He wondered whether she was in greater shock than he had supposed, for she wasn't making sense. She was now agitated, sitting up sharply, peering into the garden.

'It came through the trees at the back,' she went on, 'so no one else would see it. If I said anything people would think I was foolish or mad . . . That was the purpose, to make me seem mad.'

Perhaps he should phone John or Margaret? They would know the local doctor. He guessed Mrs Balelli needed more help than he could give.

'It moved in the dark where I could not see . . .' she went on. 'Then it would howl, or worse – this little whining noise – just below my window. And I looked down . . . it was there, looking up, with green eyes. Not looking fierce . . . No, just inevitable.'

He was sure she had the wrong word. '*Inevitable?*'

She nodded. 'It would follow for ever until I ran far away. If

69

I stayed it would always be in the dark woods – maybe round a corner in the garden . . . Always when I was alone.'

'What did your own dog do?'

'I have no dog,' she said.

He looked blankly at her. 'But I understood you had shot your own dog?'

'I shot the big dog,' she said. 'The one that was following . . .'

Edward wasn't sure he could cope with this. Maybe it was her fantasy?

'Where is it now? The dog?'

'It came to the window,' she explained. 'I ran to lock the door . . .'

'When?'

'Very early this morning . . . as I came down from my room to make coffee. It was there.' She pointed to the window beside them. 'I tried the door. It was still locked, so I would be safe. I came back. At first I did not see it, I thought it had gone . . . and then . . .' She could hardly bring herself to carry on. 'It came from *somewhere*, right against the window again – as I stood here. Almost beside me . . . and only a window . . . thin glass. I did not dare move, I did not breathe. And it stood upright, you understand, on its back feet! Taller than a man! Its head was up *there* . . . above mine. I was shaking. My hands – my fingers – I could not open the cupboard where the gun was kept. I looked over my shoulder. It was still there, watching as I tried . . . I thought the weight of it would smash the window and it would be in the room. But something happened. These windows, the top part slides down. Perhaps the catch was old . . . broken. It slid down just as I got the cupboard open and the gun . . . Even the big dog was shaken. It did not seem to understand why the window was open . . . And before it moved, to come in or go away, I had fired the gun. I don't remember but I must have done it, for there was the noise, the smell of the powder . . . And the dog was still there – upright at the window. Its head, neck, chest against the open part – as if it was about to come in. And it began to slip to the ground . . . It dropped. I could see it no more . . .

'I ran to the window. It was trying to get to its feet . . . it went a few steps, limping, falling . . . Behind I could see it trailed some blood. It went behind the cottage, to the back garden. I went to the kitchen to look where it went. It was moving so slowly, across the garden to the woods . . . It just

70

got to the trees – the first trees . . . I saw it sink to the ground, and I felt my blood go cold. It gave one howl, looking at me, looking back at the house . . . then it fell over.'

Edward had understood part at least. 'It died in the back garden?'

'Yes.'

'In the trees?'

She nodded.

'Where is it now?'

'Still there.' She was very quiet, sitting in her chair, apparently exhausted.

'Excuse me. I'll go and see.' She said nothing as he left the room.

The dog was lying as she had said, under trees that edged the cottage garden. It was out of sight of the house, since it had collapsed into bracken.

It was bigger than he had imagined. Perhaps an Irish wolfhound?

Wolfhound . . . He paused, looking at the animal. It wasn't exactly like the dogs with which he had come into contact these last few days. This had a thick coat of woolly hair and its ears were large and erect. It was a dull brown colour, flecked with black. The head seemed small on such a large body. The lips had been drawn back in death, and showed the teeth. They were long, sharp, vicious.

There was a bullet wound in its chest, in the centre of the ribcage. It could have been hit there only if it had been standing upright, as the girl had said.

Round its neck was a collar, buried in the rough fur, and made of thick leather, studded with metal buttons. He pushed aside the hair and knelt to read the nameplate. *'Balelli . . . Pietro . . . Sardegna.'*

Before Edward left, he asked her: 'Your family name is Balelli?'

'My husband's family name. My late husband. He is dead.'

'Do you live in Sardinia?'

'I used to . . . Yes, I suppose I still do.'

'In Pietro?'

She was surprised that he knew. 'Why, yes.'

It seemed clear to Edward that she had shot her own dog, and that it had been standing upright at the time. That part of her story at least was true. It didn't make sense to him, but he

71

was sorry for the girl, who was obviously in a very neurotic state.

'It would be nice if you could call and see Mrs Balelli,' he said to his sister. 'I think she's about to have a breakdown.'

'What can Margaret do about that?' complained John.

'Of course, I'll go,' said Margaret.

Later John had a change of mind. 'I'll go with you,' he said to his wife. 'I can certainly make arrangements for someone to take the dog away.' Edward had told him where the body lay.

'It's after seven. Isn't it rather late?' asked Margaret.

'Good Lord, no.'

Edward expected them to be gone for quite a while, and induced the children to go to bed with the promise of a story.

'The one about how you blew up the robbers,' demanded Henry.

'And the princess who wanted to marry you,' added Carrie.

'Oh, that one,' said Edward. But before he had started he heard the car arrive back.

'There was no one there,' John told him.

'Sure you went to the right place?'

'Of course. Tudor Cottage.'

'It's shut up,' Margaret told him. 'Curtains are drawn – doors all closed and locked.'

'The car's gone,' added John.

'We looked through the window,' said Margaret. 'It doesn't look lived-in. She must have gone away.'

'Did you find the dog?'

'We found the place. There was blood on the ground. But there's no dog there now.'

Edward frowned. 'I wonder if she phoned the vet.'

'On a Sunday?'

'Or Sergeant Parker?'

'I wouldn't know.'

Upstairs the children could be heard shouting for their story.

Edward drove off after John had left for London the next morning. Tudor Cottage was shuttered and silent. Where the dog had lain there was still a slight impression in the bracken, and a dark stain.

72

Back at the house again, he phoned the police station.

'I didn't know she'd gone,' said Parker. 'No, we didn't remove the dog. She must have made her own arrangements.'

Edward sat by the phone for quite a time. If there was any logic behind what had happened, he failed to see it.

'Thinking, Eddie?'

'Not really.' After all, what was there to think about?

'Guess what?' said John on arriving home. He looked quite pleased with himself.

'What?' asked Margaret.

'Guess whom I've just seen on the train!'

'No idea.'

'Countess Clara!'

'In the train from London?' Edward was surprised.

'First class, of course, and with a secretary and attendant. Met by cars at the station . . . But not before she'd had a word with me.'

'Whatever for?' asked Margaret.

'About you.' He was being deliberately provocative.

'Me?'

'She wanted to know what you were doing tomorrow.'

'I'm not doing anything,' said Margaret.

'That's what I told her . . . She asked if the children liked music. I said I thought so.'

'I like music,' said Henry.

'So do I,' Said Caroline.

'Is there a point to this?' Margaret had had a busy day.

'It seems she has a party going to town tomorrow. There's a special performance at the Albert Hall – some charity or something, saving animals in Africa or somewhere – and she's got a batch of tickets, and wants to know if you'd like to take these two.'

'To London?' The children danced round the kitchen.

'What time?' asked Margaret.

'In the afternoon. And they're having a meal in some posh restaurant after the concert, to which you are invited – and, in fact, so am I, as I'll be finished at the office. There are cars to take you there, and bring you back. Me, too, for that matter.'

'Won't that be very late?'

'No . . . no!' protested Carrie. 'It's our holiday.'

'Not very,' said John, 'and it's only once in a while. I said I thought it was a nice idea.'

'You accepted?'

'More or less.'

'Well . . .' Margaret thought about it.

'Mummy! Don't be mean.'

'All right.'

'What's the music?' asked Edward.

'One of the symphony orchestras,' said John vaguely. 'It's specially for children, so it won't be too highbrow.'

'What about Uncle Eddie?' asked Henry.

'I'm afraid he's not invited,' said his father.

'What! Poor Eddie! Left all alone.'

'I don't mind losing you for a few hours,' said Edward. 'I could do with a rest.'

'I'll phone and thank her,' said Margaret.

'I have thanked her,' said John. 'Besides, they aren't on the phone.'

'Are you sure?'

He nodded. 'She's just told me.'

Edward was surprised. 'How do they do business? I got the impression he was still involved with affairs.'

'Oh, they have telex, and some sort of radio system, a scrambled service, whatever that is . . .'

'But no phone?'

'Anyhow, it doesn't matter. The secretary is going to be on the train again tomorrow morning. I'll speak to her and phone you from the office with times and details.'

'What a complicated way of doing things,' mused Margaret.

'We can't exactly complain,' said John. 'But you're right. They'll have to get a phone if they're going to have a social life in the district.'

'If they want it,' said Eddie.

The phone rang while Edward and Margaret were having their morning coffee.

'That'll be John.'

'There's a car calling for you and the kids at two o'clock,' John told her. 'You're meeting the Countess inside the Hall. You'll have another passenger with you – one of the boys we met swimming. He's got the tickets and details. The Countess hopes this is convenient.'

'Which boy?' asked Margaret.

'Was there one called Marcel?'

'I think so.'

'Is Eddie there?'

Margaret called to her brother. 'He wants a word with you, Eddie.'

'You must have roused their sympathy,' John told him. 'They don't like the thought of you being on your own this evening, so you have an invite to dinner with the Doc himself, and one or two of the younger members of the family. Seven-thirty for eight. Nothing formal, just brush your hair and look tidy. We have a reputation in the district!'

'What if I'm doing something else?' asked Edward.

'Then it doesn't matter. It's nothing special, just drop in if you want to . . . *Are* you doing something else?'

'Probably not.'

The car arrived promptly at two, chauffeur-driven by a London firm.

'They don't stint themselves,' commented Edward.

'They don't stint their guests,' Margaret corrected him.

Marcel was in the car. He slid out to open the door. 'Please . . . where do you wish?' he bowed to Margaret.

Henry was overjoyed to see him. He and Carrie piled in noisily.

'Have a nice time,' called Edward.

'You too,' Margaret waved.

The house seemed stunningly quiet after they had gone, and Edward enjoyed the silence and the solitude. Later he prepared for his own excursion.

The gate-keeper stood by the open gates and waved him through. He pulled up by the front door, and Dr Shannon came out to greet him.

'So glad you could some. I am sorry we have no phone: it must be very inconvenient. I just hoped you did not have another engagement.'

He led Edward into the house.

'I've been looking forward to it,' said Edward.

He was vaguely aware of music playing in the distance, and

75

of a pleasant perfume wafting along the corridor. It was like a woman's scent, indeterminate, subtle, but there was no one near who might be wearing it.

'I am in the library – join me for a drink before our meal.'

The library was very much to Edward's taste, books lining two walls, a partner's desk – probably Georgian – by the window, and on another wall a breakfront bookcase, also probably Georgian. A drinks cabinet stood beside it.

'Thanks. I'll have a brandy,' said Edward.

Where there was space on the walls there hung pictures, mostly portraits, but with some paintings of horses, cattle, hill-farms, mountain ranges. The leather chairs were high-backed and comfortable. Everything was solid, of old materials in sombre colours. He felt at home.

'You are our first guest,' said the Doctor.

Edward raised his glass. 'I hope you will be very happy here.'

'You are right,' smiled the Doctor, 'we are. Please sit . . . they will call us when the meal is ready,' and he went on as they sat down, 'I hope Mrs Warwick did not find this outing too abrupt. I am afraid that is a problem with my cousin – she is so impetuous. Something comes into her head, and it must happen immediately. I said it would be difficult to arrange to take children to London on the spur of the moment, but she was already organizing her party and she said, "I will ask Margaret," – she calls your sister "Margaret". It was too good an opportunity to let the children hear some excellent music. It is never too early to introduce children to the good things of life, don't you think, Edward? To music and art, and adventure . . . to life itself, in fact. When you are young you absorb so easily and quickly. What you are when young you remain for the rest of your life. I cannot understand the tendency to protect children from the richness around them. If they learn when young, they are more able to cope with events. As with wine, for example: a little when a child, and one does not go to excess later. One learns to appreciate, to be able to handle things . . . the qualities that compose happiness. That has always been the feeling in our family. Welcome life with open arms – prepare for it in good time, taste it, and enjoy it. This makes for a much more open attitude to the world. Then one does not grow up with confused ideas, with hypocrisy, and a destructive sense of guilt. What do you think about that, Edward?'

A bell sounded, softly, melodiously.

'Ah! We are called to the table. That is one order I obey promptly. I fear to face the anger of a cook who has been kept waiting.'

He rose with a smile and led the way from the room. The perfume was still in the corridor, but there was no one around. The Doctor was opening a door as he added, 'One or two younger relatives of mine are joining us. I hope that is acceptable?' And as he entered the room he called cheerfully: 'Ah, my dear Robert, you are in charge of the wine.'

Four people were already in the room: one young man drawing the corks of several wine-bottles, and three girls. At first glance Edward guessed that they were in their early twenties, and were probably numbered amongst the 'attractive nieces' about whom the Countess had spoken. She had not exaggerated, for they had the dark good looks that all the women seemed to possess in this extended family.

'My niece, Paula,' said the Doctor. 'My cousin, Helena. My second cousin, Zoë.'

Edward bowed to each in turn, there being an old-fashioned formality about his host that was infectious. The girls were very like each other, and indeed, closely resembled the girl he had met at the gate. She, too, must be a relative of theirs – possibly another niece or cousin. And the girl in the swimming-pool, perhaps she . . .

'I think you have already met another young cousin of mine?' went on the Doctor.

Edward was taken aback. Did his host know about her? Would Santana have told anyone what had happened? 'I don't think so,' he said doubtfully.

The girls were smiling, reassuring and friendly.

'Indeed you have,' said the Doctor. 'My young cousin, Marcel: he went swimming with you.'

'Oh, the boy!'

'And he's with your party at the concert,' added Shannon.

'Certainly, I know him,' said Edward. 'A charming young man.'

'Please sit,' indicated the Doctor, taking his place at the head of the table. One of the girls sat between him and Edward; another sat at the other end of the table, on Edward's right, while Robert and the third girl – Zoë, he thought – sat opposite. He was gradually beginning to differentiate between the three.

'As a matter of fact, we were speaking of Marcel earlier,' said

Edward. 'We wondered how old he was. Henry had the idea he was ten: he said that was what Marcel had told him.'

The Doctor made a calculation. 'Yes, I suppose that's right.'

'Really?'

It seemed to Edward that the others were suddenly quiet. They all looked at him with interest.

'You seem surprised,' said the Doctor.

'We thought Henry had made a mistake: Marcel appears so much older. Quite mature.'

No one spoke for a few seconds, then the Doctor said thoughtfully, 'Let me think. Marcel . . . yes, perhaps he would be more than that. Looking at him, Edward, how old would you say?'

Edward shrugged. 'I don't know. Fourteen, at least.'

'You are probably right.' He turned to the girl between them. 'You know Marcel best, Paula. How old is he?'

She smiled. 'Mr Glover is close.'

'I am sure our guest prefers to be called Edward,' said Dr Shannon.

The girl smiled at Edward. 'You are correct, Edward. The boy has a younger brother of ten. That is where the confusion must be. Marcel is nearly fifteen.'

Edward sensed a general relaxation round the table, as though it had been a matter of some importance. A servant brought in a trolley of dishes. The young man opposite rose to pour the wine.

'To our guest!' The Doctor raised his glass. 'As you have seen, ladies – a very observant man.'

They laughed and drank. The dish before Edward, the wine, and the company – all were attractive and welcoming. He was being fêted, he told himself, and he wondered why.

The girl beside him had delicate, arched eyebrows, high cheekbones, a small nose, and deep, dark eyes. How could he ever have thought she looked like anyone else? Her black hair was done in a knot on the top of her head, showing a slender, youthful neck. She smiled faintly as she turned to him.

'You don't live here,' she said. 'I am told you stay a few weeks, and then leave?'

'I work abroad mostly.'

'Is it something exciting?'

'I buy and sell.'

'That is what we do.' She pulled a face. 'It seems all the world does that.' She spoke English beautifully, but with the trace of an accent which he couldn't place.

'Paula forgets the world trades to live,' said the Doctor.

'Our family lives to trade,' she teased him.

'It has its rewards,' said the Doctor.

'But it means we have to uproot ourselves from one home and make another in some new country.'

'England is our mother-country,' the Doctor reminded her.

'Is that why you have come here?' asked Edward. 'For business?'

'What else?' said Paula. 'Everything is business. My uncle is one of the elders of our family. They make the decisions, and we – like children – must trail along in their wake.'

'I suppose you could branch out on your own,' suggested Edward. 'I'm sure you would be a great success.'

The girl accepted his admiration with a smile. 'I might take your advice.'

'Don't believe her, Edward. We're like gypsies or Jews, with branches in many places. We stay in touch. If Paula, or Robert, or anyone wished to join another branch, they would only have to say the word and it would be arranged.'

'They're very lucky,' said Edward.

'You see!' The Doctor gestured towards his guest for the benefit of the others. 'And he knows: he has been out in the world on his own, without such back-up as you have. He appreciates your advantages.'

'He does not know the disadvantages,' said Robert.

There was a split second of silence, as though someone had broken the rules, mentioned a forbidden subject. It had been little more than a mutter – a low growl from the young man was how Edward sensed it – and in the silence that followed he had a feeling that a lot was being said. These people round the table spoke without words.

'Disadvantages?' asked Edward.

'Of course there are disadvantages,' said the Doctor. 'We would not be mortal creatures in an unpredictable world if we did not have problems. Robert has only to ask himself if our disadvantages – his disadvantages – are not outweighed when he remembers the alternatives.' The young man was being brought to heel, thought Edward. 'But we mustn't bore our guest,' went on the Doctor.

'You don't,' Edward told him. 'You sound like a well-organized society.'

'You have only to look at the history of minorities. In adversity, they learn to protect themselves, to retain a strict discipline, to survive at all costs.'

'But how are you and your family a minority?'

'Foreigners are always looked upon with suspicion. If things go wrong – the rains fail, or a stockmarket collapses – the outsider is suspected, made the scapegoat. We have been foreigners in many countries; we have had to be doubly alert, doubly aware, and quick to move before vengeance is meted out against us.'

'Has this happened?'

'From time to time.'

'Well, it can't happen here. Here you aren't foreign.'

The Doctor smiled. 'I would like to believe that, but we have been away so long – in so many places, absorbing foreign cultures, adjusting to deserts, to rain forests – that you cannot say we are typically "John Bull". Indeed, we do not all speak English properly: you must have noticed that. Have you not wondered where we come from? What language we talk? What, in fact, we are doing here?'

'I certainly wondered about the accent, which I find most attractive.'

'Yes, when spoken by a pretty girl! But what if it is the voice of a rival, or someone who is buying land or cattle, running your banks, or threatening your livelihood? Then this strange accent creates suspicion. Who are these people? Why should they work so hard, and become so rich? Pass laws against them . . . set fire to their haystacks . . . throw stones . . . start rumours. You see how it goes?'

'I'm a foreigner in the countries I work in,' said Edward, 'but I haven't experienced these problems.'

'You are one man. Doing well, but not *too* well. Not threatening anyone.'

'So we learn very early,' chimed in Robert. 'A lesson is absorbed with our mother's milk: "Lie low". That's the message. To survive . . . lie low.'

There was just a hint of resentment in his voice. Again Edward sensed the low growl.

The Doctor shrugged. 'Some of our young men are impatient with this need for caution. Young men like to face a challenge.

80

But that is foolish if the results are inevitable, so we ingrain in them "lie low".'

'And how do the young women respond to this challenge . . . "lie low"?'

Paula laughed. 'We have other ways of dealing with things. If mankind puts on a frightening face we absorb it. We do not confront it. That would bring disaster. We put our arms round our enemy. After all, everyone knows the way to victory is through love.'

Edward looked blankly at her. She seemed to be telling him something wise and deep . . . and yet these were sentiments he had heard a thousand times, catchphrases – Christmas cracker wisdom, at once both mocking and true. She was still laughing . . . her eyes danced. He looked round the table, then back at her. No, she was not like anyone else.

'You must not take Paula seriously,' said the Doctor. 'She is a wicked girl.'

'Is it wicked to say love conquers the alien world? The disadvantages Robert speaks of vanish. We turn them to our advantage . . . by love.'

Edward knew she was mocking him, and that the joke was shared, discreetly, at the table. It was at many levels – perhaps a family joke – and one, he guessed, that would never be explained.

'So you all work for this all-embracing organization – the family,' said Edward drily.

'Not all of us,' said the Doctor.

'My uncle has earned his retirement,' said Paula.

'Then how do you fill your time, sir?' asked Edward.

'I am busier now than ever,' said the Doctor. 'The work of an old man is to explain the meaning of life.'

'And have you found what that is?'

The Doctor hesitated, then nodded slowly. 'I think so.'

'I'd like to hear it,' said Edward.

'Another time,' said Paula. 'Now you must come with me. I am going to show you the rooms we have furnished, and you will see how quickly we have settled in.' As she rose from the table the Doctor bowed his acquiescence. She seemed to be a girl of importance in his house, her authority taken for granted.

She took Edward's arm. 'Just a quick tour,' she told the others. 'We'll be back for coffee,' and she led Edward from the room.

Where the corridor widened into a hall, she paused. 'We've put some of our bits and pieces here.' The 'bits and pieces' were a collection of pictures, icons and sculptures. Edward recognized the styles of Italy, Greece, the Middle East and Russia. Translucent vases could have come from ancient Egypt.

'These must be worth a fortune.'

'We don't intend to sell them,' she said.

He felt rebuked. 'I don't think you should keep them here. How safe is it?'

She smiled. 'Very safe. We are well guarded.'

Edward followed her along the corridor. A room to one side was filled with antique French furniture. It wasn't to his taste, but the collection was spectacular. The next had four walls of magnificent pictures.

'Now I understand why you have the wild dogs,' he said.

'What wild dogs?' She looked puzzled.

'The dogs that roam the grounds. I doubt if anyone would brave them even to get in here.'

She was frowning. 'I don't know of any dogs.'

It was his turn to frown. 'You must do,' he said. 'Big animals, like German Shepherd dogs.'

They were back in the corridor, heading for another room, but she stopped. 'The only dogs we have are guard dogs, and they are not so big, and are always kept on chains.'

'These are as big as wolves,' he said grimly, 'and they are free to go where they like.'

'How do you know this?' she asked.

'I've seen them.'

'How many? Where?'

'Two, here. In the grounds.'

'You were there?'

'I was at the gate . . . the small iron gate that leads into the fields.'

Paula nodded, looking at him in wonder. 'I know it. It is locked.' She hesitated. 'But there are no such dogs. You must have been mistaken. Tell me, was it some hot summer's afternoon when you had been enjoying a little wine?' She was mocking again.

He nearly responded to her tone. Why not forget it? Treat it as a joke . . . Perhaps he had exaggerated: *could* it have been a summer fantasy?

'No,' he said. 'I was there. I saw the dogs.' Then he remembered something. 'Perhaps Santana could tell you about them.'

'Santana?' She raised the delicate eyebrows. 'You have met Santana?'

'Yes. She was at the gate.'

'You went to meet her?'

'I was looking for something, in the field.'

'Oh?'

'I was looking for a cat.'

The big, dark eyes gave little away, but Paula appeared to be sunk in wonder, as though he were telling her impossible things.

'How do you know her name?'

'She told me. Is she another cousin?'

The girl nodded. 'She is one of our family. But are you sure? What was she like?'

'Dark . . . young . . . pretty . . . powerful . . .' He corrected himself. 'She looked powerful.'

'You remember her clearly. I am surprised you found her so attractive.'

'What makes you think I did?'

'The way you talk about her.'

'I said only . . .'

'The hidden music in your voice.' For a split second he knew exactly what she meant, how she knew – and then he wasn't sure.

'But I would not have supposed . . .' she began, then said, 'Was she not too primitive, too physical, for you?' Then she hurried on, 'Anyhow, that is not important.' She smiled. 'What is important is to put your mind at rest.'

'I don't follow.'

'If you think such animals are here, you must have fears for the children. I am told Henry and Caroline are still young, and such dogs would be dangerous.' She hurried him along the corridor. 'I must show you that all is peace and quiet, and it is safe for them to live as our neighbours.'

She was opening a door, and he realized that they were stepping out in fading light into the garden. He felt his skin prickle. Even if she didn't know what animals roamed here, he did. Her innocence would be of no use if anything came at them from the shadows.

'Look, I have to be honest,' he said. 'You don't believe me, but . . .'

'Are you afraid?' Her face in the light that fell from the open door was alive with amusement. 'I thought Englishmen were brave.'

'I couldn't help you if anything . . .'

'Very well, I will go myself. I will walk to your romantic little gate and back – and I will tell Santana when I see her next that you did not have the courage to come with me.'

She turned away, and began to walk along a path under the trees. 'Paula!' She didn't answer. 'Wait one moment . . .' She didn't look back.

He hurried after her. The very crack of a twig under his foot made his heart jump.

'Paula . . .' He caught up with her, and grabbed her arm.

She smiled up at him. 'I guessed you would not leave me, if you really thought it would be dangerous.' She kissed him on the cheek. 'Come . . . we will walk together. In such adventures, people find out the truth about each other.' She was holding his arm a little more tightly, as they moved on. He must be on the look-out for both of them, Edward thought; she had no idea what lay ahead. It was madness to take the risk, but he had no choice.

He remembered that it wasn't possible to see the house from the iron gate, hidden in this neglected parkland which in his imagination stretched endlessly.

'That was an owl,' Paul informed him.

He had heard nothing, directing his senses to ground level, fearing even the scuffle of dead leaves, remembering what he had heard once before. He kept imagining it: a rustle, low on the ground.

'It's the wind,' she said as he looked behind him.

Every nerve in his body was tight.

It was darker under the branches.

'Follow the path,' Paula told him.

'Is there anyone in these grounds?' he asked.

'No. Later a watchman goes round with the dogs.' He half-turned. 'The ones I told you about – on a chain,' she added.

He knew that something was following them by the faint sounds along the path, a little distance behind. When he stopped, the sounds stopped. Guessing what he was thinking, she said, 'There are many things in the woods at night. Little animals – mice, voles, even badgers. We are safe – or would I be at your side?'

Her confidence gradually rubbed off on him, but still he couldn't blot out the image of two dogs at each others' throats.

'Look!' she whispered. 'Just ahead. You see, all is peaceful and it is not so far.'

The path twisted between bushes, and he could see the gate opening on to the fields. The moon, flickering from behind clouds, picked out the pattern of its wrought-iron bars. He was still annoyed with himself for having been manipulated into this foolish walk.

'It's not far,' she encouraged him, again.

'This is childish.'

'Very well. We have gone far enough to prove that nothing is wild or dangerous.'

They turned towards the house, though she stopped once to say, 'Listen! It's so peaceful in this country, so beautiful . . . it's such a gentle place.' Then, when the house loomed up, she changed direction. 'I want to show you something.'

He let himself be led towards an outhouse with a large pen attached to it. The girl whispered softly into the darkness. A moment later two dogs came from the outhouse, looking sleepily at their visitors.

'Did you see these?' asked Paula. 'They go with our guard.' They were broad-chested mastiffs, powerful, but small.

He shook his head as she led the way back to the house. Inside she said, 'You are not convinced. No matter what I say, you still believe in your fierce animals. And this was not a proper search. What you must do – and I invite you tomorrow – is to walk round our garden. All of it. See what you choose. Ask any person you meet. My uncle would wish you to have an easy mind. And if someone has brought wild creatures, he will have them put away.'

'I didn't mean to cause trouble,' Edward said.

'It's important.' Paula looked serious. 'So do that, in the morning – in the clear light of day. Now we must join the others.'

As they returned to the dining-room, Edward had an odd feeling that he was walking on to a stage where a set piece had been prepared. The Doctor had on the table before him a collection of photographs, mostly of birds – building nests, feeding their young, doing a courtship dance – and he was holding forth to Robert and two of the girls. 'It's done by instinct,' he was saying. 'No reasoning. Instinct has protected the species, and ensures its continuation.' He broke off to welcome his guest.

'You aren't back on your hobby-horse,'protested Paula. She turned to Edward. 'He has this bee in his bonnet, that intellect is the downfall of mankind.'

'What do you say, Edward? Was any animal designed to live in cities, to work in offices and factories? To ignore his intuition? To become alien to his great strengths?'

'Do you know what they are?' interrupted Paula. 'One's emotions, instincts . . .'

'Voices from an age-old ancestry,' agreed Dr Shannon.

Paula poured coffee. 'Perhaps Edward isn't interested?'

Edward had a feeling that the scene had been rehearsed, and he guessed what he was supposed to say. 'I am,' he assured the Doctor.

'I am concerned that humanity has lost the use of instinct. Too much faith is put in reason, a dangerous faculty.'

'It's done pretty well up to now,' said Robert.

'It invented the flint axe,' said the Doctor with a shrug.

'And that was handy when one was attacked by a bear!' said Robert.

'Reason also produced the bronze sword,' went on the Doctor. 'Through it man learned to temper steel, and later to split atoms . . . What good will it have done to man, or the world, if he blows himself to oblivion and takes every other species with him? Reason could leave us with a barren planet.'

'Don't let your coffee get cold,' said Paula.

'What's the alternative?' asked Edward.

'He's working on it,' grinned Robert.

'You know what my uncle says?' said Paula. 'He says that when man became a rational animal, Nature made a big mistake.'

They laughed and made jokes, but Edward was sure that the interlude had been prepared. There was about it something artificial and out of key.

As he drove back he passed a car pulling out of the drive, and guessed that the family had just arrived home. Margaret was upstairs, hurrying the children to bed. 'It's late,' he heard her calling. 'Terribly late. Be as quick as you can.'

John was pouring drinks.

'I've solved it,' said Edward. 'They're some sort of a sect.'

'Who are?'

'Your neighbours. Dr Shannon has these theories . . .'

'What sort of a sect?'

'You know . . . these communities that spring up nowadays, like hippies in the past. Communities that go off to India or California or Wales, and set up an alternative way of living.'

'In Park House?'

'Why not? If they've got the cash . . . and they certainly have that!'

'I thought they were still in business?'

'They are. But they're all so integrated, packed together, in lots of ways. They look alike . . .'

'Many families do that.'

'They think alike. Even when they argue, it's a pretence.'

'You didn't enjoy the evening?'

'I did. A splendid meal – charming companions. All I'm saying . . .'

'Is that you, Edward?' Margaret called down.

'I'm back,' he replied.

'Say good-night to the children.'

'Good-night!' he shouted.

'Properly!' he heard them calling, and he had to go up.

'We had a brilliant time,' they told him. 'Marcel was great fun.'

'And his brothers and sisters.'

'Does he have brothers and sisters?' asked Edward.

'Well, cousins . . . and a wonderful supper.'

'How about the concert?'

'That was all right.'

'Marcel's my best friend,' said Henry.

'And mine,' said Caroline.

'We're going swimming there again,' they told him.

'And having a picnic at the seaside.'

'Mum says we might spend a night at Park House during these holidays.'

Something about the children's excitement made Edward uneasy.

'Good-night, kids.'

* * *

'You're not going round there again!' Margaret looked at her brother in amazement.

'I've got an invitation to take a stroll in their garden this morning. And as it's such a beautiful day, with the sun shining . . .'

'Is there some girl there?' Margaret was suspicious.

'About a dozen,' said Edward.

He wanted to check on something first, and went down to the tree-house, where the netting made an effective camouflage. He climbed up and tied a white handkerchief to the branch above. Then he collected his car from the stables and drove the short distance to his neighbours.

He had expected to see Paula, but he was greeted by a young man.

'I have been asked by my cousin to say she is sorry she is not here, but she will be in the house when you have finished your inspection, and she asks you to join her then.' He carried a heavy walking-stick. 'She wants you to take this. It will be useful in the rough patches. We have not yet cleared the estate, and there are brambles and bracken in places. And she says also you might be happier with something that could be used as a weapon.' He was smiling as he handed Edward the stick.

'Very thoughtful.' Edward weighed it in his hand and was glad to have it.

The young man took him to the back of the house. 'Most of the park is over there. But I expect you know.' He gave a polite wave.

'I'm on my own?' asked Edward.

'That was the arrangement, wasn't it? And when you return, please come in by this door. My cousin will be in a room along the corridor . . . the third on the right.'

Edward set off, the young man watching him for a moment before going back into the house. He had used the word 'cousin', but that might refer to a multitude of people in this family. Edward hoped it meant Paula.

He had gone a couple of hundred yards into the woods, along an old path, before it dawned on him exactly where he was, and that he was alone. 'A sucker for punishment,' he murmured to himself. He gripped the walking-stick and headed on, away from the house. The first thing he wanted to locate was the wall that backed on to the field, but it wasn't as easy to find as he expected, and making his way through the unkept scrubland was tedious. He used his stick to hack a path through the bushes.

At last the wall appeared ahead of him. At its base there was evidence of a track, like an animal run, probably made by foxes. It was simple to follow, and he stayed with it as far as the iron gate. Here he stopped to peer through the bars into the field. Then he stood with his back to the gate, as though looking in. There was thick bracken on one side, and he remembered the wolf-like creature that had burst through it. The memory chilled him, and he stood, listening.

Birds sang in the branches above; a faint breeze rustled the leaves. It was a beautiful summer morning in a familiar and peaceful countryside, he reminded himself.

The dog had come at him from the bracken; it had been on the point of springing when the second dog had appeared from nowhere. He remembered watching them snarling – rearing at each other as they rolled over the dusty ground. He walked slowly round the clearing inside the gateway . . . Earth and dust had certainly been scattered, but that could have been done by anyone. There was no evidence of a bloody encounter.

He moved into the bushes where the struggle had continued. What did he hope to find? Blood? Torn skin? Tufts of hair? He looked carefully through some broken bushes, but there was no sign of the thick, matted fur he thought he might find. No sign of blood.

Having one more inspection to make, Edward moved on, walking just within the wall, until he could see the trees in his brother-in-law's property.

It took him a moment to pick out the tree-house, by locating the white handkerchief in the tree above it. It was well hidden, blending with branches and camouflaged by the old fruit-netting. He was fairly sure he had now found the spot where the three girls had been lying, and he examined the bushes and bracken nearby. Tufts of fur caught in nearby thorn bushes could have been animal hair, but he had no idea how old they were and they might have been left by foxes.

As he moved away he heard someone digging; a little further on he saw a man hacking with a pick-axe at the ground around some bushes. He stopped as Edward came into the clearing.

'Hello,' Edward nodded. 'Hard going on this patch?' He received no answer. 'I suppose you get foxes here?' Edward went on. The man merely looked puzzled.

'Sorry,' said Edward, for it was clear the other hadn't understood him. 'What language do you speak?'

The man remained silent for a moment, then said, in a curiously stilted fashion, 'English . . . I speak English. No, I have seen no foxes.'

Edward guessed that he was not going to learn anything from him: in fact, nothing was to be gained by this inspection. What he had seen from the tree-house and through the iron gate bore no relationship with this artificial walk through the grounds, during which he would see what he was supposed to see . . . an idyllic, though overgrown, English parkland. He wasn't sure what else there was to see, but he had obtained glimpses here of a different world, and the two pictures didn't blend.

The digging began again behind him – a pick-axe hitting flint, an age-old sound. Edward decided to take a short cut to the house through the bushes, and had gone a little distance when he found himself in a thick tangle of brambles. He hacked his way out of one patch and into another, then he turned back to try to regain the path, but thorns made the going slow, and he had to slug his way inch by inch.

He was wielding his stick, breaking down the undergrowth, when he heard a sound somewhere ahead of him – some distance away, in a part of the grounds he had not visited. It came again almost immediately, but this time much clearer. He had his arm raised, and he froze, the stick in mid-air, absolutely motionless.

He decided he must have made a mistake, but the third time the sound reached him there was no doubting the high-pitched whine, the excited baying – still some distance away but growing louder. Impossible to judge how far away it was in this wooded and walled garden. He guessed it was only one creature – excited, inflamed – but one would be enough . . . He would have to run – no point in keeping still. It had his scent, and wouldn't need sound to locate him.

He tore himself free of the bushes, scrambled back to the path, turned towards the sound. It was now close – he could hear something racing through bracken and brambles, over dead leaves. His best chance, perhaps, would be with his back to a tree, and thank God for this heavy stick . . .

Remembering the man digging with the pick-axe, Edward ran towards him. When he'd gone a few strides, he knew he wouldn't make it, for the howl that sounded behind him let him know he'd been seen. There was a tree ahead . . . if he had time to climb it! To be even six feet above the ground . . . He heard the whistle as faintly as he had first heard the animal, and it registered as faintly in his mind. He was still running for the tree when the whistle came again. He had one hand on the lowest branch, and took a quick look over his shoulder . . . he had just to pull himself up . . .

There was nothing behind him! Nothing following. Nothing scrambling through trees. The path wound into the garden through bushes, empty, silent, serene.

It took Edward a few moments before he trusted his eyes. Then he understood. The whistle! Whatever was hunting him had obeyed the whistle! It must have spun round and gone back to where it came from . . . But was that possible? What animal, in the excitement of a hunt, could be so obedient, so manageable, controlled by such a long and invisible leash? It wasn't possible!

He waited until his hand stopped shaking, then he walked back to where the man was still chipping away with his pick-axe.

'What was that?' he asked.

The man looked up. 'What?'

'What was that in the wood? Over there – ' he pointed. 'You must have heard it. Some animal howling and running through the trees. Then someone whistled.'

The man was looking at him with the same incredulous stare.

'You must have heard it,' persisted Edward. 'Like a dog. At the rate it came, and the noise . . .'

The man blinked at him. 'You saw a dog?' he asked.

'There was one there,' said Edward angrily. 'I didn't see it, but it was there.'

The other man gave the impression of trying to make sense of that. 'You didn't *see* anything?'

Edward knew there was no point in losing his temper. He shook his head. 'I didn't see it.'

The man took up the pick-axe again. 'No dog,' he said. 'There's no dog.' He was about to start his work again when he remembered something. 'Two dogs,' he told Edward. 'Two guard dogs . . . but in the pen. Two dogs go round at night. No other dog.'

He began to dig.

Edward turned and left him. He kept to the path back to the house.

There was no one in the corridor as he went in, but he remembered his instructions: Paula would be waiting in the third room on the right.

There were doors on both sides of this corridor, the one down which he and she had walked the previous evening. He counted the doors, though he was doubtful about the first which looked as though it were merely a panel to balance the door on the other side. He decided to count it as he made his way along the corridor, and tapped on the third door.

He wasn't sure whether someone called out. He was still shaken; it would be a comfort to experience some human company. He opened the door and went in.

It was an L-shaped room, with the larger part round the corner from the door, but there was no one in sight. He moved into the other section of the room.

'Hello!' he called. 'Anyone at home?'

Sunlight streaming in at the window threw a shadow across the room, and for a second he thought someone was standing there, but when there was no movement he realized that the figure was of marble, a most exquisite Adonis, so lifelike that he could almost imagine that the statue had moved. At its bare feet lay a cloak, the stone so beautifully cut that Edward imagined it to be as soft as velvet. The model was powerful, masculine, yet its very grace made it look sensual.

Edward caught his breath. It was so unexpected, so full of vitality, with the muscles of thighs and buttocks rippling under the skin. Thick hair curled to his shoulders, both arms were held before him, and the body was naked. The ribs, the very veins, showed in faint realistic detail.

Edward moved forward, filled with admiration. As he expected, the face was classical, full-lipped, youthful.

The second figure, which lay before this Adonis, was not as exposed, for she reclined on a bed of tumbled marble pillows and feather-deep quilts, her head thrown back, gentle impressions like silk etched into the stone. And if he were an Adonis, she was certainly a Venus, a most relaxed and amorous one. Long hair tumbled on the bed beside her, eyes were closed in ecstasy, lips were parted in a delicate, sensuous face which was turned slightly to one side, showing one small ear, a fragile neck. Her shoulders were slim, high firm breasts tipped with small erect nipples. Clothing was tossed in a careless heap, revealing the rise and fall of her belly – and below, the hair between her embracing legs was sculptured in delicate detail.

Sun played on the static figures. Edward was indeed an intruder into a secret room, for this was surely a moment for privacy, this enrapt intimacy as they were forever caught in the act of making love.

He felt he should back away, but he was enchanted. He turned from the magic of the two figures to look round the room. Nothing he saw surprised or shocked him: everything fell into place. He was surrounded by the toys and trifles of love. A wall was lined with a series of paintings similar to those in the villas of ancient cities or in any modern brothel. 'Instructions for the beginner,' he thought of them, or perhaps *aides-mémoire* for the elderly; universal stimulants for many an inadequate customer. But they had merit, these particular paintings. Some were old and executed on wooden panels, others were mosaics, or scraps of frescoes. In all, it could have been a history lesson in sexual encounter.

Other pictures might have come from some European court, in more luxurious times . . . gods and goddesses – men and women in disguise – clearly enjoying each other. Satyrs chased nymphs, and nymphs allowed themselves to be caught, contentedly paying the price, sprawling across ceiling and walls, their modesty lost in the struggle with lust. The artists who had brought these extravagant creatures to life had admired every soft, round limb of the women portrayed, and had done justice to each of their taut and vigorous lovers. Gradually he took in the other items in the room: a showcase of small erotic models, reminding him of a famous – or notorious – collection put together by an Egyptian royal prince. He guessed that some of them were priceless. And there were rows of books. He didn't bother to take them from the shelves, but he guessed their contents. The visual impact was quite stunning. Slowly, in admiration and in wonder, he circled the room . . .

'Are you looking for someone?'

A young man stood by the open door. Edward thought he recognized him, but he couldn't be sure.

He was conscious of the display around him.

'I was looking for . . . Paula.' He realized he wasn't sure of her last name.

'She will be in the next room,' said the man.

As Edward passed him, he again thought he had seen him previously. He looked like Marcel, the boy who had been swimming, but must be considerably older.

'Thanks.' He went on down the corridor and knocked at the next door.

'Come in.'

Dr Shannon sat by a table with a pile of papers beside him.

'My dear Edward, I am pleased to see you. You are a little early, but Paula will not be long.'

'I seem to be interrupting your work again.'

'Not at all.'

'I'm afraid I went into the wrong room on the way here.'

'Which room?'

'The one before this.'

'Ah . . . the Gallery of Amorous Sports.' The Doctor smiled indulgently.

'It's remarkably beautiful,' said Edward.

'It is useful,' the Doctor nodded. 'Not that it is so essential for members of our family, not for close members, but for more distant cousins – young men, and young women too – it can be helpful.'

'I don't think I quite . . .' Edward let the question trail away.

'I am sure you are aware of problems. There is a price to be paid for the civilizing disciplines. Mankind dilutes its instincts at its peril, and inhibiting factors take over: conscience, training, religious teaching, the demands of society. In one way or another the human animal has been damaged by the pressures of its way of life. Unlike the animal he once was, our unhappy man of today is no longer controlled by intuition or instinct. Many things inhibit him . . . and inhibit her. The intellect takes over and confuses the pattern. You know, Edward, left to itself the intellect might bring the species to an end. It has made inroads in that direction. Animals act as the season demands – excited by touch, taste, smell. All unrolls according to the internal programme that has remained constant throughout time – a picture imprinted in the genes, describe it how you will . . . If trust is sustained in such an inner programme, then the species is assured. But if the dictates of society – these civilized demands – take control, how is man to produce his kind?

'As it is, Nature has had to concoct one universal madness to overcome man's errant ways. He has lost touch with what you might call seasonal desire – animal need as dictated only by the senses – and the civilized inhibitions are overcome only by this fantasy of "falling in love". Have you ever thought how strange it is that the human species has to fall in love? It's a fantasy that brings man and woman together. What other form of life – animal, vegetable, or what you will – what other form has to be subjected to such madness before it can ensure the continuation of its kind?'

The door opened, and Paula came in. 'You are here already?'

'Time has not been wasted,' said Dr Shannon. 'Edward and I have been discussing the need to bring back the immediate and unconscious power of attraction between man and woman.'

'Don't tell me,' she said. 'He went into the next room?'

'And now he understands how we help those who have been damaged by concepts of right and wrong, of good and bad, and what is proper in civilized society. Those who have wandered – through centuries of priests and rulers – far from their original being.'

'Original sin, I think you mean, Uncle.' She was laughing at him.

'Then sin is a necessary element for continued existence,' said the Doctor. 'For if you take away the fiction of love . . . without this so-called original sin, what does mankind have but a very bleak future?'

Paula turned to Edward. 'Next time you call I'll make certain my uncle is not around.'

'I can take a hint,' said the Doctor. He gathered up his papers, smiled, and went out.

Paula ignored him. 'Tell me, how did you make out in our garden? Did you see the whole estate? I don't think that was possible, because you were so quick.'

'I saw enough.'

'Then you know what things are really like?'

'Not really. I found the whole thing rather formal, unreal. It could have been prepared and planned.'

She looked serious. 'You're very honest. Yes, it could seem like that. You will have to drop in unannounced, when no one knows . . .'

'How can I do that?'

'Just turn up.'

'I can't.'

'Come by the back gate.'

'Which gate?'

'The one on the field, the iron one. Where you met Santana.'

'Isn't that always locked?'

'Is it?' She looked thoughtful. 'I'll find a way,' she said.

Edward wanted to talk to his brother-in-law first, and leave
John to pass on to Margaret anything he thought important.
'As I told you before, they're a sect of some sort,' he said, 'but
I'm damn sure they're not religious. I think it's some sort of
whacky sex community.'

'You can't be serious!'

'The chap Shannon – as far as I can make out, he thinks we're
at risk as a species. Mankind – I ask you! We're proliferating all
over the globe, yet he says we don't function as animals any
more.'

'That's true enough.'

'He believes we operate on a very shaky basis, biologically –
no longer directed by instinct, creating the fiction of "love" to
keep us going, gone off on the wrong track. Endangering our
future . . . and needing every sort of stimulus that the artist,
poet or anyone else can dream up!'

John was thoughtful. 'You know, Eddie, most of these guru
chaps are just a lot of talk.'

But he must have spoken to Margaret, for next morning she
said: 'Tell me about your little expedition.'

Normally Edward would have told her everything. They
didn't have many secrets from each other, but this time he was
a little guarded.

'They're an odd mixture. Charming, sophisticated and fairly
intelligent, but some of them – not all – are very odd.'

'Like what?'

'Well, Doc Shannon thinks – and he seems to be the head
man – he thinks society is sick. We have to get back to our
roots, trust primitive instincts . . . you know the sort of clap-
trap.'

'Is that a problem?'

'Well, they're next door to you. And you've got two kids.'

'Henry and Carrie are far too young to pay attention to that
sort of thing. It sounds fairly innocuous to me.'

Edward wasn't sure whether he should mention the Gallery of Amorous Sports. 'There's quite a bit of exotic art in the house.'

'Exotic?'

'Hindu gods demonstrating the most imaginative positions.'

'That's well over Henry's head for a few years to come.'

'I just thought I'd mention it.'

She looked doubtfully at him. 'Anything else? I mean, don't you like them?'

'As I said, some are charming, but others are a bit wild. I get the feeling the left hand doesn't know what the right hand is doing in that house.'

'For example?'

'Well, one of the girls, a real honey, seems totally convinced I'm suffering from hallucinations. I told her I'd seen these damn dogs . . .'

'Dear me, not those dogs again.'

'. . . And she's convinced there ain't no such animals.'

'And you're sure there are?'

'Of course I'm sure! But how can she live in the place and not know what's going on?'

'Perhaps they were there on just one occasion. Perhaps a visitor brought them.' Margaret had lost interest and was rummaging in a cupboard.

'See you later,' said Edward. 'I'm off to the village to fill up with gas.'

He had driven home the night before and left his car just inside the stables, without bothering to shut the garage doors. He was about to back out when he noticed something lying on the passenger seat, partly covered by an old raincoat.

It was a small, neatly folded package, without a name or address. He had no recollection of having seen it before, and wondered whether Margaret or John had left it there by mistake. Or was this some joke by Henry and his little sister?

There was something quite heavy inside; he pressed with his fingers in an effort to identify the shape. It was three or four inches long, rigid, and at one end it appeared to have a loop.

Edward couldn't understand why he should feel excited, but he had already guessed what the parcel contained. It was a key – old and rusty, made of wrought iron, in all likelihood the same metal which had been used to fashion the iron gate. He

97

didn't have any doubt what it was. Someone had given him the key to the entrance into Park House from the field.

He sat in the car, unable to make up his mind what to do. Perhaps he should make certain – go to the gate and try the key, see whether it turned the old lock. But he knew that wasn't necessary. It was made in the same ornate fashion as the gate, with a tiny figure above the handle. Edward couldn't make out what it was and took it to the stable door, holding it up to the sunlight. A very small, but very fierce, wolf with wings appeared to have a broad smile on its face. At least, its mouth was wide open.

'What're you doing, Eddie?' Henry and Caroline were coming towards him out of the woods.

'Nothing.'

'What's that in your hand?'

'A bit of the car engine. I'm checking it.'

He ducked out of sight, back into the stable, and put the key in his pocket. The two children appeared in the doorway.

'Can you check cars?'

'Of course.'

'I'd like to see what you do. Open the bonnet.'

'What for?'

'To get at the egnine.'

'I don't know how to.'

'Then how did you get that bit in your hand?'

'Push off, you two. I'm busy.'

'You're not doing anything.'

'I'm thinking.'

Caroline stared accusingly at him. 'That wasn't a bit of the engine.'

'Your mother is looking for you.'

'What was it, Eddie?'

'I told you.'

'It was rusty. Your car isn't rusty.' They stood looking searchingly at him. The two pairs of childish eyes were very knowing, clearly suspicious.

'It's wicked to tell lies.' Together they had a persistence he found unsettling.

'A devil will get you.' That didn't sound like Henry.

'Who told you that?'

He hesitated. 'A boy at school.' But he turned aside as he spoke.

Edward climbed into his car.

'Where are you going?'

'To the village, to pick up some gas.'

'Can we come?'

'Not this time.' He had always taken them previously.

They watched him back out. Their silent, expressionless faces were a blend of innocence with some other unfamiliar quality: a little secretive, a little hostile. It quite shocked Edward. They had always been such good friends, outspoken with each other, casual, accepting. Now a screen had fallen, as though the children no longer trusted him. Just because he wouldn't tell them what he had been holding? He must be imagining things.

Edward was uneasy all the way into the village, and decided to take them back a large carton of ice-cream. That would do the trick.

He put the key in the pocket of the car and locked it. Perhaps he should return it? He didn't relish the idea of going alone into the Park House gardens. He remembered the day before . . . and the dog he had heard – or thought he heard. And yet if the girl, if Paula, had gone to the trouble of providing him with this key . . . He felt a wave of pleasure, of anticipation.

The key was safe where he had put it. If she expected him, it would be after dark: he would decide later.

It was a long, slow afternoon, and Edward wandered about aimlessly.

'You're quiet today,' commented Margaret.

'I've got things on my mind.'

'Business?'

'Sort of.'

'You're not going to be dragged away?'

'I don't think so.' He didn't say anything to her, and felt childishly guilty. He wondered again whether to hand back the key. Wasn't he too old to be involved in such adolescent affairs? He might even mention the episode to John that evening.

'Oh, Eddie, I forgot to tell you,' said Margaret. 'John's got one of his conservation meetings this evening, and he wants me to go with him. It's not until eight o'clock, so the children will be in bed. Hopefully asleep. D'you mind?'

'Of course not.'

'It's quite important – about building on the Green Belt and all that.'

But it was after eight before she and John left for their meeting, and Henry and Caroline were certainly not asleep.

'What country are you going to next, Eddie?'

'Why do you ask?'

'I just want to know.'

'The Gulf, probably.'

'When?'

It was strange to feel that they were interrogating him, but that was what he sensed. Somehow the relationship had changed – their relaxed intimacy had gone, and Edward didn't like it. When had it happened? And why? Surely not just because he had hidden that key in his pocket.

'When?' Henry repeated.

'Can't you wait to get rid of me?'

'It's not that . . . I just like to tell people.'

'Who?'

'My friend, Marcel.'

'Did he ask?'

'No.'

'So why tell him?'

'He's been to lots of countries, too.'

'So has his cousin, and his uncle and his aunt,' chimed in Carrie from across the landing.

'What about his *mother* and his *father*?'

'His mother and father?' There was a momentary silence, then Henry said: 'They're in another country.'

'What do you think about that?' said Edward. He felt he'd got the upper hand in an undeclared war. 'How would you like it if *your* father and mother went off and lived in another country?'

Another silence. He had an odd sensation that their brains were racing like computers, looking for answers.

'*You* go off and live in other countries,' volunteered Henry.

'I'm not married,' said Edward.

'Why aren't you married?' Caroline called sharply. 'Everyone gets married. People are supposed to be married. Don't you want to get married? Don't you like girls?' There was no doubt about the challenge. A gauntlet had been thrown in his face. He stared at the open bedroom door. It was so unlike the little

100

girl . . . unlike any little girl. Almost as though she had not spoken for herself . . .

'Time you were both asleep,' he said as he went downstairs.

'Where are you going?' called Henry.

'That means both of you,' said Edward.

He sat by the sitting-room window for a while, then went out and walked on the lawn. The sun had gone down, but the hazy light of the summer evening still lingered. He glanced up at the bedroom windows. Lights were out; all was peaceful.

Without actually making a decision, he hurried down the drive towards the stables. He still wasn't sure what he was going to do as he took the iron key from the car pocket and headed into the wood. Unlocking that gate could mean opening a Pandora's box, releasing some unknown terror on an unsuspecting world. What might fly out across these peaceful fields? He visualized a pack of wolfhounds hunting and shattering the summer night: it was a disturbing fantasy. He wouldn't take that risk . . . And yet the gesture of sending this key to him was surely a promise! A shared secret between himself and the girl.

What was it Carrie had said? *'Don't you like girls?'* The truth was that he probably liked them too much. That was why he was still involved in this folly.

He made his way along the path in the dark; bushes loomed up unexpectedly, and he stumbled over unseen roots. He hadn't realized how far it was to the end of the garden and the big yew with the tree-house. He was glad to see it. Something fluttered white above, and he realized that his handkerchief was still tied in the branches.

It was a pleasant surprise to stand on the low wall, to look across the field and to see that once out of the trees it still wasn't dark; fading light hit high clouds in the far distance.

He now knew clearly what he was going to do. He would drop the key through the iron bars and leave it at that. He just hoped no one would find it before Paula picked it up, being appalled by the thought that someone might unwittingly open the gate. He strode briskly towards it – a dim shadow set back in the high wall.

He was almost there when he heard sounds . . . a faint rustle of movement, someone whispering softly, with a sense of suppressed excitement.

The idea vanished of just tossing in the key. He could see a

101

figure at the gate. A light-coloured dress fluttered. A girl whispered: 'Hello!'

He didn't recognize the voice. 'Who is it?'

'Edward?' whispered the voice.

He was certain it was not Paula. He came close to the gate. There stood a girl whom he had never seen before; admittedly very like her sisters and cousins, as pretty as they were, dark, with all the family features, a little broad-shouldered – but not Paula. Not anyone whom he knew.

'Who is that?' he asked.

'You have the key?'

He didn't know what to say. 'Yes.'

'Where is it? Take it . . .'

He hesitated. 'I don't understand. I found it in my car.'

She was suddenly insistent. 'Quick, turn the key . . .'

He took it from his pocket.

When she saw him hesitate she gestured urgently. 'Hurry . . . she is there.' She pointed into the darkness. 'Give it to me.'

She took the key through the bars and unlocked the gate. It swung back heavily, grating on its hinges. It was unbelievable to see it open.

'Come . . .' She was smiling and beckoning. 'Come, she is here.' She waved a hand again into the gloom.

Edward felt that he was walking into a trap, sensed the universal and eternal bait. Inner voices screamed warnings. They were all ignored.

'This way.' She moved ahead.

He looked over his shoulder. Who had been whispering? Who else was there? She seemed to be alone.

She was heading down a narrow path, moving into the overgrown gardens, showing no difficulty in seeing her way. Edward had no choice but to follow.

He found it hard to get his bearings; it was dark under these tall trees, and he was sure they were heading in the wrong direction, going further away from the house, passing the wired-off wreck of a tennis court, a broken-down pavilion, and a long-neglected vegetable patch. She slowed to let him catch up, pointing ahead, smiling as though they shared a secret.

A summer-house stood in a little clearing. Even in the gloom, Edward could see how charming it must once have been, built mostly of glass and iron-work, reminding him of a past century

– a time of elaborate conservatories and potted palms. It was Gothic and ghostly in the half-light.

He followed the girl round the side, to a glass door. Paint had flaked from the panels, the iron framework had lost its black gloss; all was decay and dilapidation. She stopped by the door and smiled; in an odd way Edward felt she was conveying a blessing – a pagan blessing.

She held out her hand, and he was surprised to see that she was giving him back the key.

'Other times,' she said softly, and hurried away before he had a chance to say anything, vanishing like a pale flutter in the shadows.

He stood for a moment with his hand on the door, the glass scratched and grimy, then he pressed his head against it and peered in.

It was dark inside and he could see nothing at first; then he began to distinguish one thing from another – decaying vegetation, pot plants, a dead palm, fronds, straggling ferns and pampas grass in big urns. Just inside the door was a stack of flowerpots, many broken, their contents spilling over the floor. The wreckage of years was stacked there, chill, damp, rotting. He had no wish to go in.

The other end of the summer-house was lighter, with fewer trees hanging over the glass roof. Here there was a collection of garden equipment – tools and spades – and beyond them furniture, such as hammocks and garden seats. There appeared to be no one inside.

He opened the door cautiously. The handle was loose, the glass cracked; the wooden floor creaked as he moved.

Beyond the stack of chairs was a row of upholstered sun-beds, some protected by covers and in quite good condition. This corner of the summer-house was drier and more solid. He was making his way in that direction when he heard a faint sound, and stopped in his tracks.

'Edward . . .'

He spun round.

He remembered the small figure as he had last seen her alone, smiling; he remembered her look of pleasure, and her assurance that had so fascinated him.

'Edward . . .' Little more than a whisper, the same soft purr. And now, close at hand, he could see that she was not much more than a girl – sixteen? seventeen? – a very assured girl, moving slowly, languidly . . . What was it Paula had said – 'Physical and primitive?' Dark hair melted into the darkness, eyes were calculating, making no effort to hide her admiration, amused and full of excitement, showing her satisfaction.

It was Santana. No longer in her dark skirt and blouse, peasant-style, she wore what in the darkness looked like a white smock, and came softly towards him with the grace of a woman sure of herself . . . at home in the world, close to the earth. She seemed shorter than he remembered – until he saw she had bare feet.

She murmured 'Edward' again, caressing the word. He caught a trace of the perfume he had smelt once before, equally animal, equally heady. 'You find the key?'

So she had sent the key, not Paula? He nodded. Perhaps he should have been disappointed.

'A gift for you,' she whispered.

She didn't bother to hide her appetites, nor attempt to disguise her need . . .

This time there was no iron gate between them, as she stood holding herself against him, leaning back slightly; he felt her thighs, loins, belly, pressing against him. Her head was back, looking up, her lips apart, mouth a little open, like a serpent about to strike. And then slowly she put her arms round him and dragged him into her kiss. He remembered the impact as once before – the light-headedness, the passive shock . . . the unsteadiness . . .

He knew exactly why he had been so drawn to Park House, what the unspoken magic was. This magnetism flooded through him, and he was shaken by the sensation. He threw his arms round her and pulled her hard against his body, kissing her fiercely, viciously, his hands racing over her body. She wore nothing under the smock. He released her, ignoring the enjoyment in her eyes, and untied the bow that fastened the shift round her shoulders, which slipped over her breasts. They were small, full and rounded, her nipples firm and hard. He bent to take each in turn into his mouth.

Smiling, she pushed him back, making a gentle, almost animal sound. 'Wait . . .' She pulled aside the cover from the sun-bed at her back. The hammock swung against her legs. She sat down and put her hands on his waist, pulling aside his shirt, slowly and possessively undoing the buttons, slipping it from his shoulders, laying her hands on his belt . . .

They both froze as they heard something moving beside them. It seemed to be in the summer-house itself, but then it scraped along the glass outside, and a moment later the glass door shook.

The girl moved quickly off the sun-bed and past him, pulling him back protectively behind her, racing to the front of the building. She called out angrily, and banged on the glass.

Edward followed, but could see nothing outside. He was dazed by the sudden noise and the speed at which Santana moved – like a cat, alert and fierce. She was trying to drive something away, something below the level of the windows. Her anger took his breath away.

He joined her at the glass door, but she pushed him aside. 'Go back!'

'What is it?'

'Nothing. Go back.' She hustled him behind the stacked furniture. 'Stay there.' She hurried back to the door.

Edward had seen nothing, but could still hear something moving below the level of the glass panels. The old nightmare returned: he was in this ramshackle glass-house, with cracked panes, a door that was falling apart, and fragile, disintegrating walls, while out there . . . He was in a cold sweat. In spite of all their denials he was surrounded by a pack of animals! He had seen them before, and those he had seen were killers! What in God's name could he do now? One semi-naked girl was trying to control them – to protect him!

He hurried to the side of the room and looked out. Something was crouching in the bushes, low on the ground, watching. He couldn't see the girl, but he heard the door shut, and heard her shouting again. She must be outside. Whatever it was in the bushes made a sudden movement and then it was gone . . .

In the silence that followed Edward's courage flowed back; he sensed that the danger was over, but with it all lust and passion had been drained from his body. He felt the key in his pocket. He would run for it.

He waited for a moment, catching a glimpse of the girl, outside but heading back towards the summer-house. And then he was astounded to see in a fleeting glimpse, a second figure, watching from the trees. He couldn't be sure in the poor light under dark branches, and for only a few seconds before it vanished, but in those few seconds he thought he recognized her . . . as she looked towards him, then turned away. Could it have been Paula?

But she had gone . . . and the other girl came back into the summer-house. He watched her as she entered, still wary, as though ready to spring: a huntress, silent and watchful.

Something made Edward look back over his shoulder to the glass panels where he'd just been standing. He saw the dark, low shadow below the window launch itself upright and rise to the height of a man.

He was incredulous. It was something which had already been described to him: a huge dog, wolf-like, with narrow pointed jaw and tongue lolling to one side, large ears erect, its thick hair coat pressed against the panes. The lips formed a brutish snarl, showing long teeth like daggers. Green eyes caught a flicker of light . . .

Edward couldn't move or speak. The huge beast might at any moment come tumbling through the glass.

Santana came to stand beside him, and saw the creature, its front legs against the glass, its claws scraping the window. She screamed – not in fear but rage – turned and ran, throwing the door wide open and disappearing round the side of the building.

It was more than Edward could stomach. He raced from the summer-house and along the path, uncertain as to which way he was going, fear giving him speed. He tore through the bushes, stopping for nothing, heart pounding – seeing at last the estate wall ahead, using it as a guide . . . running . . . running . . . until he saw the iron gate. He tugged it open. Thank God they had not locked it! Pulled it shut, fumbled with the key, shaking . . . turning the key, trying the gate. Locked!

He leaned against the iron bars . . .

It was several minutes before he recovered his breath, before sanity returned. There was no sound from within the Park House estate, only silence and peace.

Edward limped towards his sister's home. Out in the open it was still not quite dark.

Once in his garden, he realized that he had not thrown the key back as he had intended. Perhaps that was just as well: as long as he had it in his keeping, no one could unlock that gate. He went into the garage and put it in the car pocket, then locked the car.

He limped into the house. He couldn't remember hurting his leg, but it was painful.

Henry was calling down the well of the stairs: 'Eddie?'

'You should be asleep.'

'Where have you been?'

'Down to the garage.'

'Where else?'

'Nowhere. It's late . . . are you out of bed?'

'You left the garage a long time ago. I saw you.'

'I saw you too,' called Carrie. They were at the top of the stairs.

'What are you doing up at this time of night? Your father will be very cross.'

'We saw you go down the wood,' called Carrie. 'We were at the window.'

'It doesn't matter where I was. Get into your beds.'

'We saw you . . .'

'If you don't, I'll tell your father.'

There was a hushed conference, then he heard them move to their rooms. Shortly afterwards, the car pulled up outside and John and Margaret came in noisily.

'Guess who was at the conservation meeting . . . your friend, Dr Shannon, and his cousin the Countess.' John was quite enthusiastic.

'They're very keen,' said Margaret.

'They gave the society a whacking great contribution,' said John. 'Dead set on preserving the indigenous species, and against all these chemicals and things.'

Edward had decided what he had to do. 'I had a telephone call this evening,' he said. 'I'll have to go up to London tomorrow.'

'How long for?'

'Probably a day.'

They heard Henry call down. 'I've been awake all evening. There hasn't been a telephone call. He just made that up.'

'What the devil!' said John.

Then they heard Caroline. 'Eddie's been telling fibs all day. He said he didn't go down the wood, and he did. And that *wasn't* part of his car . . . and he didn't talk to anyone on the telephone.'

'You get them too excited, Eddie,' said his sister. 'You'll have to stop telling stories at night.'

She went upstairs to put her children back to bed.

Edward had one important commission to carry out in the village next morning before he left for London.

Henry and Caroline were even more attentive than usual.

'Where are you going?'

'I won't be long,' he told them.

'Why don't you take us?'

'Next time.'

They viewed him with cold hostility.

He bought a postcard and wrote: '*Happy Birthday – with my best wishes*', then addressed it to '*Mrs Balelli*' at '*Tudor Cottage*'. It was probably an unnecessary gambit, for when he asked for the forwarding address at the little post office they gave it to him. He recognized it as a pleasant suburb on the northern edge of London.

Back at the house, he packed an overnight bag. Margaret helped him. 'Does this trip involve your little actress friend?'

He thought it best to say 'Yes'. It was possible he might see her, anyhow.

'I am glad,' said Margaret. At times she reminded him of their mother. He waved a cheerful goodbye to the watching children, but they were still guarded and reserved.

'I'll bring you back something nice,' he called as he drove off. In an odd way that sounded like a bribe, and they were unimpressed.

He soon forgot his nephew and niece as he drove. Other things weighed on his mind, though some of them seemed too bizarre to be taken seriously. All were dominated by a single vision: the animal – wolfhound, deerhound, or whatever it was – up on its hind feet, ten feet tall and peering into the confusion of the summer-house. That was exactly what had been described to him by the widow from Sardinia. Was it just a coincidence? Two such animals in the same locality surely needed an explanation. Edward wished he had paid more attention to what she had said. At the time he had taken it for granted that it was her dog, but now he wasn't so sure . . . And yet it had had her name on its collar, or her husband's name, and their address in Italy.

He drove fast until he ran into traffic on the outskirts of London. The motorways made a big difference, and he could see he was going to get there earlier than he had expected.

He hadn't tried to get in touch with Mrs Balelli, as he didn't want to risk a rejection. He was sure that this visit would clarify many things that puzzled him. Something else she had said confused him – she had heard this dog, or some other, howling on several nights, as well as on the morning she shot it.

The address he had been given was near to Hadley Common, where large houses were still occupied by single families, and one could see fields and trees. He found the house, set in a small garden. Parked at one side was the car he had seen her drive.

A woman in her thirties opened the door; behind her in the hall a man came out of one of the rooms.

'Sorry to bother you. I'm looking for Mrs Balelli.'

Both the man and the woman viewed him anxiously.

'May I ask what it's about?' the woman said, and the man joined her at the door.

'Can I help you?' he asked.

'I'm looking for Mrs Balelli. I understood she was here . . . That's her car, isn't it?'

'Is she expecting you?'

'I don't think so. We met in Sussex where she's been staying. I was asked to help when she had an accident. She shot a dog.'

They both hesitated. This seemed to register.

'Please come in.'

They took him into a sitting-room.

'She's staying here, isn't she?' asked Edward.

'Not at the moment,' the man said. He had a slight foreign accent and seemed a little defensive.

'I was given this address.'

'She's away for a few days.'

'Can you tell me where I can find her?'

They looked at one another doubtfully. 'Perhaps you could call back . . .' the man began.

'It's very important,' said Edward.

There was an uneasy silence. 'It's awkward,' said the woman. 'She's not particularly well at the moment.'

'Is it serious?'

109

'No, we don't think so.' Then she said, 'May we know who you are?'

'Edward Glover. I'm staying in the same village. Mrs Balelli had some problems, and I hoped I'd be able to help.'

The woman spoke. 'I'm Betty Sara. This is my husband, Piero. We're old friends with Sandra . . . Sandra Balelli. *Her* husband was at school with Piero.'

'I understand.'

'She was going to come and stay later, but as she didn't feel well she changed her plans and came now.'

'But you say she isn't here?'

'She has gone to a – nursing home for a short visit.'

'I'd still like to see her. I think she'd want to see me, if she knew what it was about.'

'What is it about, Mr Glover?'

'About the dog . . . the one she shot. About what she told me.'

'What did she tell you?' The wife did most of the talking, while her husband sat and watched.

'She told me she'd been troubled by this dog – or others like it – since she arrived in England. I didn't take her seriously, but I do now. I think it's important to ask her exactly what happened.'

'You are not a doctor, Mr Glover?' said the husband.

'No. It's just – something has happened, and I think she might be able to clear things up.'

'I doubt that,' said the wife.

'Oh?'

'I'm afraid Sandra has been rather upset of late. She hasn't really recovered from the shocking death of her husband.'

'What happened?'

'He died in a fire, a little over a year ago. I think, to be honest, she is still in shock.'

'She is certainly not as I remember her,' said her husband. 'Not like herself.'

'Other things happened . . . equally distressing,' went on his wife. 'She lost her son.'

'You mean, he died?'

She shook her head. 'No, she lost him. Literally *lost* him. He vanished.'

Her husband shrugged his shoulders resignedly. 'It is no surprise that she is disturbed.'

110

'Disturbed? What exactly does that mean?'

'Did you realize she was suffering from delusions, Mr Glover?'

'No . . . I didn't know that.'

'She has been having hallucinations. She has extraordinary ideas about which she is absolutely convinced. I'm sure it's just temporary . . . the strain. To lose one's child, and then to have your husband burned to death . . .'

They sat in silence. Edward felt he had run into a *cul-de-sac*.

'What will you say to her, Mr Glover?'

'That I believe what she said about the dog.'

Husband and wife looked thoughtfully at one another. 'That might be a comfort,' the wife said. 'She feels no one understands her, no one accepts what she says.'

'I'd like to help,' said Edward.

They were silent for a few moments, then the wife said: 'I could phone her . . . but you mustn't expect too much. She isn't completely rational. Still, if you think you might be able to do something . . .'

She left them, and they could hear her phoning in the next room. She came back in. 'She will see you, but the Sister says you are not to stay long. Here is the address. It's quite close.' She handed Edward a visiting card.

They invited him to have coffee, but he was anxious to go.

A nurse warned him, 'She tires very quickly.'

'I understand,' he assured her.

Sandra Balelli looked doubtfully at him for a moment, then recognized him. 'You came with the policeman.'

'Yes. Did you have the dog buried?' That had preyed on his mind.

She shook her head.

'It's gone,' he said.

She looked into the distance, unseeing. 'They must have come and taken it.'

He realized that this was perhaps the wrong tack to have chosen. He didn't want to say anything that might trigger off the 'disturbance' about which her friends had warned him.

'I wanted to let you know I have seen some other dogs – one at least – that looks very like the one in your garden.'

111

She didn't seem surprised, nodding in apparent agreement. 'Yes. In the house . . . the big house with the walls.'

'You know Park House?' He was surprised.

'I know where the family with the dogs are living.'

'I wanted to tell you about them,' he said. 'They are next door to my sister.'

She looked sharply at him, hesitated, then said nothing.

He went on: 'The incident you described to me . . . the dog that stood like a man outside your window. I just want to say that I had a similar experience. I was in the grounds of Park House . . .'

She interrupted inconsequentially, as though she hadn't been listening. 'They lived in Sardinia for a long time. They had land, farms, vineyards – in a poor part of the country to the north. It is mountainous . . . very out-of-the-way. Of course we knew about this family. Occasionally they came to town, to functions or receptions. Not many of them . . . the elders – and some of the pretty young girls, with their dark, handsome men. My husband's family was an old family on the island, and wealthy, but the two families did not mix. There were no roads – or poor roads – in those days. Lately my husband had business in a village not far from this château of theirs. He did not meet them – he had no cause to – but he heard about them from locals. Stupid rumours . . . crazy stories that went back many years. But peasants believe such things: They are still superstitious.'

Edward wasn't sure where this rambling account was leading, but realized it was something she had to say.

'When he had to stay longer in that area – he was a geologist, you know – I went with him, and our son. There was little for a young boy to do in that primitive place. He was only nine, and when he met another boy of his own age – very charming, well brought up – I was pleased to see they played, and were good friends, and went off together, sometimes on horses which he learnt to ride.'

'Who was this friend?'

'A boy from this old family. Sometimes he came to our village hotel and had supper with us. He was very polite – well-educated.'

She stopped, as though remembering. 'Then my husband took our son by himself, when he had holidays, and I found I was going to have another child. Our boy was always so anxious to be back with his new friend, and once or twice he stayed a night at their château . . . but not often. My husband was not too pleased he should sleep there.'

'Why?'

She shrugged. 'It was his feeling, that something was strange. Our little boy began to think and speak beyond his years. Nothing was wrong, just . . .' Again she shrugged. 'Then one day we could not find him at our home. We searched everywhere. I became distracted. Someone said they had seen him going here, going there . . . Another said he had been seen a hundred kilometres away at that village . . .'

'What happened?'

'Nothing was proved . . . it was all rumour. But it was too much to suffer. I lost my baby. My husband began to believe the peasants' rumours, began to think our son had really gone all that distance to find his new friends. My husband had many powerful connections, and he found ways of checking in the château. There was no sign of our boy, nor any reason to believe he had ever been there. People in the château were charming and helpful . . . but my husband didn't believe them. It is still a country of vendetta and family feuds – if they steal a child, then honour demands revenge.'

She sat silent for so long that Edward thought she had forgotten him.

'What does it matter, people say. It is over. My baby aborts . . . my son is gone from the earth, and my husband is dead. I don't think I can succeed where others have failed. But perhaps, as a warning, they put the dogs on me.'

So that was the reason for her breakdown: she'd lost a son, and the father had blamed this family: now it appeared that he too had died.

'Did you come to England because this family was here?'

'Yes.'

'Are you still looking for revenge?'

'I'm looking for my son,' she said simply.

'But these people . . . Dr Shannon . . .'

'I don't know what name they give themselves in this country.'

'Do these people know you're here?'

'They know a great many things.'

'You think they tried to frighten you away?'

She nodded. 'They have done it. I was scared, so I left; now I am here.'

113

Then there was the pivotal question. 'But why should they want to take your son? You say they have young people of their own?'

'They have many.'

'So it doesn't make sense. Who would steal children in that situation?'

Again he thought she was going to speak, but she just gave him a wary look. 'Thank you for coming. I am tired. I can't tell you more. Goodbye.'

She pressed a bell and the nurse appeared. Edward was already going. Nothing was much clearer in his mind, except that she seemed to have given up some struggle, perhaps an irrational one. He left with the nurse, who was just closing the door when the girl called after him.

'Do you go home?'

'I'm staying in London.'

'See me tomorrow,' she said. 'Come in the morning.' She was quite unpredictable, Edward thought.

The nurse showed him out.

'At what time shall I call?' he asked.

'When you like.'

He drove off. He had intended to phone his actress friend, but decided he needed time to think things out. He wondered how much of Sandra's story was reliable and how much the product of a disturbed mind.

He booked in at a local hotel, then phoned the Sara number. The wife answered.

'I thought you'd like to know that I've seen Mrs Balelli, and she wants me to go back tomorrow.'

'That sounds promising.'

'She told me a long story. Can you tell me if I've got it right? Apparently her husband blamed this other family for the disappearance of their son . . .'

She interrupted. 'You mean the Arlettis?'

'Who?'

'The Arletti family. They had estates on the island.'

'I see. Is that the name? Well, she said her husband wanted revenge . . . There was some sort of vendetta. But she didn't say exactly how he died.'

'Part of the Arletti château burnt down . . . a whole wing. Sandra's husband was trapped in it. They found his body there.'

114

'In the château?'

'Yes. No one knew he was there. He must have broken in
. . . My guess is that he hadn't given up hope of finding his
boy. You know how Italian fathers are: his son meant everything to him. He would have killed to get him back, but he
himself died.'

'So the story's true? She's lost her family, and blames these
people who have come to England, Dr Shannon and company?'

'She says they are part of the Arletti family,' explained Betty
Sara.

'Is that the case?'

'It's impossible for us to know.'

'Is it likely the Arlettis had anything to do with the son's
disappearance?'

'It's most unlikely. Of course, we can't say this to Sandra . . .
that would distress her. But it's an old wives' tale, child-
stealing. I don't think even gypsies are supposed to do that sort
of thing nowadays.'

'That's what I thought,' said Edward.

'Are you going to see Sandra again tomorrow?'

'Yes.'

'We'd like to hear how you get on. We're most concerned
about her.'

A different nurse greeted Edward the following day.

'Please wait, Mr Glover, and I'll see if she's ready. There have
been problems. She has been in tears all morning.'

When he was shown into her room Sandra was composed,
but her eyes were red. She began to tell him again about her
son, which was clearly an obsession with her. Then she broke
off.

'I told you this yesterday,' she said.

'Do you mind if I ask some questions?' he said. 'Are you sure
the people in Park House came to England from the Arletti
château?'

'Yes.' She was emphatic.

'How do you know?'

'I had them followed. I paid an agency to watch them.'

'And you think they took your child?'

'Who knows? He has gone.'

'I see.'

'And they caused my husband to die.'

He looked incredulously at her. 'What exactly do you mean?'

'They murdered him.'

He suspected that she might be more unbalanced than he had supposed. Her story was becoming increasingly extravagant.

'Would they murder your husband?'

'Why not?' she said. 'They knew what he would do.'

'What?'

'He went to burn them.'

He was shocked by her simplicity. 'Your husband started the fire?'

She nodded. 'He told me many times what he would do. I couldn't stop him. He told me he would burn them for what they had done. They must have locked the doors so he couldn't get out . . . when they saw flames.'

'You can't *know* this?'

'The windows too were locked.'

'Were they *found* to be locked after the fire?'

She didn't seem able to see the difference between fact and supposition.

'Who knows if they were still locked then? Who would look? But I know . . . I am sure. And the dogs,' she went on. 'They had them in the grounds. Not the guard dogs that they let everyone see, but other dogs, like the one that came to my cottage. Peasants said they heard them at night . . .' Then she looked at Edward. 'You say you have seen such dogs?'

'Several times.'

'Dogs like the dead one at my cottage?'

'Yes. I can't understand how they got them into England. We have strict quarantine laws.'

'With money they can do anything.' She hesitated. 'But just dogs prove nothing. Even fierce dogs prove nothing. Even the dog at my window . . . All these alone prove nothing.'

He couldn't follow her train of thought, if there were one.

'You see what I mean?' she said. 'The Arletti family are so rich that they want special dogs to guard their property. Perhaps dangerous dogs the law does not allow, dogs that would frighten peasants . . . make them tell stories, start rumours.' She was obviously trying to be logical and reasonable.

She sat quietly by the window, then said: 'Perhaps my son went somewhere else – nothing to do with the Arletti – and got

116

lost in the hills . . . And my husband was caught up in his folly, killing himself by accident. The other things *might* all be fantasy . . .'

Shortly afterwards, she asked him to leave, thanking him politely but not suggesting another visit.

He phoned the nursing home later in the day, only to hear that Mrs Balelli had suffered a relapse. There was little point in his coming back to see her for a day or two. She was under sedation, as she had been very distressed, suffering from some alarming delusions.

'What sort of delusions?'

The matron came on the phone. 'We understand you are not related, Mr Glover?'

'No, but I am concerned . . .'

'I'm afraid we have no authority to discuss Mrs Balelli's condition.'

'I merely want to know what you consider to be her delusions.'

'We know very well what delusions are! We have had considerable experience. Suffice it to say she has been talking a great deal of hysterical nonsense, working herself into a state of exhaustion . . . and our doctors insist on her taking a complete rest.'

Edward was loath to go back to Sussex the next day, and filled in his time contacting business associates. That evening he moved into a hotel in central London and met a couple of shipping agents for dinner, but his mind wasn't on the discussions.

He thought of going back to see the Saras the next morning, but decided to phone Margaret first.

'Good gracious! Where are you? We've been trying to get in touch. I had a phone number for your actress friend and called her, but she said she didn't even know you were in London.'

'Some business cropped up . . .'

'Listen, Eddie, we had your friends from next door in for drinks last night. We thought you'd be back then.'

He couldn't believe it. 'Who?'

'The Shannons . . . or rather, the Doctor and the Countess, and a couple of very sweet youngsters. Everyone was disappointed not to see you. It was all about conservation. John wants him on the committee, but he can't at present . . . maybe he will later. The thing is, they have invited us to a meal this evening – and you, of course. We accepted for you. Will you be here?'

'Actually,' he said, 'I was just on the point of leaving London.'

'Oh good . . . see you later.'

He phoned back to the nursing home. The matron sounded annoyed to hear him again.

'I would like to leave a message for Mrs Balelli. Tell her I'm having dinner this evening at Park House.'

'She is in no condition . . .'

'Let her know when you think she's fit enough.'

He couldn't explain, even to himself, why he thought the message would be of interest to her, but he made sure they had a note of his phone number.

Edward arrived home in the early afternoon. The house was quiet.

'Where are the kids?'

'You know what they're like. They're forever disappearing.'

'This hobnobbing with next door . . . a sudden development, isn't it?' he suggested.

'Not really. John meets one of their young men occasionally on the train. Rather bright, John thinks. A very bright family . . . almost precocious in some cases, he says.'

'What's the occasion this evening?'

'Nothing special. It's informal . . . a sort of follow-up to our chat last night about the countryside. You might find it boring, so if you don't want to get involved . . .'

'That's all right. I'll come.'

Edward had several things on his mind . . . uneasy feelings for which he found it hard to account. It wasn't just that abortive expedition to the summer-house, although he sweated at the memory. What would he say about it if they brought it up that evening? Had the girl told anyone else? At least one other girl – the one at the gate – knew he'd been there. The thought filled him with a suggestion of schoolboy embarrassment.

But the real uneasiness emanated from other things. Not the animals in the garden, or the unashamed lustiness of some of their young women. It was more indeterminate . . . a sense of nothing being what it appeared to be. Perhaps Dr Shannon was too far removed from this world, too wrapped up in his theories and cranky ideas, to be aware of what was going on under his nose.

Edward wandered down the garden and into the wood, vaguely apprehensive about the children. Perhaps they were playing in the tree-house. They weren't, and his handkerchief was still in the branches. He climbed up and collected it, then stood under the netting and contemplated the high walls of Park House estate, its trees moving gently in a soft breeze – a peaceful, Arcadian, scene. It was difficult to reconcile this with his memories of the place. A grown man – he had to admit it – he had been both seduced and frightened. It wasn't a comfortable image of himself.

The warm summer spell showed no signs of breaking. All was hazy, the field shimmered, nothing stirred in the wood or across the farmlands. The little stream was a mere trickle. This was England as Edward remembered it: safe, gentle, enchanting; a familiar and temperate patch of earth which did not generate evil.

Perhaps it might be a good idea to have a chat with Margaret – tell her about Sandra Balelli? It was unlike him to have kept so many things to himself.

As he came out of the woods Henry and Caroline were running towards him.

'Where have you been?' asked Caroline.

'I've been looking for you,' said Edward.

'You've been in the tree-house.' Henry sounded accusing.

'How d'you know?'

'You've got your handkerchief.' Edward was still holding it in his hand.

'You're getting very observant. Quite the little detective.'

'We know why you've been up the tree.' said Caroline.

He was being assailed from both sides.

'You do?'

'Well, Henry does.'

'You've been spying on naked ladies,' said Henry.

'I've what!'

'Like Peeping Tom,' said Caroline.

He looked at the two children in amazement. There was no way they could possibly know that.

'What ladies?' he asked.

'You know. From next door.'

'There are naked ladies next door?' He was still trying to work out how they could have discovered that.

'Why not?' said Henry. 'Ladies like to sunbathe.'

'They sunbathe next door, do they? And you can see them from the tree-house?'

'Yes.' Henry looked coldly at him.

'You've seen them, have you?' asked Edward. 'You're tall enough to see over that wall?'

'I know they lie in the sun,' said Henry.

'Who told you that?'

'I just know.' Henry was stubborn.

'Your friend Marcel, wasn't it?'

'No, it wasn't . . . it was a cousin of his.'

'I see. So you think that anyone who goes into the tree-house wants to spy on them?'

'It's rude to look at naked people,' challenged Caroline.

'I'm going to knock that tree-house down,' said Henry. He had a flinty look about him that Edward didn't remember seeing before.

'You'd better ask your father first about that,' he told the boy. 'Anyhow, if you want to know, I was up there for quite another reason . . . I'm surprised you didn't guess it.'

'What reason?'

'I was looking for your wolf-man.'

The children were both clearly shocked, looking at their uncle with something like alarm. For a moment neither spoke, then Henry asked: 'What wolf-man?'

'The one you told me about. The man you saw who turned himself into a wolf.'

They were speechless, and Edward received an impression of two brains moving at speed . . . of alternatives, permutations, flicking through two minds, and being accepted . . . rejected . . . tested. And then Henry smiled contemptuously.

'That's rubbish. There wasn't any wolf-man, we just invented that.'

'You didn't believe it, did you, Uncle Eddie?' Caroline was smiling.

'I believe everything you tell me,' said Edward.

'It was just a joke,' said Henry. 'We made it up because you thought you were so clever with your tricks.'

'You thought those baby tricks fooled us,' said Caroline, 'so we thought we'd fool you.'

120

'You thought that? Did you, Carrie? You thought that at the time?'

'Of coure she did,' said Henry. 'We both thought that.'

'And what about the time she was crying in the bushes?'

'I wasn't crying . . .'

'When she saw the wolf watching her?'

'That was part of the joke, Eddie . . .'

He looked slowly at them, turning from one to the other. Both faces wore the same fixed grin, neither showing a real indication of amusement. 'Yes . . . you fooled me that time.'

He walked on, glancing back once to find that they were still smiling, still watching him . . . Two strangers. He was overwhelmed with a sense of loss, and then surprised that it mattered so much to him. And he had no clear understanding as to why it had happened . . . why they had suddenly shut him out of their world.

He found Margaret in the kitchen, but he was no longer able to confide in her. He could say nothing about the woman who had lost her son and husband. It involved too many other things, only half thought out; inferences not yet fully drawn, only doubtful, irrational speculations too bizarre to be put into words.

'I've just seen the kids,' he said. 'What've they been up to these last few days? Do they see the youngsters next door?'

'Yes, that's been great fun for them this holiday. The day you went to town they went riding with some of them. And they've been for a picnic . . . One of the aunts took them.'

'Anything else?'

'They've been swimming, of course, several times. I think they are getting quite good. Carrie says she can dive. One of the girls is helping her. They're very sweet.'

'I see quite a change in them,' he said.

'Well, it is two years ago.'

'No, I mean since I went to London.'

'That's ridiculous,' Margaret laughed. 'It's only a few days.'

'They're more adult – even in that time.'

'You've just noticed, that's all. Don't forget, Henry is nine next week, and Carrie has her birthday straight afterwards.' It was a family joke that the children had been born two years apart, almost to the day.

'They seem more than nine and seven to me,' said Edward.

Margaret was pleased. 'They aren't stupid, are they?'

'Anything but. In fact . . .'

'Yes?'

'Aren't they a bit in advance of their years?'

'Good gracious, no. Children today grow up so much faster than they used to.'

'They're very aware, don't you think? I mean, sometimes it's like a game of chess, dealing with them. They're thinking ahead, covering some position, knowing what's in your mind, and pretending not to.'

'I think they might be good at chess.' Margaret was busy with a batch of clothing.

'And a little secretive.'

'They would have to be secretive, if they wanted to win at chess.'

'Mind if I use your phone?'

He called the nursing home and was surprised to be greeted almost cordially by the matron. 'Mr Glover! I'm glad you called. I passed on your message, and Mrs Balelli would like a word with you.'

A moment later the Italian woman spoke.

'There are things I did not tell you, Mr Glover, because they are not your problem . . . But you will see the Arletti this evening?'

'Dr Shannon, really.'

'It is best I say something . . . so you are watchful. It is about what the peasants say, what the rumours were . . . some rumours . . .'

There was a silence, and he thought she'd gone away. 'Hello . . . yes? What did they say?'

'This is just what my husband told me – no local people spoke to me themselves. They told him some young women had been seen beyond their high walls at the château. They were not aristocratic people like everyone supposed, not the same people who went to receptions and dinners. But more disgraceful than the lowest peasants . . .'

'What d'you mean by "disgraceful"?'

'They did not dress or behave like men and women, but lived in squalor. There were animals there, of course, as any land-owner has – cattle, goats, sheep, oxen . . . animals that came and went amongst them. Eating, sleeping, sheltering in the same place. Worse than ignorant gypsies. Worse than pigs!'

He could hear that her voice was rising, and the matron in the background: 'If you get excited, Mrs Balelli . . .'

'That is what I have to tell you,' she called over the phone. 'About the Arletti – they lived like animals!'

The matron must have taken the phone, for the line went dead.

'More business?' asked Margaret.

'I'm afraid so.'

'You don't have to go back to London, do you?'

'I'm not sure.'

He went into the sitting-room, wanting to be on his own, to try to make sense of what the woman had said. But a few moments later the two children followed him in. They climbed on the chair beside him. Caroline put her arm round him. Henry was at his most conciliatory.

'We've been thinking about what you said, Eddie.'

'What's that?'

'You said you were looking for the wolf-man . . . a man who could turn himself into a wolf.'

'Right.'

'Could anyone do that?'

They were sounding him out about something.

'*Could* a man change into anything else?' Henry clarified the question.

'What d'you think?' Edward asked them.

'I don't think it's possible,' said Henry.

'And I don't,' said his sister.

'If you're one sort of thing,' Henry sounded almost coaxing, 'then how can you become something else? I don't see how anyone could believe that.'

Edward needed time to guess what they were implying. 'I'm not so sure,' he said. 'What about a caterpillar . . . *that* changes. It becomes a butterfly. Or a tadpole – suddenly, by magic, it's a frog.'

'That's not really magic.'

'All life is magic,' his uncle said. 'Birth is magic. A great deal is magic. No one can really explain the start of anything – or the nature of anything – or, for that matter, the reason for anything! So it's a very small piece of magic for a man to turn himself into a wolf – or into a bear, even. In Lapland, in Finland, and in the far north in Russia, they believe some men and women can turn themselves into bears.'

123

The children looked at him in silence. The friendly approach had gone.

'Nothing can change like that,' said Henry firmly. 'Only mad people would believe such a story.'

'You believed it,' Edward reminded him.

'That was before . . .' Henry corrected himself. 'That was just a trick.'

He slid off Edward's chair. Caroline unwound her arm. They stood for a moment, coolly looking at him. He realized that for some reason they were both very uneasy.

'And it isn't just a matter of caterpillars and tadpoles,' he went on. 'Other animals change. The snow-fox turns white in winter, then changes back in the summer time. Lots of creatures have to change in some way in order to survive.'

'That's different,' said Henry firmly.

'Who's to know what might have to happen in the name of survival? Some form of life might undergo lots of changes . . . into this, into that. And back again. Only the *appearance* changes – the creature inside remains the same.'

He wasn't sure whether they had followed the logic as he played Devil's advocate, but Henry replied sharply: 'That's a stupid argument. No man could turn himself into a wolf.'

'Ah, no. Perhaps not,' said his uncle. 'But what about the other way round?'

'What?'

'Suppose a wolf could turn itself into a man!'

The two children looked at him incredulously, then walked from the room.

They were greeted at the door of Park House by Dr Shannon.

'We are so glad you could all come. We heard Mr Glover was in London, and we feared he would not be back. And we particularly wanted to see you, as we have a confession to make.'

They were ushered into the elegant drawing-room, where the Countess rose to welcome them.

'How charming. Come in . . . sit down, my dears.'

They were made to feel like old friends as drinks were handed round.

'And now, that confesssion,' said the Doctor.

'Yes. You had better get that off your chest,' said the Countess. 'I wouldn't be surprised if Mr Glover decided not to stay when he hears it.' She waved disdainfully at the Doctor as though she disassociated herself from him.

'Very well. It appears my niece Paula . . . indeed, it is Paula who should be apologizing to you, but she is too ashamed. She has asked me . . .'

As if on cue the door opened and Paula came in.

'All right, Uncle. I'll say it for myself.' She turned to Edward. 'I feel dreadful about this. When I think how sure I was . . . and you could have been hurt, badly hurt. So could I, for that matter.'

He began to guess what she was talking about.

'I was so amused by you, Edward, when you spoke about those dogs. I thought you must have been seeing things . . . remember? I said I'd walk round the garden myself in the dark . . . but I'm very glad you came.'

'I don't follow,' said Edward.

'You were right. There are two dogs here, two *big* dogs . . . in fact, there might have been more than two. But Uncle didn't know, I didn't know . . . no one knew except a young cousin of ours, Michael. He's been here for several weeks. He came before the rest of us, and was helping to get the house ready. You see, Michael has been living in this country for some years.'

'Only *just* in this country,' the Countess added.

'Michael lives on one of the Scottish islands,' explained Paula. 'He doesn't want a life in trade or finance. He likes crofting and fishing, the simple life.'

'And Michael breeds dogs,' said the Countess.

'He breeds Irish wolfhounds,' said Paula.

'I thought they were extinct?' interrupted John.

Paula nodded. 'Almost. Michael is proud of himself, as he managed to pick up a pair in some outlandish part of the world a few years ago, and later another pair – he's not sure how pure they are – in Norway. He's managed to breed from them on this island of his. He expects to make a fortune.'

'He's got them here?' asked Margaret.

'He had,' said the Doctor. 'I can assure you, they have gone.'

'Back to his island,' said the Countess firmly.

Edward expected to feel a sense of vindication, but he didn't. 'No one knew they were here?'

'Two of the boys knew. They didn't think anything of it.

They fed them sometimes and gave them exercise in the grounds . . . As you can imagine, we were very cross. I don't think the brutes were properly trained.'

Edward remembered the dog-fight by the iron gate.

'Where were they kept?' he asked.

'In a part of the grounds you haven't seen,' said Paula. 'There's an old summer-house beyond the tennis courts, and a little further on are the stables. Michael turned part of these into kennels. We haven't started to put that corner of the estate in order yet. I don't think any of us have been down there.'

Edward had no difficulty in recalling the summer-house. So, just beyond it this cousin had a menagerie of wolfhounds? 'He sounds an enterprising fellow, this cousin of yours. I'd like to meet him.'

'Michael?' The Doctor shook his head, smiling. 'Michael has been banished to his island again. It will be some time before he is forgiven.'

'Resurrecting an extinct species?' mused John. 'Rather admirable, don't you think?'

A bell sounded.

'Ah,' said the Countess. 'Dinner.'

They went into the meal rather formally, Dr Shannon leading with Margaret, followed by John and the Countess.

Paula took Edward's arm. 'Am I forgiven?'

'Is there anything to forgive?'

'It could have been very serious,' she said.

As they followed the others across the hall, Edward heard his sister say: 'What a lot of pictures you have,' and feared the worst. It was not the room he had dined in on the previous occasion, but one in which all four walls were covered with pictures. A quick glance, however, revealed that they were nothing like those in the so-called Gallery of Amorous Sports.

'The family have been collectors for generations.' The Countess sounded almost apologetic. 'My cousin is as bad as his forebears.'

The Doctor nodded. 'These are amongst my favourites.'

The door opened.

'Ah. Robert and Zoë.' The two younger members joined them at the table. From where he sat Edward could see the excellence of the pictures round them. They were not the family portraits one might have expected, but a personal collection: obviously, one man's taste. Opposite him was a large woodland scene, with a pot-bellied Silenus riding on a donkey and clutching his wine-skin, his bald head crowned with ivy, followed by a group of dancing satyrs padding at whose heels was a panther. Next to it was another Silenus, this time older and covered with a growth of hair; snub-nosed and looking much less human, he still conveyed great sensuous vitality.

'I see my pictures interest you,' said Shannon.

'They do indeed.' Edward would have liked to ask about them, but the conversation was concerned with the meeting they had all attended in the village. Conservation was an obsession with John, and Dr Shannon appeared to share it. The countryside had to be preserved – the flora and fauna at all cost. Fox-hunting was a practice of social snobbery which should be discouraged. Trees were to be planted, old English trees such as oaks and elms. Even the less attractive forms of animal life had their champions round the table.

'There's been a scare about adders,' said John. 'A visitor on the old rail-track was bitten last August. He was perfectly all right, but you should have seen the headlines in the local paper! You would have thought we were all at risk . . . There was a "Kill an Adder" campaign.'

The Doctor shook his head. 'All forms of life have a right to exist. We all depend on one another. There is a balance which we are in danger of destroying.'

'I don't like to think of adders in the garden with the children,' protested Margaret, but saw John frowning at her across the table.

'My dear Margaret,' said the Doctor, 'everything shares this one mysterious essence: Life. There is only *one* life energy. *We* have it, *animals* have it, *vegetation* has it. Life pulses through all creation. To take life is to destroy part of ourselves.'

'And yet,' said Edward drily, 'we all take life. Life lives on life. We eat plants, meat, fish. It's impossible to exist without destroying other forms of life. It's a sort of pyramid, isn't it? I mean, that panther – ' he pointed to the picture on the wall – 'wouldn't think twice of gobbling up a couple of chickens.'

'Really, Eddie . . .' began John.

'But he's right,' agreed Paula firmly.

'Of course he is,' said the Doctor. 'Energy, life itself, the ability to survive, come only with the absorption of energy from beyond ourselves. That is the pattern of things. And if we needed adders to eat, that would be a different matter. Transferring life from species to species is one thing – from grain and grasses to beef and lamb, and from those to us, perhaps. But we should be aware of the significance of this transference . . . this consumption. In a way the acts of eating and breathing are holy. We are taking the essence of life into ourselves. We shouldn't do so lightly . . .'

'My much respected uncle,' interrupted Paula, 'what about this salmon? Do we say prayers over each mouthful? Or may we have a glass of wine, and just enjoy it?'

The Doctor gestured. 'She is right as usual, my niece . . . Forgive me.' He turned to his guests.

'And I guess you have reached a conclusion,' persisted Edward.

'Many,' said the Doctor. 'Perhaps the chief conclusion is that surely all life, all forms of it, be they never so unusual or bizarre, have a function. All should be allowed to exist; even the most alien to us . . . to mankind . . . should be given the respect that Nature requires, and should not be hounded to oblivion.'

There was a moment's silence, then Edward said, 'I'll drink to that!' And Margaret protested, 'Oh Edward! Really! You'd drink to anything.'

The silence was broken in a burst of laughter.

Edward made a mental note to remind his sister and her husband of what he had previously told them: their neighbours – some of them at least – had the craziest ideas.

But the pictures were not forgotten, and after the meal the Doctor conducted his guests round the room.

'This, as I am sure you know, is Pan. One recognizes him by his horns and goat's feet. He's a Greek god of the mountains and valleys, worshipped by shepherds, and inclined to appear suddenly, frightening travellers – hence the word "panic".'

The Pan in question danced as he played on his musical pipe.

'Whatever is this?' asked Margaret, who had moved to the next picture. 'It looks like a mixture of goat, lion and serpent.'

'That's exactly what it is,' said Shannon. 'A chimera.'

'Whoever dreamed up such things?' she said.

'Our ancestors,' the doctor said. 'People of a very early age. They have been with us forever, these creatures. We have these images imprinted in our beings from how many millions years ago . . . I suppose, from when we first experienced them.'

'You don't think they really existed?'

'Not as in those pictures, no. But the animal kingdom has not always been as we know it today. As the world is constantly changing, so we and they change. Nothing is permanent. Species have merged with species . . . or rather they have divided from common ancestors: we know that to be the case. Such manifestations as this chimera may be just a faint echo of a racial memory.'

They passed before a winged crocodile . . .

'Every corner of the world has its dragon,' said the Doctor. 'Man must have met him some time.'

A graceful mermaid rose from waves, and next to her, centaurs galloped over wild country.

'Half man, half horse,' commented Edward. 'You think they too existed?'

'When you think a horse was once as small as a dog,' said the Doctor, 'anything may have been the case. Myths are a form of history – primitive, but with their own truth, coaxed from the recesses of the mind, poetic, requiring interpretation. These pictures are an artist's version of earlier visions. And so it goes back for ever and ever.'

'Sounds like a prayer,' said Edward.

The Doctor glanced at him. 'Perhaps that's what it is.'

He would have continued – Edward could see a wall of unicorns, tritons, fauns and satyrs – but the Countess would have none of it.

'That's quite enough for one evening. If anyone wants to see more, Dr Shannon will arrange conducted tours every other Sunday. No charabancs . . . Coffee in the other room, my dears. This way.' She swept everyone before her.

'What did I tell you?' said Edward later. 'Didn't I say he was nutty?'

'I thought he was very interesting,' protested Margaret.

'The trouble with you, Eddie,' said his brother-in-law, 'you're too materialistic. If you can't explain something in scientific terms, you say it doesn't exist.'

'Don't tell me you two think those fantastic creatures exist!'

'Well, not today.'

'Or ever existed!'

'You heard what he said . . . they are part of a myth.'

'Part of a superstition. Peasants' stories.'

"Night, Eddie . . . it's late. And the old boy gave us quite a drop to drink.'

'Turn the lights out when you go up,' said Margaret.

'You turn them out,' said Edward.

He sat in the sitting-room in the dark, trying to recall the evening. He had been told something important, but couldn't quite put it together. Was that all they were – peasants' stories? The woman in the nursing home had also spoken about peasants' stories. He wondered whether mankind was still making myths, and if so, what they were? Did they involve such a bizarre mixture of creatures? Were dragons and centaurs still stalking the world in one form or another?

Margaret was right. The wine had been plentiful. He stumbled up to his room.

'Why don't you like them?' Caroline was standing by his elbow at the breakfast table.

He knew exactly what she meant, but he pretended ignorance.

'Who?'

'The people next door?'

Edward had been alone, taking his time over his coffee, when the children had joined him – silent, unsmiling.

'Who says I don't like them?'

'We know you don't.'

Henry stood beside his sister, nodding gravely.

'I think they are very interesting,' said Edward.

'*They* like *you*,' said Caroline. It was almost an accusation.

'Who told you that?'

'All of them.'

'Paula likes you,' said Henry.

'Did she say so?'

'She always asks questions about you,' was his answer.

'And what d'you tell her?'

'I said you were all right,' Henry shrugged.

Caroline chipped in. 'Henry told her you thought yourself very clever. You always did silly tricks, and thought we didn't see when you cheated.'

'Whom else do you speak to next door?'

'Everyone,' she said.

'Paula says we shouldn't talk too much to Santana and her friends.' Henry pulled a face. 'She says they're a bit crude.'

'Crude?'

'Promiscuous.'

'That's a big word for a small boy,' Edward told him drily.

'Why shouldn't I learn to use proper words?'

'Does your friend Marcel use words like that?'

'Of course. He's very grown-up.'

'I've noticed,' said Edward, wondering why the children were there. It was a strange feeling to find himself fencing with such small and innocent opponents. He stirred his coffee. Caroline hadn't budged from his side.

'Why don't you like them, Eddie?' The same question, but her tone had changed. She called him 'Eddie', coaxing him gently, using, Edward felt, at this very early age, some feminine weapons. It was best not to take her too seriously.

'I can't like everybody.' He smiled at them both.

'Which people do you like?'

'You'll have to give me notice of that question.'

Henry was scathing. 'You see!' he said. 'You're being clever again.'

It was like talking to two tiny adults in disguise. Their experience might be slight, but their intellectual agility was surprising.

Margaret walked past the open door. 'Let your uncle have his breakfast in peace,' she called.

They didn't move, waiting until they heard the kitchen door close.

'Anyhow,' said Edward, '*you* must like it in Park House. You're there all the time.'

'It's our summer holidays,' said Henry. 'It's something to do.'

'You used to find plenty to do here at home. You used to have lots of friends come round.'

'When?'

'Last time I was back on leave.'

'We were much younger then,' said Henry.

Edward looked grimly at them. 'Yes, you certainly were!'

Hearing the kitchen door open, they left him. Whatever the message was that they had to convey to him, he had probably choked it off.

But he was wrong, and they confronted him several times that morning – always, he noted, when he was alone. He was surprised to find himself on the defensive, so he decided to turn the tables on them.

'What do you do there all the time?' he asked.

'We're not there all the time.'

'I suppose you go around with that friend of yours, Marcel?'

'No, we don't.'

'Sometimes,' Henry corrected his sister.

'There are lots of others more our own age,' said Caroline.

'Marcel is too grown-up,' said Henry.

For some reason Eddie was glad to hear them say that.

'Your mother says you go swimming?'

'Yes, but they won't let us swim unless there's an adult with us.'

'What about Marcel?'

'He's not adult enough,' said Henry.

'We'd be safe with him,' complained Caroline. 'He's a good swimmer.'

'But that's the rule,' said Henry. 'That's what they say.'

'Who says that?' asked Edward.

'They all do. An adult must be in charge.'

Caroline's face lit up, and she grabbed her uncle's arm.

'Eddie! Eddie! You can come! If *you're* there, we can swim all the time.'

Henry looked at her with some admiration. 'Yes, that's right. We could.'

'Oh, Eddie! Please! Do come. Why don't you?'

They were suddenly hopeful, hardly able to hide their excitement. Edward wondered why.

'I'm busy,' he said.

'*Eddie!*' The intensity of the plea surprised him.

'Uncle Eddie! Please1 . . . We really *ought* to swim.'

'I'll think about it,' he said.

He did think about it. Indeed, he found himself thinking about little else other than his nephew and niece and the family in Park House. And he also found it hard to explain why he should be so uneasy. After all, the cause for past concern had been resolved. The reason for genuine alarm – those damn great dogs roaming about in that walled garden – had been explained, and the dogs had gone back to some Scottish island. And the other matter, the original trigger for his involvement – that story the children had told him about a man turning himself into a wolf – now appeared to be their idea of a joke. He should have expected something like that . . . the thing was, they had told it and acted it with such conviction. He could have sworn Carrie had been terrified at the time. They must have rehearsed it thoroughly. Had they really gone to that trouble just to get even with him?

He didn't see them again until the afternoon.

'Have you thought about it, Eddie?'

He turned, to find that they had followed him to the stables.

'About what?'

'About coming with us, swimming?'

There was a relentless persistence about them.

'I'm still thinking.'

'You are slow.' They looked at him contemptuously.

He had always been thought of as quick-witted. He remembered school reports: '*Mercurial*'. Coming from an English public school, that was something of a criticism. Now these children thought he was 'slow'. Edward wondered what scale of measurement they were using. Whatever it was, it had been recently acquired, picked up probably at Park House. That could easily be the case, he mused, for there was a special atmosphere there. They all seemed to share a special awareness . . . like a flock of birds which would suddenly fly off together or a herd of animals which would race off at the scent of a predator. Did they also hear, see, smell, with greater perception? The Doctor had been saying something like that, something about trusting to primitive intuitions . . .

He realized the children were waiting for his answer.

'Why don't you ask your father to take you?'

'He's at his office all day.'

'Ask your mother.'

'She doesn't like swimming much,' said Caroline.

'The people want you to take us,' said Henry.

'Why?'

'They like it when you visit.'

'Why?' Edward could be persistent as well.

Henry shrugged his shoulders. The children glanced at one another. For a brief moment they were their old selves, not knowing what to say, nor how to handle him.

'I suppose they just like to see you around,' said Henry lamely.

They made one more attempt to extract a promise from him. 'We can go swimming tomorrow, in the morning. We've asked.'

'Whom did you ask? Your mother?'

'Of course not. We asked the lady.'

'She's in charge,' said Henry. 'The Countess said you have an invitation.'

'It's a nuisance to get the car out for such a short distance,' he told them.

'We don't need the car,' Caroline said. 'We don't need to drive . . .'

Henry interrupted her. 'Of course we do,' he said, sharply, and Caroline nodded slowly.

But Edward didn't commit himself. He felt that their anxiety might make them give away something . . . what?

But they didn't, remaining very self-contained. He saw them heading for the wood, whispering together, turning to look towards him, then standing for a moment, watching, almost motionless in the shadows of the trees. It was impossible to guess what they were thinking.

Another thing puzzled Edward. Why did neither Margaret nor John appear to notice any change in their children? Surely parents should be more conscious of their children than a mere uncle?

'They're as thick as thieves this summer,' he suggested to Margaret.

'They are, aren't they?' Sometimes she had a distant and indulgent smile when she spoke about her children, and he noticed it now.

'They're rather more secretive, though, aren't they?' he added.

'Oh, they were always like that,' she said. 'It's a sort of Mafia: these two and their friends against the grown-up world.'

'That's another thing,' he said. 'I don't see many of their friends round here nowadays.'

'I suppose they all play with those new friends at Park House,' she said.

'Do their old friends go there?'

'I suppose so. Perhaps not as much as ours do. After all, it's so convenient for them. Just next door.'

'You don't think they're overdoing it?'

'I think Countess Clara would soon send them packing if they became a nuisance.'

It was clear that Margaret saw no reason to feel concerned

134

over her children, and Edward began to wonder whether he had been exaggerating the position.

'They want me to go to Park House with them tomorrow. They aren't allowed to swim there unless there's an adult with them.'

'Very sensible,' said Margaret. 'Are you going?'

'I might. It depends what else crops up.'

Something else did crop up. He returned from the village to find Margaret looking for him.

'Do you know anyone called Sarah?'

'I don't think so.'

'She was on the phone for you. She's calling back.'

The phone rang shortly afterwards.

'Same lady,' called Margaret.

Edward took the phone.

'Is that you, Mr Glover?' The woman at the other end of the line hurried on. 'It's Betty Sara. I'm very sorry to trouble you like this, but you gave the impression you were concerned about Mrs Balelli.'

'Has something happened?'

'She's discharging herself from the nursing home.'

'When?'

'Today . . . tomorrow. I'm not sure.'

'Is she all right?'

'She says she's well again. She insists she's cured . . . whatever that means. She suggests it has something to do with your visit.'

'I don't follow.'

'I don't understand it myself. Perhaps it's because you showed her some sympathy. But she appears brighter, stronger . . . more determined. She says she's not frightened any more.'

'Have you any idea what she means?'

'You know her stories . . . about what happened. I think she believes some people have tried to stop her from investigating her husband's death.'

'She sounds a little manic . . .' Edward felt uneasy, but it was not really his business.

'Exactly. She's been talking about you since you left, and she believes you could help her. She speaks of you as a "new strength".'

'I don't know what to say. I hardly know her.'

135

'I know, it's very embarrassing. I'm phoning to tell you that she will very probably call. I thought it best to warn you.'

'Thank you.'

'She tells me she is going back to the cottage.'

'Here? To this village?'

'Yes. I think I've persuaded her to stay a day or two with us, if she does that, her mood might change, and she might go into the nursing home again. If not, I'm rather afraid she'll be back there.'

'I don't see what I can do.'

'We shan't let her come alone, even if she does decide to go. We'll drive down with her, and see she's all right. As I say, I thought it only proper to let you know.'

Edward sat by the phone, trying to make sense of the call. Margaret found him there. 'So you did know the lady?'

'I met her in London.'

'Problems?'

There was nothing he could tell her. 'I don't think so.'

For some reason Edward wanted to hear what Mrs Balelli had to say, though he told himself that he ought to forget the whole affair. His was only a morbid interest.

He went into the garden, and found Margaret was in one of the greenhouses.

'Looks as though I've cleared my desk,' he told her. 'It's all free time. Where are the kids? I'll take them for that swim.'

'I don't know where they've gone.'

They were starting to call for the children when Henry walked out of the wood, followed by Caroline.

'Right . . . let's see how well you can dive,' said Edward. 'Into the car.'

'Where are we going?'

'Next door, of course.'

They looked at him in dismay. 'But you said . . .'

'I know – and now I'm saying something different. Do you want to go?'

'I'm not sure if they'd like it if . . .' Henry was thinking fast.

'Okay,' said Edward. 'You do what you like. I'm going.'

'Going by yourself?'

'Why not? You said I had an invitation.'

He moved to where his car stood on the drive. The children hurried after him, both unaccountably concerned.

'What's the problem?' asked Edward. 'I thought you came and went as you pleased.'

'But if they think *you're* coming . . . They like to be ready for grown-ups.'

'I'll handle that,' said Edward. He climbed in. 'Coming?' They didn't say anything as they took the seat beside him.

They drove the short distance and pulled up outside the iron gates. A woman came from the lodge, peered at them, then stood back to let them through.

There appeared to be no one else about as the car stopped outside the house.

'They might be resting,' Henry made it sound like a criticism of his uncle's decision to arrive without prior warning.

'I know the way,' said Edward. 'We don't need to disturb anyone. Follow me.' Edward headed for the house. The other two trotted at his heels, glancing nervously towards the big windows that overlooked the drive.

'Trust your uncle,' Edward encouraged them, wondering why they were so apprehensive, as they walked along the corridor.

'We should let them know . . .' began Henry.

'This is the way, isn't it?'

'Yes, but . . .'

'Press on,' said Edward.

There was no sign of anyone in the hall; no sign of anyone in the corridors. Doors to left and right were shut; the rooms beyond were silent. For a house with so many inhabitants, it struck Edward as strange, but there were many things in Park House that puzzled him.

They turned down a second corridor and a woman came towards them with a welcoming smile. The sigh of relief from the children was almost audible.

She was middle-aged, with a sharp-nosed, severe expression, and a bun on the top of her head. Edward had no recollection of previously having seen her, as she greeted him. 'So you have managed to bring them, Mr Glover? We did not think you could come. How nice . . . now they will continue their swimming lessons. This is a pleasant surprise.'

She took over the children who gravitated to her side, both smiling with satisfaction.

'You know Robert, of course?' She turned to indicate a young

137

man who had followed behind her. Edward recognized him as one of the dinner party. They shook hands.

'I'm acting as chaperon for these two.' Edward nodded towards the children.

'No, no,' the woman said. 'There's no need, I shall be there. You go with Robert. They are listening to music in the conservatory. Do you like music, Mr Glover? I believe there are others there whom you have met several times. We will finish in the pool in about an hour, and shall collect you from there.' She was brisk and emphatic. 'Come along, you two. We must join the other children.' She led them away.

Again Edward was aware of the children's smiling faces; they shared a secret satisfaction.

'This way, Edward.' The young man led him politely down the corridor. 'It is nice to meet you again.'

Edward had a sense that in some way it was all a charade, and that he was the victim of an elaborate trick. But as he followed Robert into the hall, he couldn't for the life of him guess what that trick might be.

He had expected – from what the woman had said – that Paula would be there, but he saw no sign of her in the conservatory. Not that it was easy to see in the room; a number of people were sitting in little groups in a dim light, under plants and palms and amongst screens of flowers. He was also aware that the pleasant perfume – which was always present in the house – was particularly noticeable; a mild, sweet vapour which could have come from the flowers, but which he was sure did not.

Robert took him to a group on bamboo chairs, half-hidden in an alcove of plants, where there were a couple of empty places.

'You remember Zoë . . . and perhaps Angela?' He was greeted warmly, but in hushed voices, as though he had come in after the orchestra had started to play.

There was indeed music, a synthetic, soft, continuous murmur, without a theme that Edward could follow; a gentle background. He could see no equipment, and couldn't make out from whence the sound came, but it was all round them, comforting and pervasive. The quality of the sound was good, and the music was undemanding and relaxing; it would have been easy to fall asleep. If this was the family entertainment, it wasn't particularly exciting, and Edward was more interested in peering through the half-light to see who was there. It was possible that Paula might be in one of the other groups scattered around.

The room was reminiscent of a Victorian conservatory, decorated with intricate iron tracery on walls and roof. The glass panels overhead had been screened, but the panels round the room revealed the corridor, and a courtyard massed with flowers. It was claustrophobic to be so hemmed in by this luxuriant foliage, surrounded by cascading flowers and potted plants. The heavy perfume contributed to this feeling. Edward shifted in his chair; it was not an atmosphere in which he felt comfortable.

He was surprised when the music stopped, the light brightened, and those around began chatting together. They turned to him, including him warmly in their conversation.

'What a pleasant surprise! We did not expect you. We thought you were caught up in business affairs.'

'I'm sorry Paula is not here,' said the girl beside him. 'She will be disappointed, but she has administrative duties. Paula is one of our younger directors, a very intelligent young lady.'

But it was a stilted conversation, as though they were using a foreign language.

One of the men in their party had disappeared and now returned with a tray of drinks. Edward saw that those around had similar refreshments.

'It is a special cordial our family makes. You would call it a liqueur. Please tell me what you think of it.'

It had a bitter-sweet flavour, and tasted slightly alcoholic.

'It's very pleasant,' said Edward.

The others accepted the compliment, and raised their glasses to him.

'How long do you stay on this holiday?' they asked. 'When do you have to go back to your work?'

'I'm not sure,' he replied. 'I may have to leave sooner than I expected.'

'What a pity.' They seemed genuinely interested. 'And when do you come back again?'

'Not for another two years.'

They made sounds of regret. 'That is a long time. Do you know which part of the world you visit next?'

He was surprised that they knew so much about his affairs.

'I have business in the Gulf,' he told them. That was certainly

139

true, but for some reason he carefully avoided giving a proper answer. 'Do any of your family come from the Gulf states?'

They looked round vaguely. 'Yes, we think there are some.'

The lights dimmed again. 'We hope you like the rest of the music,' they whispered. 'It is not a long piece. We often enjoy it.'

He hadn't been ready for the concert to start again; in fact, he would gladly have called it a day. But the rest of the party were sitting back with distant expressions, some with eyes closed, or looking up at the glass ceiling. Besides, as Edward moved, he was conscious of a great lethargy in his limbs. His whole body felt heavy. Perfume and music wafted round him hypnotically. His eyelids drooped. He had to struggle to keep awake, and he sensed that others were already asleep – or in some sort of superficial trance. When he managed to move slightly, the girl beside him opened her eyes, and smiled tenderly at him. Perhaps that drink had been more alcoholic than he thought. There was a dream-like quality about the place, faint shadows falling around them in the dim light. The girl had closed her eyes again. Her head hung back. He saw the soft curve of her cheek, her slender neck, the dark hair that fell to her shoulders. She was only a foot or so from him, breathing softly, totally relaxed. They might have been the only two people in the room together.

Edward experienced a strange sense of isolation. He would have liked to put his arms round her, but resisted the impulse, guessing they were under some drug, a form of intoxication, though the only symptoms of which he was conscious were the weight of his limbs and an overwhelming desire to sleep.

He gave up the struggle to keep awake, aware only of the gentle rise and fall of the music, of colours that came and went like vapours around him, of a sense of comfort and a peace of mind that removed all strain and tension from his body. He was still unable to lift his hand, but that was of no importance.

And then he realized to his surprise that he was not asleep. It was a totally different sensation. He was resting, lying on the surface of a great ocean, buoyed up by some force below: warm, safe, and in some familiar place. His eyes were not properly open, but he knew exactly where he was and could see the heavy leaves of the palm that hung above him, the screen over the glass roof. He could turn his head slightly and see the relaxed bodies of the others around him . . . the sweet outline of the girl beside him. With an effort and with enormous concentration of will and physical strength, he could even raise his head a little, and see the room ahead, the listening audience – some more somnolent than others, some apparently entirely unaffected by music, perfume or drinks, and listening as an audience might do at any concert.

Perhaps he could sit up . . . Edward tried but failed. An inner weight proved too much. In part of the room ahead, glass panels divided them from the corridor, where someone was strolling past. One or two figures stood just out of the corner of his vision, but others were close against the glass, peering in at this silent audience, as a man might look into a goldfish bowl. With one more effort, Edward turned towards them . . . only a fraction of an inch, but enough to bring them into vision. And yes, they were indeed there . . . three figures, watching with casual interest the reaction of those within.

For a few seconds the watchers roused no wonder or amazement in Edward. He took them in at a glance, his mind stretched to its utmost with the effort he had made. They stood there beyond the glass, two of the three with tongues lolling out of long, wolfish jaws, moving slightly as their yellow-green eyes roved slowly over the scene, with ears pricked in easy attention, grey hair bristling from exposed neck to the lower ribs – indeed, all that was visible as they stood upright in that posture he had seen once before. Their black paws rested on the glass panels, long yellow-boned claws slipping slightly as the effort of standing in that unnatural, upright posture told on them.

For a brief moment there seemed to be nothing surprising or unnatural about them. The haze of other-worldliness that swirled around Edward suggested that such a vision was nothing uncommon. It was only as the images sank into the recesses of his brain that the enormity of what he observed swept over him, and he struggled against the power that imprisoned him.

He tried to shout . . . he wanted to wake those around him, alert them to the danger. They were so incapacitated, bound like this, and at the mercy of such terrifying creatures! Fear welled up inside him, demanding a great primitive scream to his kin, to his tribe, his species. A yell to put them on their guard – to arm themselves with stones, axes, spears, swords, guns.

It was a moment of panic, but his cry was a mere sob. He

could hear it as he came fully awake . . . a gasp for breath that appeared to rouse those beside him. They sat up in alarm and looked towards him. The music faded, the light flickered. They realized that something was wrong.

'What is it?' asked the girl sitting by him. 'What happened?'

It was difficult to speak, difficult to turn and point . . . and as he did so, he saw that no one was there. No one outside in the corridor, nothing pressed against the panel, certainly no animal looking in. Instead, in the very space the creatures had occupied there were standing a few of the family, chatting. Three, he counted; beyond them another couple was walking past.

'Did something happen? Is something wrong?'

They gathered round him with concern.

He shook his head. 'I thought I saw . . .' He hesitated. They were watching with anxiety. 'I'm sorry. I wasn't used to that drink. I must have been dreaming.'

'I'm sorry if you have been upset.' The girl beside him took his hand.

'I'm fine.' He kept turning towards the glass panels. It had been so vivid! He could have sworn he had seen . . .

'I must collect the children!' He struggled to get up. It was suddenly imperative! *They* were in danger too . . . *That* could be what this image had meant.

'There is no need,' the girl told him. 'When they have finished they will come here.'

'I have to go!' He was insistent. There had been three wolves . . . three standing upright as he had seen in the summer-house at night . . . as Sandra Balelli had described the creature the night she shot it. And he had seen them clearly.

'It would be a great pity to go now,' said the girl.

Edward had difficulty in standing.

'Are you all right?'

'Yes.' He swayed slightly. The girl was concerned, gently holding his arm.

'Perhaps, if you wait for a few moments . . .'

He was convinced that there was no time to lose. He had a sense of appalling danger, though he couldn't visualize what the danger might be, what exactly he suspected. It had the quality of a nightmare about it . . . He kept seeing the semblance of the three creatures, relaxed, casually looking through the panels – in that bizarre and unnatural position, standing like men. And they were not dogs . . . No one could mistake

142

that long thin snout, the red tongue lolling from the partly open jaws, the big canine teeth . . . They were not even the Irish wolfhounds that had been banished to the Scottish islands!

'I'm sorry, I *must* go . . .'

Overwhelmed by a protective urge towards Margaret's children, he tried to hurry through the family groups towards the door. He felt as though he had been shaken from a deep sleep and was not yet fully awake as, unsteadily, he caught at the back of a chair.

'Let me help . . .' The girl was still with him, leading him through the little groups between them and the door. Those they passed watched with puzzlement, as though he were a little drunk.

The girl opened the door for him, and the air in the corridor began to clear his head. The heavy perfume was less intense.

'I shall come with you.' She closed the door after her.

'There's no need. I'm perfectly okay. It was just . . . I think I must have fallen asleep.'

'This way,' she said.

She moved away, taking him with her. As they passed the onlookers by the glass panels, Edward looked at them wonderingly. Two young women and a man stood together. One of the women smiled. 'I hope you enjoyed the music,' she said.

The man bowed. Edward looked back, to see that they were still watching, frowning thoughtfully, as he and the girl turned out of sight.

He didn't recognize the passageway into which they had turned.

'Where are we? This isn't the way to the pool.'

'It's a short cut,' she told him.

He felt lost. He wanted to go the way he knew. There was something horribly inexplicable in this house, although he appeared to be the only person aware of it. Something primitive . . . bestial.

'Are you *sure* this is the way?'

'Of course.' She smiled her reassurance.

He hesitated.

'Come along. We're nearly there.'

He followed, uncertain, fists clenched. He couldn't understand what it was he feared, or why he was so tense. She pushed open some swing-doors, and he saw they were at the far end of the swimming-pool. The noise was sudden and surprising, as he stood in the doorway. No one in the big room noticed them. Children were running, shouting, jumping in the water, swimming, splashing, screaming with laughter. It was so unlike the pictures in his mind that Edward stood shock-still. It took him only seconds to pinpoint those for whom he looked. Henry was jumping into the water at the deep end; Carrie was being taught to dive.

He stood watching, momentarily disorientated; it was so totally different from what he had feared.

'You will find your nephew and niece somewhere in this crowd.' He had forgotten the girl by his side.

'I've already seen them.'

'And how are they?' She seemed to know of his alarm, though he had told her nothing.

'They appear to be all right.' He was cautious, guarded . . . somehow he could no longer trust his senses.

The children saw him: Henry waved, and Carrie called, 'Watch me, Uncle Eddie! I can dive!'

He stood, not wishing to move, his back against the doors, only half believing what he saw . . .

'Watch me! Watch, Eddie!'

Carrie dived, and came up spluttering, very pleased with herself. Whatever might be the danger he had feared, it did not seem to be here.

Edward was content to stay where he was, letting relief wash over him. To have been so desperate and now to relax, surrounded by this hubbub of life and vitality, was a heady pleasure.

'Do you wish to stay? Or do you return to the music?' The invitation was attractive; the girl still held his arm.

'I'll take them home,' said Edward. 'Their father will be there, and he likes to see them before they go to bed.'

She grimaced in disappointment. 'Of course. We will see you here before you go, I hope?'

'I would like that.' Again he had the vision of animals upright against the glass, and wondered how he could speak so casually. It was like telling a lie – his outer calm was a hypocrisy.

'You don't know when you leave, do you?' she asked.

'Not exactly.'

'But not for a few weeks?' Was she coaxing, or questioning?

144

'I'm not sure.'

'Please come to see us when you have time. We don't know many people in the district.'

She gave him a smile and went away. Edward leant against the wall. He must have been more shaken than he had supposed, and he whispered some sort of prayer as he watched the children climb from the water. The lady with the bun of hair on the top of her head spoke to them, and pointed to where he stood.

'Come on, kids!' he called.

They disappeared into cubicles to change, then raced cheerfully to join him. He had seldom seen them looking so healthy and relaxed. They grabbed his hands and skipped by his side as they left.

'That was great, Uncle Eddie!' Caroline hugged his arm.

'The lady says we can swim properly, so we can come by ourselves next time,' Henry told him.

Whatever was the reason they had wanted him to accompany them on this visit, it had been achieved. They seemed very pleased with themselves.

'I might go for a swim myself,' Edward said.

They looked doubtfully at him.

They were about to drive away when someone called 'Edward!', and Paula hurried from the house.

'I've just heard what happened,' she said. 'I'm very sorry. My uncle is very angry. He would like to apologize.'

'I'm sorry. Apologize for what?' asked Edward.

Paula looked swiftly at the children. 'Could you come and see him? Or if you're taking the children home first could you come back later, perhaps? Come for a drink. In half an hour?'

She stood looking after them as he drove away.

John and Margaret were already pouring drinks as Edward arrived home.

'I've got to go back,' he informed them.

'Whatever for?'

'Something the old boy wants to tell me.'

'We've been here for years,' complained John, 'and none of our neighbours have insisted on *our* company.'

'Sorry.'

The children burst into the room.

'How was it?'

'Great! We can both swim!'

'And dive . . . Can't we, Eddie?'

He nodded. 'They've learnt a lot in a short space of time,' he said. Henry gave him a quick look.

Edward drove back to his neighbours' house to find one of the young men at the door. 'They are waiting for you,' he said. 'In the study. Second door.'

He was careful not to make a mistake with the rooms again, as he knocked.

'Come in.'

Paula was waiting.

'I thought your uncle was here,' said Edward.

'He's coming.' She looked worried, tapping her fingers on the table.

'What is all this? I don't know of anything which merits an apology.'

'It is very serious,' she said. 'Very bad manners, to say the least.'

'Tell me.'

She was nervous. 'We are new to this country, you know. Some of us don't know how to behave . . . especially young people.'

'Like the girl at the back gate?'

'Nothing like that . . . Some of our scattered family come from other cultures where things are permitted which would not be allowed in England.'

'I don't know what you're talking about.'

'You are being polite, but other English people might react in another way. There could be trouble . . . it would be embarrassing. My uncle was angry. If it had been another person, not you, who was our visitor there could be a scandal.'

'I'll give you thirty seconds. If you don't tell me what's going on, I'm off home.'

She took a deep breath, glancing uneasily at him.

'Have you noticed the perfume in the house?'

'The perfume? Yes. Why?' He was surprised.

'Did you notice it this afternoon?'

'Yes, as a matter of fact, I did. It was quite strong.'

'When you brought the children, my cousins took you to listen to the music in the conservatory?'

'Yes. And now you mention it, the perfume was stronger there. But it wasn't unpleasant. I didn't object.'

'You didn't recognize it, of course?'

146

He grinned. 'I don't use perfume myself.'

'But nobody mentioned it to you?'

'No.'

'Nobody told you that it's prepared from seeds and foliage in other countries? Countries where some members of my family have lived for generations, and whose way of living they have adopted?'

'No, no one mentioned that.' He was beginning to guess what was coming.

She hesitated. 'It is probably not a prohibited substance in this country, because it is unlikely to be known in Europe. My uncle says it is not known as a drug even in the land of its origin.'

'The perfume floating through the corridors is a drug?'

'It is very diluted there, but in the conservatory it is quite concentrated. It heightens appreciation of the music and gives sounds a richer quality. Indeed, it gives richness to all the senses. And it also stimulates the imagination, the memory – it liberates certain functions of the brain. My uncle can tell you about that.'

'I don't think a whiff of your special incense did me any harm.'

'It is more than incense: it affects people in different ways. It is all very well for my cousins and others to use it as they wish – they have become accustomed to it over many years. But it was wrong to take a stranger there, and to say nothing, to give no warning. Some people become very distressed. They may see things . . .'

'Like what?'

'Things that aren't there, I mean. Images, visions, colours . . . more or less anything.'

'I see.'

'Things that are hidden deep in the mind. Sometimes things they do not wish to see.'

'Suppressed in the subconscious?'

'You know?'

'I know of other substances – chemicals, drugs, also gathered from flowers – that have the same effect.'

'But no one told you what to expect, Edward. No one asked you if you wanted to take that risk.'

'I follow.'

'They gave you something to drink?'

'At the concert? Yes. Don't tell me . . .'

'That is a similar substance. It induces sleep . . . one becomes relaxed . . .'

'You certainly do!'

'So you were aware of it? I do not think it is forbidden in this country, where it is not known, but that is not the point. They should have told you . . . asked if you permitted it.'

Edward tried to apologize for his hosts. 'Don't forget, they didn't expect me. I led the children to believe I wasn't coming; then I changed my mind.'

She looked thoughtfully at him. 'The drink can be hallucinatory. The rest of them are familiar with it, as with the perfume, but a stranger might have a bad response, and could be quite alarmed. People can imagine devils; it can recreate one's worst fears.' She spread her hands helplessly before her. 'You see how serious it is? Such stupid behaviour could cause great distress.'

She waited for Edward's response. It was a long moment, and he was on the point of speaking when something made him check himself. What could he say? That he had seen three wolves through the glass panels? At their ease? In her house?

'You went to collect your nephew and your niece,' she went on, 'immediately after.'

He nodded.

'What made you hurry to them like that?'

Perhaps he should tell her. Why didn't he? She was so concerned to help. 'I'm not sure . . . Time to take them home, I think.'

She was watching him, puzzled. 'Was that all?'

He smiled. 'Don't forget, I've been around in a lot of strange parts of the world myself. I've shared pipes of brotherhood with the best – or the worst – of them. Maybe I'm immune to opiums and the like.'

'You weren't . . . distressed?'

'I was damn sleepy. My strength just drained away and I couldn't stand straight. Just as well you've told me what it was . . . I thought it was too much Scotch! I was going to cut that back a bit: thank God I don't have to!'

Paula didn't take her eyes off his smiling face. 'I'm glad it was you,' she said. 'Someone else might have created a scandal.'

The door opened and Dr Shannon hurried in.

'I am so sorry,' he said. 'I have just been told you were here.'
He shook Edward's hand.

'It's all right, Uncle,' said Paula. 'It's not such a big problem
as we expected.'

Dr Shannon looked enquiringly at Edward. 'You were in the
conservatory?'

Paula answered for him. 'Edward was there, yes, and he was
given something to drink. But I don't think it has done him any
harm. He is made of sterner stuff.'

'You had no ill-effects?' asked Shannon.

'I was just a little intoxicated,' Edward assured him.

'Really? No illusions? No hallucinations?'

'Nothing to speak of.'

'How fortunate. The first time I indulged I was very frightened. I had just finished an *affaire*, and I had pushed the lady
out of my mind, but one glass of the stuff and she was by my
side, accusing me, shouting about my inadequacies, my impo-
tence, and finally beating me on the head with a stick! You
really say you didn't even have an uncomfortable moment?'

'Perhaps I imagined my nephew was drowning,' suggested
Edward. 'I know I felt I had to go and see how he was.'

'And that's all?' The Doctor and Paula waited. Something
was clearly very important to them. Edward wasn't sure why
he lied, but he nodded.

'But I have to admit, I didn't care much for the music!'

They all laughed in what was a moment of relief.

'Nevertheless,' said the Doctor, 'it was unforgivable behaviour. Those who were to blame have been severely dealt with.
Our difficulty is that, with such a diverse community – rather
like a kibbutz, our family coming from such scattered places, as
far apart as China and Peru – we are ill-prepared for the way
some of them live.'

'Forget it,' said Edward. 'No harm done.'

They wanted him to stay, but he excused himself, saying his
sister was waiting. They accompanied him to the front door,
waving and laughing, as he drove away. He found it hard to
understand their concern. They'd no way of knowing that he'd
seen three wolves.

'Well, what was it Dr Shannon wanted to see you about?' asked
John.

'The funny thing about your neighbours,' said Edward, 'is the number of times one thinks there's something odd going on, and it turns out to have a perfectly ordinary explanation.'

'Like what?'

'Someone's breeding wolfhounds or spraying the place with hallucinatory drugs . . .'

'What!'

'As I said – perfectly ordinary explanations.'

'Don't be silly, Eddie,' said his sister.

He nodded. 'It does sound a little bit far-fetched.'

'What did he have to say?'

'Actually it was Paula who said most of it.'

'Paula? Is that the dark, pretty one?'

'Sounds like her,' agreed Edward. 'She's also very bright.'

'What did *she* have to say?'

'Well, keep this to yourselves, but they go in for minor narcotics . . . at least, some of them do. Paula and Uncle were annoyed that I'd been exposed to the stuff.'

'Not for the first time, eh, Eddie?'

'So I told them. The responsible members of the family want to merge with the local community and don't want scandals . . . either with dead dogs or dope.'

'Don't be flippant, Eddie. It's a serious subject.'

'I wouldn't worry, Margaret, they are very careful with the youngsters. I watched them in the pool. Young people are important to them. I have a feeling they consider them particularly valuable.'

'Most of us do,' his sister said drily.

He glanced round. 'Where are the kids?'

'Gone to bed,' said Margaret. 'They wanted to say good-night to you, but it was late.'

'I'll take a look,' said Edward.

'Don't waken them if they're asleep,' called Margaret as he left the room.

He stood at the foot of the stairs in the dark; there was no sound from above. He was about to turn away when he heard a faint whisper, he wasn't sure whose voice it was. He listened, but there was silence on the landing. He went up a couple of steps, then stood motionless . . . There wasn't another sound. But there had been something about that whisper – as though it were a warning.

There was still no further sound. It would have been unlike

them to keep quiet for so long if they had been awake. He would see them in the morning, he thought, feeling for the lower step.

'There's no one there.' It was Henry's voice, in a hushed whisper. 'It's all right.' There was a flurry of movement above.

'Why did they want him?' Carrie was clearly wide awake.

'They didn't say.' Henry sounded as though he was on the landing, at his sister's door.

'Will they tell you?'

'It's not important.'

'But why?'

'To watch him, I suppose.'

'To watch him?'

'To see what he's doing.'

'Oh.'

There was a pause. 'To find out what he thinks,' whispered Henry.

'Will he tell them?'

'No. But they can find out. They know about people in all sorts of ways – how they look, how they smell . . .'

There was another pause, them Carrie said bitterly, 'Why doesn't he go away?'

'He will.'

'When?'

'Soon.'

At the foot of the staircase, Edward dared not move. He couldn't believe the children were speaking about *him* in such a cool, calculating fashion. They must be discussing some stranger – and an unloved stranger at that. Someone they wanted to be quit of . . .

'Where will he go to?' whispered Caroline.

'He said the Gulf.'

'Not to the old home?'

'No,' said Henry softly. 'You mustn't speak about that.'

There was a silence. Edward stood in the dark, a sick feeling spreading through him.

'Why do they have to worry about him?'

'Because of the joke.'

'The joke you told him?'

'Yes. He might start to guess.'

'Who else did you tell?'

151

'No one else has paid any attention, but he does. And then the things he saw . . . he may wonder about them.'

There was a moment's silence, then Carrie asked softly: 'So we must be careful?'

'Yes. He pretends . . . he doesn't tell the truth. They aren't sure what he *really* thinks. He's very clever, you know.'

When Carrie spoke next it was almost angrily, a moment of accusation. 'You should never have told him about the man!'

'That was before we knew anything,' said Henry.

A door opened below, and a light went on in the hall. Someone moved swiftly across the passage above.

Margaret saw Edward on the stairs, and was about to speak when he put his finger to his lips, tiptoed down to join her, and whispered: 'They're asleep.' They went back into the sitting-room together.

'I'll have that drink now.' Edward poured a whisky.

'You all right?' asked John. 'You look a bit shaken.'

'I've had a long day,' said Edward.

He had made up his mind what he was going to say to the children next morning, working out questions that might take them off their guard, phrasing his words carefully. He was hurt as well as angry, and he wanted to ask them what the hell they had been talking about last night. But there was no sign of Henry or Caroline at breakfast.

'Are they up?'

'Ages ago,' said Margaret. 'I heard them talking about Beachers Farm. They must have gone across there.'

'That's the other side of the fields, isn't it?'

'Yes. There's a path.'

He walked through the wood to the tree-house. He guessed he was wasting his time, but nevertheless he climbed into it and scanned the fields. There was no sign of the children, but he was conscious of Park House close at hand. If they had come this way they might also have gone to play with friends there. The thought made him uneasy, and he wondered why. Was it the knowledge of that diluted perfume wafting down those corridors – could they too suffer from hallucinations? That didn't seem to be what disturbed him – but he couldn't think what else it might be. He still smarted at the knowledge that

152

they were looking forward to the day he left and went back to work . . . How easily one's vanity could be hurt, he thought.

When he returned to the house, Margaret had gone out but had left a note for him.

'Phone call for you. The Italian lady. She's back in Tudor Cottage. Wants to know if you can drop in and see her this morning.'

Edward was surprised to think she had returned so soon. Perhaps her friends, the Saras, were with her.

But when he drove over she was by herself.

'Come in, Mr Glover. How nice of you to come so quickly. Excuse the mess. I've been putting things away.'

She looked very different from the sad, distressed woman to whom he had spoken in the nursing home. Her hair was tied on the top of her head, an apron over her dress, her sleeves were rolled up, and there was an air of busy activity.

'I'm making coffee,' she said. 'Please join me.'

She had a pile of papers on a desk beside her, and had been tearing them up and tossing them into a basket.

'I am getting rid of many things,' she said. 'You might call it "Cutting one's losses", or "Seeing the light".' She went through to the kitchen where the smell of coffee greeted them, and talked brightly as she poured it into cups.

'I am not sure what I said when you came to see me.' She pulled a wry face. 'I was not myself. I may have suggested stupid things.'

'You told me about your husband and your son.'

She stirred her coffee; the brightness died.

'Yes,' she said. 'It was very sad. I went a little out of my mind with shock when our boy vanished. And I believed what my husband told me. He suspected terrible things . . . he was in such pain about his son that it was easier to find some people we could blame. It was easier than feeling guilty. In such misery we invented scapegoats.'

'I see. And the things you told me about the Arletti family?'

'That was fantasy. Because they were apart from the local people and kept to themselves, peasants started rumours . . . told country stories. It was the same in the old days: if someone was different – an old man or an old woman – ignorant villagers would say they were witches or heretics. That is what we did, Mr Glover. We found strangers we could blame, and we put all our hate, our suspicion and anger on to them . . . because it was too heavy a load to carry in our own hearts.'

153

'And when your husband died?'

'Then I carried a double burden. I became obsessed with the idea that these people had to be destroyed. When they left their château, after the fire, I followed them, living only for revenge. But my suspicions were quite unreal . . . without evidence.'

It was like listening to someone who had undergone a conversion. Those she had thought of as devils, she said, could very well have been angels. After all, they had befriended her son, they had taken no proceedings against her husband – not even questioning his presence when he was found dead in the burnt-out wing of their house. Their legal representatives had not claimed that he was there with criminal intentions. The suggestion had been that nothing could be proved one way or another, and it was not worth the expense of taking the matter to court. The Arletti family had then begun to evaporate . . . some had gone to one part of the world, some to another. Over a period of months they had left the château in little groups. She thought the place was empty now, and was merely supervised by a single custodian.

They went back to the front room, where the sun was streaming in at the window, and there was a smell of burnt paper. A heap of ashes lay in the grate.

'It is best to have done with this matter. All the stupid papers we collected, anything that supported us in our folly – once burned, I shall forget it.'

Other papers were heaped on the floor. Edward picked up one of them.

'You see, we collected everything. We read into the most innocent words meanings that were not there.'

'These look like notes from a lecture,' said Edward.

She glanced at it. 'It was something I found in my son's room. He could not have understood it. But they gave their young people much to think about. They always seemed very clever and advanced to us.'

Edward nodded. 'They seem like that to me,' he said. He read a few lines. 'Dr Shannon talks like this.'

'There was no Dr Shannon there. This was a talk by Professor Arletti . . . so my son told us.'

Some passages were underlined, with notes made beside them in a youthful hand. Edward read them aloud. '*Humanity in danger. The species has lost its reliance on instinct. Become intellectual. Neglect of the senses. Self-destructive. No other species* destroys its own kind. They fight for supremacy of the herd – for sexual power – but they don't kill. The loser backs off to challenge later . . . The species is thus kept vital and in good health. But mankind has broken this natural pattern; it has to protect itself with artificial structures – morals, ethics, religions, principles. Poor substitutes for animal instinct. At the mercy of man's intellect the whole world could now be destroyed. He has gone off on a terrible path.'

Edward looked up at the woman. 'Your son must have found this very boring?'

'He didn't tell us. We found them in his room when he had gone.'

Edward skipped through other pages. 'The intellect is fallible and will lead to man's destruction, and perhaps to that of the rest of the world . . . Yes, Shannon talks this way. But why worry children with this? What's the point? Shannon's only solution would appear to be the cultivation of man's primitive powers – those we share with other animals.'

The woman gave a little shrug. 'We did not think that important.'

'Perhaps not.' Edward collected the papers. 'D'you mind if I keep these?'

'I was going to burn them.'

'I'd like to look through them.' There didn't appear to be anything revolutionary or even original in the notes. But he wondered whether Henry was being fed this simplistic doctrine . . . or even Carrie?

'I was anxious to see you,' Sandra Balelli said. 'I couldn't remember all I had said to you about your neighbours.'

'They aren't really *my* neighbours,' Edward explained. 'They are next door to my sister. I'm here once every two years; this is the nearest thing to a home I have in this country. I come here . . .' He broke off, then said, 'I have a niece and nephew. I have been a bit uneasy about them, I don't know why, since hearing your story.'

'I'm sorry about that.'

'It's not just your story but other things. Suggestions. Something vague but, well, sinister. Then when you told me about your son . . . your husband . . . And now you tell me it was all fantasy?'

His voice tailed off. He looked at the grate . . . at the paper ashes. 'The children have changed,' he said, after a moment.

'How?'

155

'They seem much older, more mature. Secretive . . .'

'What does your sister say? Or her husband?'

'They don't notice a thing.'

'You could be imagining it all . . . like we did.'

'I've heard the children whispering together. We've always been good friends, but now they want me to leave. I think it's something to do with the people next door.'

'Why do you think this?'

'I heard them talking together when they didn't realize I was there.'

He had a strange feeling that she believed him, but that she didn't want to endure such a belief. 'You could have made a mistake,' she answered, staring at the blackened ashes in the fireplace.

In the silence that followed Edward guessed at what had happened. Sandra Balelli had gone as far as she could go – indeed, to the edge of insanity – in her assault on those she took to be her enemies. Perhaps she now felt it was hopeless to continue: that way madness lay. Now she intended to be quit of all that had haunted her these past months. Clearly she wanted no further part in his investigations.

But this backtracking, he sensed, had a purpose. Was she protecting herself? Physically? Mentally? She had envisaged a terrifying world – and had failed in her challenge to it. So now she was backing off, reconciling herself to her tragic losses – was that it? Was she denying what she had hinted at before, labelling it a fantasy, as a way of staying sane? If so, he didn't blame her, but he knew she was no longer his ally.

Still, there were things he hoped to learn nonetheless.

'What *were* those stories you spoke about? The stories you said the peasants told about the Arlettis?'

She gestured. 'It is a backward part of Europe, you know, and many generations behind the times. Visitors see only the new holiday places on the coast, but in the mountains, where the roads are poor, it is centuries out of date.'

'That was where they lived? Where they had this château?'

She nodded. 'The Arletti family had been there for a long time – rich, with the power of their wealth. But they did not mix. In such a situation people made up stories, saying they were evil, against the Church, against morality, carrying out wicked rites and orgies. Animal worship . . . sorts of superstitious things.'

'You said they *lived* with animals?'

'Of course. But they would have to. They too were farmers of a sort, and all farmers live close to their animals in those parts. They had their cattle in byres under the château, and sheep and goats herded into the grounds, behind the big walls. In those hills it is bitter in winter. Animals are wealth, and farmers care for them as they do for themselves.'

Edward gathered the papers together and stood up. 'Do you mind if I take these with me?'

She hesitated, loath to leave loose ends, anxious to end a nightmare. Edward hurried on: 'I'm intrigued by the similarities between Dr Shannon and the Arlettis.'

Her expression changed briefly – part an awakening, part dread – then she shrugged her shoulders. 'If you want,' she said.

She went with him to the door. 'You will forget any silly nonsense I may have told you in the nursing home?'

'Of course.'

'We've been looking for you,' said Henry.

'Where have you been?' asked Carrie.

'I have a life of my own,' Edward grinned. He pushed the bundle of papers into his inside pocket as he left the car.

'What's that?'

'Business.'

'You're on holiday. You're supposed to stay till the end of next month,' said Carrie.

'I don't want to outstay my welcome.' He was still smiling, watching to see how they would take the news.

'That's silly,' said Carrie.

'Do you want me to go?'

'Why do you say that?'

'I thought you might be getting too grown-up for my jokes.'

They looked soberly at him, then Henry said: 'We like your jokes . . . Anyhow, we thought you might like to take us to the coast.'

'That's a bit far at this time of day.'

'Or perhaps the Forest. That's only eight miles.'

'I'll think about that.' Edward headed for the house.

Henry called after him, 'Where are you going?'

He tapped his pocket. 'I told you. Business. I have to read these papers.' They watched him doubtfully.

Edward went to his room and locked the door. He had no idea what he expected to find in the bundle of notes, but he sat down to read them systematically.

There were a few pages in the same boyish hand, annotating the same simple 'back-to-nature' philosophy that he'd read before. There were also cuttings from some local newspapers, a dog-eared weekly given over to farming details, local weddings, court cases and Sardinian football. There were also letters, some torn from other newspapers, some hand-written, others typed and formal, with a mass of cross-references. It was undoubtedly part of an investigation by Sandra Balelli and her dead husband into the mystery of their lost son and, indeed, the details of other missing persons in that part of the island.

At the end of the correspondence someone had written, also in Italian, that this was no recent phenomenon. Men and women had vanished over the years for as long as the families of Sardinia had carried out their murderous feuds, although nowadays it was nothing like it had been in the past. One did not have to look further than the ethics of the island: an eye for an eye. A knife in the back, or a shot from behind a rock . . . It was an easy matter to tip a body over a cliff, into an abyss. *'Do not look to strangers in this matter,'* said the writer. *'People vanish in these hills – especially young men wishing to prove manhood. Do not invent theories of fantastic happenings. No one steals our young, no one is guilty of bizarre practices. We ourselves are the explanation of the mysteries of our own land.'*

Edward read the letter again. It supplied solutions to questions that he had not asked. But once they had been raised, he found it difficult to ignore them.

He looked back at the letter and made a note of the writer's name: 'N. Stefani'. He thought he had seen the same name in one of the other papers, and checked back. He found an article by Professore Nello Stefani, and he made a slow and careful translation of it. The professor, if that was what he was, was analysing the stories and legends of the district. In no place was there any mention of the Arletti family, but it dealt with a number of current rumours and superstitions which the professor linked to myths and fairy stories in other countries:

We are not the only peasant community to believe – or perhaps to half-believe – in strange and supernatural events.

Other cultures have their own stories of fantastic creatures, half-man, half-horse, mermaids and the like. They are deeply embedded in the subconscious of the human mind. Perhaps they reflect a time when such creatures truly did exist. Or, more likely, a time long before the state of life in the world as we know it historically. A time before man was indeed man – when life was in flux, when it was possible to mix and merge the different forms: animal, mineral and vegetable. It is only logical to admit that at one time all life shared a common origin. Before the specialization that exists now, there must have been many experiments, many failed attempts by the creative power to establish life in the ever-changing environment on a hostile planet, ranging from the vaporous power of the solar system to the lifeless ice-caps of the glacial epochs.

Edward wasn't absolutely sure that he followed the argument, but the man seemed to be intimating that nothing was impossible, because anything could have been a reality in the long history of the universe's evolution. He had a vague feeling that in some way the professor was an apologist for the Arletti philosophy, no matter how crazy it appeared, and he wondered whether the professor was one of that family. Was he in fact Dr Shannon under another name? After all, according to Sandra Balelli, Shannon and Arletti were one and the same – or was that one of the statements that she no longer wished him to dwell on?

He read again through everything she had given him. When he had finished, he was very careful to fold the papers, tuck them into his inside pocket, and carry them about with him for the rest of the day. Later that evening he put them in his briefcase, which he locked – a thing he did not normally do in his sister's house.

The following day Edward required a little time to himself, preferably with the rest of the house empty. Even a quarter of an hour would be sufficient. But that turned out to be surprisingly difficult to arrange, since either Henry or Caroline always tagged along behind him. He suggested various expeditions to them. He would give them money if they went to the village for ice-cream. On this warm morning they had no desire for ice-cream. Okay, so why didn't they go and play with their friends? They were too busy. Doing what? he wanted to know.

'You're not the only one with business,' Henry told him.

'We're busy too.' Caroline looked him straight in the eye. He went down to the stable, and they followed at a distance. He pretended not to notice, and headed for the wood, doubling back through the bushes. Shortly afterwards he had the satisfaction of seeing them hurry out of the wood too. It was as though he was playing a child's game, but what was at stake was far from childish. He had been back in the house for about ten minutes when Henry came in, flushed and a little breathless.

'What are you doing?' It was an accusation.

Edward grinned innocently at him. 'Making a few notes,' he said.

Carrie followed her brother into the house, equally surprised to find her uncle there. 'How did you get back?'

'I've been here a long time,' he told them.

They looked at him with suspicion, knowing they had been outmanoeuvred.

When Margaret came back from shopping, Edward greeted her with concern. 'Sorry, love,' he said. 'I've got some bad news. Bad for me, that is. I've got to go.'

'What!'

'There's nothing I can do about it.' He gave a gesture of resignation. 'I know it's messing things up. I tried to get out of it, asked if I couldn't delay it a bit. I've looked forward to being here with you, John and the kids. But there's too much at stake.' He'd made sure the two children were with them. 'Sorry, kids,' he said.

'But what happened?' asked Margaret.

'They phoned from London,' he explained. 'This agent. There's been a cock-up somewhere along the line, and one of our commissions has gone astray. Looks like I'm the only one who can sort it out.'

'Oh Eddie, I'm so sorry. I don't know what John will say. Why, you've hardly been here at all!'

'Nearly three weeks,' he said.

'That's nothing . . . When did they phone?'

'Oh, about twenty minutes ago.'

'You were in the woods,' said Henry.

'We saw you go,' said Caroline.

'Well, I took the call,' smiled Edward. 'Don't forget I was in here when you came racing back.'

It was a trick! They thought they had him now. 'We were just outside . . . we would have heard the phone!'

160

'You were in the woods,' said Edward. 'I saw you going, as I was hiding. Then I dodged back here.'

'What for?'

'I thought that was the game. Lucky I did, don't you think? Or I would have missed that call.'

'But you can't have done, not in that time! You were out of sight for only a minute!'

'Don't be silly, children,' said Margaret. 'We're all sorry to see Uncle Eddie go. But if he has to, that's it.'

'He doesn't have to!' scolded Caroline.

'Believe me, kids, I'd much rather spend the next five weeks here with you. We could have gone swimming next door . . . picnics, lots of things.'

They looked scathingly at him. Caroline turned on her heel and went out. Henry followed her.

'They *are* upset,' said Margaret.

'I'll make it up to them next time,' Edward told her. 'These two little ruffians mean a hell of a lot to me.'

Edward spelled out the details to John during the evening meal. 'I can't give you my exact movements, because the agents don't know just where along the line things have gone astray. I'll probably make Dubai my headquarters, but my guess is, I'll be spending time in both Abu Dhabi and Kuwait. I'll tell you what, when I know exactly where I am, I'll be in touch. I'll give you a call.'

Caroline and Henry had come down to say good-night to their father. They stood by his side, eyes fixed on their uncle, grimly suspicious.

'We were in the garden,' said Henry, 'just outside. We didn't hear any phone call.' His parents ignored him.

'When are you going?' asked John.

'I shall go up to London tomorrow.'

'What flight?'

'I'm not sure, my agents are booking it.' He shrugged. 'And at this time of the year it's going to be damn hot out there.'

He didn't look at the children, but he sensed their unblinking stare.

* * *

Edward travelled light and his luggage fitted easily into John's car next morning.

'The Porsche is paid for to the end of the month, so you might as well use it.'

Margaret was momentarily tearful. 'We see so little of you, Eddie.'

'I'll be back.' He kissed her. 'Just another couple of years . . . God, won't these two be enormous!' He tousled their hair, but neither Henry nor Carrie responded, even when he kissed them.

'You haven't told anyone else you're going,' said Henry.

'No one else gives a toss,' he said.

'Park House,' Henry reminded him.

'Give them my regards.'

Edward waved as they drove away, and wondered how long it would be before his message was delivered next door. He had thought about spending the day with his actress friend, but that might have been risky. Someone might phone her, and she wasn't particularly good at keeping things to herself. Besides, he wanted some place to store part of his luggage. But he took her out to dinner that evening. She was delighted, though cautious. 'Things haven't stood still,' she told him.

'Of course not.'

'Freddy . . . you remember Freddy?'

'Vaguely.'

'Well . . . and then I'm in this wretched TV soap . . .'

'I've seen it. You're great.'

'D'you think so?'

'It's fantastically popular.'

When he phoned her in the morning from the airport she told him, sounding intrigued: 'Somebody phoned you twice. They said it was very important, and wanted to speak to you. I told them you were on the plane to Dubai.'

'Thanks, love.' Edward was glad he had told her the time and flight number: surely no one would investigate further than that? Later he took off for Rome, still with his Dubai ticket in his pocket. When laying a trail, it was worth the expense to be consistent.

Part 2

Edward spent most of the flight studying the papers he had taken from Sandra Balelli. It was important to glean from them every scrap of information about names, places and times. As the aircraft prepared to land, he put his notes away, and hoped that Sandra would stick to her apparent resolution to forget any further thoughts of investigation or revenge. Her life might then be in less danger.

He changed planes in Rome.

It was several years since Edward had last been to Sardinia, and he remembered it as a hot, dry country, much less sophisticated than the Italian mainland: mountainous, massed in strange rugged outcrops. These were not particularly high but were sinister and uninviting, with long, lonely valleys. Inland, away from the crowded coast, villages had been sparsely dotted over barren rocks; one could travel miles without seeing a soul. He wondered whether time and the package holidays had changed all that.

As his Alitalia flight from Rome flew over the long rectangle of an island, he could see narrow coastal plains like pencil lines along the edge of the Tyrrhenian Sea, flattening out into tablelands, with a fringe of meadows and green thickets. Occasional bathing resorts were dotted along the shore, but clearly the big island had not been urbanized in the way other Mediterranean islands had suffered.

From that first re-introduction he was aware how empty the vast land still was, devoid of cities, with hardly a town of any size that didn't cling to the coast.

The last time he had been here he'd represented a mining consortium, and had been confined to the south-west of the island. This time, after hiring a car at the airport, he headed inland and north, and was soon into desolate country. Stopping a couple of times to ask his way, he was pleased to find that although he wasn't sure he understood fully what was said to him, those to whom he spoke had no difficulty in following him.

There was a long drive ahead and he had no intention of completing it before dark. He booked in at a roadside hotel for the night, where they were used to visitors from the Italian mainland, though few other 'foreigners' passed this way, he was told. At dinner he was given much advice – often conflicting – about the best roads to take. There was general agreement that he was going to *una bruta zona*, and that there were much more rewarding places to visit on the island.

He left early next morning, with the sun already hot, glinting on the rocky sides of gorges as he drove through. The hills were of granite, giving hard, sharp outlines to the countryside; the landscape grew increasingly barren and forbidding.

After midday he left the main road and drove over country tracks on the top of a bleak plateau. Later he descended to scrubland and low mountains. He saw no one for miles. When he reached the village it was much as he had expected: poor, scattered and empty. He booked in at its solitary hotel on the corner of a big, dusty square, in front of a Romanesque church in need of repair. He hadn't eaten since breakfast, and was given a meal of pasta and salad.

The manager proved helpful. He knew the address Edward had hoped to find; he even knew of the professor. A learned man, of some standing in Rome itself – now retired to a villa outside the village – some ten kilometres outside – on a poor road, however. But – and a shrug of regret – so many roads were in poor condition. Not as in Piedmont, which was his own part of Italy. But what could one expect in such a backward and impoverished land?

The professor would probably be having a little nap at this time of day. Perhaps if the signor telephoned him in about an hour . . . ?

Edward went to his room and waited. When he finally spoke to the professor, the voice at the other end of the line was thin and high-pitched. It was also very wary.

'You have come from England to see me?'

'I have been reading several of your publications, professor. I find them very stimulating. I wondered if there was any chance of talking to you about them. Perhaps you would care to dine with me?'

There was a pause, then the high-pitched voice asked, 'What books of mine have you come across? Have you read my thesis on the prehistoric monuments of Sardinia?'

'No, I'm sorry I haven't seen that. I look forward to doing so.' Edward cursed himself for having failed to do his homework. He should have looked up the man's record. He had been in too much of a hurry.

'You say you are English. You speak Italian. Do you read in translation?'

Edward wondered what the intention was behind the questions.

'I've read several articles, mostly in newspapers, and a number of letters you have written to journals on the island. They sound very analytic – debunking fantastic mythology. I found this very interesting.'

'I see. You have read only newspapers? I see . . . You are staying in the village?'

'At the Moderno.'

'I shall call you later,' and the professor put the phone down immediately. But he was as good as his word, and called back just when Edward was beginning to wonder whether he had been too impetuous.

'I am free in an hour,' said the professor. He sounded cautious. 'I prefer not to travel, but you may visit me. I presume you have the address. They will tell you at the Moderno which direction to take.'

Edward was thanking him as the professor rang off, equally abruptly, probably already regretting the permission he had given.

The manager drew a map. 'It is a villa with a garden and a vineyard. The vines are poor: it's too high for grapes. But you will see them.'

Edward was glad of any landmark as he went over the stony track that led out of the village. He passed a few people coming in from the fields, one or two cars driven at speed, and a couple of overladen donkeys. Things were changing even in this remote area – but only slowly. A few farmhouses were scattered over the hills, and the occasional peasant's cottage appeared in lonely isolation; several looked uninhabited.

There was no difficulty in identifying the professor's villa, standing back from the road on the edge of its small vineyard. A few trees shaded its terraces, and exotic flowers led up to the doorway. It was an unexpected corner of luxury and civilization in a bleak country.

The professor stood on the veranda; a small, spare man with thinning white hair, very spry, jerky and beady-eyed, reminding Edward of a large bird. He shook hands guardedly, and stood summing up this stranger, politely questioning him in English. It took him a long moment before he stood aside to invite Edward into his house.

Edward had brought his file of papers, having made sure it was carefully edited. The only documents other than those written by the professor were innocuous.

He opened the file. The professor was taken aback.

'My goodness,' he said, 'you have indeed many of my letters.' He glanced through them. 'I have to say I had forgotten this correspondence. I write to newspapers about many things. This is from some time ago . . .'

'I found them fascinating,' said Edward.

The professor nodded thoughtfully, and a little of his frosty defence thawed. 'It was a corrective to other articles. There is much superstition in the world today. Yes, even now. Much religion is merely superstition; philosophies also. Many foolish people condone it, encourage it. Indeed, some villains make a living out of it – academics, mostly. Third-rate minds, who have no true creative force. I have writings by such people . . .'

He led Edward into a study lined with books, and hurried to search the shelves.

'To be frank,' said Edward, 'it's *your* theories that interest me. You wrote about something which had perhaps happened locally. Was there an incident that sparked off this correspondence?'

The professor frowned. 'I remember nothing unusual. There is always chatter, from quite intelligent people who should know better.' He still frowned thoughtfully.

'What exactly does that mean?'

He gestured dismissively. 'They like to frighten themselves with talk of devil worship. What does that mean? We are all pagans at heart. The divine teachings have their pagan roots – still very powerful. So it is folly to single out others as dangerous people: we are all dangerous.'

The professor had relaxed and was no longer glancing suspiciously at his visitor. The difficulty for Edward was to keep him to the point.

'So "others" – as you call them – *were* considered dangerous?' he suggested.

'Of course. There were letters to papers . . . I see you don't have them . . . which spread alarm. I remember now . . . about missing persons. Good God! This is not the only place with missing people! Rome is full of missing people; so, I am sure, is Paris. So is your own city, London. But missing people on this island must have been spirited away! They must have been abused! The supernatural must be to blame! Not us, oh no – not parents, or law-makers, or poverty! *Our* missing people must have been abducted by *strangers*, who need them in some mysterious way, who live off them, who require not just their youthful energy, as a capitalist requires workers. No, this is different. Our *disparues* have vanished into thin air! They have been used as pure energy, to bolster up some decaying, decadent culture. Alien, of course; outsiders, of course; maybe even from outer space! As I said in one article . . . ah yes, I see you have it here . . . "*Look no further than the family quarrel, look at our history of crime and feuding. If people vanish, look in the ravines that split our granite mountains. There you will find the evidence, there are the bleached bones of your mystery.*"' The little man sat down sharply. He had run out of steam . . . but it had been a vehement few moments.

Edward wondered where it left him, but he had no time to ask questions. The professor looked at him sharply.

'If you are not engaged for this evening, you may have my invitation to stay for dinner.'

He was much quieter at the evening meal.

'Let me clarify some things,' he said. 'When people don't understand something they invent a story to explain it. Maybe a little of the story is a fact, but most is mystery and magic. We don't understand life or death, so we make up stories about them. In the same way, on a lesser scale, people explain private and public mysteries with myths. Perhaps, as an ignorant people, we on this island believe more, and act on our superstition. Primitive communities do this obviously; civilized communities do it under many disguises. The stories that I objected to were blatant nonsense – a mystery was made out of ordinary things. Some drunken man thinks he sees something . . . a child comes home with a story of the miraculous . . . a young man goes missing . . . a certain group of people, a family or one of our smaller racial groups . . . does not join with the common culture. Out of that springs a whole fantasy! Stones are thrown, people insulted in the village . . .'

'Are you talking about the Arletti family?'

The cautious look was suddenly back on the professor's face. He hesitated, then he nodded slowly.

'That was the latest incident. They were cultured people – though I did not know them personally – made to feel under threat, abused physically as well as verbally in the village, at the market . . . and worse, at their own gates – to such an extent that they kept them locked! And suspicion falling on them for a galaxy of crimes! No wonder many of them no longer wished to live amongst us and drifted away, until there was but a handful left. And now, I believe, they too have gone, after that strange fire . . . the death of an unfortunate man obsessed, I am told, by the idea that his son had vanished through their machinations. Very sad, very sad. Not the way to conduct affairs in a civilized world. But, of course . . .' he shrugged with resignation, 'I don't think we are entitled to say we are civilized, in such circumstances.'

Edward sat silently, wondering to what extent he too had looked for a bizarre explanation to a simple problem. Two children whispering in the dark did not warrant all his suspicions. What had he expected to find in this sparse corner of Europe? An explanation for a distracted woman's obsessions – obsessions she herself had now renounced? Had he allowed vanity to sway him? Probably his nephew and niece really found him a bore and wanted to be quit of him on that account. Children grow up; uncles become tedious.

'There is, of course, something to be said for the other side,' the professor was continuing tentatively. 'The local people feel they have suffered, and must blame someone. They have indeed suffered many burdens . . . very sad, heavy burdens . . . and they may think they have cause to blame that family. There *was* one unfortunate occurrence.'

'What was that?'

'The Arletti employed staff occasionally, as other landowners do. In one case, a girl who worked in the house . . . a clever girl, doing accountancy – administration of some sort – and seemingly happy for many months . . . became very strange, a little mad. Local people swore it was due to the treatment she had been given.'

'How did she go mad?'

'A break-down . . . delusions . . .'

'Delusions?' That struck a chord.

'So I understand . . . psychotic delusions. Her personality disintegrated. It is not a subject I am familiar with, but I gather she was out of touch with reality . . .' He hesitated, then added: 'That could, of course, happen in any place to any person. Nothing can be understood in such a case, unless the history and background are known. It was ridiculous to accuse the Arletti family. But the unfortunate thing is that hers was rumoured to be not the only case.'

'Who else did it happen to?'

'Some time before, I am told, to a young man from another village who tended sheep for them. When this information became common there was no stopping the local outcry, and a series of malicious incidents drove the family to leave.'

'So two people who worked for them . . .'

'Two out of quite a number.'

'Two became deranged?'

'Correct. And, oddly enough, deranged in much the same way.'

'Suffering delusions?'

The professor nodded. 'There followed a wave of fear and hate. It was impossible to write letters – I would not even have dared to name names. There is no way logic can confront primitive fears. According to my neighbours, the strangers had caused two young people to go mad. Maybe there were more, they said. Maybe all those stories and suspicions were true . . . maybe the Arletti were wicked . . . perhaps witches and sorcerers still existed . . . why not? Nothing dies out, does it? It merely goes into hiding, changes shape, flowers again in another place, in a more favourable climate.

'You see, young man, we have not yet quit ourselves of our primeval past. Inside us still live the savage and the ape, maybe also the insect and the reptile. We go back to the origins of life.'

'That sounds like Arletti doctrine.'

The professor looked quizzically at him. 'Very possibly. They had access to the truth, as we all do . . . although I am careful nowadays not to give an apology for them in these parts. Certainly not to my friends and neighbours. To you, it is different: you will be gone tomorrow, or the day after. I can say what I suspect to you. I don't know why you are so concerned

171

. . . No, don't tell me, it is not my business. I am glad to say these things without reservations. A little conversation does me good.'

'You have been a great help,' said Edward. 'I wonder . . . can you tell me where I might be able to see this girl?'

'What girl?'

'The girl who had the breakdown. She's in this village, isn't she?'

The professor was back to his birdlike jerking, staring beady-eyed. But he said, 'Yes. I think I can find you that address.'

He left the room, and Edward heard him talking on the telephone, the high-pitched voice considerably lower, and now in Italian. Nevertheless he could understand most of what was said.

'No, I don't think it is for anything sensational . . . A young fellow, quite pleasant . . . One might say, a gentleman . . . No, I did not ask, but I think he studies something, possibly our prehistoric monuments . . . Yes, he is interested in the superstitions, and I told him about the girl . . . I have forgotten her family name . . . Oh yes, Onelli . . . How is she? That's good, an improvement . . . You have recommended that she stays with her people, and she has started work . . . Well, well, much better . . . Oh, I'm sorry to hear that. Does she go for long? H'mm. Let us hope she gets over that . . . I shall let him know.'

He came back into the room rather pensively, and sat eating an orange before he spoke.

'The girl is Sylvia Onelli. They are quite wealthy farmers, and she has had some further education. As I said, she went to work with the accounts. I spoke to the doctor, her family doctor, who says she is improving. They allow her to go out to work – nothing taxing, kitchen work. She has a regular check with the specialists in Caglaria. It's just over a year since she had her trouble.'

'That sounds as though she is on the mend,' suggested Edward.

The professor made a grimace. 'He says the girl disappears from time to time, and no one knows where she goes. She returns in a filthy state, and has clearly been sleeping rough, somewhere in the hills. She comes back scratched and bleeding . . . It is very worrying for the parents, but for much of the time she is perfectly sane.'

172

'What am I to do?' asked Edward.

'I will give you the parents' address. I shall phone them in the morning. It is too late now. Then I shall phone you at the Moderno to tell you what the arrangement is.'

'You are very kind.'

'I trust this is not for some newspaper?'

'Certainly not. I'm investigating similar stories – rumours, more exactly – in England. They bear some resemblance to the stories here. I am interested to see whether there are any common denominators.'

The professor nodded; he appeared to be satisfied.

'And why do you particularly wish to see this girl?'

'She may be able to tell me something, well, rather like the experiences I've collected at home.'

'So it's not only a backward community of peasants who indulge in fairy-tales,' said the professor drily. 'A highly educated people such as you have in England spread the same bizarre stories.'

'I'm afraid so,' said Edward.

The professor almost smirked. 'Humanity changes little, in spite of the veneer,' he said.

He telephoned Edward the next morning.

'I have called the girl's father, and they are prepared to let you speak to her.'

'I'm very grateful.'

'The Onelli farm is north of the village. The Moderno people will tell you where.'

'Thank you.'

'They expect you within the hour . . .' The thin voice trailed away, but the professor had something further to say. He gave a cough. 'One small point. Apparently the girl is looking forward to seeing you, but one has no idea what she expects. She knows you are English . . . For some reason she has put on her best clothes.'

'I see . . . Well, thank you again. I'll be on my way.'

The manager at the hotel was equally explicit and helpful, and he drew another map. The farm – like most of the others – was difficult to find, along rough, single, tracks.

* * *

As the professor had said, the family was waiting for him, having seen Edward from a long way off, lurching over potholes and raising a trail of dust. The father came to the track to greet him.

'You understand the situation?' he asked.

'Yes. I appreciate this very much.'

'Perhaps you will be able to help our child.'

Edward hoped that they did not suppose he was some sort of a doctor.

The farmer took him into the front room of his home, where his wife – plump, black-dressed, with a sad, bewildered smile – made a little bow of acknowledgement. Edward shook hands, feeling he was there under false pretences but determined to persevere.

The girl, sitting by a table, looked up with a smile. She was radiant, absolutely beautiful . . . There was no sign of any abnormality about her.

'It is nice of you to come,' she said. 'Please sit down.'

In an old-fashioned Italian style both parents remained for a while in the room. But shortly the farmer muttered something and left, and a little later the mother waddled after him, but left the door open.

'I have to tell you that I know I have been ill,' said the girl. 'The doctor has told me about it; so have my mother and father. My friends told me extraordinary things I said or did. I must say it sounded ridiculous to me, but I had to believe them, although I couldn't remember anything. It's as though they were speaking about a stranger. Have they told you any of these things?'

'No.'

'What did you wish to speak about then?' She was surprisingly direct and artless. Wide eyes gave her an appealing innocence. She was so unlike anything he had expected: it wasn't easy to think of her as psychotic. What had the professor said: 'A little mad'? That was certainly difficult to believe. Perhaps it was true that she had put on her best clothes, for she was simply but charmingly dressed.

It took him a moment to collect his thoughts.

'I heard that you were working for the Arletti family, and you had a breakdown.'

'It's true I was working there. I had a lovely time, and I'm sorry that it is all over.'

174

'Why is it?'

'They've gone away.'

'Do you know why?'

'Not really. People were cruel, and said the most vicious things about them, people who knew nothing about it. They used me as an excuse, and said my illness had been caused by my work. What did they mean? Was I working too hard? Was it too demanding? Surely *I* am the person who would know? I was happy there. They were people who understood, who loved music and the countryside and natural food and wine; who loved life. They weren't like the uncouth fools in the village . . .'

'Sylvia!' Her mother called from the next room.

'But they *are* fools, Mother,' Sylvia replied. 'They are ignorant and lazy and drunken and greedy, and I hate them for what they have done. I have lost the work I enjoyed, and my friends have gone.'

'You were a bookkeeper there?' asked Edward.

'Yes. I had an office in the house. The old man was a professor – like Professor Stefani. He wrote and spoke about many things.'

'To you?'

She laughed. 'Of course not to me! I was only employed there, I was not one of the *family*. Not even one of the relations who came from many parts of the world to attend the conferences they held. They called it "a revival of the old ways and the spirit".'

'I like the sound of that,' said Edward. 'To be revived in the old ways and the spirit.'

She became thoughtful. 'It was a phrase I overheard, something they often said: "The old ways and the spirit".' She was silent for a moment, then the smile returned. 'But I assumed you wanted to discuss my illness?' Before he had time to answer she went on: 'It's an odd way to become a person of interest, isn't it? Just because you have a certain illness? Doctors and specialists were fascinated – especially in the hospital. My breakdown was something special. They don't know much about it . . . or why it is caused.' She grimaced, part amused, part puzzled and deprecating.

'I really wanted to ask you about the Arlettis,' he said.

'Very well. I like to talk about them.' Her pleasure was evident.

'How long were you there?'

'Six months.'

'Did you hear stories about them?'

'Only rubbish! I was there every day, I would have seen if there had been orgies or squalor,' Sylvia said dismissively.

'Did they stable their animals in the place where they lived?'

'Underneath, in special buildings. That's quite normal.'

'Were they unusual in any way?'

'They were polite and cultured: *that's* unusual here.'

'Sylvia!'

'All right, Mother.'

'Did you know that a family thought the Arlettis had something to do with their lost son?'

'I heard that. Of course, one would be very sorry for them, but such suggestions were untrue.'

'Were you there when the fire started?'

'No, I had left. People tell me that happened after I was ill.'

'So you know nothing about it?'

'No. Is it important to you?'

'I'm trying to piece together several accounts,' Edward said.

'You may believe only my account,' she said, smiling. 'I am the only stranger who was there.'

'The only one?'

'Well, there were one or two others, but they were working on the land – in the hills, with sheep and cattle. I was the only ordinary person in the house.'

'Why do you say that? Weren't the Arlettis ordinary as well?'

'They were very special people, with special knowledge . . . and special hope, very special. Now they have been driven away, it is a great empty space.'

The mother came back anxiously into the room. 'Perhaps that is enough,' she said.

'Don't worry,' laughed the girl. 'I like to speak about it. It makes things easier.'

'Do you still suffer from this breakdown?' asked Edward.

'I wouldn't know. I forget some days, they tell me, just as I forgot everything that happened when I was ill.'

'You sound very wise to me,' said Edward.

She laughed at him. 'Because I am, Mr Englishman. I learnt to be wise when I worked with them. I hope I shall keep their wisdom all my life.'

He was fascinated by Sylvia, finding her quite unpredictable.

'Where is this château?' he asked.

'Where I worked? About fifteen kilometres from here. Over the ridge – down in a valley. A beautiful sheltered place, surrounded by hills and rocks. I think there was a monastery there many hundred years ago – trust the monks to find a nice place in which to build their home. There are hills just beyond, where they took their cattle, wild and desolate. It has everything, that place, although the ground is stony and no crops grow . . . But it is splendid, picturesque, dramatic!'

'Is it hard to find?'

'Very. Why?'

'I would like to pay it a visit. If it's as splendid as you say, I'd hate to miss it.'

'You would never find it,' she said doubtfully.

'The man at my hotel draws me maps. He drew a map to show me the way here. I'll ask him to draw a map to show me the way to the Arlettis' place.'

Sylvia was quiet for a moment, suddenly a little remote, as though she had forgotten him. Then she said, '*I'll* show you the way.'

Her mother hurried into the room, but the girl brushed her aside – once again her smiling, amused self.

'We will not be long, Mother,' she said. 'I am sure you can trust Mr Englishman to look after me.'

'That is not the point.'

Her father came in from the farmyard, and turned to Edward for assistance. 'She is not herself.'

'I understand,' said Edward, 'and I am happy to go alone.'

'I insist,' said the girl. 'A stranger would get lost. You have to walk the last kilometre. A man once fell down a gully there. What would our neighbours say if they heard we had neglected to look after our guest? No, I shall be all right, and I will show the way.'

She went out ahead of the others, the parents standing uneasily by the door. Then the father shrugged his shoulders. 'She is obstinate. Perhaps it is better to take her, and bring her back.'

'Sometimes she has disappeared on her own,' whispered her mother to Edward.

'So I've heard,' he assured them.

'Keep an eye on her. Don't let her slip away.'

Sylvia was standing by the car as they came out of the house.

177

'Come along!' she called. 'I am safe. It is Mr Englishman you should worry about – out there in that strange, wild place!'

She mocked her parents with a laugh, but they still looked uneasy as Edward climbed into the car beside her, and they drove away.

It wasn't until they were sitting together in the car that he noticed her scratched hands and broken nails.

'How did you do that?' he asked.

Sylvia's face clouded. 'I think I fell,' she said.

Scars ran along the back of her hand, and it was hard to visualize how they could have been caused by a fall.

'Perhaps it happened when you were ill?'

But she was too honest to accept that. 'No,' she said. 'It has been done recently, but I don't remember how.'

Edward didn't mention it again, and her momentary concern vanished; she pointed to places as they drove past, and had a comment to make about most things. She was a very beguiling companion, laughing and chatting, as though simply out for a drive; but he noticed she covered her hands.

'There's someone still guarding the château, isn't there?' he asked.

'Oh yes, a caretaker. But pay no attention to him, he's very simple.'

'I see.'

'They were sorry for him, and gave him work.'

'Have you been back to the château since the family left?'

'Why should I?'

'How do you know the simple man is there?'

She hesitated. 'Everyone knows that.' A few minutes later she was laughing and joking as before.

It was slow going over the rough track, and the further they went the more neglected the road became. Edward remembered something else he wanted to ask. 'The Arlettis had a number of animals?'

'Of course. They bought and sold them.'

'Mostly cattle?'

'Yes. Also sheep, pigs and goats.'

'Did they breed dogs?'

She looked at him in surprise. 'Dogs?'

'We call them Irish wolfhounds.'

178

She shook her head thoughtfully. 'They did not have dogs.'

There were great dips in the road and outcrops of bare rock showed through the surface.

'Is it as bad as this all the way?'

Sylvia shrugged. 'Soon there is a place to leave the car. After that we must walk.'

They came under the shadow of high rock; the track clung to the side of a ravine, at the bottom of which was the dried bed of a mountain stream. As the sun vanished so Sylvia's mood changed and she stopped talking; her smile died.

'You must know these parts well,' Edward said.

She nodded. A moment later, she asked, 'What are those dogs like? The wolf-dogs?' She seemed to be trying to remember something.

'They're very big.'

As they came out of the ravine, a green patch of meadow lay ahead, bathed in sunshine. In the forefront was a collection of buildings; the wing of one was roofless and blackened by fire. The property was surrounded by a high, thick wall of white stucco, peeling in places to reveal granite rubble below. A small iron gate appeared to be the single entrance.

'That was their home.' Sylvia must have been disturbed by the sight, as she spoke with a little difficulty.

'Are you all right? Do you want to stop?'

She stared across at the buildings. 'I want to go on.'

Edward was concerned; it seemed to him she now found talking an effort. Words came thinly, from the back of her throat.

'I'll drive you back,' he told her.

She was almost angry. 'There is no need! Stop . . . you must leave the car there.' Edward turned the car into a wide sweep to one side of the track, which could have been a disused quarry.

'Now we must walk,' Sylvia said, but she remained in the car for a moment, and he saw her gripping the car door tightly. He would gladly have turned back; the strain on the girl was obvious. He tried to distract her. 'It's in a splendid position,' he said, looking towards the house. She didn't reply; he felt that she didn't even hear him.

They started along the track. The château – although that was a grandiose name for what was no more than a very large and sprawling farmhouse – could be clearly seen from where they were, but to reach it they had to follow the winding path to the bottom of the ravine, then up the other side, crossing a stone bridge. Winter torrents would probably wash right over it, but that day it was an idyllic spot: no wonder the girl had enthused about it. Now, though, she said nothing, but walked by his side, rubbing the back of her scarred hand and looking abruptly at the rocks above, then back to the buildings.

There was no sight or sound of anyone else as they made their way side by side along the rough road. Sylvia began to make a soft panting sound, as though she had been running.

'Do you want to rest?'

'Of course not.'

She hurried on, moving ahead of him, her quick, short steps growing quicker, developing into a steady rhythm, a lithe, almost loping walk – probably the best method over these barren hills.

At the foot of the ravine they crossed the bridge and began to climb; the château was directly above them. Part of the way up, the path divided.

'This way,' Sylvia said. 'We will go to the gate.' Each word now appeared to be an effort, and she no longer looked at him as she spoke.

The track followed the other side of the ravine. She turned sharply to left and right, looking over her shoulder, then back again.

'What's the matter?'

'What?'

'Are you looking for something?'

No answer. She went up the slope almost at a trot. It was as much as Edward could do to keep pace with her.

She hurried across a grassy patch towards the gate, and on reaching it she grabbed the iron bars. Her knuckles showed white. Edward looked at her anxiously. He could see no reason for this change in her – this sudden alarm.

'Listen, it's not important. I've seen the place, and I can come here again myself. It's better to go back now . . .'

The girl tried the handle of the gate, but it was locked. A heavy metal bell hung above it, chain attached. She reached up and pulled at it, impetuously. The sound echoed across the courtyard and died away. Nothing moved. She was staring fixedly at the house.

Edward didn't know how the hell he would cope if she had a

180

breakdown in this benighted place. He didn't even know what form such a breakdown might take. He should never have come here with her – the sight of the house must have triggered off some memory, and her personality had changed. He must persuade her to return to the car.

He put his hand on her arm. 'Let's get back . . .'

She shook him off, and pulled the bell-chain angrily again. 'He must let us in! I know he is there!' It didn't even sound like her voice. She shouted through the bars: 'Come at once! You hear! Come and open!'

He might have to drag her away, Edward thought. She was becoming more disturbed the longer they waited.

'I will tell them about you!' she shouted across the yard. It was the quality of her voice that decided Edward; a shrill, challenging cry. He took her arm . . .

The side door of one of the buildings opened slowly, and as they watched a man stepped cautiously into the sunlight, peering across at them. He was broad and short, bald, with the wide, nervous eyes of a simpleton. He hesitated, silent.

'Let us in!' called the girl. 'It is Sylvia, you know me. Let us in!'

He screwed up his eyes in concentration, and shuffled towards them, but he stopped after a few steps, and she had to call again. It was a slow process, coaxing him to the gate.

Finally he stopped a few feet away and looked at each of them in turn.

'Open the gate,' Sylvia told him. He had a bunch of keys tied round his stomach, and played nervously with the key-chain, knowing what was expected but unable to bring himself to step nearer. The delay infuriated the girl: she shook the gate, baying at the man – a voice without words, an undisguised howl of anger.

Edward was appalled as he watched her. It was hard to believe that this was the girl who had laughed and joked with him in the car.

'I have seen all I want,' he said desperately. She ignored him, gripping the gate, a spasm seeming to race through her body, holding on for dear life . . . or clinging on to sanity, Edward wondered? He must help her; he had brought her there, so he was responsible. He tried to attract her attention, calling: 'Sylvia! Sylvia!'

At last something seemed to penetrate the mind of the man

on the other side of the gate. He looked at the girl with a new awareness; recognition came into his childish eyes, which blinked at her in alarm.

'You are not to come in! I know who you . . .'

He turned and shuffled away, quick but ungainly, to the door he had left open, going in without looking back and slamming it behind him. The echo of bolts being shot home rang across the yard.

By his side the girl threw back her head and howled. It was no cry of despair, nor even of anger. It had no human meaning or content, but was the cold, alien sound an animal makes, meaning much only to another of its kind.

As Edward heard her, he felt his skin prickle and something inside him grew thin and cold. He was too shaken to move. Strength had gone, flowing from his limbs. She was only a few inches away – this pretty girl, her trim, attractive body pressed against the iron gate, her dark hair falling over a delicate neck. What an incongruous moment to be aware of such charm!

Once, twice, a third time, and oblivious of the man beside her, she threw back her head and gave a long, wild howl that sounded into the hills round them.

With difficulty Edward suppressed the urge to turn and run. He caught a glimpse of her eyes that no longer had any contact or understanding, as though she in turn failed to make anything of him.

He said, 'For God's sake . . .' and was going to plead with her, to try to bring her to her senses – literally, to her senses! – but before he could, there was another sound in the distance, one that could easily have passed as an echo of her own call. A long drawn-out sound – the cry that one animal might make to another: the call of a wolf . . . or the answering howl . . .

The girl let go of the gate, no longer trembling but very taut, alive . . . Edward was aware how lithe she was, how fit – how powerful for a girl. She ignored him . . . he might as well not have been there. As she stepped back from the gate and turned away, she no longer stood upright but, arching her back agilely, lowered herself, on to the balls of her feet like an athlete, except that she bent lower, her arms falling forward, as though representing the front legs of some creature – not quite touching the ground, but low enough to give the impression of an animal.

In that posture . . . strangely graceful but with something

182

lethal in her every movement . . . she went loping off. It was the only word he could use to describe the way she went, at speed, heading for the cliffs above the ravine – leaping over rough ground and not looking back until she was on the ridge above his head. Then she stopped, turned and saw him as though for the first time. As he watched, her mouth pulled up on one side, lips lifting to show teeth; the sound she made carried to where he stood, petrified. She snarled a warning . . . or a threat . . . then she turned and disappeared over the ridge.

Edward stood, as though stunned, watching the break in the ridge where she had vanished but knowing she would not come back. She had left her home with him, an attractive, charming girl, as normal as any he had met . . . and she had turned into an animal. Was this what the children had meant in Sussex, so long ago? Was this how Henry had seen a man turn himself into a wolf? For that was what she appeared to him to be . . . a wolf, climbing between the rocks, scrambling over the edge of the ravine, absorbed in her own inhuman world, aware of him only as an intruder – an enemy.

He realized he was trembling as he held the bars of the iron gate, resting his head against them, waiting for what seemed a long time until his shocked nerves regained composure, whispering to his bewildered self, 'Oh God . . .'

He felt the need of human contact, any human contact . . . even that of the pathetic creature who had run from her in alarm. Perhaps *he* would know what had happened and could explain.

Edward rang the bell at the gate, keeping it sounding continuously, even gaining comfort from the noise. The door of the outhouse opened, but the little bald man stayed where he was, and watched.

'She's gone,' called Edward. 'She's run away – what happened to her? Do you know who she is . . . what went wrong?'

It was a staccato monologue, the man in the shadows saying nothing, but peering into the hills and clearly very nervous.

'She's been ill,' called Edward. 'Did you know? Have you seen her like this? Has she done this before?'

The man stepped out only to get a better view of the ridge.

'Can you help me? I have to get her to her home.'

The other man either didn't understand or didn't want to. He took a last look into the hills, then went back into the house and rebolted the door.

Edward, feeling more isolated than before, had to summon up all his courage before he could force himself to climb to the top of the ridge. He reached it with hands cut on the sharp granite, and stood on top of a rocky ledge. A plateau of rocks and stones, cut across by a maze of ravines, lay before him. In the distance was a range of hills rising to mountains on the far horizon. Before him lay a wilderness of scree and stunted trees, with patches of summer grass; wasteland, cut off from the rest of the world, moon-like, derelict. No movement, anywhere.

He went cautiously back down the slope to the path, taking a last look through the gate. All was silent within.

He dreaded his return to the girl's parents, but what could he do? She had run off, and he had been unable – afraid – to follow. It was possible she had done something like this previously. Anyhow, he had to face them, and probably the professor as well. It was the only way to get the girl some help.

He set off along the track, down to the bridge, crossed it and reached the path that would lead him to the car. It didn't occur to him that he might not be alone as he moved into the shadow of the ravine. His hands were still trembling slightly and his heart sounded loud to him as he walked at a good pace. The sooner he was back at the farm, the better the chances of a search-party finding the girl.

He had a strange sense that there was someone behind him, and for a second hoped it might be the girl . . . but when he looked he saw no one was there, and he hurried on.

The sensation persisted, however, and he found himself glancing over his shoulder every other minute . . . he remembered that Sylvia had done the same. He reminded himself drily that a neurosis was not infectious. Rounding a bend he came to a dead stop, as a thin trickle of stones and dust filtered down from above. He peered up at the rocky outline, but saw nothing. Nothing moved. There was no sound. It could, perhaps, have been a bird?

He went on even more cautiously. Was she following him, somewhere above?

Ahead, the cliff dipped and lowered. If she *were* there, that was where he would most likely see her. He approached slowly. If only there was a chance of coaxing her back with him! The sound of rolling stones convinced him . . . she was there! A rock bounded down the cliff-face ahead of him, hit the path, and plunged off it into the dried bed of the stream below. He

stopped, motionless: if he had been a little further ahead . . .
Could it have been an accident? A rock dislodged by chance?

Another boulder, with rubble in its wake, landed on the path behind him. He spun round as a figure above darted out of sight, behind rocks on the edge of the cliff. That was no accident!

He turned and broke into a run.

Immediately, from above, he heard a chilling sound – the howl of a wolf! And just ahead . . . a second howl! His imagination ran riot! Somewhere on the ridge above, running parallel with him, hunting him . . . A pack of wolves!

Something whistled through the air, missed the path, and plunged into the abyss. He didn't stop to look but raced ahead. His life might depend on it. He reached a low dip in the cliff and was briefly out of shadow, as the sun lit up the track. A second path – a goat track probably – ran parallel to his, half-way up the cliff. A figure sprang from the rocks and loped along it, over boulders and gullies, animal-style, arms almost touching the ground, head lowered, looking down on him, yelping. A noise that announced a kill.

It was the girl – transformed, vitalized, moving with the grace and assurance of an animal, and beautiful even in this insane pursuit, her clothes ripped, her skirt torn, hair falling over her face. The tragedy of it! The destruction of such a charming creature! Surely, if he were to appeal to her . . . ?

He stopped and called.

'Sylvia! I want to help. Come back to your home . . .'

She too stopped, hands on the rocks before her, lank hair hiding her eyes.

'Come on, love. Your own people . . .'

Her face was transformed as she snarled at him. There was no mistaking the signal . . . She might have been a tigress at that moment; for a second she might have leapt down on him. He wished she had; he would have fought her, dragged her to the car . . . But she didn't move, just curled her lip as a dog might, tossed back her hair, never using her hands like a human being but keeping them low on the ground.

A stone whistled through the air and hit the rocks beside him . . . Another figure, more or less upright, was on the top of the cliff: a man, torn, ragged, dishevelled.

A second stone went over his head, and Edward ran towards the car. He had almost reached it when a third stone bounced off the track and hit him. Much of the force had gone out of it, but the sharp edge of granite cut into his leg, and the pain was excruciating. As he managed to drag himself into the driving-seat, he saw the blood on his shoe. The last thing of which he was clearly conscious was the howling of an animal . . . the sound of triumph!

They patched him up in the hotel.

Edward was aware of a doctor putting away some instruments, and a woman bandaging his leg. Also in the room he was fleetingly aware of the girl's father and mother. He tried to speak to them, but only English words would come. 'I'm sorry. Sorry. She ran away . . .'

They led the farmer's wife out, weeping.

The next time he awoke Professor Stefani was there, bird-like and critical.

'They should never have let you take her there! What were they thinking of? The stupidity! They knew very well the psychosis . . . it is not my speciality, I know nothing about it, but any grown person would know the girl was not in any way cured. She may never be cured! In fact, I don't know whether such a thing as a cure exists for ailments of the mind.'

All Edward could do was to repeat, this time in Italian, 'I'm sorry. Something happened to her. She changed . . . she spoke in a different voice. She wanted to get in at the gates.'

'What are you saying, young man?'

'She became hysterical . . .'

'She is out of her mind. They should know that.'

'She seemed so sweet, so sane.'

'That of course is the problem. Demented people can appear completely sane until the moment comes. Then, for no reason, *poof!*' He threw his hands in the air. 'It is not my province, of course . . . They should have known.'

Edward must have slept again, and when he came round it was already growing dark. He was surprised to see the professor still with him, sitting alone in a corner of the room, reading a paper. He saw Edward stir and rang a bell, ordering something to drink.

'A little brandy might do you some good,' he said.

'This is very kind of you,' said Edward.

'Not at all. You are a visitor, I sent you to these people: I am

186

responsible. Besides, there are things to ask you for my own information.'

The brandy arrived, and life crept back into Edward's limbs. As he sipped the drink, and later took a little minestrone, he told the professor what had happened.

'The change was remarkable, and without warning – although I think she had been growing a little nervous, tense. She was looking everywhere . . . and she stopped chatting and laughing. But it suddenly came over her. I couldn't see a reason, not a valid reason.'

'She was back at the cháteau,' said the professor.

'Is that a reason?'

'Who knows? But she should never have gone there.' He was picking his teeth with a toothpick. 'You know, of course, what has been wrong with her?'

'No.'

'But you have seen it, just as the doctors in the hospital described! My guess is that her father and her mother know all about it. I suppose this always happens on the occasions when she goes missing.'

'She has always come back?'

'Oh yes. In my opinion, in a few days' time she will return home.'

'Thank God for that,' said Edward.

'Don't blame yourself,' said the professor. 'It is a formidable and a very rare condition.'

Edward looked across at him expectantly, but it was a long time before the professor spoke. 'You know what lycanthropy is, of course?'

'I've never heard of it.'

'You surprise me. It's a condition of insanity in which the patient believes himself to be a beast.'

Edward put down his glass. Images tumbled together in his mind. 'A beast?'

'Exactly. He, or she, believes it, and acts as one. What did you say she appeared to be? A wolf? Very probably that is what Sylvia Onelli thinks she is: a wolf.'

'Oh my God!'

'It is unfortunate,' said the professor. 'In her case it comes and goes, and she is not permanently under this misapprehension. But when she is, that's how she acts, that is what she is

187

'. . . a wolf.' He was thoughtful for a few moments. 'You say, she ran on all fours?'

'Near enough. She tried to.'

'She would think she *was* on all fours. Nothing would convince her she was not an animal. She would do nothing that such an animal could not do. I imagine she was not the person who threw the stones?'

'The man did that.'

'Yes . . . you see, a wolf cannot throw stones. It has no hands.' The professor spoke quietly, thoughtfully. Edward was too sickened to speak.

'It's a pathological condition,' mused the professor. 'I suppose best described as a type of hysteria. In some cases the person attempts to eat the food the animal eats. As she is a wolf, she craves to eat like a wolf.'

'Poor kid.' Edward was overwhelmed with pity.

'Indeed . . . Let me fill your glass.'

The professor settled himself again. Edward felt he could do without the details, but he knew he had to hear everything. Was it possible some of the mysteries were about to be clarified?

'In the old days people would say that such a man or girl was possessed. They were believed to show certain symptoms: as I remember, a yellow complexion, hollow eyes, and a dry tongue.'

'The girl was nothing like that. All the time, even when she behaved like an animal, she stayed beautiful.'

'H'm, yes. She has had this condition for about a year. Perhaps in time . . .' He was silent for a few moments. 'It takes different forms in different parts of the world. In tropical countries, victims may believe themselves to be tigers, in others, hyenas or leopards. But oddly enough, the commonest form is belief in becoming a wolf. In fact, the word "lycanthropy" means exactly that: metamorphosis of man into wolf.'

'What causes it?'

'Ah! What causes any mental illness? As I say, I have not gone deeply into the subject, but I imagine there will be a family tendency. Perhaps a tendency of nationality or race.'

'That doesn't seem likely in this case.'

'No, true . . . But one never knows what is inherited from one's past. On the other hand, certain infections may cause disorders, or feeble-mindedness.'

'She's a quick, intelligent person.'

'My guess would be a traumatic experience. Unbearable stress, perhaps over a period, and culminating in an impossible situation. Yes, she might have undergone an intolerable shock.'

They hadn't turned on the light, and now sat drinking in the dark.

'An interesting case,' said the professor thoughtfully.

Edward, remembering the girl struggling with herself, fighting to resist overwhelming impulses, to remain sane, was moved with compassion and made no comment. He was very tired. He tried to move in bed, and found it hard to lift his leg.

'The doctor says you will take some time to get over the wound,' the professor told him. 'I shall go now. You must sleep.'

'Who was the man with her?' Edward asked. 'The other figure I saw up above, in the hills?'

'They say he is the shepherd.'

'And he's suffering from the same thing?'

The professor shook his head. 'He, too, had a mental problem certainly, but of a different sort.'

'That's damned odd,' said Edward. 'Two of them – different, but equally destructive. Both local people working for the Arletti.'

'Yes, that *is* unusual, but not necessarily significant.' The professor remained impartial.

Before he left, Edward asked him: 'Tell me, would you say the girl is dangerous?'

'That depends. What will motivate her? What does a wolf eat? What a wolf eats, so must she. If it is starving, and the opportunity arises, I am sure a wolf will hunt, kill, and eat most flesh – including people.'

He bowed his good-night as he left the room.

Within a few minutes Edward was asleep.

It was very dark when he woke. At first he wondered why he had come so swiftly and alertly awake, and he lay listening . . . His room overlooked the village square, and he could see through one corner of his window, where the blind had not been properly drawn, that moonlight bathed the church. It must be very late.

There wasn't a sound from the hotel below, but there was a

movement – a faint sound – from closer at hand. Someone was in his room!

His instinct was to jump up, but paralysing pain shot through his leg. He lay, hardly breathing, letting his eyes become accustomed to the gloom, ready for anything.

A floorboard creaked, as though someone had frozen on it. A few seconds' pause . . . then the sound again. He could see no one. The noise came from the shadow by the door. Ignoring the pain, he reached for the bedside lamp and switched it on.

The girl, dirty and dishevelled, was only a few feet from him, her hands outstretched. She looked different: her eyes were no longer blank, but full of alarm.

'I came to find you,' she whispered.

She tiptoed to the edge of the bed and sat, covering her face with her hands. A moment later she looked up.

'How did you know I was here?' asked Edward.

'They told me this morning.'

'Why have you come?'

It was a very simple confession. 'You know I have been ill. They told me at the hospital, but I did not believe them until today. Today I made myself break through the dream. I saw I was an animal . . . a wolf.'

'This is true?'

'Yes. While the mood is on me, I *am* a wolf. But I saw you today, and part of me knew I was hunting you . . . I beg you, I don't want to be a wolf.'

She looked pathetic, tear-stained and filthy, with her clothes ripped, her breast bare, her skin lacerated, her hair earthy and bedraggled. 'Now I realize what I am, I think I have a chance.'

Edward wasn't sure what to believe. He had seen her go berserk once – she might do so again.

'What can I do?'

'You came to see me to find out about the Arletti family. That was why you wanted to go to the château. You know things about them, don't you? If you know things I know, then I am not mad . . . and this wicked thing that has happened to me will vanish.'

'Yes, I did want to find out things about them.'

'Why? Because they are magic?'

'Magic?'

'That's what they say. It's their spell. They say you must

190

never break the magic, never turn your back on the mystery, and the charm is the charm.'

She looked so earnest and so sincere, clutching her hands before her, as if in supplication. 'I can tell you about them,' she said. Her eagerness was heartbreaking. 'I was a little besotted by them from the first. I thought they were wonderful, and I wanted to be like them. I must be honest: there was one of the younger men – ' She broke off with a gesture of resignation. 'Yes, I was a little bewitched.'

Grotesque though it was at this moment, Edward felt a pang of jealousy, then wondered at his own stupidity. He had a sudden recollection of his own recent infatuation: there had been a quality amongst the women in the Shannon family which he also had found hard to resist.

Sylvia began to speak again. 'Only gradually did I see exactly what they were – what they could do.'

'What could they do?'

'They are not people, you know.'

'No?'

'Not *human* people. They look like it for much of the time, but that is a disguise . . . a camouflage. They pretend to be people, for in that way they survive. If men knew what they were they would kill them, hunt them for fear or for sport – for they really *are* animals. Not like me, who only believe I am. They are animals like wolves, but as I say, they are magic. They can change. They come out of one skin into another, change from men to beasts. In that way they are safe. The beast is the real thing; the shape they take on, that is the face they present to the world. That is why men treat them as men. Did you know this?'

'The Arletti family are wolves, not men?' He tried to make it sound reasonable. *Could* any of this be possible?

'Yes, all of them. And there are branches of this family, they come and go across the earth. Not so many of them now as they are a weak and dying species, so they need strength from outside. As an old fruit tree needs to have grafts implanted from healthy young trees, so this species needs to interbreed with men and women. Then their children – the next generation – have the magic. But the people they use – the men and the women – I fear may go mad.'

He looked at her now in amazement. Her blue eyes were filled with sincerity, her hands pleaded with him to believe. She had found in him another human soul in a wide and empty world who knew the truth she had discovered, and which had driven her beyond the edge of sanity.

A little of the intensity had gone out of her: she had achieved some relief in telling her story. She continued softly, almost rationally, putting together the pieces of her past – or her imaginary world?

'I know why I became a wolf: it was to protect myself. To be like the others. If they were animals under the skin, I had to be one.'

'Do you want to be one now?'

'Not at this moment. But who knows? It may happen again. You can help me . . . if there is only one other person who knows what is true, and can share it with me, then I am not cut off – I am no longer isolated. You can tell people I am speaking the truth. I am ill only because no one believes . . .'

She had put into words fantasies Edward had wished to keep at bay, fantasies that had both enthralled and repelled him, that intellect had rejected, but that some other part of his being had seemed to understand. He felt he was being led step by step towards intolerable conclusions. What was she *really* telling him? He had to be sure.

'What did you mean – the Arlettis could *change*?'

'Oh yes, I have seen them change from men and girls into wolves, and back when they had to mingle with the world. They are like chameleons – the skin changes. The outer creature is one thing, then another. There is an old word for them: they are werewolves. It is not just an ancient story, though they are not exactly as the fairy-tales would say. They are another species which might have died out, as the huge lizards of the Ice Age have gone, but they found a way to grow like parasites on the blood of mankind, with subtle violence, quietly, as a fungus lives on the life it drains from a tree. They and their kind survive only because they are not known.'

Edward laid his hand on her arm. 'Are you sure this is all true?'

She gave him a quick glance. 'I know. I was there. I saw it happen.'

He felt hopeless, guessing there was nothing he could do now to help her. There must be some way of easing her distress, some treatment, some drug . . . Perhaps her doctor . . . ?

Looking anxiously at him, she went on: 'They go back to the

early time. They have to survive on earth while man is dominant, just as they did when other gigantic creatures were all-
powerful. They lie low, live in hidden places, absorb fresh blood
. . . and wait. They will out-distance man.'

'I think I know how to help,' he said. 'Give me a hand.'

She helped him out of bed; it was a painful struggle. 'Wait
here,' he said.

It took him ages to go down the short flight of stairs, and it
was equally long before he could rouse the doctor at the other
end of the phone. When he returned to his room she was sitting
in the armchair. She had washed the dirt from her face and
hands, and was relaxed. It was as though she had come home
and knew she was safe.

He lay down on the bed again. The pain in his leg left him
helpless; he could scarcely move. From where he lay he thought
the girl was asleep: her eyes were shut and she was breathing
softly, steadily, her hair pushed back, her dress primly
adjusted, seemingly at peace. He wondered how that could be
so, with such a maelstrom of memories – or was it of wild
fantasy? – in her head.

But he was wrong. She wasn't asleep. She opened her eyes
and looked across to him.

'I have been ill for over a year, they say. Of that time I
remember very few things. I pray that in that time I have not
given them a child, fathered by them and able at will to change
to a wolf.'

The idea, even as an unreal image, chilled him. He sweated
as he thought about Caroline and Henry.

It took a long time for the doctor to react to his call, but at last
headlights flashed past under his window and engines revved
to a halt. It sounded as though a whole fleet of cars had braked
to a theatrical halt outside the Moderno, though it proved later
to be only two.

A few minutes later the sleepy but startled manager knocked
on the door. He entered, began to speak to Edward, saw the
girl now curled up in the chair, and hurried out.

'I know you had to tell them,' she said.

There was a rush of feet on the stairs and the door was
thrown open. Two uniformed policemen barged in, the manager hovering behind them. At the head of the stairs stood
another man in uniform.

'What the hell's this?' demanded Edward. 'I simply asked the doctor to come.'

'It is out of his hands,' said the manager. 'Things are too serious.'

The girl hadn't moved. She sat looking up at the two policemen who stood over her.

'You will have to go, Sylvia,' said the manager.

'Come along,' said one of the policemen. 'You'll be all right. We'll look after you.'

'I'd like to see my mother,' said the girl.

'We'll get her,' the policeman told her cheerfully. 'This way. Car's waiting.'

She went out between the two of them, without looking towards Edward. He was aware that he had been guilty of a betrayal, and he felt sick.

'Help me down there,' he said to the manager. 'There's something I have to tell her.'

It was a slow, agonizing passage from step to step. The girl was in the manager's office when they went in, and Edward was appalled to see she had her arms before her, locked in a pair of handcuffs.

'For God's sake! Does she have to have those?'

The policeman shrugged. 'Regulations,' he said. 'She's all right now, but who knows what could happen?'

One of the other officers called to him from outside.

'Keep an eye on her, please,' the man said as he hurried out. For a moment Edward was alone with her. He was going to try to explain what he had hoped would happen, but she brushed aside his apologies.

'Memories of my time are coming back,' she said. 'That is a good sign, I am sure . . .' Then she looked up at him with one of her radiant smiles. 'Will I see you again, Mr Englishman?'

He nodded, finding it hard to speak. What else could he have done? But it felt like treachery. 'Of course you will. Now that you have told me . . .'

'I remember some things very clearly,' she interrupted. 'In that household they did many things that were unusual. All the time they played music – that's nothing, I know. But it could make you very sleepy. And they had this sweet smell in the rooms and corridors. You know what they said it was? A mild drug.'

Edward could hear the cars starting up outside, doors opening and shutting. There was some shouting and orders given, operatic-style.

'They're coming back,' he said. 'I'll find out where they're taking you . . .'

She still wasn't listening, but with an amused smile of recollection she said: 'And several times . . . I can now see them standing there . . . it was so strange, and yet I took it for granted as just part of the magic . . . One or two of them, upright – as if they were still men and women, front paws on the wall as they watched someone at play, great tongues falling from their open jaws, yellow-green eyes turning to me, and showing no concern that I had seen their secret. They must have known I would lose my own senses, and so no one would believe me, even if I told them.'

Edward's skin prickled, and a sense of sickness swept over him. The jigsaw puzzle had been pieced together, and the picture was one of sheer horror! He resisted the urge to grab hold of Sylvia, to keep her until she had answered the questions that flooded into his mind, as the police officer came in.

'All aboard,' he said cheerfully.

'Who was standing?' Edward asked her urgently. '*What* did you see standing?'

She was leaving the room with the officer, but she turned to smile at him comfortingly, as though she were the one concerned about him.

'But I told you,' she said. 'The Arletti, so often, standing upright like us . . . yet wolves.'

As the officer led her out he turned to Edward and winked knowingly.

Edward heard the car engines race into life, and tried to hurry to the door. But he couldn't move for the pain in his leg, and the police had gone in smoke and dust before he reached the square.

Edward could scarcely walk for the next three or four days, during which time he had several visits from the professor. But now he couldn't speak to anyone about his suspicions . . . in fact, there was only *one* person to whom he could talk, and he found himself thinking about her most of the time.

As soon as he was fit he drove to the hospital in Cagliari, where Sylvia Onelli was housed.

'She is not here,' he was told.

'I know she is.' He gave the admittance number. The officials scrutinized this and took him aside.

'You are Mr Glover? The Englishman?'

'Yes.'

'I'm afraid you can't see her.'

'Why not?'

'It has been particularly requested.'

'By whom?'

'By her father and mother.' He looked at his papers. 'Also by her doctor.'

As Edward was about to protest, the man added: 'Besides, she is not here. She has been moved on.' It was a patent lie but Edward could see he wasn't going to get anywhere. He handed his car in at the airport.

Part 3

'Eddie! How wonderful to see you! Whatever happened?' Margaret ran down the steps at the front door as he paid off his taxi.

'We sorted out the problem quicker than we thought.' He grinned and put his arms round her.

'Have you been to the Gulf and back?'

'No . . . Last-minute change of plan. We met in Rome and put the business back on its feet.'

'So you're here to finish your holiday?'

'If that's okay?'

'You know it is. It's wonderful to see you.'

'Hello, kids.'

They were standing at the top of the steps, just inside the doorway, clearly taken aback, yet looking at him fixedly, motionless and – or so he thought – suspiciously.

'Not back at school yet?'

'I thought you'd gone away,' said Caroline.

'And you were right. Now I've come back.' The last time he'd arrived they had raced along the drive to meet him, throwing their arms round him. 'Getting a bit confusing, isn't it?' he said. 'All this coming and going.'

They didn't smile.

'Where did you go?' asked Henry.

'I'll tell you all about it when I get my breath back.'

'Yes,' said their mother. 'Give Uncle Eddie a chance to recover. The Middle East is a long way off.'

'He didn't go there,' said Henry drily. 'He said he was going. He told everyone he was going. But he went somewhere else.'

'Where did you go?' asked Caroline.

'He's just told us. Rome. In Italy,' said Margaret.

They went into the house, and the children followed. He felt their unwavering eyes on him, watching every move. They had been cheated once . . .

'He always does that,' said Henry. 'Says he's doing something, and does something else.'

'There was nothing wrong with his car *that* time,' said Caroline.

'What time?' asked Margaret, as she was pouring cups of tea.

'And no one *else* heard the phone ring,' said Henry.

'Now you're being childish,' said Margaret. 'I told you to put your cycles away. Go and do it.'

They were loath to leave Edward, watching him grimly as they went out of the room.

'How nice to see you!' Margaret lifted her cup in salutation. 'John will be pleased. What happened?'

'It was all very simple and straightforward,' he smiled. 'Nothing much to tell. Nothing exciting.'

Margaret wrinkled her nose. 'I hoped there'd be a bit of high finance to pass on to my neighbours. I saw one of the Shannon girls in the village – I don't know which one, they are all so alike, aren't they? The children must have told them you had to dash away, since she seemed to know all about it. John thinks you're gun-running or something. He's being very good about it, but he hates the thought that you make so much more money than he does!'

'He doesn't know his good luck,' said Edward. 'He has you, and the kids.'

'I think he just takes that for granted,' she said.

'What have they been up to?'

'Carrie and Henry? The usual, I suppose. Come to think of it, I'm not sure what they've been doing since you went. They're so much more independent now. Of course, they spend a lot of time next door.'

'Doing what exactly?'

'Playing with their kids, I suppose. They are such very nice people.'

'Have you seen anything of them?'

'Not really.'

'No more dinner parties?'

'No. But I'm sure they'll want one when they hear you're back.'

'How long will that take?'

'Rumour goes through this village like a dose of salts. They'll hear it on the grapevine.' Mixed metaphors never bothered Margaret.

'Have you still got the Porsche?' he asked.

'It's in the garage. John didn't have the nerve to drive it.'

'I'll just pop down to the garage in the village with it.'

He saw Henry and Caroline coming out of the wood as he drove off.

'Where has he gone?' they asked.

'To the village,' said Margaret. 'I think he wants to check the car.'

She didn't notice the suspicion, nor the contempt, in their eyes. But then she'd no reason to look for either.

Sandra Balelli listened impassively to Edward, then sat for a few moments before speaking. 'But you say the girl is crazy?'

He nodded. 'Oh yes, at least some of the time, but she had her own mad logic.' He stood looking out over the neatly trimmed lawn and the tended flowerbeds, aware that Sandra was looking at him. He had no idea what she might be thinking.

Then she said: 'If they are a dying species, and need to breed with us, with people, that would be why they took children. Those stories have been around for many generations in my country.'

'You get legends like those all over the world,' he told her. 'That hotch-potch of myths and old wives' tales is oddly consistent. But Sylvia certainly believes what she said to me.' He hesitated, turning to the girl beside him. 'She said something else, just before they took her away, about the château she had worked in. She said it always smelled of perfume . . . and that music played through the house.'

'Many houses might have music and perfume,' Sandra said.

'And then she told me about the people she had seen in the corridors. That brought back the image so vividly – of wolves, standing like people, upright, at ease, casually watching something. She mentioned their tongues hanging from their open jaws . . . their wolves' eyes watching.'

Sandra interrupted, suddenly angry. 'As she's out of her mind, she could say anything.'

He nodded. 'Except that I have seen the same scene myself.'

'You have seen what?'

'At Park House, amongst the Shannon family. Or do we call them the Arletti?'

'I don't believe you,' she said desperately.

'I had it explained to me later,' he went on. 'They use drugs which cause hallucinations. If you aren't used to them, you are liable to see the things you are trying to suppress – trying to hide in your subconscious. Perhaps wolves masquerading as men and women is a common fantasy?'

He could have said more, but she raised her hand. 'Mr Glover, you know I do not wish to speak about this family. I also think that you know why. In a few weeks' time you leave, and stay away for two more years . . . Why don't you just enjoy what's left of your holiday?'

John was already home when Edward got back. 'You young rascal! This is splendid! Great to have you back.' The welcome was so genuine, Margaret and John so loving – could he not trust them with his outrageous suspicions? John's good sense would bring things down to earth. This might be the time to share his grotesque fears.

'Margaret tells me you didn't get further than Italy.' That was indeed true. 'What the devil have you been up to?'

'Gun-running,' said Edward.

'So she told you, did she? Loyal little wife!'

The two children slipped into the room.

'And where have you been this evening?' went on John. 'I thought you'd gone to the garage for a check-up on your expensive car, and I phoned, but they hadn't seen you.'

'I had one or two things to do . . . just wrapping things up.'

He was aware of the children watching him.

'A man of mystery,' said John. 'Well, we delayed drinks till you came back.' He busied himself with the whisky decanter.

'We knew he hadn't gone to the garage,' said Henry. 'He always says one thing, and does another.'

'Not always,' protested Edward.

'Where did you go?' Caroline was direct.

'That would be telling,' Edward grinned at them.

'I know how to find out,' said Henry.

'That's interesting. How?'

Henry looked grimly at him. There might have been only the

202

two of them in the room. The boy's animosity was almost painful.

'You don't know everything, Uncle Edward,' he said softly. 'Oh yes, everyone thinks you're very clever. People realize that, now, but they won't make the same mistake twice.'

'Nice to get the warning,' said Edward. He managed to sustain an inane grin as he spoke, but he sensed the malice in the threat.

'What are you talking about?' John carried the drinks to the table. 'Here you are, you two. In honour of the event, I've poured you a couple of powerful lemonades.'

'What event?' asked Henry.

'Your uncle's return, of course.'

'Some people think he never went away,' said Caroline.

'I could show you my air ticket,' said Edward.

'You can book a flight, but not go on it,' said Henry.

Edward looked at him. 'That is a very adult statement. It shows a remarkably developed sense of deception.'

'I don't know what you three are on about,' said John. 'But cheers, all of you. And now, off you go and watch television, you two.'

As they left, Margaret came into the room.

'Lots of things have happened while you've been away, Eddie,' John told him. 'They want to put a by-pass round the village, through Castle Wood. We're going to fight it, of course. That wood has been common land for hundreds of years; a breeding ground for wild life . . .'

'And for generations of bastard children,' added Margaret.

'Ignore that,' John went on. 'We've started an *ad hoc* committee. I'm on it, and your buddy next door, Shannon. Conservation is his middle name. He's promised the cash for any legal aid.'

'He's on your committee?'

'He certainly is. Preliminary meeting in one hour.'

'Where? At Park House?'

'At the King's Head, as a matter of fact. Want to come?'

'I'm not on the committee.'

'It's informal tonight.'

'Okay. Might be interesting.'

'They don't know you're back, do they?' asked Margaret. 'Next door?'

'I guess they will do by now,' said her brother. 'I'd better go and say good-night to the kids.'

Caroline half-shut her eyes. 'I don't want to talk to you.'

'Why not?' asked Edward.

'You don't love us.'

'Why do you say that?'

'You don't tell us anything.'

'Like what?'

'You don't tell us the truth. And you don't play any more games.'

'We're playing a game now, aren't we?' suggested Edward.

'It isn't a game,' she said sharply.

'Carrie!' Her brother called warningly from his room.

She turned her face away and said nothing.

'All right,' said Edward, 'I'll go and talk to Henry.'

He sat on the edge of Henry's bed. 'Carrie says it isn't a game. What's not a game? What does she mean by that?'

The boy looked coldly at him. He was not to be cajoled or tricked. The room was in darkness, but by the light from the landing Edward could see clearly the veiled, hostile eyes.

'It's silly to play games,' said Henry. 'It can be dangerous.'

'Trust me,' said Edward. 'I can look after you.' He hoped to make that sound reassuring.

But Henry was contemptuous. 'Can you look after yourself?' he asked.

In the face of such antagonism, it was hard to keep up any pretence.

John called from the hall below. 'You coming, Eddie? We're going to have a snack before we go.'

''Night, kids,' said Edward. The sense of unease lay heavily on him, but there was nothing he could say to their mother or father. Nothing that would make sense.

When it was time to leave, Edward told his brother-in-law, 'You go ahead, I'll come in my own car. I'll probably want to leave before the end.'

'Okay. See you later. We're in the room behind the bar.' John drove off, and ten minutes later Edward followed.

The committee members were well into their stride as he

slipped into a seat at the back of the room, and they didn't notice him amongst the other spectators. The babble of voices calmed down as someone called them to order. It was Shannon, just out of sight, but speaking with quiet authority.

'There are many principles at stake,' he said. 'Some of us have different priorities, but we are all united against this proposal. For my part, I fear the loss to animal life that has survived in this land for thousands of years. Not just life we are conscious of – not just foxes, badgers, birds, owls and the like – but also many tiny forms that remain in woods and wasteland. If mankind continues to destroy and urbanize, what will be left for our fellow creatures? For insects, ants, bees, for the unseen and unknown? We must not behave as tyrants in Nature, we do not have that right. Nature is a pyramid: one form of life depends on another. If we destroy one small part, we cannot calculate the harm we are doing to the whole.'

There was a moment of throat-clearing. This wasn't an argument that was going to cut much ice with the authorities.

'A good point,' came John's voice. 'Now I think we should have a look at this map they've sent us, and see what they have in mind.'

Edward stayed for half an hour, during which time the Doctor was fairly quiet, pressing only for the 'right to survive'. 'We are not gods who can condemn other creatures to oblivion,' he reminded his fellow committee-members.

'You didn't stay long,' said Margaret.

'They'll be there till midnight,' Edward told her.

'How's it going?'

He shrugged. 'Maybe they'll delay things a little, but my guess is we'll have the whole world concreted over sooner or later.'

'So you're on Dr Shannon's side?'

'What? Yes . . . I suppose so. We can't be totally irresponsible, cutting down rain-forests and the rest of it.'

'Castle Wood is scarcely a rain-forest.'

'You know what I mean. Shannon is correct when he says we don't have a right to obliterate other forms of life.'

'What if they're dangerous?' said Margaret.

'That's different,' said Edward. 'We'd be damn silly not to protect ourselves.'

John arrived back with a vague invitation.

'Shannon saw you slip away. He's sorry to have missed you,

and suggests we go next door for drinks or a meal. He says they owe us hospitality.'

'Do they?' asked Edward.

'Not exactly, but the Countess did bring a couple of their youngsters to play.'

The invitation became firm next day, Henry arriving with a note.

'They want us to go tonight,' said Margaret. 'I've phoned John at the office and he says it's okay with him. How about you, Eddie?'

'Suits me.'

He wondered at the urgency . . . what did they want to learn? What had the children told them? He wondered how much they already knew . . . or guessed. Suspicions were mirrored in the eyes of both his niece and nephew, and there was now no doubt in his mind where these adult and alien intelligences came from. Certainly, Henry and Caroline were spies in his camp, but at the same time they unwittingly brought back information in much that they said or did.

'Just one thing I'd like to ask,' he said to Margaret. 'Every time I visit your neighbours I drink too much . . . or the company goes to my head. I'm not used to this socializing.'

'What *are* you talking about?'

'Or it could be that heady perfume. Promise you'll keep an eye on me, like you used to do when liquor first beset my teenage years?'

'It was girls that intoxicated you, little brother.'

'That too . . . So stay close.'

'Eddie, really! I thought you fancied that girl – the clever one, Paula.'

'As a matter of fact, I do. It's a chaperon I want. Just don't come home without me.'

Margaret told John as they changed, and he laughed. 'Good Lord, what's got into him? Women used to be his favourite pastime.'

They were surprised to find they were not the only guests. Several cars were already parked outside the house; the main doors were open, and lights shone on to the driveway. Inside, they were swept up by the Countess and taken to meet the 'next Member of Parliament for this constituency . . . from the Green party!' There were also a couple of landed gentry, a local lawyer, and various people whom Margaret knew by sight and with whom John had some acquaintance.

'All after my own heart,' the Countess informed them in a loud whisper. 'All determined to save the world from exploitation and disaster.'

Dr Shannon joined them. 'I'm so glad you could make it. You can see why I wanted you here this evening. We've really got to make a stand against this mindless destruction by the authorities.'

It might have been one of dozens of dinner parties . . . it seemed so ordinary; a collection of respectable citizens hoping to put together a pet scheme. In this room of animated guests, clutching drinks and talking non-stop, was there room for monsters?

'It's Edward, isn't it? I hope you haven't forgotten me.'

'Of course not.' One of the girls he had met on the previous occasion he had dined there was standing beside him – one of the 'attractive nieces', he wasn't sure which one. Besides, she appeared older than when he had last seen her.

'It's Zoë,' he guessed.

She smiled. 'Correct.'

Across the room he caught sight of Paula, absorbed in conversation with a good-looking young man.

'One of our local landowners,' Zoë explained, catching Edward's glance. 'We think he could be influential.' It all seemed so mundane.

'You've been abroad?' suggested the girl.

'Yes. I had business.'

She nodded with approval. 'When you work for yourself you never stop. Where did you go?'

'Italy,' he said. 'That's a country you know well, isn't it?'

She looked at him in surprise. 'No. Not really.'

A servant appeared and the Countess called them to come into dinner. It was all a pleasant mixture of etiquette and informality.

'My aunt has given us places,' said Zoë. 'Look . . . we're sitting together.'

Paula was at the far end of the table – now expanded to take a score of diners – and her partner at the meal was the good-looking landowner. She looked across at Edward, smiled and waved, before resuming her discussion. Beside him, Zoë fluttered attentively, her conversation a mixture of casual chatter and seemingly innocent questions, which Edward was careful how he answered. He also had difficulty, above the chatter, in keeping up with the conversation at the other end of the table, and he was glad when the meal was over and they returned to the drawing-room. At least, some returned there, while others went into conference in a side room. 'Please forgive us. We have one or two ideas to crystallize.'

To his surprise, Edward was joined by the Doctor.

'Could I have a word in private?'

'Delighted.'

Shannon led him down the corridor. 'My study,' he explained, and when they were there he said, 'You haven't been to see us since your business trip.'

'I've been back just a couple of days.'

'Dubai, wasn't it?'

'Rome, actually. I wrapped it up there.'

'Ah, yes. The children said something about that.' His smile was warm and friendly, yet Edward sensed it as an apparently harmless move in a dangerous game. 'Anyhow, it's good to have you back. Our other guests are well-intentioned, but I must say I like a loner. That's how I think of you, Edward . . . a loner. Slipping out of your own community into a wider world, seeing things from different angles . . . One realizes there are many ways of *doing* things on this planet, many ways of *being* . . . not just one right way. Your way of living makes for open-mindedness . . . even sympathy.'

'That's a big build-up,' Edward grinned. 'Can I live up to it?'

'I hope so. We may need your help.'

'I'll do my best.' He wondered what was coming.

'You know Sandra Balelli?'

That almost caught him off-guard. 'I've met her.'

'She comes from Italy. From Sardinia,' said the Doctor.

'So I understand.'

'As you know, we are from many countries, and one contingent at Park House used to live there.'

'In Sardinia?' Edward had to think quickly: what to admit, what to deny?

'Apparently she is somewhat disturbed, this lady. And in the past it has come to our attention that she has been telling unpleasant stories, spreading rumours. Younger members of our family are angry. She has suggested scandalous things

208

about them, accused them of all sorts of depravity – of vileness and bestiality . . . You don't know about this?'

'I can't say she has said anything like this to me. Besides, she has been under great stress – her son vanished and her husband died. That could explain any odd behaviour.'

Shannon frowned. 'You think that's it?'

'What else?'

'I shall reassure my young kinsmen,' he said, rising from his chair. 'We don't want any unpleasantness.' Edward followed him to the door.

'I must admit,' said Edward, 'that I myself would feel like she does – having lost her son like that – if anything happened to Henry or Caroline . . .' He didn't finish the sentence, but nodded his farewell to Shannon at the door.

'You'll find your friends in the end room.' The Doctor pointed down the corridor. 'Please give them my apologies. You must excuse me.' He returned to his study.

What had been said? What had Shannon wanted to learn? It was difficult to tell. Clearly they knew about Sandra Balelli, but they didn't seem sure what he, Edward, believed. Was that important?

He walked along the corridor. Ahead, another corridor intersected it, unlit. Someone whispered from the shadows, and he caught sight of a girl's face. It was Paula – not looking like herself, but white and anxious.

'What's the matter?'

'I must speak to you.' She took his arm; he let himself be led into the unlit corridor. A few steps and they were by an alcove with potted palms and elegant furniture.

'What is it?' Edward asked.

Her hand was tight on his arm. 'I think you *know* about us,' she said. 'Things no one else knows.'

Had it been pre-arranged that he should be shuttled from one approach to another? Or was he becoming paranoid and inventing conspirators to sustain his bizarre suspicions?

'What things?'

'I think you know.' Paula seemed to be making an effort to control herself. 'Everything isn't what it seems in this house. You know, you have guessed. The children have as good as told me.'

'Those two? They're very young. They often get hold of the wrong idea.'

She ignored that, as she went on, 'You know we have come from many countries, some from Italy. From Sardinia, where you have just been?'

'Whoever told you that?'

'It's true, isn't it?'

'I can't think where you got that idea!'

Again she brushed aside his denial.

'We have some cousins from there. They call us "cousins", but they are second cousins, many times removed, and so different. We are not the same.'

'In what way are they different?'

'Surely you know? Surely you have seen!'

She wanted him to say what he suspected, to say clearly what he feared, what fantasies obsessed him. Edward hesitated.

'There's someone coming,' she said hurriedly. 'I mustn't be seen talking to you . . . Pretend . . .' She put her arms round his neck and her lips on his. Pretence vanished. A shock went through him, and he was trembling as she drew back. 'It was the Doctor. I know he suspects me,' she whispered.

It was a set-up! A double-act between the two.

'I know what he is, and the others like him. They take cover amongst the rest of us.'

'Paula . . . what are you saying about him?'

'You don't trust me!' She looked at him in dismay. 'Surely you suspect? Did you not listen to that poor woman from Sardinia? What did she tell you?'

'You know about her?'

'So you *do* know!' It was a moment of triumph. 'Admit it! We can work together, before he finds out. Don't you think you should take risks for the sake of other people?'

Edward knew he wasn't thinking as clearly as before. Was it just her disturbing proximity? He had a moment of alarm, a faint reeling sensation, as though he were drunk. Surely he was not going to be a victim of the most basic trick of all!

'Is there perfume in this corridor?'

'That's not important. We won't stay here. My room is nearby. We have to work out a plan . . .' She was moving away, and he was being taken with her, as though some of his will had evaporated. Was it possible, he wondered vaguely – *had* he found someone he could trust?

He went down the darkened passageway, happy to be with her. There was an unreal quality about the moment.

210

'This room,' she whispered. 'They will never come here.'

Then he heard Margaret calling, 'Eddie! Eddie . . . where are you? We've been looking for you everywhere.'

'Don't answer,' the girl whispered urgently.

He had asked Margaret not to leave without him. Why had he done that? What had he anticipated? His head bobbed above the mounting waves of unconsciousness . . .

'Eddie, are you there?'

'Won't be a moment, Margaret,' he called.

He felt Paula's hand tighten painfully on his arm.

'I'll have a word . . .' he whispered.

'Wait,' said the girl.

'I'll be back.'

He thought she wouldn't let him go, as her fingers dug into his flesh. No woman should have that strength. He didn't recognize her: her face puckered, no longer white and drawn. The pathos had vanished, and in its place was anger. The contempt was almost a snarl.

Edward stumbled as he went down the corridor. Margaret was turning to go.

'There you are! Where have you been?' She glanced down the darkened corridor, seeing the quick flurry of a coloured dress.

'Eddie! Really!'

He walked unsteadily beside her, and she took his arm. 'What have you been drinking?'

'Not a lot.'

She stopped. 'What was that?' she asked.

'What?'

'That noise!'

'I didn't hear anything.'

'Like a howl . . . Something howling.'

He looked at her in astonishment.

John was waiting. He took one look at Edward. 'I'm driving,' he said.

'You've got some funny ideas, haven't you, Uncle Eddie?'

They'd followed him into the garden, where he'd settled himself in a deck-chair under the beech tree. Carrie was playing with her doll. He hadn't seen her do that for some time now, but she was concentrating on it, apparently absorbed in its

211

dress, bending over it so that he was unable to see her face. Henry stood watching Edward as he leaned back, his eyes half-closed.

'What sort of ideas?' he asked lazily.

'You think things other people say are stupid.'

'Very likely.' He pretended to be falling asleep. Why had they followed him? They must have something important to say.

'Adults don't usually believe in magic.' The boy was skirting around the subject.

'Well, you know I'm magic,' said Edward. 'Only a magic man could do my famous tricks.'

'I'm talking seriously,' Henry rebuked him.

'I'm listening,' said Edward. 'Prod me if I fall asleep.'

'The really funny ideas you have,' Henry went on doggedly, 'you don't talk about. You even pretend you don't think them.'

'Slowly,' Edward interrupted. 'I've had a couple of beers at lunch, and I can't follow anything complicated.'

'Yes, you can,' said Carrie sharply.

'Oh! So you're with us?' Edward opened his eyes. She stared at him angrily. He guessed she knew exactly what he was doing. She turned back to the doll.

'Press on,' he encouraged Henry.

'Even if you don't tell anyone the strange theories you have . . .'

'Theories? That's a good word!'

'Anyone can tell what those ideas are from the way you go on.'

'Ah, deduction by the observation of actions. Tell me, how did you get so clever these holidays? Is it because you mix with such intelligent children as Marcel next door?'

'We hardly ever see him.'

'Why not?'

'He's a bit too old for us.'

'You used to play with him.'

'But he's too old now.'

'You mean, he's growing older faster than you are?'

They looked at him, startled, guessing they'd fallen into a trap. If they had, Edward wondered what it was. It wasn't one of his setting, although he had been presenting a picture of a relaxed and inattentive man, hoping for a moment when the guards were dropped and something of significance might accidentally be said. The only trouble was, he didn't exactly see what the significance was.

'No one can grow older faster than anyone else,' said Henry very carefully.

'That's what I always thought.' Edward sounded unconcerned. 'But it looks as though young Marcel has managed it. Too old to mix with you nowadays, eh? In a matter of a few weeks.'

'I didn't say that,' said Henry, defensively.

'Anyhow, it's a pity,' Edward continued. 'He seemed an interesting fellow, polite and civilized beyond his years. A good influence, I would have thought. But you still spend a lot of time next door. Whom do you play with now?'

He guessed they had intended to find out something from him – that that was the reason for this encounter. Though it was extraordinary that he should be fencing in this fashion with a child.

'We play with Pierre,' said Henry.

'And Hilka,' added Caroline.

'Who else?'

'Ivanovich. Boris. Damo. Natasha. Lots of them.'

'I see. They sound a bit foreign.'

Again, the hint of alarm in their eyes, as they looked at their uncle with caution. He pretended to be half-asleep, but he was lying in ambush.

Henry chose his words carefully. 'They come from other countries. Is there something bad about that?'

'Of course not. We're all brothers under the skin, aren't we?'

Carrie's childish fingers clutched her doll.

'What does that mean?' asked Henry.

'We're the same at heart,' explained Edward cheerfully. 'English, French, Russian . . . it's all one. Human beings – African, Greek, Eskimo, you name it – are just superficially different, due to different environments. You know, a lot of sunshine or not enough, different diets, that sort of thing. You must learn about that at school.'

'We do,' said Henry.

'Just mutations,' added Edward sleepily.

They weren't sure they had heard properly. There was a moment's silence. Edward thought they were going to move away: Carrie glanced up, ready to go, but Henry stood firm. It seemed to Edward an act of courage on the boy's part, and his

213

heart went out to him. One part of him wanted to shout out, 'For God's sake, stop playing games. It's too serious. Too dangerous.' But there was nothing he could say; they had probably been schooled to meet any challenge. The skirmishing had to be continued. There was so much at stake . . . *They* were at stake, he guessed.

'No,' said Henry. 'Not mutations. That is a biological change.'

'Did they teach you that at school as well?' asked his uncle.

'Yes,' said Henry.

'Good school,' mused Edward.

'Anyhow – ' Henry, like his father, could cling to a line of thought, decided Edward grimly – 'they have these foreign names because they all come from different places. They live in scattered lands; they were split up long ago. You know this.'

'Do I?'

'Dr Shannon told you.'

'So he did.' Edward closed his eyes again. Perhaps this was the moment to take them off their guard. 'There was something you wanted to ask me,' he said.

'Yes,' said Henry. 'Have you told anyone else your theories?'

'My funny ideas?'

'Yes.'

'I haven't spoken to your mother or father,' said Edward slowly.

'Of course not,' said the boy. 'But to anyone else? Does anyone else believe the things you do?'

Edward shook his head. 'I don't think so,' he said. 'I keep my thoughts to myself, as long as they are just speculations. I would tell the world only if I were absolutely sure. And perhaps not even then: there's no point in alarming people unnecessarily. In fact, if I could be sure my nearest and dearest were not in danger, I might even forget the whole experience. Write it off as a nightmare.'

'Everyone is safe,' said Henry.

'I doubt it.'

'So you would still tell other people if you could prove you were right?'

'I'd have to, wouldn't I?'

Could the boy follow such a speculative argument . . . such a hypothetical set of concepts? He seemed to.

'I wish you wouldn't, Uncle Eddie.' For the first time an emotion seemed to overcome the boy's strict discipline.

214

'Sometimes you have to pick sides,' said Edward. 'You have to make a stand. I mean, we have to fight disease, don't we? Mankind is vulnerable. We can be destroyed from within.'

The moment of concern had gone, and the boy now wore a calculating look.

'But you haven't told anyone else?'

'Not as yet,' Edward nodded.

Without looking at them, Caroline stood up. She headed towards the woods and Henry followed.

Edward watched them disappear under the shadows of the trees; they didn't look back.

'You seem to cast a spell over my children,' said Margaret. She had set a garden table with cups of tea.

'What d'you mean?'

'They follow you around. They're always watching what you do. You're a source of endless surprise and interest to them. They don't hang round John like that, nor me. You appear to fascinate them. Do you still tell them stories?'

'I think they know all my stories. As a matter of fact, I think they can read my mind.'

'You know, Eddie, there's an aspect of you that's still very young – I nearly said childish. You sometimes give the impression of being on the same wave-length as my two.'

'They are very important to me,' he said.

'You should get married, little brother. You'd make a good father.'

'I'll think about it.'

He spent the rest of the day waiting – he knew they were going to return. There was unfinished business. Their discussion had been the groundwork; whatever the project was, it had yet to be put into practice.

But they were a long time in coming back, and he had almost decided his intuition was mistaken when he saw them walk out from the woods.

'Well, kids, whom did you play with today? One of your foreign friends?'

They were not to be drawn. Both were very sure of themselves – very much in control.

215

'We've been thinking about the things you've been saying,' said Henry. 'Perhaps you really *do* know more than anyone else.'

'Recognition at last!'

'Perhaps you *are* a bit magic.'

'Watch this penny – I put it in this hand and . . .'

'We've thought of something to give you a proper test.'

'Test my magic?'

'Test lots of things.' There was a smile, hinting at superiority, on Henry's face. 'That is, if you're brave enough to try.'

'Do I have to be brave?'

'Well, it *is* a test.'

'I see. What is it? What do I have to do?'

'We can't tell you now, but we'll meet you at the top of the path in half an hour.'

'The path to the woods?'

'Yes. We'll wait there till you come.'

'Then what do we do?'

'That's a secret.'

He tried to read their faces. They both smiled back at him; at ease, confident, giving nothing away.

'Who worked out this test?'

'We did. Will you be there?'

'Why not? Okay, kids, see you.'

They went into the house, and from the hall a little later he saw them sitting in the kitchen. There seemed to be no reason why they should want to wait this half-hour before the test; they didn't appear to be making any use of it.

He glanced out of the window. John would be home soon; the day was losing some of its summer light.

He didn't speak to the children, but walked up the stairs and loudly closed his bedroom door; then he tiptoed down again and went quietly into the garden, keeping under cover of trees and shrubs as he hurried to the stables. Then he went cautiously down the path towards the tree-house.

He had contemplated climbing up into it, but guessed that would be the first place they would search if they decided to look for him. A thick and stubby yew grew on the other side of the path. It didn't give him the vision he wanted, but it would provide good cover. He tried not to work out the implication of what he was doing. It didn't stand analysis.

He found a stout branch half-way up the yew, and wedged

himself behind the trunk. He could see only partially, through a curtain of dark evergreen. He guessed the area to watch lay between the tree-house and the field. Beyond that were the dried-up stream and the wall round Park House, but he could see neither.

It was a good five minutes after the appointed time before he heard anything, then Henry started to call: 'Eddie! Uncle Eddie! Are you there? We said stay at the top of the path . . . Eddie!'

Caroline joined in.

The shouting died, and he could hear them hurrying towards him. They stopped a few yards away, whispering together, and a moment later he heard one of them running back towards the house. He guessed Henry had stayed, and saw the boy walk past, peering up into the tree-house, stopping underneath it, standing patiently, waiting.

It was five minutes by Edward's watch – but it seemed a lot longer – before Carrie came running back.

'He came down here,' she whispered. 'Mummy saw him go into the wood.'

'He didn't wait where we said,' said Henry coldly.

'Why? He doesn't know what the test is.'

'He does things like that . . . To be clever.'

'What will happen?' Caroline sounded anxious.

'I know where he is,' whispered Henry. He called towards the tree-house. 'We know you're up there, Eddie. You have to come down . . .' They stood, looking up expectantly, and a long silence followed. Edward had a feeling that something moved along the path behind them, but he wasn't sure. Just a rustle of leaves. The children either didn't hear, or paid no attention.

'It's no good, you'll have to come down,' Henry continued. 'You can't sit up there all night.'

'You can't stay for ever,' echoed Caroline.

They waited for a few more minutes, peering up, then there was a whispered conference. Edward could see Henry begin to climb towards the wooden platform, coming and going from his view. From somewhere along the path the rustle of leaves was repeated, more distinctly this time. Edward peered through the yew branches, but there was no one in sight. A breath of wind might have disturbed dry undergrowth.

Henry stopped just below the tree-house. 'Come on, Uncle

217

Eddie!' he called. 'This is wasting time. Don't you want to do the test?'

He was slow to take the last few steps up the tree, but finally he disappeared under the old netting. A moment later he put his head over the side. 'He isn't here!'

'Are you sure?' His sister sounded childishly incredulous.

'Of course.'

'Is he in the tree above?'

They scanned the branches overhead, but it was obvious there was no one there.

'Where can he have gone?' called Caroline.

They looked simultaneously towards the fields. There was a puzzled silence, then Henry said, 'He can't have gone there.'

He began to climb down, then stopped. 'Listen! Someone's coming!'

'It must be him,' whispered Caroline.

'Come up . . . Quickly!' Henry called to her.

The footsteps were quite close. Whoever it was, made no attempt to disguise his approach.

Caroline scrambled into the tree-house, Henry dragging her under cover, apprehensive and excited. Edward could see little along the path, but he heard the footsteps, and then the fainter noise . . . the rustle of leaves as before . . . something moving through the undergrowth, suddenly moving at speed, leaves disturbed, twigs snapping, bushes shaken as in a sharp gust of wind.

The footsteps stopped; there was a moment of hesitation – a split second of silence.

'Are you there, Henry?' called John's voice. 'Carrie? Is that you?'

'Daddy! Daddy!' shouted Henry. 'We're here! *Be careful . . .*'

'Daddy!' screamed Caroline. 'Daddy! Daddy! Daddy!' She was beside herself, jumping up in the tree-house, shaking the sides, trying to throw aside the tangled netting. It was a moment of panic. Edward looked on in wonder.

John came running down the path. 'It's all right, I'm here . . . You're okay. What's the matter, Henry?'

The boy looked down at his father at the foot of the tree.

'I'm sorry, Dad, we didn't know it was you. We heard someone coming, and Carrie got scared.'

'You shouldn't play down here,' John scolded them. 'Not when it gets late.'

'No, Dad, we won't.' Edward could glimpse Henry staring along the pathway.

'You'd better come down,' called John. 'Can you manage or shall I come up?'

'We're all right, now we know it's you.'

'For heaven's sake, who else could it have been?'

The children climbed down, John reaching up to catch them. He couldn't explain why, but he held each one tightly in turn.

'I know they can be appalling,' he said to Margaret, 'but they really are the most important things in my life.'

'What about me, darling?'

'Well, of course.'

It was a good ten minutes before Edward joined them in the house.

'Where have you been?' asked John.

'I took a stroll,' Edward told him. 'I had a rendezvous with your kids, but they didn't turn up.'

'We did,' said Henry. 'You weren't there.'

'I waited by the pond for twenty minutes. Was it some sort of a joke?'

'I said "Wait at the path", not "the pond".'

'*The path!*' Edward looked surprised. 'I thought you meant the pond . . . Right, we'll have to do the test another time.'

'It's too late,' said Henry coldly.

'You knew where to go,' said Caroline. 'You knew very well. You played one of your tricks.'

Henry took her arm and began to lead her away. 'He thinks he's clever . . . but he's not as clever as other people,' he said.

'What people?' Edward smiled. It was just possible he might goad them into saying too much.

'Never mind. They'll think of something.'

'Like what?'

'I won't tell you.'

'What *are* you three talking about?' asked Margaret. 'Who wants something to eat?'

She moved towards the door, and John joined her.

'D'you know what I saw?' he asked her. 'Down in the wood, just before I found the children? You know those foxes that used to be in the field? The ones we thought had gone? Well, they haven't, they're still there. I saw two of them, in the garden . . . in the bushes close to the path. Gave me quite a fright. Great big creatures they looked in the half-light. I must have scared them off, for they turned tail and raced for the field. I thought they were heading straight for me when I saw them first, but then they spun round, and in a flash they were gone! Vanished! Splendid to know we are so close to wild life.'

They were leaving the room as Edward said, 'Did you see their tails? Their brushes?'

John looked thoughtful. 'Come to think of it – I don't think I did. It wasn't all that clear. They were in the shadow.'

'Supper in five minutes,' called Margaret.

'I'll pour you a drink, Eddie,' said John. Together they left the room, passing the children who were standing just outside.

'What d'you think about that?' Edward asked them.

They returned his stare unblinkingly.

'Foxes, eh? Lying in wait? And do you know why they turned away as your Dad said – first going for him, then turning tail? Because they still have this well-developed sense of smell. Not like us. Mankind has lost it.'

Hostile and unmoving, they never took their eyes from his face.

'But these creatures – foxes, as he thought – in the shadows, they still have retained this sense,' Edward went on. 'So they realized that the person coming down the path was not the one they had expected. They smelled him. Smelled danger, so to speak. I mean, what would you have done if anything had happened to your father? Where does loyalty lie?'

Not by so much as a flicker of an eyelid did either child suggest he or she had understood a word.

'After all,' he said softly, 'family is the ultimate unit, the most important thing. You are born into it, you create your own, pass on to the next. It's a river that never stops flowing. Don't contaminate it.'

Small, motionless faces watched him coldly.

'You know the story of the Trojan horse? Do they teach you that at your school? You can bring corruption as well as danger into the heart of your own camp. You have the look of innocence, so no one suspects . . . except me.'

'You always think you are so clever,' said Henry. 'You shouldn't have come back. You should have stayed at your work.' He was starting to leave the room, but saw Carrie hadn't moved. She sat, her eyes still on her uncle, puzzled, frowning. Edward wondered to what extent she had understood; to what extent that heightened awareness – like a coiled spring in her little head – had followed argument and implications. At six . . . seven?

'Carrie!' Her brother tugged at her shoulder, and she followed him out.

In the kitchen, John handed his brother-in-law a glass.

'Mind if I join you on the train tomorrow?' said Edward. 'I need a day in London, I've got work to finish.'

'Splendid! We'll have lunch in town.'

Edward came back in the early afternoon, concerned to avoid travelling back on the same train as John, and carrying a small case which he covered by holding his newspaper over it. He drove into the stables before slipping the case into the boot of his car, then he made sure it was locked, put the key in his pocket, locked the boot, and put that key in another pocket. It was all done with great care.

He walked up to the house, where Margaret met him.

'A successful day?'

'I hope so.'

Henry and Caroline viewed him from across the lawn.

'Hello, kids. Not playing with your mates?'

'We have other things to do,' said Henry.

'They've been around all afternoon,' Margaret told her brother. 'You see, they aren't next door all the time.'

'I wonder why?' said Edward drily.

'Don't be silly. They like it here.' She went into the house, and he heard her busy in the kitchen.

'What was that box?' asked Caroline.

'I beg your pardon?'

'The box you put in the car?'

'I have work to do, you know.'

'What was it?'

'My briefcase.'

'Made of wood?'

'How did you know?'

'We saw it.'

'From this distance?'

'We were round the other side of the house.'

'I see. Spying?'

'What is it?'

'That's my business.'

'It's locked.'

'Of course. Perhaps it's valuable . . . There may be money in it.'

They looked contemptuously at him. '*You* don't lock up money, Uncle Eddie. You're too rich.'

'That's what you think.' He tried to make a joke, but they weren't to be diverted. He would have to be even more cautious.

'Why did you lock your car?'

'I always do.'

'You never do.'

'I do from now on,' he told them.

They disappeared shortly afterwards. If they were watching him, he warned himself, he had better watch them.

They went into the wood, and he didn't doubt they had gone to Park House. Nevertheless he checked, following the path as far as the tree-house. There was no sign of them, so he went back to the stables and collected the case from the car. Since it was better that Margaret didn't see him, he went in by the side door and up to his room. He was being needlessly cautious, he told himself – but nevertheless he locked the bedroom door before opening the case.

The automatic shotgun was one of a type he had sold in several countries over the years. It was by no means the most up-to-date, but he knew it to be reliable, easy to handle, and adequate for his purpose. It clipped into the case, and ammunition slotted into a separate compartment. It was a demonstration model with which he was familiar, and he had checked it with the selling agent that morning. Looking at it again was only a nervous gesture, but he carefully noted the bits and pieces, and even read – as if for the first time – the maintenance and cleaning instructions.

He heard Margaret call: 'Cup of tea, Eddie?'

He replaced the weapon, and double-locked the box.

'Coming, love!' he answered.

He put the case on the top of his wardrobe, out of sight, pushed back against the wall.

In an odd way he felt there had been a declaration of war.

But if the children were on the side of the enemy they now ceased to show any hostility. They appeared to have forgotten their differences with their uncle, and were unusually friendly. There was no more discussion about the briefcase, no suspicious looks, no veiled comments. They were right back to their previous relationship – teasing, playful, even warm.

'It's their joint birthday next week,' Margaret reminded him.

'I haven't forgotten. I've got them each something.'

'Nothing too elaborate, I hope?'

By 'elaborate' he knew she meant 'expensive'.

'Not really,' he said. 'I had to get rid of some yen.'

He wondered whether the change of attitude on the part of the two children had anything to do with their birthdays, but he dismissed the idea. Neither of them was at all mercenary. If there were a reason behind their friendliness it must have another cause. He went along with them, appearing to join in with their games, never referring to the fact that for the next couple of days they spent time with him, rather than visiting their many friends next door.

But he did venture one comment. 'I'll bet the Park House people have got a surprise for you.'

There was a momentary silence, and a cautious look to see what he meant. 'A surprise?'

'I mean for your birthday.'

'They are taking us out for the day, later on.'

'Where to?'

'We don't know.'

'It's a secret,' added Caroline.

The subject was dropped, and the three of them arranged to drive to Castle Wood that afternoon. 'We'll go and see where they want to put this road.'

But when the time came for them to go, only Caroline was waiting for him in the stables.

'Where's Henry?'

'He said he wouldn't be a minute.'

Edward backed the car out of the garage. 'Where did you leave him?'

'In his room . . . changing his shoes.'

They waited for five minutes before Henry came running down the drive.

'What have you been doing?'

The boy was breathless, trying to hide his excitement.

'I was looking for a map,' he said. 'A map of Castle Woods.'

'Not changing your shoes?'

'No. Why?' He was surprised.

'You should get together with your stories,' said his uncle.

Again there was a moment of uncertainty, as though a facade had cracked, but as they drove off the friendly atmosphere returned, and Edward fostered it.

Castle Wood was a belt of common ground, overgrown and unused – a home for the bird and animal life of Sussex. It was a very carefree expedition, and they stayed longer than intended. This was how his relationship with them should be, Edward thought.

They flopped into chairs in the kitchen when they reached home.

'That was great, Uncle Eddie, great!'

'I've had a call from John,' Margaret told him. 'He ran into Shannon on the train. There's a special meeting in the village this evening, and they want the wives to go.'

'Including you?'

'If that's all right with you? The children will be in bed.'

'Okay by me,' Edward said.

John phoned again later to say he was having a meal with the Shannons, and would see Margaret in the pub about nine that evening.

'What are you going out for?' complained the children.

'You'll be all right. Eddie's here.'

They didn't like their routine being changed, but they went to bed after supper, with only the occasional grumble. 'You're sure you'll be in *all the time*, Uncle Eddie?'

'Of course he will,' said Margaret. She didn't leave until they were asleep.

After she had gone, Edward walked through the quiet of the place. The house had been built in the last century, designed for the comfort of a large Victorian family, and John especially enjoyed its spaciousness, although he admitted that it wasn't fully used. 'We should do something with the cellars,' he would say. 'They run under the whole place. We could at least stock up the old wine racks down there.'

'We drink quite enough,' Margaret would inform him.

Edward could understand John's pride in his house, as he returned to the sitting-room, poured himself a whisky and settled down before the television set. It only partly held his attention – artificial comedy and artificial laughter – and he gradually became aware of another sound.

Someone was moving about upstairs.

He turned the set off and sat in the darkening room, listening. The faint movement was repeated. He wasn't sure which room it was in – perhaps in the corridor – but someone was walking softly, trying not to attract attention. Margaret had told him the children were asleep – but how could anyone else have got in, and on to the landing above, without his knowing? Well, it was a big house, and a second staircase led up to the upper floor from what had once been the servants' quarters.

Edward picked up the poker that lay beside the empty fireplace – better to be ready for anything – and gently opened the door.

The wide staircase curved up from the hall ahead; a dim light had been left on outside the children's doors. There was no sign of anyone above; he could see the landing and the two doors. He stood, holding his breath and wondering whether he could have been mistaken, when the soft sound came again. It was directly above him, and someone *was* walking.

He leapt up the stairs, two at a time, the poker gripped very firmly. A fit and powerful young man, he'd been in many a rough corner these last few years, and there was little he felt he couldn't handle in this relatively law-abiding country.

At the top of the stairs he saw Henry in his pyjamas, shock-still, looking at him, taken aback by this sudden appearance.

'What the devil d'you think you're doing?' Edward was surprised to find himself so angry.

'I just got up.' Henry appeared to be looking beyond him, down the corridor.

Edward spun round. Caroline stood in the shadows that led to the back of the house.

'What is this? What's going on?'

'We just got up,' repeated Henry.

'What for?' Edward was very suspicious.

225

'To look around,' said Henry vaguely. He didn't seem to be concentrating. 'To see if everything was all right.'

'Of course it's all right. Did you wake Caroline?'

'She awoke herself.'

'I 'woke myself,' the little girl repeated.

'Both together? Both walking about?' He was incredulous.

'Yes.'

'Then get back to bed! Get back at once. I shall certainly tell your mother about this!'

They didn't say anything, nor did they hurry but went slowly past him, not giving him a glance, to their separate rooms.

'And I don't want to hear another peep out of you! Understand? Not another word!'

Edward waited for a moment, then went downstairs. He was surprised to find how disturbed he was. His heart was thumping – surely an exaggerated reaction? Up and downstairs, at speed admittedly, shouldn't be enough to make his heart race!

He stood by the sitting-room window, getting his breath back, peering into the gathering dusk, sipping his whisky; very alert, and listening. There was no sound from above. Perhaps they had been upset because both their parents were out . . . they might be nervous. What other explanation could there be?

Edward put down his drink and walked briskly to the back of the house – to the kitchen and scullery, and into the old butler's pantry, with its array of ancient bells. He tried the doors and windows; they were all shut. He tried the little back door in the playroom. One was inclined to overlook that.

The handle had been turned, and although the door looked as though it was closed, any pressure from outside would have opened it. He locked it now. There was also a chain, which he slipped into place. Perhaps Margaret had forgotten to check it? The children had been upstairs; no one else had been down here.

After that he went round the ground floor with double care, but nothing else was amiss. Back in the sitting-room, he didn't put the television on again but sat with his drink in the dark, leaving the door open, certain that in that way he could hear any whisper or movement in the house. He wasn't quite sure what he was listening for.

By this time, he supposed the meeting would be in full swing in the pub, and he wondered how long it would be going on.

A moment later someone ran along the corridor above.

'It's all right, Uncle. It's only me,' called Henry. 'I'm going to the bathroom.'

He heard the boy go back to his room.

'I'm going to the bathroom, too,' called Caroline.

Edward went to the foot of the stairs and called up: 'Stop fooling about. It's late.'

They had sounded more excited than nervous.

He went back to the darkened sitting-room, and for a moment he thought cattle had found their way into the garden. That had happened before when the farmer nearby had left a gate open. It was hard to say in the gloom, but he could have sworn a cow – or perhaps a sheep – moved through the bushes by the stables. It was low on the ground, it could have been grazing. Then he lost sight of it: perhaps it had gone back into the bushes, or perhaps he'd been mistaken? Edward pressed his face against the glass in an effort to see across the lawn. Nothing moved. He must have imagined it.

He heard the children whispering together upstairs . . . then there was silence. He wondered what they were doing and went quietly up the stairs. Henry was at the landing window, shading his eyes and peering out, much as Edward himself had done.

'What are you doing out of bed again?' he demanded.

The boy spun round. 'Nothing,' he said, clearly excited. 'I thought I heard something. It was nothing.'

Edward joined him and looked out. The same stretch of garden lay below him – the bushes beside the stables, and the banks of rhododendrons and azaleas that ran along the road to the village. A car passed and its headlights threw patterns through the hedge, spraying the far end of the garden with fleeting brightness. Again he was sure something moved through the bushes, grazing – or keeping cover – while the lights raced past.

'What's that over there?' said Edward.

'I didn't see anything.'

'Close to the ground.'

'What did it look like?'

'A sheep . . . or a goat.'

'I'm sure that's what it is,' Henry gabbled his agreement, his eyes dancing in the half-light. 'They have sheep in the farm . . . and a lady keeps goats.'

'Did you see it?'

227

'No.'

'Get into your bed.'

'Right. I was only looking.'

Henry climbed into his bed, and lay back with his eyes tightly shut.

'Don't get out again,' said his uncle.

The boy didn't answer.

Edward was certain this wasn't the end of the incident. He waited in the hall below. A moment later Caroline ran from her room.

He shouted angrily, 'Get back to your room.'

She disappeared along the darkened corridor to the back of the house. She must have gone to one of the rooms over the kitchen, or she might have gone down the back stairs to the kitchen itself.

'Caroline!' he shouted.

There was no answer.

'Perhaps she's gone to the bathroom,' called Henry.

'Rubbish!'

'She often does.'

There was no mistaking the amusement in the boy's voice, as if he were taunting the man – amusement and superiority, a sense of power, authority.

'I'll get her,' he said, appearing at the top of the stairs.

'Stay where you are!' shouted Edward. He couldn't understand the tension that gripped him.

'I know where she's gone.' Henry ran after her, also disappearing into the dark. There wasn't another sound.

'Henry! Caroline!'

No reply. Edward was about to go up after them, but changed hs mind and hurried to the big windows in the sitting-room.

Perhaps he was growing more accustomed to the evening light, for he could now see everything more clearly. And he had been right! There *was* something in the garden, and it could very easily be a sheep or goat – except that it moved too fast, from cover to cover – from bush to bush, moving through shadows, lying low, then picking itself off the ground, making another dash, closing in on the house, using it as a focus.

The mistake he had made was that there was not just *one* such scurrying shadow . . . there was a second, until then undetected, moving and dropping suddenly, its dark, rough hair blending with dark earth, then up with a quick rush over

228

open ground to the next patch of bushes, closer to where Edward stood by the long windows of the darkened sitting-room.

For a moment he remained surprisingly calm, telling himself it was as he suspected, his nightmare realized. And as he stood there he saw there were not just two such creatures – other shadows loped round the edge of the garden. He counted . . . three, four. A whole pack!

He was aware of a puff of air through the house, coming from the kitchen. A door banged. He raced through, and found the door was wide open! He locked it and took the key.

'Henry! Caroline!' He tried to keep his voice steady as he shouted again. There was no answer, but footsteps ran down the stairs and into the hall. He heard smothered laughter. Another door opened. Edward ran into the hall and slammed the front door, locking it and pocketing that key also.

There was muffled laughter in the sitting-room, and as he went in the children dodged out from behind the door. He didn't go after them. The windows were now open! He didn't see anything as he closed them . . . but gravel on the path below sprayed as something scrambled past.

Edward was aware that his fingers trembled as he searched through the telephone book. He found the number of the pub where John was at the meeting. The noise of running and suppressed laughter upstairs distracted him, but he made the call.

It seemed a long time before anyone answered.

'King's Head.' A man's voice sounded above a background of noise and laughter.

'John Warwick is at a meeting there.' Edward spoke surprisingly calmly. 'I have to speak to him urgently.'

There was a pause, then the man replied: 'Don't think you've got the right place, mister. There ain't no meeting here this evening.'

'It's a special meeting,' Edward knew the children were now in the hall, 'called by Dr Shannon.'

'Not here, it isn't,' said the voice at the other end.

'This is urgent,' insisted Edward.

'Sorry I can't help,' said the voice.

'Do you know where he is?'

'Sorry, mate.'

229

'If you see him will you tell him to get back home as fast as he can?'

'Understood.' The line went dead.

He went into the hall, but the children had gone. There was no point in calling for them: they were beside themselves with excitement. He could hear running and spluttered laughter in the rooms above. That didn't concern him. It was the downstairs doors and windows that absorbed his attention, and he hurried round checking them. All was well.

He went back to the sitting-room window. No more movement in the garden. Another car passed from the village; headlights revealed no hidden shapes.

Of course! Why had it not occurred to him before? His car! He had only to get into it and he could be out of this place in less than a minute. All the shadows he had seen had been on the one side of the garden; the way to the stables was clear.

The children were still running about upstairs as he went through to the kitchen, whose door was nearest to the stables. It would be a fast sprint to the garage, but he could do it.

He unlocked the door he had previously locked, and opened it gently. There was no movement, no sound from beyond. He waited for a moment, his eyes adjusting to the dark. The garage doors were open; he could see his car. He stepped cautiously on to the gravel path. There was a grass bank on the other side of the path: he would be able to run soundlessly once he was on that. A couple of steps and . . .

A soft snarl . . . a low grumble in the back of an animal's throat, and Edward stopped dead. Strength flowed from him. Again – louder – fiercer. Then a rush along the gravel path and chilling yelps of excitement!

He turned to see the door closing behind him . . . He threw it open, and Henry went sprawling back against the wall. Edward slammed the door, locked it, leant against it, shaking, waiting for an impact that didn't come.

'You wanted the doors shut,' Henry protested innocently.

Edward didn't reply: the betrayal was too obvious. He made sure he took the key as he hurried towards the stairs.

Henry followed as he went up to his room, but the boy stopped at the door, making no further pretence of going back to bed; watching Edward stand on a chair, reach for the top of the wardrobe and bring down the wooden case.

Something was wrong – it was too light and the key was in

230

the lock. As he threw it on the bed, the lid fell open. The ammunition was still packed into the special compartment, but the gun was gone! Edward couldn't believe it! He had carried the key in his pocket all the time. When could anyone have taken it? *Who* could have taken it?

Henry stared at him, expressionless.

'Have you been in my room?' Edward asked, still bewildered.

'You said it was just a briefcase,' said Henry. It was an oblique answer.

'Where's the gun?' Edward demanded.

Henry shook his head.

'Where is it? Give it to me!'

Henry ran from the room.

Edward began to go after him, then stopped. It was useless; he wouldn't have time. He couldn't force Henry to speak. There had to be some other way to protect himself.

He needed help . . . should he try to get in touch with John again? Or the police? What could he say? That two children were trying to kill him? That a pack of wolves surrounded the house?

The children were downstairs; he could hear their running and excited whispers. It was hard to tell where they were. Then he realized with horror that they were on the cellar steps. They must have opened the door to the rooms below . . . the boiler room, the wine cellar, the old coal shoot which opened into the garden! They didn't even try to run away as he pushed past them, smiling their pleasure in this wild game. He shut and bolted the heavy wooden door, with sockets out of their reach.

They were at the top of the steps when he came up, still smiling mockingly. Edward had a sudden insight: the children were puppets on strings, their excitement hysterical.

They followed him to the sitting-room, watching him turn the telephone dial.

'All the windows and doors are shut,' said Henry. 'What are you worried about?'

'You *said* it was your briefcase,' remarked Caroline.

A voice answered at the other end of the phone.

'Listen,' said Edward. 'This is urgent . . .'

The girl recognized his voice.

'You know where I live? My sister's house.'

'Who's that?' asked Henry sharply, his smile vanishing.

'Can you get here as soon as possible? Remember the dog? *Bring your shotgun!*' He put the phone down.

'Who was that?' insisted Henry.

'It was nobody,' mocked Caroline. 'You don't know anyone . . . and you've lost your gun.'

He looked blankly at them. Total strangers in a familiar guise, aliens, mocking or hostile, hounding him to his death . . . 'Hounding'!

A door banged somewhere in the house.

'What was that?'

'*Perhaps* I forgot to close them all,' said Henry. The smile was back. The game was on again.

Edward heard the noise in the back rooms, in the corridor, at the top of the cellar steps, over the stone-flagged floor.

He tried to leave the room, but the children barred his way.

'It's nothing,' said Henry.

There was a sound on the floorboards that he had never heard before . . . something was *padding* over bare boards!

'Nothing, Eddie . . . nothing!'

He threw them aside and raced up the stairs, with time for only one shocked glimpse down the passageway to the back of the house. In the dim light he saw a surge of movement, heard a sharp yelp of triumph! He was up at the top of the stairs before the dark shapes reached the hall, slammed shut his bedroom door and groped for the key . . . he should have known it wouldn't be there!

He dragged a table against the door, propping it under the handle, then pulled the mattress from the bed and rammed it against the foot of the door.

'It's all right, Eddie.' Henry was just outside. 'You can come out!'

The handle turned gently, stopped, then moved again slightly. He was having difficulty in turning it.

'What's the matter, Eddie?' the boy called. 'What's wrong?'

Edward didn't answer. He pressed against the door, his hands shaking.

Caroline called: 'Uncle Eddie, it's all right. Henry and I wouldn't be here if there was anything dangerous. You'll be safe.'

'We'll go back to bed,' said Henry. 'Mum and Dad will soon be home.' They appeared to move away. After a moment of silence, something lurched itself against the door. The frame shook. Beyond it, just a few inches away, Edward could hear the sound of animals sniffing round the edges of the door, and a low involuntary snarl. A couple of seconds later the door shook a second time. It wasn't going to hold.

Edward crossed to the window. The garden below was now empty. He pushed up the sash. It was a long way to jump . . . The door behind him shook loudly. He tried to push the bed against it, but it was too heavy, so he piled two chairs on top of the mattress, then scrambled on to the window-ledge. He would have to land properly.

The lights of a car approached from the village, slowing as it neared the entrance; he watched it turn, headlights shining down the drive.

There was a sudden silence from outside the bedroom door. Then soft whispers. 'It can't be.' That was Henry's voice. 'They said they'd be late.'

'It's someone,' said Caroline. 'He really did phone someone.'

The silence was shattered by a gun-shot. Outside the door there was a wild scampering of feet, as attack gave way to flight, aggression to fear. Subdued baying sounded from the floor below . . . from the back of the house, the kitchen, then from the garden under his window. Dark shapes disappeared under the trees towards the stables. They turned as a body – a pack – into the woods.

They were gone.

Edward pushed aside the barricade from his door, and went down to the hall. The car was at the front door, and the woman in the driver's seat, her shotgun in her hands, was still on the alert, the window beside her wound down. A smell of gun-smoke lingered.

It was impossible to thank her, but he tried.

'Thank God! You were just . . . another minute . . . Did you see them?'

'See what?'

It was hard to tell her. 'Remember the dog?'

She nodded.

'They were in the house . . . running about . . . wild. The children let them in.' He was puzzled. 'Why did you shoot, if you didn't see anything?'

'You had sounded so alarmed. If there *was* one of those dogs here . . .' She shrugged. 'So I shot. I thought it would be a loud noise, anyhow. It would frighten anything off.'

'I'm sorry I had to involve you.'

'Just so long as no one else knows . . .' she said. 'Besides, my business here is finished. I go home next week.'

Edward was aware of the front door standing open, the children in the entrance.

'Who is she?' asked Henry.

'You'd better go,' said Edward softly.

She didn't ask why, but started the engine, turned and drove off. He watched her, then went into the house. He sensed the change in atmosphere. The excitement had evaporated.

'Who was that?' repeated Henry.

'Someone I know,' he told them.

'Why did she have a gun?'

Caroline didn't wait for his answer. 'You told her to bring it, I heard you. On the phone.'

'Your mother and father will be home soon. You'd better go back to bed.' There didn't seem to be any point in telling them this; such normality had no place there.

'What's her name?' asked Henry. But when he didn't reply they went slowly, suspiciously, to their rooms. Edward sensed they were as depleted as he was himself.

He went to his room, restoring it to order before he heard a car outside and John and Margaret came into the hall.

'We got a message from Dr Shannon to get back as soon as we could,' said John. He appeared distant and unfriendly. 'He had a message from someone you had phoned.'

'Shannon? He passed that on to you?' asked Edward.

'Of course.'

'I phoned the King's Head.'

'We had our meeting in the other pub, the George. Shannon took a room there.'

'I see.'

'What was it about?' John sounded distinctly cool. Something had angered him. Surely not just Edward's phone call?

'Are the children all right?' asked Margaret.

'They're in bed,' he told them. 'It's not that . . . I thought there was something in the garden.'

'Something?' John sounded unimpressed.

Edward shrugged. 'I thought there might be a break-in.'

They looked sceptically at him.

'Don't tell me that's why you brought a gun into the house?' said John. 'You didn't have arms and cartridges because you anticipated a break-in this evening!' He was clearly trying to restrain his anger.

'You know about the gun?'

'Of course I do.'

'Where is it?'

'I've got it in my desk. Locked up. And there it stays until you are ready to remove it from the house . . . which I suggest you do first thing in the morning.'

'*You've* got it?'

'Good God, man! The children found it when they were playing! Fortunately they had the sense to give it to me!'

'They *found* it?'

'It's not up to me to say anything about the way you make a living. If you buy and sell arms, that's your affair. I disapprove, but it's not my business. But it *is* my business when you bring your merchandise into my house . . . with my children running about. And you didn't have the common sense to lock up the damn thing – I think that was disgraceful! I want it out of the house – bullets and all – as soon as possible. I really think you have abused our hospitality. I would never have expected it of you.'

John went into his study and closed the door.

'Really, Edward,' said Margaret, 'it *was* rather irresponsible. The children could have killed themselves. You know that, unlike John, I don't mind what your job is, but please don't bring anything like that into our home again.'

She went upstairs, and he saw her go into each of her children's rooms.

'How are they?' he asked.

'Fast asleep,' she told him.

He glanced in at them before he went to bed. Both looked angelic.

He didn't see John in the morning; apparently he had left for an earlier train, but Margaret had the gun.

'Please make sure it's out of the house before John gets back.'

He made two neat packages, the gun in one, the ammunition in the other, with a note to the agent: '*Many thanks. Order follows.*' There was never any difficulty finding clients for that model.

As he drove back from the village post office he wondered

what to say to the children. He needn't have bothered. Henry was waiting for him as he put the car in the garage.

'You didn't have to worry,' he said reassuringly to his uncle. 'Nothing would have happened to you.'

'You really think that, do you?' said Edward grimly.

Henry spread his arms in an innocent gesture. 'Nothing happened to us. It was really to show that there was no danger. Appearances are deceptive.' Such a comment from a child of his age!

'Who told you that?'

'Everyone knows that. It just shows there is no reason to suppose things that are different from us are necessarily dangerous.'

'That sounds like something you've learnt by heart.'

'Things around us are not all enemies.' Henry smiled gently.

'There is room in the world for all of us, as Dr Shannon says,' suggested Edward.

'And he's right. They are peaceful people, they want to live and let live. No harm would come to anyone.'

Either the boy had been so indoctrinated that he believed what he said, or he was corrupted beyond recovery. Edward hoped it was not the latter.

'Listen,' he said. 'What if I told you there had already been harm, great harm? People driven out of their minds, lives destroyed, people used, their vitality channelled from its natural course all to sustain a form of life that is dying, that should be dead? An infection which has to be wiped out like a plague?' He was surprised by his own intensity.

'I wouldn't believe you,' said Henry simply.

'Why not?'

'Because I've been shown the truth,' he said.

'I see.' Edward guessed how important that was. 'What about Carrie – has she been shown the truth as well?'

Henry shook his head. 'She is too young.' So there was still hope for the little girl. 'She will be shown later in the year,' Henry went on. 'She just follows as though she's . . .' he groped for the word . . . 'hypnotized,' he said. He seemed so open, so honest. Was this a change of heart?

'One thing you ought to know,' Edward told him. 'Like any animal, they will kill if they have to.'

'That's a lie!' Henry looked angrily at his uncle, then ran back to the house.

236

'What's the matter with Henry?' asked Margaret later. 'He was quite tense and unlike himself. What did you say to him?'

'He didn't tell you?'

'No.'

'We had a talk. About last night.'

'If I were you,' she said sharply, 'I wouldn't say any more about it . . . especially not about the gun.'

There was a strained and unhappy atmosphere about the house. Edward excused himself. 'I've got one or two things to do,' he said, as he left her.

The following morning, as John was about to leave, a car turned in at the gate.

'Good lord,' said John, 'it's Sergeant Parker again. What the devil can he want? Ask him, Margaret. I don't want to miss my train.'

The police car stopped in the drive, and the Sergeant heaved himself out. Margaret went to have a word with him, then turned and called: 'Off you go, John! It's Edward he wants to see.'

'What? Again?' muttered John. He drove off, filled with curiosity, as Edward came out of the house.

'Sorry to trouble you,' said the Sergeant. 'I take it these are yours?' He was holding a small bundle of papers, and Edward recognized one of them as a note he had written to Sandra Balelli.

'That's mine,' he said.

'One or two of the others, I think, sir. If you like to look at them?'

Edward recognized cuttings from the Italian newspapers, and a summary he had made of them. There were queries of his on some of the papers Sandra had given him.

'Yes,' he said. 'Some are mine, some Mrs Balelli gave me. Why do you ask?'

'When did you give her these papers, sir?'

'A few days ago, after I got back here. What's the matter?'

The Sergeant looked uneasily at the children standing on the steps behind them, and dropped his voice. 'There's been a tragic occurrence, sir.'

'Sandra Balelli?'

'Yes, sir. Found in her garden, on the ground, just below her bedroom window. That was wide open, and off the hook. Of course we can't say exactly, not just yet. An inspector is on his way from Tunbridge Wells. But at first glance it seems pretty clear she jumped.'

'Jumped!' Margaret was startled.

'Yes, Mrs Warwick. And for a cottage it's a fair height. I understand she was rather an unusual lady . . . nervous type.' He turned back to Edward. 'Do you know if she has any relations in this country?'

'She has friends. I know where you can get in touch with them.'

'That will be helpful, sir.'

'Is that the lady who came here with a gun?' They turned to look at Henry, who was calling loudly and clearly, a youthful innocence in his voice.

'With a *gun*?' repeated his mother.

'Yes. Uncle Eddie knows about that, don't you, Eddie? She came here late at night with a gun, when you and Daddy went to that meeting. She shot it. We all heard it . . . Carrie, Eddie and me. She just sat there in her car, in our garden, where you are now, Sergeant Parker. And she shot her gun.'

'What are you *talking* about?' Margaret looked at him in amazement.

'That's right, isn't it, Eddie?' The innocence still sounded in Henry's voice, but his eyes were hard and calculating.

Edward nodded.

'Are you sure?' Margaret could hardly believe it.

'Yes. She did come that evening.'

'Whatever for?' asked Margaret.

'I'd phoned her earlier. I wanted to speak to her . . .' he indicated the papers lamely . . . 'about these.'

'She came here, did she, sir?' asked the Sergeant.

'Yes. She didn't stay. It wasn't necessary . . . it was too late.'

'And is it right what young Henry says? She fired a shot?'

'Yes.'

'Whatever for?' repeated Margaret.

'I think it was an accident,' said Edward.

Both Margaret and the Sergeant looked doubtfully at him.

'Perhaps she was shooting at something?' suggested Henry. He was very sure of himself; more so, Edward felt, than his elders. 'Perhaps she saw something in the garden – in the dark? Things can look very scary in the dark. Perhaps she thought she saw something and shot at it? What d'you think, Eddie?'

238

'I doubt it, but it's possible.' Edward was conscious of the boy's mockery.

'Anyhow, she just drove away when Eddie told her to. Actually, she just did anything he said.'

There was a moment's silence as the Sergeant struggled with his thoughts. 'How long have you known her, sir?'

'Since the day you asked me to come and help you with her,' said Edward sharply.

'I remember. You were very helpful the day she shot her dog.'

'Correct.'

'On that point, sir . . .' The Sergeant was hesitant. 'I wonder if you'd be kind enough to come back to her cottage? You might be able to give us a bit more help.'

'Could you be more explicit?' said Edward. He didn't like the implication.

'A matter of identification, in a way.'

'Surely she doesn't need identifying?'

'Very true, I could do that myself. It's more identification in another respect . . . another identification, so to speak.'

'*I* saw her,' said Henry loudly. 'I'll come. I could identify her.'

'Certainly not,' said Margaret.

'That isn't necessary,' the Sergeant reassured her.

'I'd like to,' said Henry.

'Henry!' His mother was shocked.

'I can help Eddie,' the boy said. He didn't take his eyes from Edward. 'I saw everything he saw. I'd like to go with Mr Parker.'

'The lady's dead, you know, Henry,' the Sergeant said. 'Jumped from a window. She doesn't look very nice.'

'But it's important, isn't it? I'll come with you, I might be able to help.'

'That's enough, Henry!'

Henry turned and ran into the house. They heard a door slam.

'Shall we go, sir?' asked the Sergeant.

'Go ahead,' said Edward. 'My car's in the garage, I'll follow you.'

'Where are they going?' asked Caroline, as the cars drove off.

'I'll tell you later,' said Margaret.

* * *

239

The body was as Sergeant Parker had described it. Sandra Balelli lay on the narrow flagstoned path that ran behind the cottage, directly below the bedroom window.

'I've closed it,' explained the Sergeant. 'It was swinging in the wind.'

A police constable from the next village was standing by.

'Not often we get an incident like this,' explained the Sergeant. 'We need all the help we can get. Bit neurotic, wasn't she, sir? Least, that's what I thought, last time we was here.'

'What was it you wanted me to help you with?' asked Edward.

'Ah yes, sir.'

They moved closer to the body. It was extraordinary to be looking at the rigid figure of the girl he had been chatting to so recently. Her clothes were those she had been wearing when he last saw her, and her hair was hardly out of place. He noticed she had her shoes on . . . She might have been asleep, apart from the fact that her eyes were open.

'How long has she been dead?' he asked.

'We'll have to wait to find that out,' said the Sergeant. 'But I'd guess she did this last night.'

'How did she die?'

'Well, we've been careful not to move her, we've got to wait till the Inspector gets here. But I'd say she broke her back, landing like that on them stones.' He motioned to Edward. 'At first, we wasn't sure she was dead and I started to pick her up . . . just her head, you understand. That's what I wanted to show you, in view of what had happened.'

'What d'you mean?'

'You remember the dead dog, sir? She shot her dog, and when I started to lift her . . . Look at this.'

He gently raised her head; Edward moved in beside him.

'Good God!'

Two scars, deep and hideous gashes, ran from the base of her neck down her back. Her clothes were ripped and clotted with blood.

'What are they?' asked Edward.

'Can't say, sir,' said the Sergeant, sounding a little uneasy. ''Course, I could say what they look like.'

'They look as if they were made by the claws of an animal,' said Edward.

'That's what I thought. An animal . . .'

240

He gently lowered the girl's head.

'How far down her back do they go?' asked Edward.

'Can't say, sir,' said the Sergeant. 'But I guess all the way. I don't want to shift her, not till the doc's seen her, anyhow.'

Edward moved round the body, whose legs were stretched out on the ground. He carefully rolled her on her side.

'Better not do that,' said the Sergeant.

'Look!' Edward pointed. 'The scars run right down her back.'

They both looked up, aware of someone watching from the corner of the cottage. Henry was standing there, staring at the body the men were holding.

'How the hell did you get here?' said Edward angrily.

'I was on the floor in the back of your car,' Henry answered quietly. He didn't take his eyes off the figure on the ground.

'What has the boy seen?' whispered Parker.

Henry heard him. 'The marks,' he said. 'Everything.'

'Bad for him,' said Parker. 'Shouldn't have been watching.'

'I'd like to go home,' Henry said. He looked very shaken.

'It's possible the Inspector might want a word with you,' the Sergeant told Edward as he shepherded the boy to the car.

'I'll be pleased to do anything I can,' Edward assured him. He was anxious to talk to Henry, but the boy disappeared as soon as he arrived home, even before his mother had a chance to scold him.

'He can't have gone next door already,' protested Edward.

'He may have,' said Margaret.

Caroline shook her head. 'He wouldn't go without me.'

But she was wrong, and Edward later saw the boy climbing back into his own garden. He was pale, and looked as though he might have been crying – something he very seldom did.

'Why didn't you take Carrie with you?' asked Edward.

Henry looked at him – a vague, blank look. 'They were very sorry to hear about the lady,' he said.

'Oh. You told them?'

'Of course. They always want to do what they can for everyone.'

'Nothing anyone can do for her now, is there?' said Edward coldly.

'It would've been better if she'd stayed at home.' Henry turned away as he spoke: usually the boyish stare was deliberate and unflinching.

'*They* didn't stay at home, did they?' Edward reminded him. 'That lot have come here from all over the globe. And they

241

could just as easily disappear again – to some other part of the world.'

He hadn't expected Henry to answer, but the boy said, 'Some have gone already.'

'What?'

'They come and go.'

'New people have come?'

'No . . . but some have gone.'

As they walked through the woods towards the house, Henry said: 'I wish *you* would go, Eddie.'

'I beg your pardon?'

'Why don't you go back to your work? You'd be all right then.'

'I'm all right now.'

'You would be safe.'

'Safe? What d'you mean . . . safe?'

'The lady was a friend of yours?'

'I knew her slightly.'

'You told her some of your ideas.'

'So what?'

'People get frightened,' said Henry.

'I don't see the connection.'

'If you get frightened, you do things you don't mean to.'

'I'm pretty stable,' said Edward drily.

'I mean *other* people.'

'What are you trying to tell me, Henry?'

'When you come back on your next holiday – it's every two years, isn't it? – things will be different. You'll be safe then.'

'Does that matter to you?'

'Of course.'

'How safe was I the other night, when you opened the doors? How safe was I if *I'd* come down this path instead of your father, the night before?'

Henry glanced up at him in surprise.

'Oh yes, my lad, I know all about that!' He was ready to move on, but Henry stood where he was.

'D'you think she could have cut herself when she jumped?'

'What with?'

'The edge of the window? The gutter? Something?'

'What do you think?'

The boy hesitated, but said nothing.

'Did you tell *them* about the scars?' asked Edward.

Henry shook his head.

'So there you are!' said Margaret. 'You were told not to go with Sergeant Parker. I don't know what your father will say.'

Henry made no attempt to excuse himself.

Caroline glared across at her brother. 'You've been to see them! Why didn't you take me?'

'I had to do something else,' he said. It was the first time Edward had seen any sort of a rift between the two children.

For the rest of the day the boy was continually at his back.

'Are you spying on me?'

'Of course not!'

Edward didn't question it, for there was no longer hostility or suspicion in Henry's voice and look. Carrie watched from a distance, sulky and uneasy.

'Henry and Eddie are being horrid,' she told her mother.

'What are they doing?'

'Being horrid.'

'Don't worry. You're both going with your friends tomorrow for your birthday picnic.'

'Do I *have* to go?' asked Henry.

'Of course you must! What a thing to say! You'll love it. The Countess has gone to a lot of trouble to arrange it, and it's very kind of her, so don't start being silly now.'

Henry mooned uneasily around the kitchen.

'Why don't you want to go?' she asked him.

'I just don't.'

'But you're always playing next door, and they're taking you to the seaside! You can swim . . .'

'Are you going?' he asked his mother.

'Of course not. It's just for the children.'

'The Countess is going.'

'It's her party.'

'*And* some of the others.'

'That's enough, Henry. You're being childish today.'

'I'm glad I'm going,' said Caroline.

Henry looked at her, frowning. 'If Carrie goes, I have to.'

* * *

243

Later, he returned to the subject. 'I know what would be a good idea!'

'What?' asked Margaret.

'They said I could invite anyone I liked, so why doesn't Uncle Eddie come too? They're always asking about him. Dr Shannon is going, and Paula. I'd like to go if Eddie goes.'

Margaret looked at him doubtfully. 'You'll have to see what your uncle says. He might not want to go to a children's picnic.'

'And he's a very good swimmer,' said Henry. 'He can go to the rescue if anyone is drowning.'

'What d'you say, Eddie?' asked Margaret.

'I'll think about it,' Edward answered.

'Please, Eddie.' Henry held on to his arm, and Edward was touched by the boy's concern.

'I don't want Eddie to come,' said Carrie. 'He'll spoil everything.'

'I said, I'll think about it,' repeated Edward.

He tried to fathom the change in Henry. Was he sincere, or was this another ploy? What was it he had said about going to the rescue if someone was drowning? Was that an image which had bubbled up from the boy's subconscious – did he fear drowning, or some other danger? Did he think he needed someone to protect him? That was unlikely, but Edward couldn't be sure. They had been very convincing in their intrigues, these children, and this could be an ambush of another sort.

Nevertheless he said, 'Okay, I'll come along for sandwiches on the beach, cold tea and a freezing swim.'

'Great!' It was hard to believe that Henry's relief wasn't genuine – and there was also no pretence about Caroline's annoyance.

'Why did you have to ask him!' She slammed the door.

'What's got into her?' asked Margaret.

Henry followed his uncle out into the garden. 'Carrie can't help it,' he said.

'Why not?'

He clearly found it difficult to explain. 'It's not what she really thinks . . . not what *Carrie* thinks.'

'All right, then,' said Edward. '*Who* really thinks like that?'

Henry looked cautiously at him. 'You know,' was all he said.

Edward guessed he had a big fish on the end of a line: he had to play it carefully and appear uninterested as Henry followed

244

him to his car, parked in the stables. He lifted the bonnet and thoughtfully examined the engine, while Henry looked on. It was several minutes before the boy spoke.

'Do you think they could really do anything bad?'

'Like what?'

'Anything,' said Henry.

'H'mm.' Edward appeared to fiddle with the mechanism. 'You mean . . . like push someone from a window?'

He saw Henry wince. 'I don't mean that,' said the boy.

'Rip your skin?' suggested his uncle.

The boy was horrified. 'They wouldn't!'

'With animal claws?' Edward straightened up and looked at the boy.

Henry screwed up his eyes, as though blotting out an image.

John caught a later train next morning as it was the children's joint birthday, and the exciting ritual of present-giving was carried out at the breakfast table. It was in fact Henry's birthday, but the family had established the custom of sharing the celebrations – after all, Carrie's birthday was merely two days later. Edward gave Carrie a cassette-player and Henry a camera. They were both delighted, and for a short time everything else was forgotten. But their father had to go to work, and it would soon be time to leave for the picnic, as the Countess would be calling for them. The carefree mood of the morning vanished. They were children carrying a burden.

Henry prepared himself slowly, and watched his uncle anxiously.

'Can I come with you in your car?' he asked.

'Come along, Henry,' called his mother. 'You'll go with your friends, and the Countess.'

'I'll follow behind,' Edward told him.

The Countess arrived with a station-wagon and half a dozen children. 'The rest have gone ahead,' she informed Margaret. 'The Doctor has one car-load, and Paula has another.'

'Where exactly are you going?' asked Margaret.

'We have bathing cabins near Normans Bay,' said the Countess.

'Oh yes, I know it.'

'Don't expect us back until quite late,' said the Countess. She noticed Edward at the wheel of his car. 'Hello, Edward! Where are you off to?' she called.

'I'm Henry's special guest,' he called back.

For a split second the Countess was taken aback, then she smiled. 'How nice.'

'I hope that's all right?'

'But of course!'

She drove off with the children.

'You know the way?' asked Margaret.

'Like the palm of my hand,' Edward said. He was about to follow the station-wagon when a second car turned into the drive, and Sergeant Parker eased himself out.

'Glad we caught you, sir,' he said. 'Inspector Gray's making enquiries about the death of Mrs Balelli, and he thought you might be able to help.'

'I'm just about to leave . . .'

'This won't take long, sir. 'Morning, Mrs Warwick,' he called to Margaret.

'Okay,' said Edward. 'What can I tell you?'

'Actually,' said Parker, 'the Inspector would like you to come back to the cottage.'

Edward spent a tedious morning explaining his acquaintance with Sandra Balelli.

'Can you tell us anything about the dog?' the Inspector wanted to know.

'What?'

'The dog she shot. I understand you saw it.'

'Yes . . . over by the trees.' He pointed.

'You don't know where it was buried?'

'No.'

'It's rather puzzling. There were marks on her body which we believe were made by such an animal.'

'A dog?'

'It would have to be, wouldn't it? A very big dog, admittedly, but it's unlikely any other animals as large as that would be roaming the Sussex countryside.'

'Sorry, I can't help you,' Edward told him.

'You don't know of such a dog?'

What on earth could he possibly say? Edward shook his head slowly. He was very conscious of the passage of time and that Henry would be on his own. But why should that be significant? Except that the boy might think he had deliberately left him, it might seem like a betrayal . . . and at this stage Edward wanted nothing to happen that might upset his fragile confidence.

The Inspector had a few more questions, but Edward guessed he knew he was on the wrong track.

'Thank you, Mr Glover,' he said at last. 'You have been very helpful. Are you in the country much longer?'

'Another couple of weeks,' Edward told him.

Parker, who ran him back to the house to pick up his own car, was apologetic. 'He has to cover all these points, the Inspector . . .'

It was noon before Edward drove off towards the coast.

The bay where the picnic was being held was sheltered by a series of sand-dunes. Edward pulled off the road at the top of the hill and looked down at the beach. It wasn't difficult to locate the Shannons' party; it occupied a number of huts, and spilled on to the grass and sand before them. About a dozen children of varying ages were playing on the beach, running in and out of the sea, lying in the sun, shouting, swimming, even building sand-castles. It couldn't have looked a more traditional English outing.

To Edward's surprise there were also half a dozen adults. He had gained the impression from Henry that there would only be three. He could make out the figure of the Countess in a deck-chair, pouring herself a drink from a bottle, with Shannon in a chair beside her. Two younger men lay on the sand. He couldn't see Paula, but another girl was standing with the children at the edge of the water. Carrie, having a splendid time, was on the shoulders of one of the bigger boys, diving into the sea.

Even from where he sat in the car, Edward felt an air of relaxation about the scene. They looked totally at ease, which was something he had never before experienced with the Shannons – as though a great burden had been lifted and now everyone was on holiday.

The thing that concerned Edward was that he was unable to locate Henry. He had a pair of binoculars in the car, and with them scanned the beach. Paula, he saw, was sunning herself just beyond the others, but there was still no sign of Henry. Edward wasn't particularly concerned; nothing could be wrong, for Carrie was splashing in the waves, laughing her head off with the other children, and she most certainly wouldn't have been so happy if her brother were in any trouble.

He lowered the glasses, puzzled, and drove down to the beach huts. Cars were parked behind them, and Edward backed in alongside. Henry, in his bathing trunks, was sitting in the shadow of the huts.

Edward went to join him, and saw the boy was unsmiling, tense. And a little distance away, watching Henry continuously, was one of the young men whom Edward had already met. He remembered his name: Robert.

Henry saw him and jumped to his feet.

'Eddie!' He ran towards him. Robert looked as though he were about to prevent him, checked himself and turned to stare at the newcomer.

'How's the birthday picnic, my lad?' Edward was aware that he sounded unduly hearty.

'Eddie! Where have you been?'

'It's a long story; I'll tell you later. I had to tell the police all I knew about poor Sandra Balelli.' He was also aware of the impact that had on the other man.

'Hello, Robert!' he greeted him, cheerfully.

Robert, uneasy, rose to his feet and indicated Henry. 'We had to keep an eye on him,' he said. 'I'll tell the Doctor you're here.'

'Keep an eye on him?' Edward questioned coldly.

'He was a little difficult . . . excited.'

'Of course he's excited,' said Edward firmly. 'It's his birthday, isn't it?' Robert looked stonily at him as he moved away between the huts.

'What's the problem?' Edward asked Henry.

'I didn't do anything,' said the boy.

'Come on, chum.' He took Henry's hand and walked round the huts to join the party.

'Edward!' The Doctor waved to him. 'Glad you could make it.'

'Come and join us,' called the Countess.

'Having a problem with the lad?' asked Edward.

'He was a bit upset,' said the Doctor. 'Missing you, I think. He's all right now.'

'We've some smoked salmon and salad,' said the Countess busily. 'I'm afraid the rest of us have eaten.'

'What do you recommend, Henry?' Edward asked the boy. 'What did you like best?'

'I didn't have any,' said Henry.

'He didn't feel like eating,' the Doctor said. 'But if he's better now, how about beef, cheese – anything you fancy, Henry?'

There was a hamper in one of the beach huts. 'Mind if we help ourselves?' asked Edward.

'Go right ahead . . . and there's plenty of wine.'

Edward watched Henry gulp down a plate of sandwiches. 'What was the trouble?' he asked again.

The boy didn't want to answer. He shot a glance towards the adults.

'They can't hear you,' Edward assured him.

Henry shook his head in contradiction. 'They hear better than we do.'

What sort of an implication was that, Edward wondered. 'What happened?' he whispered.

Henry shrugged. 'They were asking questions.'

'What about?'

The boy looked away.

'About me?' suggested Edward.

The nod was almost imperceptible; he was very edgy. 'And about the dead lady,' he whispered.

'Time you went into the sea,' said Edward loudly, as a shadow fell suddenly across the entrance to the beach hut. Henry stood up dutifully and ran off, and Edward turned to see Paula in the doorway.

'Edward! I didn't know you were here!'

'Just arrived,' he grinned. 'I got caught by the police! How long had I known the dead girl . . . that kind of thing.'

'The poor woman from Sardinia? That was very sad.'

'Hold on,' said Edward. 'I'll be back in a moment. I promised Margaret I'd keep an eye on Henry when he was in the sea.'

Paula would have liked to detain him, but he hurried off after the boy, who was already in the water. None of the other children went near him – not even Caroline, who looked at her brother from a distance with annoyance. Edward wondered whose emotions she was carrying . . . probably those of everyone else in the party. Henry was the outsider, no longer sharing a communal intuition, as a flight of birds might do . . . or a pack of animals. Once excluded, the outcast didn't survive for long.

'Okay, Henry!' shouted Edward. 'Let's see that running dive

of yours. I'll bet none of your mates can swim as long under water.'

No one fell for the ploy. The intellect guiding them was much too adult.

But Henry played up to his uncle and put on a show of laughing, shouting, and plunging below the waves. Caroline – perhaps least able to disguise her emotions – called out coldly, 'Eddie always spoils everything.'

'Do you remember me, sir?' One of the older boys joined him. 'I am Marcel.'

'Of course I do.' Edward wouldn't have recognized him. He looked at least two years older than when they had first met.

'I'll look after Henry. He'll be all right, if you wish to join the others.' The adults were watching from the huts.

'Then I leave him in good hands,' said Edward cheerfully. 'And keep an eye on Carrie as well. I'm responsible for them both.' He felt he had made things very clear as he walked up the beach.

Paula was lying on a rug apart from the others as he joined her.

'They were cross with Henry,' she said, as he sat beside her. 'He was behaving badly, but they were too hard on him. I told them so.' She glanced critically at the Doctor on the other side of the huts, and again Edward had the feeling that she was different from the others. 'He seems to be enjoying himself now,' she added. Henry was running along the beach, Marcel by his side. 'You can relax.' She turned with a warm smile to Edward, lying with her leg just touching his. It was pleasant that she was so much at ease with him.

Paula frowned as she remembered something: 'My uncle says you are a man without compassion. What does he mean?'

'I've no idea.'

'I would have thought you very compassionate – look how you tried to help Mrs Balelli.'

'What do you know of that?'

'There's talk, of course. Just rumours.' This time she looked at him with amusement.

'Perhaps Dr Shannon thinks I lack compassion because I *am* concerned about people like Sandra Balelli . . . people unable to defend themselves . . . children, for example.'

'I'm not sure I understand.'

'I'm glad to hear it,' he said.

Robert joined them, carrying a bottle of wine and glasses. 'We've just taken this out of the ice-box,' he said, as he poured the drinks and prepared to sit with them.

'We're having a private chat,' Paula told him, and Robert moved back to join the others.

'What's so private?' Edward asked.

'Some of the family are moving on. I suppose you know that?'

'Someone told me.'

'They are too concerned about what people think, too sensitive. I don't consider that's healthy, do you?'

'I suppose newcomers – outsiders. . . .are always like that, particularly if they don't blend.'

'We would have blended. We've always done so before, sometimes for centuries.'

'So now they move on? Because they don't feel comfortable in the district?' Edward wanted to be sure he had understood.

'One has to avoid hostility.'

'What hostility?'

She hesitated. 'One senses it in children. Henry, for example: he was close to us – so sympathetic, he could have been one of the family. Then suddenly he changes, withdraws from us, is wary – almost an enemy. One wonders why?'

'Children grow up, think for themselves,' said Edward. 'Suddenly they see below the surface, and may be disturbed by what they see.'

'What could young Henry have seen?'

'He hasn't told you?'

'He tells us nothing now.'

'So he's being pressurized?' suggested Edward.

'Is he?' She sounded surprised.

'If a child is excluded like that . . .'

'Oh really!'

'Surely you noticed? He was ostracized. Even now, who plays with him?'

'I saw one of the boys.'

Edward looked along the beach. 'I don't see any sign of them,' he said. 'That's odd. I think I'd better check.'

'Why are you so concerned?'

Edward stood up to get a better view, but sand-dunes and the grassy bank obscured the rest of the bay. Though he was

251

tempted to stay with her, he said, 'I'll take a look,' and moved away. The others watched him in silence.

He climbed to the top of the first sand-dune, and saw Henry only a couple of hundred yards along the beach. He was with Marcel, but two other older boys had joined them, and they were playing a game. From this distance it wasn't clear how much Henry was enjoying it: he was trying to get past the three bigger boys, trying to head back towards the picnic, while they would run to bar his path, sometimes holding hands to form a barrier, skipping in front of him, catching him, pushing him back, laughing, giving the appearance of a friendly competition. Henry kept a brave face, but there was a growing desperation about him as they repeatedly out-manouevred him.

Edward watched for a few moments, then waved. A relieved Henry caught sight of him and waved back. The three bigger boys looked round and saw Edward on the dunes behind them. As Henry ran towards him, Marcel followed. 'Did you see how good he was at that, Mr Glover? I'm sure he would soon have got past.'

The boys went on ahead; Henry walked at Edward's side.

'What was that all about?'

'It was a game,' said Henry. 'To frighten me.'

'Why?'

'In case I try something.' He wasn't able to be more explicit.

Edward left the boy at the water's edge with the other children, and was on his way to rejoin Paula when the children began to shout. They were pushing Henry out of the sea.

'He hit me!' One of the boys was pointing angrily at Henry, as the rest of the group rounded on him.

Henry looked bewildered by the attack. 'I didn't!' he protested.

Carrie's hostility to her brother had vanished; she was now strained and anxious. She had her hands to her mouth.

'What happened, Carrie?' Edward asked. They all turned to look at her.

'He hit someone,' the child told him, but she seemed to find it hard to say.

'Better come with me, Henry.' Edward led the boy up the beach. 'Why don't you play along there, on your own.'

'I did nothing,' he said.

'That's okay,' said Edward. 'Along there, you'll be out of sight.'

He went back to join the adults.

'You were right,' he agreed cheerfully with Robert. 'My nephew is letting his birthday go to his head.' He lay down where he could see Henry collecting sticks a few hundred yards along the beach. Edward closed his eyes as though idling in the sun. From time to time he engaged Paula's attention. For some reason he didn't want her to notice what the boy was doing.

Henry had carried his little bundle of sticks into a hollow in the sand. Close by, the occupants of another beach-hut, strangers, had cleared away their things and were driving off, leaving behind the embers of a fire over which they had boiled a kettle. Henry began to coax them back to life, finally carrying a smouldering stick from there to his own collection. He lay with his head on the sand, blowing the flame to life. Gradually the heap of sticks began to burn.

'What's the child doing?' called Dr Shannon sharply.

Edward pretended to notice for the first time what was happening. 'Practising scout-craft,' he called lazily.

'He is starting a fire,' said the Doctor angrily. 'That's dangerous. He must be stopped.'

'It's well away from everything.' Edward was unperturbed.

The Countess let out a wail

'All it needs is a gust of wind and the whole area could be ablaze,' said Shannon. 'The grass is bone-dry.'

'What wind?' asked Edward.

Shannon jumped up and hurried towards Henry, crouched over his flame.

'What are you doing, boy! Put that out at once!'

Henry looked up, surprised, then grinned faintly. 'Don't you like fires?'

'Put that out! You're putting lives in danger!'

'Look,' said Henry. 'It's quite safe!' He picked up one of the sticks, and those around Edward seemed to catch their breath. No one spoke as Henry held it above his head like a torch. 'You see!' The look in his eyes had changed. He was no longer hiding fears, he was assured, triumphant.

The Doctor backed away. 'I have told you . . .'

'Take it . . . Hold it . . . You'll see it's safe,' Henry said, offering it to the Doctor, who seemed mesmerized, unable to touch it.

From the beach the other children came running up, stopping as they saw Henry. The flame was flickering out, and thin smoke rose from the burning stick. 'You see, it's hardly alight. You know what you have to do to keep it going? It needs oxygen. This is the best way to do it!' He waved the stick before him, and the flame came alive again. 'There! See that? You try!'

Shannon turned away. 'Edward!' he called.

Henry ignored him, grabbing up a second burning stick and holding them together, then scrambling to his feet.

'Here's another game to play, Marcel!' he called. 'You try it!' He raced towards the other boys, his eyes bright, his grin wide, a little demonic, Edward thought. They saw him coming, and for a couple of seconds the older children hesitated, transfixed as the Doctor had been. Then they turned and ran. Henry let out a shriek of laughter. They scattered before him, to the huts and into the sea. Only Carrie stood where she was, motionless, as her brother challenged those round her.

'Edward! You must do something before there's any harm done!' The Doctor tried unsuccessfully to hide his anxiety.

'These sticks are hardly alight,' protested Edward, but he had got to his feet. 'Henry!' he called.

The boy didn't seem to hear him, as he raced after those who had tormented him and made a dash toward Marcel. The bigger boy, frightened, turned and fled into the sea. *'Henry!'* Their alarm was a ridiculous over-reaction, Edward thought, but the game had to be stopped. As the boy came running past the beach huts, and the group of adults backed off in alarm, Edward caught hold of him.

'Okay, son,' he said. 'You've squared the match. Let me have those. That's enough.'

'Can we go home now, Eddie?' asked the boy.

'Good thinking,' said his uncle.

'Why did you do that?' asked Caroline. She and Henry were sharing the passenger seat beside Edward.

'They'll see I'm not helpless,' Henry told her. 'Maybe now they won't try anything!' He turned to his uncle. 'I wish you hadn't sent your gun away, Eddie.'

There was a silence, then Carrie said: 'Don't you like Marcel any more?'

'I hate all of them,' said Henry.

She was still critical. 'That wasn't nice. You know they don't like fire.'

'What's that?' asked Edward.

'That's right,' Henry nodded. 'They don't have fires in their house.'

'But it's always warm. They cook . . .'

'They never have a flame. Not a naked flame,' said the boy.

How valuable they were, these children! He must listen to them.

'You mustn't do anything dangerous,' he said to Henry. 'Not on your own. I know it's your birthday, but you're still only nine.'

Henry nodded gravely. It was hard to know what he was thinking.

It was the following day before Edward had an opportunity to question his nephew further.

'Why did you go wild like that?' he asked.

'I didn't like them celebrating,' said Henry. 'They were glad that lady was dead. I never guessed they would be like that, and it made me mad. They were so pleased with themselves, and I thought it was cruel. They saw this, and then they were angry with me.'

'What about Carrie?'

'She doesn't understand.'

'And you understand?'

'I understand now what they were trying to do to me, but I don't understand about them. Except that they're not the same as us.'

It was strange to have found an ally in this unexpected quarter – this serious-faced little boy of just nine years. It was also strange, thought Edward, that he and Henry never discussed the nature of the dangers that faced them: perhaps they were too horrifying. Their neighbours in Park House didn't come into the world of logic, of cause and effect. They were subject to other laws, and it was difficult to think reasonably about them. The implications were frightening.

Edward strolled about the garden, trying to clarify his thoughts. What were these other laws? Where lay their weakest points? Living, as the Park House family appeared to do, as a clan, a pack, must impose its own constraints. And this mutation at will, provided it was truly in their power, must burn up enormous amounts of energy. An act of transformation would

255

leave any animal depleted. Even when a bird flew – something as natural as that – it converted vitality at a great rate; so what must be consumed when metamorphosis took place? If these creatures had this power, if they could change as he believed they did change, what organic stress they would undergo! No wonder they appeared to age as they did. Different species have a different time-cycle. A dog is old in its teens; a man in his seventies. In the few months their neighbours had been there, they might have aged that number of years! Come to think of it, he had noticed many of the younger ones seeming to mature – it was probably less easy to spot as they grew older.

Again Edward reminded himself that he had no conclusive proof, no evidence. Just hearsay from a woman who had since died; visions from a girl who might be out of her mind; interpretations of his own that might be wrong. Well, that was as close as he was likely to approach to any sort of truth.

Henry stayed near him, trailing by his side: distant, thoughtful. And when Edward drove to the village, Henry went with him. Carrie avoided them.

'Why d'you think she's being like that?' asked Edward.

'You saw her at the picnic,' said Henry. 'They used to leave her alone before, and I was the one they spoke to. I did the things they told me to, the things they put in my head.'

'Didn't they trust her?'

'They said she was too young: later on, perhaps. One day they were going to ask to take us on a long holiday to another country. That won't happen now. I think they're going to leave themselves.'

'Why?'

'They say it was a mistake to come to England. They need places with space.'

'I see.'

'And I think they are afraid of you . . . of things you might guess, and of rumours that might start, as they did in the last place.'

When they returned to the house Margaret was at the front door.

'You've just missed a visit from our neighbours,' she said.

They looked at her in amazement.

'The Countess called. They've taken Caroline for the day.'

'Is she next door?' asked Henry.

'No. They've gone to London. It's a special occasion.'

'You shouldn't have let her go! Not to London! Not without me!'

'Don't be so silly! They didn't ask for you, anyhow.' Margaret looked sharply at him.

'You shouldn't have let her go,' Henry protested again.

'That's ridiculous! They've gone to see a dolls' museum. Boys aren't generally interested in dolls' museums.'

Henry looked blankly at his mother.

'Don't worry,' she said. 'I'm sure they'll make it up to you another time.'

Edward and the boy gravitated to the tree-house and looked across to the Park House gardens, silent in the afternoon sunshine.

'I know why they've taken her,' said Henry. 'They know that as long as they have Carrie, I won't dare to say anything to anyone.'

'They can't keep her,' Edward told him.

'They won't *need* much time, if they're leaving,' said Henry. He was quiet for a moment, then he said, 'I hope they don't start to talk to her as they did to me.'

'What does that mean?'

'With that smoke and perfume in the room, they whisper to you, and you believe them. I believed they were gentle, that they wanted only to share a place in the world, in peace. I believed they would harm no one. Perhaps they'll tell Carrie that I'm not to be trusted, as they said about you.' He kept his eyes on the trees beyond the walls. 'I must get her away.'

'She's in London.'

'That's just what *they* say.'

'Even if she's in the house, it would be impossible to get in.' Edward's heart went out to the boy. 'We'll think of something,' he promised hopelessly.

At the evening meal John asked, 'And what time is my gadabout daughter coming home?'

'The Countess didn't say,' Margaret told him.

The phone rang as if on cue.

'It's Carrie,' called Margaret, 'and the Countess. They want to know if she can stay the night?'

'What? At her age?'

'They're having a wonderful time, apparently. Would you have a word?'

'You handle it. Where are they?'

'The Dorchester, I think.'

'Good lord!'

'Right,' said Margaret into the phone. 'We'll see you some time tomorrow.'

'She's a bit young to start staying out at night,' grumbled John.

'It's just once,' said Margaret.

'Where did they phone from?' asked Henry.

'From London, of course,' said his mother.

Edward caught the boy's eye, and he said no more.

He couldn't find Henry the following morning.

'He got up early,' said Margaret. 'I don't know where he is. Probably in the garden, unless he's gone next door to see his friends.'

Edward thought that unlikely, but he walked through the woods. As there was no sign of the boy, he scrambled over the low wall, and went cautiously across the field towards the iron gate. He was on edge, ready for anything – he had vivid memories of this gate – as he peered through the bars, but all was silent beyond; a drowsy langour pervaded the place; insects hummed, and in the distance there was the occasional sound of a car engine or a door shutting.

He tried the handle, but the gate was locked.

'Henry doesn't seem to be around,' he told Margaret. Half an hour later Henry turned up, his clothes very dirty.

'How did you get into that state?' asked his mother.

'I was just playing.'

'Where were you?' she asked.

'In the wood.'

'Eddie didn't see you there.'

They all had cold drinks, then Edward followed Henry outside.

'Where were you?' he asked.

The boy hesitated. 'I think she's there.'

'Where?'

'In the house.'

'How d'you know?'

'I saw her at a window. Someone pulled her away.'

'You can't see the house from the road.'

'I was in the garden . . . at the back.'

'Not possible,' said Edward. 'The gate's locked.'

'I can get in. I'll show you.'

The prospect chilled Edward.

They took the ritual walk through the woods again, into the field, and up to the gate. Edward could hardly believe he was back there.

'Were you inside?'

'Yes.'

'And nobody saw you?'

'They were too busy,' said Henry. 'They're loading trucks.'

'What about the dogs?'

'What dogs?'

'They have guard dogs.'

'I've never seen them.' Henry looked doubtful.

'Well, I have. Several times.'

Henry frowned. 'I think they try to confuse people. So if anyone got the idea they'd seen animals, they could say they kept guard dogs.' He put his hand through the bars, reached behind the wall, and withdrew the key. 'They put it there for me,' he explained. 'We used to come and go this way.' And he unlocked the gate.

If a nine-year-old boy wasn't alarmed, why should he be, thought Edward, but he broke into a sweat.

'She was at one of the windows,' the boy went on. 'I'll show you the room.' He pushed open the gate. 'Shut it behind you,' he said, 'in case somebody sees.'

Edward was appalled. It felt like stepping into a cage!

Henry dropped to his hands and knees, and crawled through the bushes. Edward started to protest, but the boy had gone. He crouched down and followed.

'This is the way I came this morning.' Henry lay still for a moment in the undergrowth. 'On the other side of these trees, we can see the house.' He squirmed away again. Another twenty yards and they could see the back of the building.

Two men were carrying furniture from a back door; they disappeared round the side of the house.

'This is pointless,' said Edward. 'There's nothing we can do.'

'I've seen her,' whispered Henry. 'She's not in London. She was at that window . . .' He pointed to a room, one floor up. Edward peered at it.

'There's no one there now.' Perhaps the boy was letting his alarm get the better of his good sense? Edward should never have allowed him to come here. He looked at his watch; he would give this escapade another five minutes.

A figure crossed the room, pausing at the window. It was a girl.

'That's not Carrie,' whispered Edward.

'It's her friend,' said Henry. The girl was the same age as Caroline, and about the same height. It looked as though she was brushing her hair, standing side-on to the window. She vanished for a few seconds then came back, this time putting on a wide-brimmed sun-hat and turning every now and again into the room, as though talking.

'There's someone with her,' whispered Henry. She turned her back to the window as she was joined by a second figure, but it wasn't Carrie. Paula stood there for a moment, putting her arms round the girl before leading her away.

'They've gone,' whispered Edward.

'They'll be back,' said Henry. 'You'll see. Carrie *must* be there.'

They lay for another ten minutes in the bushes, but no one appeared at the window.

'We can't stay,' said Edward, but the boy was unwilling to move. 'We have plans to make,' urged his uncle. 'We're wasting time.'

Henry nodded, waited for a further few moments, then they crawled back the way they had come.

'You keep just missing people,' said Margaret. 'That's the second time. Your friend Paula was here.'

'What?'

'She was sorry not to see you.'

'When was this?'

'About ten minutes ago. She came with Carrie.'

'Carrie's home?' Henry looked at his mother in disbelief.

'Yes, they're back from London. They had a lovely time.'

'Where is she?' demanded Henry.

'They've gone again,' said Margaret. 'Paula brought Carrie

260

with this little friend of hers. They're having some special occasion . . . a going-away party. I didn't quite understand what's going on next door, but I think somebody's leaving. Sorry, Henry, but it's girls only,' she said.

'Carrie was here and she's gone again?' Henry repeated.

'She's having a busy time,' agreed Margaret.

'What was this little friend wearing?' asked Edward. 'A big floppy hat?'

'How did you know?'

'Just guessing,' he said.

It was beginning to grow dark as Edward drove down the lane to Park House. He wasn't sure he believed this story of a party, and was surprised to see lights blazing from the windows. Coloured lanterns were slung along the drive; even the gates were laced with fairy-lamps, glowing under the figures of the dancing wolves. He heard music through the trees, and a burst of childish laughter. Clearly, Carrie was not on her own.

He arrived back home to find John and Margaret ready to go out.

'We hoped you hadn't forgotten,' they said to him. 'We have another meeting. It's rather important – Green Belt, you know.'

He had forgotten. In fact, he couldn't remember their having told him about it.

'Will Shannon be there?'

'Sure to be.'

'What about this party?'

'That's not his province. The Countess handles that.'

As they climbed into the car, Margaret called, 'Henry was very tired. He's fast asleep.'

They drove off and Edward walked to the foot of the stairs. Henry was at the top, already dressed.

'You passed the house, didn't you?' he asked. 'What did you see?'

'There's *something* going on,' said his uncle. 'Lights all over the place. And music.'

'Were there cars?'

'Where?'

'Outside the house? If you have a party, there must be cars.'

Edward was doubtful. 'Parents just bring their children, and

261

call back for them – they don't leave their cars. Besides, you can't see from the road.' But it was a good point; he was surprised what consideration he gave to what the boy said – it was like dealing with another adult.

Henry joined him in the hall.

'You shouldn't be up like this.' It didn't mean anything, but Edward felt he had to say it. There was a fine line between frustrating the boy, and letting him do something reckless. He appeared totally compelled; driven probably by his own special knowledge of his neighbours, by a fear, born out of insight. The thought of Caroline in their company obsessed the boy: he might do something foolish, and put himself in danger.

'We have to think this through, Henry. There are only two of us . . .' and he didn't add that one was only a child. 'We might be totally wrong. There could be an explanation for everything. Think what we would look like.'

'I know about them.' Henry was quietly sure. 'They were going to help me to join them in some way . . . and I wanted that too. They didn't hide things from me: they didn't need to. I *have* to get Carrie out.' There was a chilling finality about that.

'But how? It's a huge place.'

'I've been all over it. They never stopped me going anywhere . . . not while they trusted me.'

'We can't just walk into a party and demand . . .'

'No, they wouldn't let us take her.'

'We don't even know how many there are in the house.'

'They've been leaving these last few days,' Henry told him. 'That's why they've taken her. As long as they have her, they know I won't say anything, I won't make trouble for them. They're using the time to slip away.'

'So what can we do? We haven't even got arms.'

'I have arms.'

'Henry! Be sensible.'

'Better than guns.'

'Where?'

'I'll show you.'

Edward followed him into the darkened garden. This must be make-believe: he could have no arms with which to face a roomful of people, or a pack of animals.

The stables were also in darkness.

'Don't turn on the light,' said Henry.

'Why not?'

'You never know with them,' said Henry as he rummaged at

the back of the garage. He came out carrying a bundle of sticks. 'You saw them at the picnic?' said Henry. He had two bundles, each about a foot and a half long, packed tightly and bound with wire and string. 'You know what fire means to them – they were terrified. Not just the children, all of them!'

'I know they were upset . . .'

'They are destroyed by it! Only human beings understand fire . . . we're the only animals which aren't afraid.' He sounded utterly confident.

'You expect to walk in with two torches and take Carrie away?'

'If I set these on fire, no one will come near us,' said Henry.

Edward had to be careful. 'Okay, we'll have to think about it. But first, give them a chance to bring her back, like they said . . . in the morning, first thing. If they don't turn up with her, I promise, I'll come with you – torches and all – straight into Park House.'

It was a moment before the boy spoke. 'All right. Maybe that's best.'

Edward had expected a struggle, but Henry came back with him to the house, left his torches by the kitchen door, and went to his room. It seemed that the heart had gone out of him.

Edward sat by the window, looking out over the darkened garden, remembering vividly the previous occasion when he had been left with the children. This time there would be no dangerous intrusion; the boy had been shocked out of his infatuation, was no longer bewitched. Indeed, he appeared to be consumed by his antagonism towards those who had so charmed and bedevilled him. God knows what this must have done to the mind of someone so young, thought Edward. How had he coped under such stress? Yet he seemed balanced enough and reasonable in everything but this obsessive concern for the safety of his sister. Perhaps he blamed himself that the little girl might be in danger? Anyhow, Edward was resolved that he would stand by what he had said to the boy: if they didn't bring Caroline home the next morning, he would go and fetch her.

He went through to the kitchen to make coffee. Upstairs all was peaceful. He had begun to heat the kettle before he noticed that the torches were no longer by the kitchen door. He turned off the heat and ran up to the boy's room, but he knew already: Henry had gone.

He swore at himself as he raced down the garden path. He should have guessed. If no one would go with him, Henry would go alone.

There was just a hope that the Park House gate was still locked – but it wasn't even shut. Perhaps Henry had left it ajar in case he had to run for it? The boy would have taken the same path as he had done earlier in the day. Edward didn't bother to conceal himself, but pushed through the bushes. Music drifted from the house and lights shone, but the back was in darkness. He almost fell over a figure in the bracken.

'No noise,' whispered Henry. 'Someone just passed.'

'This is senseless, Henry. Be a good lad. I promised you . . .'

'Tomorrow will be too late,' said Henry quietly.

'You don't *know* that.'

'They've taken two cars away already, and more are going. In the morning the house will be empty.'

'Be serious! Why would they harm Carrie?'

'Didn't the Italian lady tell you – the one who lost her son?'

'What do you know about that?' Edward was shaken.

'They used to speak in front of me, I told you.'

Edward was overcome by revulsion. He looked towards the darkened house, where music and children's laughter came and went with the night breeze. What to believe? Nothing the boy implied, nothing he suspected himself, made sense. Surely there was a rational explanation for everything?

Something was odd about that music . . . and the laughter. Both rose and fell, in a repeated pattern . . . lifeless, artificial.

There was a simple solution. 'It's recorded,' he told the boy.

'Why would they do that?'

'There aren't any children there,' said Edward. The trick was suddenly clear to him – but for what purpose?

'How do we get in?' he asked.

'I'll show you.' Henry stood up and headed for a corner of the house. A concreted slope led below ground-level, past garbage buckets, to a wooden door. 'They never shut this.' Henry slid it aside. 'It goes into the cellars,' he said. Edward followed him. Inside it was very dark. From somewhere above, music played. For a few moments they stood silently, listening.

'Music . . . but no one dancing,' whispered Henry.

As if on cue there came a burst of children's laughter, which sounded even more hollow and meaningless now they were inside.

Henry closed the door behind them.

'Do you know where we are?' asked his uncle.

The boy whispered. 'Yes. Follow me.' They moved cautiously along a white-walled corridor. A short distance ahead were stone steps. 'It's the old servants' stairs,' whispered Henry. 'It goes to the back kitchens. They don't use them much.' He went ahead, carrying his two unlit torches, and Edward followed. They stepped into a scullery, with old-fashioned stone sinks against the wall.

'The real kitchen's through there.' Henry eased open the door. There was a light in the room beyond, but it was empty. Plates were piled on a table. Now, thought Edward, they might come face to face with anyone.

'Look at the stoves.' Henry pointed. Edward couldn't think what he meant. 'No gas – no naked flame.' That seemed to give the boy confidence.

'We want the next floor,' he said. He led the way into another corridor, the music loud in a neighbouring room. Doors to either side might open at any moment . . . They appeared to be heading for the central hall, but Henry turned down a second-ary corridor. A narrow flight of stairs faced them. 'This was for servants, too. It goes to the top floors.'

It was like being in the heart of a jungle . . . and Edward was following a boy who didn't understand the risks, with no defence but a bundle of twigs, looking for Carrie who might or might not be in a particular room. And if she weren't? He didn't dare let his mind dwell on it.

Every wooden step creaked . . . they might be challenged at any moment. On a brightly lit landing, carpeted, and with the familiar perfume, they tiptoed towards a door at the end of a short corridor.

Henry listened outside, then said, 'It's empty,' and went in. It was barely furnished – a bed, a chair, a mirror. Henry picked up a handkerchief. 'That's Carrie's.'

They looked into the other rooms on the landing, but they were all empty.

'Everyone's gone,' said Henry.

But that was clearly not the case, for in spite of the charade on the floor below – the lifeless recording of a party – there came the sound of people moving, of something being trundled into the hall, of muffled voices – the voices of men, not children.

Henry made his way back to the landing, where the main

staircase led to the hall below. A window overlooked the portico, and they were almost caught in a blaze of lights as a car circled the drive, stopping just outside. Doors opened and shut; the engine was kept running, and there was a hurried conversation in the hall. From the window they watched the car being loaded with baggage, and people climbing in.

'The Countess,' whispered Henry.

They counted four others.

'One man . . . three ladies. Not Carrie,' Henry said softly.

The car disappeared down the drive. The front door closed; voices receded.

It was the crude deception that angered Edward. What was it for, all this pretence? A contrivance to keep a child as a hostage? Was it, in fact, as Henry suggested, their method of escape, of making sure the boy kept his mouth shut? Could the explanation be as far-fetched as that?

'We must look downstairs,' whispered Henry.

Edward was prepared to take the boy's word for it. His inhibitions had gone: he didn't give a damn whom they ran into. The so-called Countess had invited his niece to a party – and he had seen the woman drive off – hardly the image she had created for herself . . . But a persistent voice within whispered caution; he had previously been caught dangerously off-guard on these premises.

They were a few steps from the head of the staircase – the room with the noise and music could be seen opposite – when a couple of men came along the lower corridor, wheeling a number of metal cases – filing cabinets, computers, electrical equipment. Edward waited until they had stacked them by the front door and disappeared into the rear of the house. He signalled to Henry and they were about to descend when the door opposite opened and a woman came out, holding Caroline by the hand. There was something odd about the little girl; passively, she allowed herself to be led, her eyes blank and partially closed, as though she were half-asleep. They too disappeared along the corridor.

'The back stairs,' whispered Henry.

They headed for the kitchens the way they had come. Half-way down the narrow stairs they heard voices, coming from behind a thin wall beside them.

'Stay with her,' the woman was saying. 'It's nearly time to go. Keep her in your room.'

266

Another voice said, 'Come on!'

'That's her friend,' whispered Henry.

'The one with the hat?'

Henry nodded.

On the edge of the landing they heard the two girls passing. Caroline said nothing, but the other girl was chattering away: 'Soon we'll all be gone, to a lovely place . . . lovely holiday.' A door opened and shut.

From now on they would have to move fast.

'We'll take her out the way we came in,' Edward whispered. 'Through the kitchens, into the cellar. Got that?'

Henry nodded. He seemed absolutely certain as he led the way back to the room they had first visited. Carrie and the other girl were at the window as Edward came in. Neither appeared to recognize him.

'What do you want?' asked the girl. She was still wearing her wide-brimmed hat, and she didn't seem in the slightest alarmed.

'Come on, Carrie.' Edward took her arm.

'She's supposed to stay here,' said the girl, as he hurried her towards the door. 'You mustn't take her!'

Henry appeared in the doorway.

'What do *you* want?' said the girl sharply.

He ignored her. 'We have to go, Carrie,' he said. She gave him the same blank look. He took her other arm and they led her out of the room. Passively she went with them. '*Run!*' said Henry.

The other girl followed them into the corridor. 'You know what will happen to you!'

It was a threat; Henry turned to stare at her. 'You kill people,' he said coldly.

'You know what will happen!' Her voice rose. She was bound to be heard.

'This way!' Edward hurried Caroline along the corridor.

'You mustn't take her!' the girl shouted. 'You are not supposed to be here!' She started to scream.

They scrambled down the narrow stairway, with Carrie between them, and raced through the kitchens. At the top of the steps to the cellars a stack of cabinets and the trolley blocked the way. In the shadows beyond, coming up from below, a couple of men carried a heavy container.

'Who's that?' someone shouted.

'The other way,' whispered Henry urgently.

The two men came up the steps, as Henry led the way from the kitchens, and they were suddenly in the main corridor, heading towards the hall. Outside they saw the lights of a car arriving.

'This way!' said Henry. He pulled Caroline with him, and Edward followed. The place had seemed a maze to him once before . . . now it was a spider's web.

'Where to?'

'The pool . . . there's a way out from there. Sometimes it's open.' Henry led the way, hurrying Caroline beside him, her feet flying like a marionette at speed, jerked into action by invisible strings. One passageway resembled another as they turned into a second then a third. The boy seemed sure of his way through the sprawling building. But he suddenly slowed. Ahead lay an intersection; voices sounded; they flattened against the wall as figures ran past. More voices . . . this time further away.

'They've searched the pool,' whispered Henry. 'They've gone somewhere else.'

All they could do was to hope that was the case; it was a chance they had to take.

They joined the main corridor, which Edward recognized as leading to the swimming-pool. It was brightly lit and – thank God – empty. As they hurried towards the swing-doors, Caroline began to yell, one wild shriek after another. It was so unexpected that they both stared at her. The corridors echoed with her terror.

'Carrie! Stop it . . . stop it!' Edward shook her, her head falling backwards and forwards, blank-eyed and senseless. She still screamed.

Henry spun her round and hit her, flat-handed, across the face. She looked incredulously at him, then she began to cry . . . slow, soundless, tears.

'I want to go home,' she said.

'Thank God!' thought Edward. It was the first emotion she had shown since they found her.

They each held a hand, and ran with her between them to the annexe that housed the swimming-pool.

'There's a door at the back,' directed Henry, and they scrambled over a pile of empty crates, packing cases and cardboard boxes heaped against the wall. The little girl held their hands tightly now – frightened, but alive to what went on around her, as they pushed their way to the half-open door.

But something moved. Something just outside. Something low on the ground, in the dark, merging with the night; indistinct, held in check by a leash.

And behind that was a young man.

'It's Marcel,' said Henry.

Edward felt ice in his veins. 'He's got a dog,' he said.

Henry shook his head. 'It's not a dog.'

The swing-doors behind them were thrown open and they turned to see the two men they had seen in the hallway burst in. A third came in behind them: it was Dr Shannon. In the corridor behind him they could see half a dozen other figures.

Shannon came to a halt as he saw them. He managed a smile. 'Here you are,' he said. 'And you've taken our little guest.'

'She wants to go,' said Henry.

'So, Henry, you are no longer our friend. It isn't often those who have been close to us become our enemies.'

They were being cautious, they didn't rush them . . . yet there must have been about ten of them, mostly young men, who could easily have overpowered a man and a boy. But they were looking round, uncertain. What did they suspect? Was there any possible defence?

Basic principle – go on the attack, thought Edward. 'Call off your dog,' he said.

'Oh yes, my dog. We are not without protection against intruders.'

'Right now!' called Edward.

A couple of the men began to edge towards Caroline, who covered her face.

'You know our problems . . . at least some of them.' Shannon sounded reasonable. 'You could have helped us, Edward. We would have gone without this unpleasantness, if you had had more understanding. But as usual, as so often, you were prejudiced. Now, I don't think there is very much I can do to reach a solution. If only you had . . .'

His voice trailed away, and there was a silence in the room. They were all looking at Henry.

'The boy is mad!' said Shannon.

Edward turned to see Henry striking a match. It was a pathetic gesture . . . it didn't even light at the first attempt. Then a flame flickered.

'It endangers all of us,' cried Shannon, without taking his eyes off the boy. It was hard to understand that such a tiny flame could so distress him.

Henry held the match to the bunch of twigs. There was a drift of smoke, a faint glow as leaves shrivelled . . . Long seconds passed before the torch took light, and they all stood stock-still, watching. They could have rushed the boy while the twigs still smouldered. Edward took the torch from him.

'Light the other one,' he said to Henry.

He held the flame before him, shielding it as it guttered, and moved towards the watching men.

They backed off.

'We have several of these,' he said. 'Lethal as bombs.' Would the fear last? Flames burn out.

'Get these people out of here,' he called to Shannon.

The man hesitated. 'What people?'

'These two bastards for a start,' ordered Edward.

The little crowd at the door had spilled in to fill the entrance, whispering, urging the Doctor, 'We have to go . . . let us go.'

'We can't,' said Shannon.

They pleaded with him.

'We can't let them leave,' he told them.

They moved in behind him, agitated by watching the burning flame . . . yet Edward sensed their determination.

'You see we are many,' said Shannon. 'Put out the flame and go.'

'Contradicting yourself, aren't you, Doctor?' called Edward. 'Put out this flame? What then? You can't leave us, you've just said so – not with what we know!'

'We can have an agreement.' Shannon watched the flame; it was beginning to die. If they were going to get out, they would have to move now.

Edward called: 'Stick close!' He took Carrie's hand and moved into the house, towards the swing-doors, Henry following. Those facing him quickly scattered round the pool. Edward hoped they could make it through the house again; any other way was cut off. But they moved as he had not expected. Perhaps it was that shared communal instinct, like a flight of birds taking off, for without words or signals they moved together, closing in on the children, avoiding the torch Henry carried and snatching at his clothes.

Edward tried to fight them off, but they grabbed Henry.

Marcel, coming in from behind, had one powerful arm under the boy's chin, round his neck. His torch went spinning.

No one moved. Time froze. Then Henry coughed and slipped out of Marcel's grip, as paper flared. The torch lay somewhere in that debris . . . A flame leapt from nowhere and ran along the litter by the pool. Even now they could have pitched the whole ragged bonfire into the water, but reason deserted them, and figures were suddenly running aimlessly through the smoke.

The children were ignored; Edward dragged them aside. The fire spread like a wave, sweeping through the annexe, blazing litter toppling into the water, floating in the pool.

There was little chance of escaping through the house now; in a panic-stricken knot, the others had made a dash for that exit. Crates piled by the door caught fire, and something exploded with a blast of hot air.

Edward again tried to shepherd the children to the garden door, but smoke rose from the rubbish piled there. Yet it was the only way out, and they would have to take it.

'Into the pool!' he shouted to the children. They obeyed him at once; even in that chaos he was moved by their faith in him. All three submerged themselves, and scrambled out, soaking, water streaming from them. 'Okay,' said Edward. 'One at a time. Back in the pool, Henry. Stay there till I come for you.' He had a feeling the boy would stay till doomsday.

He picked up Carrie and put her over his shoulder, wrapped his shirt over his face and plunged into the burning rubbish between himself and the door. Someone had shut the door again, but he put his shoulder to it and it swung open. The cool night air was unbelievable! Every nerve, every fibre, cried out in gratitude.

He put the little girl on the ground.

'Back in a tick, love,' he said.

It was best not to give himself too much time to think about it: the fire just inside the doorway had taken a fresh hold and the blaze was formidable.

He jumped into the pool beside Henry.

'Okay, chum, here we go!'

As they climbed out of the water he could see that the annexe was now engulfed in flames, and the fire had spread to the house itself. They had chosen the best way out.

Henry was heavier than his sister, and Edward had to steady

himself against the wall. Smoke rolled round them, blinding him, filling his lungs. More people suffocated than burned to death, he reminded himself. He tried to stop breathing, even through the shirt he had wrapped round his face, but he staggered as he headed for the door . . . The world spun . . . His legs were giving way under him.

He counted the paces to the door. He could see nothing, but if he was going in the right direction . . . Smouldering debris clung round him. He pitched forward . . . The last thing he remembered was that they had fallen on soil . . . Thank God for that, on sweet, sweet soil.

He would happily have remained unconscious, but someone was calling his name . . .

'Edward! Edward!'

It was a girl's voice, calling urgently, and he came out of oblivion to find Henry beside him, Carrie in the bushes, well away from the fierce heat, and a shape – only a vague, flickering outline – on the other side of the line of flames.

'It's Paula,' said Henry. There was no enthusiasm in his voice.

Edward struggled to his feet, and gradually the world stopped spinning. The heat was intense. Windows splintered, the walls cracked.

But the flames dipped and he could see the terrified girl in the doorway, holding out her hands. He tried to go to her, but the fire drove him back. There was no way he could help.

He heard her calling: 'They kept me here, as they tried to do to Caroline.'

Now he believed he understood. They had taken her into that family . . . He had always thought she was different.

Henry was by his side. 'That's not true,' he said.

Edward broke off a heavy branch from a shrub nearby, and began to beat down the flames that surrounded the figure in the doorway.

'They didn't keep her,' protested Henry. 'She's one of them. She's to be the next Countess.'

The flames were scattered, and smoke blew aside. Another shape moved behind the girl. It was impossible to see who it was in the smoke. Paula was only a few yards from Edward, and on a slightly higher level. One jump and she would be safe.

'Jump!' he shouted.

'Don't save her,' said Henry. His voice was dull, flat, lifeless; a judgement was being passed. *'Don't help her.'*

Edward went into the heat, as far as a man could tolerate. He thrashed at the burning patch, sweat streaking off him, with no idea where the strength was coming from. He beat the flames back by a good two feet . . . Now, surely, she could make it?

'Paula! It's your only chance. Jump now!'

He didn't see clearly what happened as he reeled back from the flames, blinded, coughing, almost passing out, but he was aware of the lean shape . . . long, grey, lithe and compact . . . coming through the smoke and flames with a spring that cleared all danger. Its paws hit the ground four-square only a few feet away, then it turned its dark, yellow-eyed head towards him in a split-second of enmity, and made off in what was now the familiar loping stride, into the shadows . . . into night.

He was never sure what he had seen.

He *was* sure he saw the second shape, fractionally later. But that fraction had been vital, for suddenly flames flared along its back, and there was a smell of scorched flesh. The howl was one of anguish, as it too raced into the darkness of the garden, flaming hair tracing its passage as it fled round the side of the house.

Edward also remembered dragging Carrie further from the flames, and Henry crouching by his side as he finally collapsed.

And it was Henry who stood guard over them, and ran to the front of the house later as help arrived.

'A remarkable lad,' Sergeant Parker told his Inspector. 'The village should be proud of him.'

Edward had no idea how he got there, but he was lying in his own bed.

'We do have an ambulance service,' said John. He was relieved that, apart from some burns on the legs, his brother-in-law was little the worse for his appalling experience. It was miraculous, thought John.

'And we also have our own fire-fighters,' added John. 'All volunteers, you know. They took a fair time getting there, but there was no alarm from Park House. That shows how danger-ous it is not to have a telephone.'

'How are the kids?'

'They're playing in the garden.'

'How long have I been here?'

'Well, the doc said you were fit enough to be brought home. They took you to the old cottage hospital first. Casualty cleared you: only minor burns. They said you were terribly lucky. Henry got his clothes singed . . .' He dropped the jocular tone. 'I don't know how to thank you, Eddie. You're a bloody hero. Margaret was in tears when she heard.'

'Heard what?'

'What you did.'

Edward hesitated. What had anyone said? Indeed, who could have said anything? Who knew anything except Henry?

'What exactly . . .'

'Don't be so bloody modest. You went into that place, into the flames . . . brought out Carrie . . . went back for Henry.'

'Did Henry tell you?'

'Well . . . actually he confirmed it.'

'Then who told you? Carrie?'

'Good lord, no. She was out to the world. She doesn't remember a thing. That child was sleeping when the three of you were found. No, actually, there's a bit of bad news to tell you. Fortunately the house was almost empty . . . I didn't realize the party was a going-away party. They must have told me, I suppose, but I didn't cotton on. The whole family next door was leaving . . . some change of plan. I suppose it was very lucky, for almost everyone had gone before the fire broke out. Only the Doctor was there when it happened. He was doing a final check, just about to bring Carrie home, but something happened and the place went up. Lucky you and Henry were around.'

'Dr Shannon told you this?' Edward was bewildered: it didn't make sense.

'He didn't tell me, he told the first chaps to arrive . . . I think it was the farmer from across the field. And two of the ambulance team.'

'I don't follow.'

'I'll tell you what he said about you,' said John. 'He said you saw him still in the annexe, that big swimming-pool – which was totally destroyed, I'm afraid. He'd just managed to get there, before the fire cut him off. He knew there was no one else left in the house, and he saw you carry out both children. He realized he wasn't going to make it, but he says you tried to get back to help him. That's when you blacked out.'

'He said that?'

'Yes, poor bastard, shortly before he died.'

'Shannon *died*?'

'They found him on the front drive, half-way to the gate. He had a car waiting, and was going to join the others, in Malaya or somewhere. There doesn't seem to be a definite address. Anyhow, they couldn't move him. They couldn't save him.'

'Why?' But Edward had already guessed the answer.

'Poor devil! His back was burnt to the bone. They don't know how he got as far, or lived so long . . . anyhow, long enough to tell them what you'd done, and how grateful he was.'

'Shannon said that?'

'Yes. And he said something else. They weren't sure they heard him properly, but it sounded like, "It was a small price to pay to be sure the others were safe." I suppose he meant his family . . . I mean, if they hadn't left before, most of them would be dead.'

Well, that wrapped it up, thought Edward. No one could really say anything. His family was safe.

'Was he the only one they found?' asked Edward. 'There wasn't someone else with him?'

'I gather he said there was no one else. Why?'

'I don't remember things all that clearly . . . but I thought I saw someone else.'

'In the house?'

'Yes. I thought two got away.'

John shook his head. 'I'm surprised you remember anything, old son, after what you went through.'

Edward wanted to get up, but Margaret insisted that he stay where he was. 'The doctor is calling in later. See what he says.' She tried to restrain her admiration and gratitude, but it overwhelmed her. Edward felt like a trickster. 'The man was dying . . .' she wept, 'and apparently all he kept saying was that you were a hero.'

The most important session was with Henry, who came and sat at the foot of the bed, serious-faced, adult-eyed.

'I told the policeman I went down to collect Carrie from the party. I said I hadn't been invited, and I was a bit jealous. I told him I was scared of the dark, so I asked you to come with me. I went in, and Dr Shannon went to get Carrie. He came back with her. All the other people had gone, so had the children from the party, but we got trapped by the fire and couldn't get out. You saw the flames and came running in at the back door. And you carried us out, first Caroline and then me. I said I didn't know what happened to Dr Shannon. But people say that he's dead.'

Edward nodded.

'The policeman will be coming to see you, Uncle Eddie,' he said.

Edward gave him a quick look. 'I'll tell him the same story.'

'Anyhow, I suppose that's really what happened,' said Henry.

'What about Carrie?'

'She doesn't remember anything . . . at least, not properly. She really thinks there *was* a party. She remembers music and lights . . .'

The boy sat silently for a few moments. There was something more he wanted to say. He spoke quietly.

'Did you see them jump through the fire? Paula as well?'

Edward nodded.

'And you saw what they were? What they turned themselves into?'

He nodded again.

'I told you I saw a man turn himself into a wolf. You said that wasn't true.'

'I take it back,' said Edward. 'That's one trick I can't do.'

The boy gave a faint smile, the first his uncle had seen for a long time. Then he said thoughtfully: 'I don't think we should tell anyone what we know. They wouldn't believe us. Anyhow, they've all gone away now.'

'I shall probably tell one person,' said Edward.

'Why?'

'It might help to put her mind at rest.'

'Will she tell anyone?' Henry was cautious.

'I don't think so. Besides, she lives a long way from here.'

'Who is she?'

'A girl I met. Anyhow, I think she knows most of it.'

Henry nodded gravely. 'We don't want to frighten people, you know . . . spreading this sort of story.'

Part 4

It wasn't yet ten o'clock in the morning, but the day was already unbearably hot. Fortunately things had gone smoothly; the transporters had been loaded without problems and had left with their loads of scrap, mostly damaged armoured vehicles. A trail of dust and sand indicated where the convoy had reached. A second cloud suggested that he was about to receive visitors.

From the open door of his caravan, the air-conditioning going full-tilt behind him, Edward watched the two trails pass each other. He used the caravan as his office, living and sleeping in the big tent beside it. He had a very comfortable feeling that they were ahead of schedule; this summer, he guessed, he'd be able to get away a little earlier.

One of his security men waved to him and called, 'Royal mail . . . post.' The fellow must have damn good eyesight, thought Edward; or perhaps a great deal of wish-fulfilment. His crew, isolated as they were, must look forward to news as much as he did.

And the man was right.

The courtesies over, Edward was left with a stack of letters on his desk. Most of them were business ones, which had taken several days to reach him. They could wait a little longer.

There were two others to be read first: one from Margaret. He would recognize her hand anywhere. The other had an Italian stamp, but the address was not in the writing he had hoped for.

As usual, Margaret's was all about her family, about the village, about the way John had headed off the by-pass. Mostly it concerned her children.

They loved your birthday presents. It's hard to believe it's over a year since they saw you. They chat about you so much, especially Henry. You really shouldn't have given him a word-processor. But I suppose nowadays children are so advanced. After all, he is ten . . . Hard to believe. Anyhow he uses it all the time. And Carrie thinks the music is fabulous. I see from your last letter you're going to be in Rome much of this year: I hope that doesn't mean a shorter holiday with us. We wondered why you were setting up this office in Rome. John, of course, says it must be a tax fiddle, but then, he would. I think sometimes he gets a bit miffed when Henry talks about you so much. John's been made one of the senior partners – over the heads of some of his friends, so that's done his ego a power of good . . .

Given a sheet of writing paper and a pen, Margaret could give range to her passing thoughts. Edward found it relaxing to listen to his sister's familiar voice without the need to reply.

And you'll never guess what's happened to Park House! It's been restored, of course. The Shannons are abroad, I've no idea where. They must have sold it because it's now a retirement home. Isn't that a sign of the times? All that vitality next door, those pretty girls and splendid-looking young men, and now! But do you know, Henry says he prefers it. He plays chess with some old chap there on occasions. He says visiting there is a trip down memory lane! But he also says that, 'Park House has gone from the satanic to the ridiculous'. He gets his quotations mixed! I've asked him if he wants to add a line to you, but he says he's writing to you himself. All our love . . . Look after yourself in 'them foreign parts' . . .

He looked through the letters on his desk, but there was no sign of one from his nephew.

He opened the envelope with the Italian stamp. He had hoped it too might contain a note as well as the main letter, but there were merely several pages from Mrs Onelli, written in formal fashion but bursting with gratitude. She tried to restrain it, to be balanced and reticent in the way the English appreciate, but it was hard.

Much had happened. Her daughter, Sylvia, was so much better – indeed, people meeting her now could not guess that anything had ever been wrong with her. Her thanks and her husband's thanks were offered in abundance to Mr Glover. Sylvia still flew to Rome each month, and saw the doctor there without fail, but she no longer needed drugs. All they appeared to do was to talk for an hour or so, but Sylvia had had no attack, no trouble, for over seven months. Of course, there might be a setback later on, but that was less and less likely. She could now speak about her strange imaginings:

Ever since she spoke to you about being a wolf, things have improved. But Mr Glover, I see no reason why you should have taken this task on your shoulders – it is not your responsibility. Taking Sylvia back to see that house did not bring on her illness; she had suffered it before, so there was no obligation for you to have gone to all this expense and trouble to arrange this wonderful treatment – and to take on the cost. I tell Sylvia the least she should do is to write and thank you. But, do you know, she just laughs and says she will thank you when she sees you! She enjoyed seeing you in Rome at Christmas time and last Easter. Next time I think you will find a great change in her . . .

He skimmed through the rest of the letter for any scrap of news about the girl.

One other very good sign, I am told, is that Sylvia has been able to help the unhappy man from the next village who worked as a farm-hand for the same people. To be able to do that without becoming depressed shows how well she is today.

Edward put the letter with the others in the file marked 'Long Term Projects'. He had scored out 'Long Term' and written in place 'Life Time'. Edward liked to think of himself – he admitted to his vanities – as both cryptic and explicit. Sitting there in the middle of a desert, one had time on one's hands to play games.

He was about to turn to the business mail, when, 'Good Lord!' he said aloud. 'How stupid! Of course – the word-processor.'

He flipped through the envelopes. It wasn't difficult to find Henry's.

Dear Eddie,

I've decided I'm going to be a gun-runner like you, but I think it's best not to tell my father yet. You can see how splendid this computer is, with the word-processor and print-out being my favourite things. I do my homework on it.

Mother says she's told you about Park House. I went through it a lot when it was just a ruin. The swimming-pool had to be demolished. It was too dangerous to try to rebuild; anyhow none of the old ladies or gentlemen would want to use it. The rest of the place is restored, but I used to wander about in it before anyone bought it. I never tell anyone what it reminds me of . . .

Did you tell the lady what happened? It's over a year ago now, and it seems like a fairy-tale. I wonder where they are? I sometimes wonder if they existed? Carrie has completely forgotten. I asked her once, and she only remembers the party she went to, with crowds of children and music. I think it's best to leave it like that.

I'm looking forward to seeing you this summer. It would be nice to talk to someone who knows. Isn't it strange how legends (I won't say which legends) have existed in so many parts of the world, and always the same story – you know, about people who could change like that. If you have so many myths, I think they must have a reason; 'no smoke without fire'. Golly! what a fire we had! So I think we (people) should have realized there might be some truth in the old stories.

Nowadays, anything about wolves catches my attention. We had a lesson in school about a boy who looked after his sheep, and he thought it was a good joke to run and tell the villagers that a wolf was killing his sheep. They came to help him, and he laughed at them and said it was a joke. He did the same thing a second time, and they came to help again.

But later on, a wolf really did come and attack his sheep, and when he ran for help, no one would come. They didn't believe him. And he lost his flock. I thought that was very interesting.

Edward grinned, and wondered where to file that letter. As with so many things appertaining to Henry, it didn't fit into anything precisely. He'd have to open another file; after all, he had plenty.

It was after twelve o'clock, he noticed. He poured himself a Scotch, put his feet up on the desk, and began to letter the new file, with heavy black print on brown cardboard: *'Cry Wolf'*. Should it have an exclamation mark or a question mark? Was it an instruction or a statement? Or something between the two? A fragment of a mystery?

He wasn't sure, and left it as it was.